Rodney Leon still enjoys island-life, though he also ventures to countries further afield and without any specific destination once there. Under the old adage, travellers don't know where they are going and tourists don't know where they have been. Rodney hopes he falls under the former category. His love for St Gilberts grows with every passing year. It may be a speck of land lost in the vastness of the Indian ocean, but to Rodney it will always be the place to which he belongs and to where he will always return, even if only in his imagination.

To anyone who ever believed in me.

Rodney Leon

Blue Water Blue

Austin Macauley Publishers™
London • Cambridge • New York • Sharjah

A CIP catalogue record for this title is available from the British Library.

ISBN 9781398459281 (Paperback)
ISBN 9781398459304 (ePub e-book)
ISBN 9781398459298 (Audiobook)

www.austinmacauley.com

First Published 2022
Austin Macauley Publishers Ltd®
1 Canada Square
Canary Wharf
London
E14 5AA

To the many friendly fellow islanders who helped me in my quest to share a slice of sunny, tropical life with those shivering in chillier climes. I thank you all from the bottom of my heart.

Thank God for tourists.

Before tourists, I thought that all the local women who slept with me were less interested in me than in simply taking advantage of my single status, nice secluded home, which is not overlooked by nosey neighbours, and my lack of family connections on the island. On St Gilberts, everyone lives with their extended family in houses that bump walls with listening and watching neighbours and so, casual sex is far from casual; it has the potential to be a cast out of family and community wrecking minefield. Not that that prevents us from doing it.

Speaking of sex; many married couples here would rather risk pulling out than endure the tutting and red-faced shame of buying condoms at the local pharmacy (there isn't any other type of pharmacy here) where they know everyone and where everyone knows them.

"Only one packet this week?"

As for vaginal lubricants and Viagra, God knows how those few brave couples pluck up the front to buy anything like that. Even single men like me know that their condom purchase will be common knowledge before they reach home, perhaps with an angry parent waiting for them at the door presenting an outstretched hand to collect the sinful items. I am only half-joking, of course; all parents were once young themselves, and there's a limit to how many people can fit in a one or two-bed home and how many babies, even Catholics, feel that they can afford to feed and clothe.

I often feel more of a connection with the tourists that I meet than I do with my fellow Gilbertise. Tourists are outsiders, *andovers*, and, despite having lived here all my life, that's exactly what I feel I am too. I am surely the least connected man on St Gilberts having only two real relatives who would actually own up in public to being anywhere near related to me. I'm not a criminal and yes, as I said, I was born and brought up on St Gilberts and have never left its shores but I guess you don't have to be that different to be marked out as 'different' and to find yourself on the outside looking in.

My dad was Gilbertise but he moved to the US to become something of a celebrity as a major league basketball player before injury ended his career. Before that had happened, he had married my mum, a blonde Swedish beauty who was also into sports; she was a national swimming champion in Sweden, Front Crawl, I think. My dad brought her back to see the little island where her husband was born and brought up, she fell in love with the place, so they stayed, built a beautiful clifftop villa, had me and then three years later got themselves killed on a Cessna flight to a small outlying island. They'd left me in the care of Aunt Mert before boarding the plane so she was stuck with bringing me up, but, anyway, back to tourists. I am a tour guide and companion to tourists and I was supposed to meet Tracy in the Three-In-One at 2 pm. I would have gone to her hotel but that would have meant sneaking past the manager who had banned me from the place.

I know I said I feel a sense of empathy with tourists but I often equally wonder if they are not only from another country, but from another planet as well. The phone in my pocket buzzed, a text message, and, speaking of the devil.

Tracy's cheeks burned as the cleaning staff hoovered around her room. She had literally shit the bed the previous night, not badly, but enough, and no matter how she had tried to sponge it away, the marks were still there for those surly cleaning girls to see and judge her for. She felt bilious and another bout of diarrhoea seemed only a light cough away but at least that dreadful fever and nausea had passed during the fitful sleep she'd finally collapsed into in the small hours of the morning.

Just when this trip was starting to provide a bit of action, she'd gotten the trots and now she was afraid to go more than thirty feet from a toilet and surely both she and her room stank, or was that just in her head? The cleaning girls were pulling the sheets off her bed and making a bit of a job of it. As if on cue, the soiled sheets were pulled back and the stains revealed, they both turned as if synchronised and looked at her and both showed expressions of undisguised contempt. Tracey shrugged her shoulders in apology and rubbed her stomach in way of an explanation but their expressions neither lightened nor forgave. Damn them!

She was going to have a word with Janet who'd organised this 'adventure trip' for her. The St Gilberts optional stopover reroutes to Mauritius was ill-advised. The place was pretty enough, stunning even, but it just wasn't ready for tourists yet. The hotels and amenities were basic and the customer service, right across the island was, as far as she was concerned, surly to the point of contemptuous. The place had at least one redeeming feature so far—Rodney.

A day earlier, she had been lounging by the hotel pool trying to fend off the attentions of a young bartender when a shadow falling across her face had made her look up. A tall figure was silhouetted against the bright blue sky and it was only when he squatted down at the side of the sun-lounger that she realised he was not staff. He had smiled into her face showing a set of dazzling white teeth that contrasted nicely with his brown skin. He was young, maybe mid-twenties, trendy in a scruffy surf-bum sort of way, dishevelled and a bit wild as if he had just gotten out of bed. She always went for the bad boy look and this one had it in spades, he also had, beneath the tousled hair and behind the stubble, an extraordinarily handsome face and the most remarkable aqua-blue eyes she had ever seen. They were intense and lent an edge to his easy-going confidence.

"I hope you don't mind me saying, but that colour of bikini looks really great on you; is it last season's?"

He was joking, of course, making fun of her, but there was no malice in it, just unsophisticated flirting. He had approached her but she got the impression that he wasn't the type of man who was ever going to try too hard to pull a woman and would probably breeze off the moment she set him the usual hoops to jump through. She was intrigued. She smiled invitingly.

"Thanks for saving me from Henry; he's nice enough but…"

"A bit pushy," he finished the sentence for her and she giggled as if sixteen again. After that, it all happened so fast, a few drinks and some banter in which she realised his English was excellent. He was both funny and provocative and though he teased her he got away with it with considerable charm. He got her to leave the pool and follow him down to the beach. As she followed him, she felt an imperceptible loss of control to him as he directed the pace that things were going to develop between them. An hour and a half later it seemed natural to invite him into her hotel room and they underwent a humorous subterfuge to sneak in without any of the hotel staff seeing him; apparently, Rodney, (and she'd learnt in their brief time together that it was always Rodney, not Rod, no nicknames or abbreviations on St Gilberts, perhaps it was an island thing), had gotten on the wrong side of the hotel manager once, but they were laughing as they entered the room and when the door closed behind them, they turned to face each other at the same time both suddenly serious.

She had a bottle of duty-free vodka and, as he poured them each a glass, she went to the bathroom shower to wash off the sweat, suntan lotion and sand accumulated over the afternoon. When she returned to the bedroom that combined as a lounge, she was wearing a white towelling robe and nothing else. She picked up the glass he had poured for her and stood looking up at him; God, he was tall; after clinking glasses they both took a sip then placed their drinks down and moved close together. In that second, she wanted him inside her but he put his hands on her shoulders and held her so he could look straight into her eyes. She looked down but he held her chin and finally their eyes met and locked. There was a fine black line encircling the blue-green iris of his eyes, it corralled the colour intensifying it so she felt as if he was seeing more than she wanted him to, more than he should.

"Why did you really come in here?" she asked, but he avoided the question with one of his own, "Why did you invite me in?"

"What else could I do? Close the door in the face of the good Samaritan who saved me from Henry?"

His eyes never wavered, "Is that what I did—save you?" She didn't answer straight away but leaned in towards him so his hands unresisting, slipped down from her shoulders taking the robe with them. Naked she stood facing him, her chin up, not shy but defiant.

"Not yet," she whispered and slowly unfastened his shirt and then his shorts as he stood looking down her body, stroking her hair and the back of her neck. It was still damp from the shower and he caught the apple scent of her shampoo. Finally, when she drew down his underwear, he heard her breath catch; she looked up into his eyes as he stepped out of them, free at last. She stood, and without speaking they faced each other. Their caresses at first gentle became harder, gripping tight and urgent as if the world was about to end within a minute—within the second. The bed was behind her and he pushed her back and then held her arms so he could lower her down slowly.

She made to sit up but he stooped down over her, forcing her to lie back and slowly he ran his tongue from her nipple down across her belly and further down still. She tensed feeling vulnerable and suddenly shy but even as she started to resist, something inside her let go and her muscles relaxed and she fell back. She imagined those intense eyes staring at her body and in her mind's eye she saw her own body as he was seeing it now. He was incredibly attractive and yet it was not his looks that stirred her but the fact that here was a man who could have had his choice of women but he had chosen her and now her naked body was driving him into lustful sexual desire, even frenzy. She found more sexual stimulation in being desired by men than in any physical attraction that she, herself, felt towards them, even when they were as beautiful as Rodney.

She wanted to be lusted after, rather than to lust over others herself.

She had a sensation of falling but not landing. Detached, and yet in the moment, her senses so heightened she could feel the bending of a single hair on her inner thigh as his breath passed over it. She looked down her own body and saw his eyes focussed downwards then his head slowly dipped between her legs…

But that was yesterday.

There was no way she wanted Rodney to see her today, she felt a wreck and her stomach was still iffy despite the Imodium tablets she'd thrown down. She had a nice memory of St Gilberts and it would be a shame to spoil it; besides, who was Rodney? His looks aside, he clearly wasn't wealthy and why was he lurking around the swimming pool of a hotel where he clearly wasn't welcome? Yes, the fact he was barred from the hotel was perhaps all the proof she needed that perhaps this dicky stomach was going to help her dodge a bullet.

He hadn't asked her for money or stolen anything from her room but maybe that was to have happened later on as he reeled her in. *A gigolo perhaps*? He had the looks and chat. She didn't even know his family name but she did have his mobile number and composed a brief text cancelling their arranged afternoon meet up in a bar in town, she cited her sickness as an excuse and pressed send. Her flight to Mauritius was early the next day anyway and she had a lost night's sleep to catch up on.

It was a relief to have the afternoon free to spend with Andy and Nahil in the Three-In-One for our usual Saturday session but Tracy's message was still disappointing and puzzling. A bad stomach? Really? I thought everything had gone really well the previous day and certainly well enough for a follow up but then I remembered back, yes, she had seemed keen enough but she had also been a bit distant and into her own head at times, we hadn't connected on anything other than a physical level. Perhaps I had missed some cues and messed up somehow? Maybe I don't know foreigners all that well at all.

As we got the first round of drinks laid out in front of us, news came in on the small television over the bar that a tsunami was moving across the Indian Ocean and was due to hit our island in the afternoon. Yeah, some advance warning that! Still, it didn't sound too serious and we all decided there and then to go and watch it come in.

It was a bizarre way to spend a Saturday afternoon, sitting on Kasper's Edge waiting for a tsunami to reach us, but we weren't afraid, we were having a picnic. We had a grandstand spot to see the wave coming in, though it had been a bit of a hike to get there. After scrounging a lift from town and past my house and then onto the turn-off, we'd walked the rest of the way along the rough narrow track through the woods and we were still brushing the needle-like casuarinas leaves off our shoulders when we broke through into the bright sunlight of the open grassy area of the cliff edge known as Kasper's Edge. From there, we could eat, drink and watch events in safety as the wave came in towards St Gilberts.

A steady breeze in off the sea slip-streamed our faces and pushed back the heavy hothouse scent of the island's lush vegetation behind us. It was that fresh sea breeze that gave us the sensation of being somewhere high even before we'd reached the edge and could see the ocean stretched out below us. I squinted north, first at the blue of the sky and then at the darker blue of the sea. The water was unusually calm. There was no reef to protect this part of the coast and so rollers travelling all the way across the vast ocean from India struck its shore day in day out, but strangely not today. I looked back towards my two friends, Andy and Nahil.

"Nothing brewing yet," murmured Andy.

"Early days," I replied though it was an effort to even say that; I was so relaxed.

"I need a drink, Rodney." Nahil looked down at the bag I was carrying. A flat grassy spot close to the edge was selected and we stretched ourselves out, popping bottles and opening the packets of sandwiches and joking about nothing in particular.

We were talking in English out of habit. Andy was an Englishman, but a year on St Gilberts coupled with the determined efforts of Nahil, his girlfriend, to integrate him into island life and her life meant that he could understand most conversations in Creole and even dish out backchat in it too. But his pronunciation was heavy and this, coupled with his occasional tendency to stammer, made understanding him hard work so we tended not to put him through it. Anyway, my English is good, actually, probably better than his; well, it is in my opinion at least.

We were the only ones who had thought to view the incoming wave from the cliff top but then anyone living lower down and close to sea would be finding higher ground above their homes just in case the wave came in higher than our local TV station had predicted. Besides, Kasper's Edge and Al Solere, the area from the foot of the cliff running down to the sea, have never been popular spots with locals, me included. In fact, the wide expanse of scrub at the base of the cliff below us had once been home to a settlement. A previous tsunami had long ago washed it away and drowned all but one of its inhabitants.

After being the scene of so much death and destruction, the place is now only associated with bad luck and evil spirits.

"Give me another beer." I said, and groaned at the warmth of the bottle placed in my hand; nevertheless I flipped the top and took a swig.

"We'd get a better view from St Francis Mount," said Nahil.

St Francis Mount was the rocky promontory eastside of the bay; it was to our right as we looked down towards the sea. A small white limestone church of the same name stood derelict on the top of it. I looked across at Andy and saw his eyes narrow as he calculated the distance. I could tell that he thought we'd be pushing our luck a little to scramble down the narrow path to the beach, dangerous enough in itself, and then to cross the expanse of shrub and sandy beach to the mount.

"And suppose the wave comes in when we're still on the beach?" asked Andy.

"Then we run like hell," retorted Nahil. None of us had any idea how high the wave would be and I wondered if it would top St Francis Mount, then decided it wouldn't, the two previous tsunamis had left it untouched and the news broadcast hadn't said anything about this wave being especially big. I thought if we reached the mount and the wave turned out to be high, the water would simply encircle the hill stranding us for a while. However if the wave turned out to be really high then... Andy and I looked out to sea and then across to the white church, and shook our heads. Anyway, it would be a hell of a walk in the sweltering heat with no shade and the beers already as warm as tea.

However, after we had downed a few more of the beers and a little more of the rum, a crazy combination if there ever was one, we started discussing the idea again. Nothing was happening out to sea and the drink had made us confident and reckless. We drank a little more until Nahil suddenly, and rather unsteadily, stood up and edged towards the narrow zigzag path that led down the near vertical cliff to the flat plain below. Without waiting for us, she started to make her way down. Being the nearest to both her and the path, I set off in pursuit with Andy close behind. The path was both steep and narrow so we had to bend our knees and lean back as we made our way down. Long ago someone had driven metal rings into the rock and threaded a rope through to act as a handrail but I would not like to have trusted Andy's or Nahil's weight on it, let alone mine. Nahil was halfway down when Andy shouted, "Where's the sea gone?" Then, "How long's the tide been out?"

None of knew, we'd all been too busy talking and drinking. All three of us looked to the horizon at the same time.

"Shit!" I said, seeing the dark line moving fast and rising as it drew towards the shore. Curling foam formed a white line at its crest and its height was still rising. Nahil stood rooted to the spot but Andy was yelling at us both with authority in his voice.

"Back up. Now! Come on, run like hell!"

I had already turned and could feel Nahil's pull on the handrail just behind mine. *Please God, don't let it break now*, I prayed and I felt the strain in my legs as I pushed myself back up the path. It felt like one of those dreams where the bogey man is coming up fast behind you but your legs are dragging, as if through molasses. Andy kept looking back over his shoulder, concerned about Nahil, and I soon caught him up and barely managed to control the urge to push around him. We were now all focused on our feet and the path ahead, but we could hear a low rushing noise, a sort of drone with a hissing top note. Andy reached the flat again and I arrived seconds behind him but breathing twice as hard. I turned to reach my hand down to Nahil but she was a tough Island woman and ignored my proffered hand, trusting instead to her own hold on the rope handrail.

"Jeez, wou-would you look at that?" Andy's stammer surfaced briefly. By then we were all standing at our picnic site, our eyes locked on the approaching wave. It was like no wave I had ever seen before. Instead of breaking and collapsing on the beach as usual, this one rose like a grey wall and just kept coming. There was a strange sparkly thing going on along the top of the crest as if it was sparking with electricity and, God, was it high. We only realised just how high it was when we looked towards St Francis Mount, and its little church, then we got a sense of just how high the wave was. The church and its small graveyard now existed as an island amid a roiling sea. As the wave approached towards us and towards the cliff where we were standing, I experienced genuine fear.

"Will it reach us?" Even I heard the croak in my voice.

"No chance," said Nahil, cocksure as ever. Action man Andy led us to slightly higher ground where we could still get a good view of the wave approaching the cliff below, jeez, it was fast! We watched and listened in horror as it hit the cliff face with a thunderclap like a god almighty ocean roller hitting a reef. A second later, spray hit us like a slap.

"Effing hell, it's still coming up," shrieked Nahil. We looked to see if we could get even higher up the path and once again, Andy led the way.

There was a small hummock to our left; it was covered in brushwood and we took the path that led through it. The path snaked right then left and then ended at a wooden bench backing up to a rock face which went up sheer another fifteen feet or so. Andy stood on the bench, balanced on the back of it, and got a handhold on the rock face checking if it was climbable. It was obvious he knew what he was doing but I was not sure if Nahil and I would be able to follow his lead. As if he had read my mind, he let go and jumped back on to the bench again.

"Let's see if it's still rising?" He said it over his shoulder already on his way back towards the edge for a look.

"Yeah. It's still rising but more slowly. There's still a good twenty to thirty foot of cliff to spare."

Even so, that still made the water level something like eighty feet from the base of the ridge. If we had set out five minutes earlier, or if the wave had come five minutes later, we wouldn't have stood a chance. We stood rooted to the spot and then, about ten minutes later, another wave came over the back of the first but it went no higher than the first wave. We waited for a further fifteen minutes, rooted to the spot, without seeing any further waves but still waited where we were, not convinced of our safety.

For long minutes, none of us spoke. The water level started to fall slowly at first and then to drop surprisingly quickly. Our nervous energy drained away like the sea, leaving us tired and listless. We sat on the grass and hardly a word passed between us as we each got our breath and our composure back. We were curious to see what had happened to the rest of the Island but it took an effort to drag ourselves away from the ridge and head back down, Nahil spotted a tamarind tree with clusters of long brown pods ready for picking.

"Rodney, get me that bunch there," she commanded, pointing up at a cluster well above her head.

"Yeah," Andy chirped in. "Get me that bunch next to it while you're at it." Being tall can have its advantages and I reached up easily.

"Bit bloody hot to be walking in this sun," I said passing around the seed pods. We each split a pod and chewed on the sharp citrus taste of the brown paste inside and spat out the large seeds.

"So, what's the deal with Al Solere? Who the hell builds a church where no one lives and no one goes?" asked Andy. I told him the story about the ill-fated village. Local history such as it was, told us St Gilberts had previously suffered two big waves. The first, in 1706, swept away all but one of the inhabitants of Al Solere, along with their homes leaving no sign that they had ever existed apart from the little church on St Francis Mount. The only survivor was a young fisherman called Marcel Leste who, luckily for him, was away from the village engaged in bedroom gymnastics with the wife of a fisherman who was conveniently away on a neighbouring Island at the time.

The second big wave, the tail-end of the same tsunami that struck Sumatra on 26 December 2004, struck us the following day. Like the first-strike in the 1700s, the second wave struck the Northern tip of the island again, but by then Al Solere was a place only populated by ghosts. No sane person would dream of setting up home in the area now. It wasn't just the threat of further tsunamis; it was the spirits of the drowned villagers' that prevented locals from even visiting the place now. Surprisingly, the previous tsunamis had left the rest of the island relatively unscathed and we expected much the same today. The bored reaction of the other customers in the Three-In-One to the news to this third coming was typical of the island as a whole—they saw it as a non-event, well it hadn't been a non-event to us.

Andy asked, "I can't understand how only one person survived. How come only one person was away from the village that night? Surely in a village of what; one hundred? Two hundred? Three hundred…?"

"Not that many," I corrected him.

"OK but even so, surely on any night of the week a few people were away boozing, shagging, visiting relatives, in hospital or fishing or something?" We considered in silence; the event was part of island folklore. The sole survivor, after encouragement, had described his memories of his life in the village to town elders, his lost life there before the wave obliterated it, to provide a written memorial of the lost community. The document, written in Creole, was still on view in the museum and local teachers still tell schoolchildren about it, or at least mine had. Nahil suddenly quoted Marcel Leste's reply when asked how he felt about the loss of his home, village, family and friends, and way of life, in one night. A dumb question of them to ask him in my opinion, but Nahil must have been paying attention on the day they covered it in school.

"It was God's will," she intoned.

"Religious then," Andy commented, adding tersely, "Some God." Nahil's head snapped round, she looked shocked and I knew why.

"Don't go bringing bad luck on us all," I said. I'd said it as if in jest but I was serious, gris-gris, local magic, was not something you ever admitted you believed in, yet you always wanted to stay the right side of it in fact, of all religious stuff. I caught Nahil's eye and we both looked each other out. Andy was quick on the uptake and knew Nahil well enough by now, he held up his hands in surrender.

"OK, no sweat."

Just then I remembered something my teacher had said all those years ago about Marcel Leste's tale and his reply to that dumb question, "It was God's will." Well, that was the official English translation from Creole shown in the museum but my teacher disagreed. He had studied the manuscript personally and insisted a more accurate translation would be "It was God's judgement". Both Andy and Nahil were looking at me surprised and then I realised I had said it out loud.

"God's judgement?" Andy echoed. "Judgement on what?"

But Nahil cut in before I could answer, "Who cares, let's get back before it's dark."

We got up and started walking again but I couldn't help thinking about Al Solere and I was sure we weren't done with it yet, or maybe it wasn't done with us, and that was an uncomfortable thought.

The next day, I felt optimistic. Tracy had left on an early plane and my day was now clear. I felt a small tinge of guilt for not seeing her off or for not feeling more concerned about her but that was soon gone as I got myself a glass of orange in the kitchen and put the kettle on for tea to follow. I was walking towards the veranda when I heard the sound of a motorbike coming down my drive.

It was Andy returning my old Honda 125. I'd lent it to him the day before the tsunami so that he could take Nahil for a spin somewhere. I hadn't asked him where he was going or for why, but thought he was a lucky bastard to have someone like Nahil to ride pillion with him. As he came up the stairs to the door, I already had it open it to let him in. He threw the ignition key up to me and I just about caught it, my coordination still not fully returned from the previous night.

"Did I disturb something?" he asked.

"Er, no, definitely not," I replied not catching his drift.

"Weren't you seeing some blonde girl?" he stage whispered.

"She's already gone, this morning, in fact."

"You two fall out?" he asked, both eyebrows rising.

"No, she had bad guts or something," I replied. "Where's Nahil?" I asked him back.

"Shopping with her aunt in the town. I dropped her off before coming here."

"Any damage from the tsunami?" I asked.

"Well, I asked Mervin. He's always got his finger on the island's pulse, knows what's happening, or about to happen. He told me it was a damp squid, a few people's boathouses got damaged, two small jetties destroyed, a telegraph pole washed over, and sea water all the way up Kerror Street as far as the tobacconists but that was all." I nodded.

"Well, are you going to invite me in or what?" He said it with an exaggerated note of exasperation in his voice. I stood back and waved him in with a grandiose gesture. Andy had been in my house many times but it always takes first-time visitors by surprise, for two reasons; first it is beautiful. Designed in the traditional island style, it has deep, shady wooden verandas around two sides of building looking out to sea. The large central open-plan living area has lots of teak and a high cathedral-style ceiling that helps keep the place cool and airy since it doesn't have aircon. It has four bedrooms, three bathrooms and is part surrounded by a well-stocked garden initially planned and started by my mother then added to by Aunt Mert and then finally by myself. The second surprise to most visitors is that the house belongs to me, the 26-year-old beach bum, scourge of St Gilberts' virgin tourist industry.

A large framed poster-size monochrome photo hanging on the main living room wall always helps me explain to first-time visitors how I came to own such a house. The photo is a skilfully taken portrait of a young couple both in their late twenties with a small baby of one year old. The two adults are stretched out on a rug on a polished wooden floor. The child sits on the father's chest the mother lies behind the man but with her head also resting on the man's chest her left arm stretched across both the man and the child. The photo is a close-up so only the torsos of the adults are in the frame. The child is smiling and the relaxed smiling faces of his parents gave the impression that they have just shared a joke. The way they lean in towards each other adds to the impression that they are close and still in love and that the child is loved too.

The couple in the photo are my parents and I am-was the child in the portrait. My parents were both professional athletes and both attractive. My father's was black even for a Creole, and though not obvious from the photo was six foot ten inches tall. Not outstanding for a US basketball player, which he was, but enough to turn heads when he was on or away from the court. Once in the Three-In-One an American tourist had found out that my father had been six toot ten.

"Well, by rights you should be taller than him, son," the man had exclaimed between gulps of beer.

"Every new generation has an inch or two on the previous one." He said it as if it was a scientific fact.

"Look, if you had spent all your youth in front of a TV or computer screen, eaten junk food and saved all your energy for growing tall instead of walking up and down all those bloody hills every day to school." His voice had raised an octave to deliver the final point, "You could've made seven foot!"

“Thank god for St Gilberts hills then,” I’d replied and meant it. Being around six foot six inches tall is already tall enough to mark you out in St Gilberts and in my experience that hasn’t been a good thing. I’d regularly been bullied on the school playground because of my height, unusual aqua-blue eyes and mixed parentage. On a small island where everyone is interconnected you don’t have to be that different to be seen as an outsider. I had the physical and mental scars to prove it.

Even now, if I’m in the Three-In-One and hear a tourist mutter the word ‘basketball’, I am paranoid enough to think that they are talking about me. Though, to be honest, one visitor actually remarked to my face that I was built more like Usain Bolt than a basketball player, which I took as a compliment even though I have neither Bolt’s muscles nor speed.

My mother had been a stunning, statuesque blond from Sweden with the sort of shoulders that came from competitive swimming at a national level.

The choice of monochrome highlights in the portrait the contrast in skin colour between my parents. The child is a little lighter than the father, but still darker than the mother my skin colour is somewhere between the two opposites and so the colour of the child draws and melds the three of them together. It is as if a little colour from each of the parent’s makes up the child, which, I suppose, is exactly what happened. I was all that remained of the photogenic family in the portrait.

My parents had both died when the small inter island plane they were in crashed into the sea somewhere between St Gilberts and La Roche Island. Their legacy to me was the house and a trust fund they’d prudently set up for me in case the worst happened. It put a modest amount of money into my account every month. The house was worth a fortune but I could never sell it; so much of my parents had gone into its design and into the garden around it and to me it is my only link to the family I lost. The trust fund provides just enough to live on, to eat frugally and pay the usual bills, but not more than that. Finding work to make more is not easy on St Gilberts. Aunt Mert always claimed the trust fund was the ruination of me.

“They’ve turned you into the lazy good-for-nothing that you are becoming with that trust fund,” she said regularly, or words to that effect.

Andy made his way straight to the veranda and flopped down on to one of the padded chairs and bounced up again as the cushion recoiled his weight.

"A free day then," he said as he poured himself some tea from the pot I'd just made. He looked down on Anse Raffin beach and then towards the sea that was starting to take on a translucent blue shade.

"A good day for a boat ride," he suggested.

"What did you have in mind—a bit of fishing?" I asked.

"We can if you want to, but no, actually I was thinking of going around to Al Solere to see the after-effects of that tsunami at sea level." I thought for a second, would my stomach stand up to a good buffeting on the waves in its current state? I placed my hand on my stomach and decided it would cope. It would be interesting to check Al Solere beach out from the sea, something I'd never done before.

"I'll take some juice," I said.

"Juice!" Andy stared at me. "You sick or something?"

I laughed and went to my room to change into shorts and a clean tee shirt.

We went to Andy's house on the Honda, me driving and Andy riding pillion. It was all downhill so I stayed in second not trusting the brakes. Our combined weights produced a fair amount of momentum but I've done the trip many times before, often with the added weight of Nahil sandwiched between us however, even with just the two of us the clapped-out shock absorbers bottomed-out as we hit dips in the road. Andy's house, in contrast to mine, is ultra-modern, all light ceramic floor tiles, white walls, and modern chrome fittings. Unlike mine his is easy to maintain and I envied him that about it. We walked through the house and I noticed the air was cool inside. One of Nahil's tee-shirts was draped over the back of a light-coloured sofa and there were a couple of used whisky glasses on a low table. Andy snatched up a bottle of sun lotion and smeared it over his face neck and arms and tossed the bottle to me. I smeared some on to, although my skin is much darker than his it still gets burnt especially if I am out on the sea in a boat for too long and, besides, I liked the smell and feel of it on my skin. We entered the kitchen with its gleaming marble and stainless-steel worktops and exited out of the rear door using our hands to shade our eyes from the brightness of the sun outside. I reached in my pocket for my shades. Tourists may love my aqua-blue eyes, but I find that my peepers are not too keen on bright sunlight especially when it is reflecting off the sea into them. The blurb on the side of the frames said the sunglasses would block out one hundred per cent of the UV rays and I prayed that they would.

There was a garden of sorts behind Andy's house that sloped steeply downwards towards the beach. Almost at the point where the garden reached the sand of the beach there was a small stone built shed with a large up and over door facing the sea. Andy turned a key in the lock grabbed one of the handles and hoisted the door up. We could both see a dark low tidemark around the building where the sea had lapped around it the previous day but everything inside seemed much the same as the last time I had looked inside. There was small rigid hulled Inflatable Avon Sea Rider it was on its trailer ready to be pulled down the beach and into the sea. Together we rolled it down to the waterline and launched the boat into the sea. Andy pushed the trailer back up to the shed while I kept a grip of the trailing rope painter. I was in the sea up to my calves and the water was slightly cooler than the air above and as clear as bottled Evian. The coarse white sand lifted in swirls but settled quickly again over my submerged sandaled feet leaving the water clear again. Andy came back and stepped into the back of the boat when he was inside, I pulled it out a bit further out to sea and climbed in over the side myself. Andy opened the small toolbox and took out the knife he always wore for diving or fishing he told me it was a shorter version of the knife worn by US Navy Seals. It had a black sheath which he strapped to his calf. The sheath had groove cut out near the bottom exposing a small cutting section of the blade so the wearer could cut a rope on a moving inflatable without unsheathing the blade. Apparently, it helped prevent accidents to both boat and passengers.

"Expecting trouble?" I said, more to wind him up than anything else.

"I bloody hope so," Andy shot back. "I'll go mad if I don't get some action soon" Andy started up the outboard and we moved off heading northwards along the coast.

The sea breeze on our faces was refreshing and I felt the last of my hangover slipping away.

"How was Tracy?" Andy asked.

"Like I said, she had some bug or something," I replied.

"No, I meant how was she to actually be with, did you like her?" Andy corrected.

"Yes, she's great, but…" I hesitated.

"But?" Andy prompted.

"But I only saw her for a day, or so, and now she's gone," I answered.

Andy snorted in exasperation, "Bloody hell, I wish I'd never asked!"

We chuckled a little and I opened two bottles of beer. After a few gulps I felt much better, that stuff about the hair of the dog really is true after all. As we moved further from the shore the swells grew larger and the Avon started to skim and hit waves turning the light refreshing spray into a soaking shower. It was breezier too and we had to shout a little louder to hear ourselves above the background noise. Though Andy had the outboard almost full out when I looked back to the shoreline, we appeared to be making hardly any progress at all. A low peninsula of land jutted out ahead and we had to steer out to sea to get around it.

"This rock took the steam out of the Tsunami deflecting it before it reached my place," Andy shouted over his shoulder as we drove into the waves head on. Once we had passed the peninsula Andy turned in parallel to the shore again. We were level with Anse Lolas or Lolas Beach which is its more usual name these days, a long sweep of white sand fringed by palms, spreading Takamaka and feathery Casuarinas trees. A couple of dark-skinned figures wearing bathing suits were walking along the beach and because of their colour I took them to be locals till one of the girls took her hat off and long blonde hair cascaded down. Hell, the tourists were sun-baking themselves darker than us! I stowed my empty bottle in the back of the Avon and Andy passed his empty back over his shoulder but kept looking forward as he gripped the wheel with his left hand. A high rock marked the end of Lolas Beach it was part of an outcrop that rose straight out of the water and up to forty or so feet high. The rocks levelled out on top to provide a comfortable viewing spot over the beach and it was a popular venue for energetic picnickers and, early on weekend evenings, for young lovers who lacked a place of their own. The local name for the place was Memory Hill though I suspect Conception Hill would have been more descriptive of the action it had seen over the years. I had even enjoyed a few tumbles up there myself when I was at school and when Aunt Mert still shared the house with me. The next beach, called Derallar, was a poor man's version of Lolas Beach. The vegetation was shrubbier and grew down towards the water's edge where the sea could reach it at high tide.

My attention was now on where the land ahead widened out again once more blocking our forward passage and forcing us to head out to sea to get around it. This marked the north eastern outer reach of Al Solere. Once we were past the outstretched arm of rock which extended a hundred meters or so, we would be able to see St Francis Mount and its little church on top. Beyond that was the stretch of beach leading up to the backstop of Kasper's Edge the limestone cliffs we had picnicked on the previous day. Once again, the Avon began to rear up as it rode the incoming waves and, just after I had wiped the spray off my shades, we took another soaking as the spray came up from the prow. We rounded the outcrop and went ahead parallel to the shore to where we thought the sea was deeper. Sharp rock formations just a few feet below the surface surprised and startled us as they suddenly appeared to rear up at us. Andy slowed the Avon's engine and looked over the side.

"There's a shelf of rock running all along this beach," he said shaking his head.

"Good job we're in this thing even a small fishing boat would get holed sailing over this stuff." Then, as we came level with St Francis's Mount Andy steered the Avon in towards the shore so it surfed the incoming waves. Once again submerged rocks showed under the water running out from the St Francis Mount as if it had sent out under water roots into the sea.

"Wow, will you look at that!" Andy exclaimed looking towards the beach but I had spotted the devastation almost at the same moment. Uprooted trees, broken branches, palm fronds, loose boulders and seaweed littered the beach. The deep blue water turned aquamarine as we reached the shallows and the white sandy beach with the St Francis Mount to our left. It was the same story all the way up the beach and the two hundred yards or so to the cliffs we had scrambled up in panic just the previous day. It was even possible to see how high the sea had reached up on the cliffs themselves and I found myself clenching my jaw, it wasn't so far from the top. As we grounded the Avon and stepped out, I felt a tingle of fear.

"Did you have the news on this morning?" I asked.

"You're wondering if another wave is due, aren't you?" Andy said.

"Yes, I am, are you?" I answered.

"Come to think of it, I wasn't, but they did mention on the telly that aftershocks were a possibility?" However, he still got out of the Avon and started walking up the beach. I shrugged my shoulders and followed him. Without the wind and spray in our faces, we now felt the full force of the sun and the smell of suntan lotion started to fill my nostrils.

"Who the hell would want to set up a village here?" Andy asked. I shook my head to show it wouldn't be my choice of location either.

“I heard they always were a bit weird, must have been the inbreeding,” I said circling an extended finger over the top of my head. “Bloody isolationists!” I added, suddenly remembering the word I’d heard on CNN TV the previous week and pleased at getting a chance to use it in another context.

Another “hmm” followed from Andy his eyes still scanning the carnage along the beach. Isolationists the word repeated itself in my head and I smiled, I was proud of my fluency in English. My parents had used English within the home so I was exposed to the sound of it from birth. Now I actively sort out new words to add to my vocabulary, the longer the word the better. I was sure that my English was better than some of the British tourists I met visiting the Island. Their surprise at my fluency always gave me a bit of a buzz.

“Isolated isolationists,” I suggested.

“Hmm,” was Andy’s only response to that as well. “Did anyone else on the Island use the church?” he asked.

“Good question,” I replied, “to be honest I don’t know, but I doubt it, for one it’d be a bloody long walk on a hot Sunday morning just to sit in the middle of an unfriendly congregation.” I looked up at the white church and felt a sense of foreboding that left me uneasy as if something was about to happen. I almost mentioned it to Andy but then decided against it.

St Francis Mount looked huge close up from sea level. We moved in towards it and as we did so the church slipped from our view. I started to walk around the hill. Its position seemed at odds with the surroundings. A large hill plonked down close to the sea at one end of a sandy beach. It looked to be of limestone the same as Kasper's Edge and, like the cliff it was big and solid enough to withstand the full force of the tsunami. Over the centuries it had also gathered enough earth on its summit to support vegetation and trees which now grew thickly over its surface. Behind the hill, where it pointed towards the cliffs, I found what I had been looking for, a set of steps cut into the stone leading up to the top of the mount and the church itself. I started walking up them thinking if another wave came, then at least I'd have a fighting chance of making it to the top before it reached us. Without looking back I heard Andy start up the steps behind me. From the cliffs the previous day the Church had not looked in such bad condition, deserted yes, a bit broken-down certainly, but still a pleasing focus for the eye. Close up the ravages of time and long neglect were unmistakable. The building material of crushed coral, limestone and cement had kept its white colour but the building itself was little more than a shell. Sections of roof tiles and possibly the underlying timbers had caved in. The overgrown stone flag pathway surrounding the church was covered in layers of bird droppings showing who the new dominant inhabitants of St Francis Mount Church were. Scattered around the church, seemingly in no particular order, were dozens of gravestones of varying size and design, some of them tilted over and some fallen flat. Surprisingly the vegetation had not overgrown them maybe the soil was too poor, or the sun, wind and general conditions too harsh.

"I wouldn't have thought the soil would be deep enough for graves," Andy commented as he stepped over some of the fallen stones. Suddenly I considered what we were doing we were walking over gravestones in Al Solere the infamous, haunted Al Solere. It was only the bright overhead sunshine and a pinch of pride that prevented me from suggesting to Andy that we head back to the boat. That's if I could have reached him. He was happily scrambling about exploring obviously engrossed in the novel surroundings. At last, something of interest for the action man with too much spare time on his hands. That was something else we had in common. We both had an income that enabled us to live—but not to live it up. Andy helped me with maintenance and restoration work on my house he also did some fishing and diving. However were it not for Nahil I doubted he would have stayed on St Gilberts for as long as he had. I sat on a rock watching him stalk purposefully around the graveyard but when he headed off to walk around the church itself, I got up and joined him.

"Apart from the roof, this place could withstand a siege," he said. I looked at the solid walls and the high windows shuttered over, too high even for me to look in to.

"Have you ever been inside?" Andy asked.

"Are you joking?" I said. "I've never even been up here before."

"Never?" Andy sounded incredulous. "You mean as a kid you never went exploring?"

"I explored girls, mate, not frigging cemeteries and churches." Andy shook his head. What he didn't say his look implied, had he grown up on St Gilberts he would have explored every inch of the Island before now. The island did not offer much in the way of a challenge even to a schoolboy explorer. If Andy thought that exploring was normal then I felt the opposite. His jibe highlighted that in some respects he was still typical of many tourists. Like them he was always rushing about his curiosity on overdrive checking out things just for the sake of it. I'd heard visitors' talk of how they travelled miles just to get a photo of a mountain or of a sunset across the sea. Many took photos of my house from the sandy beach Anse Raffin below pointing their cameras up at my cliff-top veranda with its frame of pink, red, lilac and orange bougainvillea cascading down around it.

"Well, now's your big chance," said Andy as we reached the solid wooden door. It had a hasp with a formidable looking padlock through it. One of those solid jobs made up of layers of hardened steel riveted together, a bastard to saw through, not that I was keen to try.

"Are you going to kick the door in?" I asked half afraid he was going to say yes.

“Who put the padlock on? It’s not that old by the look of it?” He asked holding it in his hand turning it as far as it would go against the hasp so he could examine it both sides.

“I think it was Father Thomas from St Mary’s Catholic Church,” I replied adding when I saw him frown, “the one up the street from Three-In-One.” Andy was no churchgoer.

“Then I guess I’d better not break it then,” he said turning. As he dropped his hand away from the padlock he looked over towards the sea. “Shit!” He exclaimed running towards the edge to get a better look.

“Tide’s coming in, let’s get the Avon higher up.” We both ran down the steps and headed around the hill down towards the sea and the Avon. We needn’t have worried; the sea was still a few yards away but we each took a side of the Avon and walked it up past the high watermark so only another tsunami could reach it. Andy stooped and raided the toolbox under the central seat in the Avon. He took out a jemmy bar, a pair of pliers, and a small coil of wire. He was just about to shut the seat lid when he stopped and reached in to get a rubber-coated torch. We returned up the beach and up to the church door. Taking the pliers and coil of wire, he cut off a piece about four inches long of the wire and bent it at right angles to form an elongated ‘L’ shape. He flattened the short leg as best he could with the pliers then cut another and slightly longer length of wire. On this he fashioned a crude handle by bending one end of the wire into a loop, he worked on the other end producing a small series of kinks in the wire.

Preparations complete, he inserted the short leg of the ‘L’ shape wire into the bottom of the keyhole. He kept a light tension on the leg of the ‘L’ wire and slipped the kinked wire in over the top of the other and into keyhole. He worked it back and forth across the pins. Within seconds the tension on the ‘L’ shaped wire turned the lock barrel. Keeping the tension on the remaining wire he dropped the kinked wire and reaching down unfastened his knife and slipped the tip into the key slot and gave it a half turn. Withdrawing the knife, he pulled down on the padlock and it snapped open.

“Bloody hell, you worry me sometimes—in fact you worry me most of the time,” I exclaimed but I was secretly impressed. Another string to his bow, was there no end to his accomplishments? It was enough to give me an inferiority complex.

The door was stiff on its hinges and creaked horribly like something from an old horror film when we pushed it inwards. The brightness of the sun outside meant the interior of the church was just a black hole to our unadjusted eyes despite the criss-cross shafts of light that pierced through the gloom from holes in the roof. Andy snapped on the torch but it didn't help and he switched it off again. Carefully we stepped inside and stood still slowly looking around to help our eyes to adjust to the dim light. I guess all churches have an atmosphere of sorts but this one was different, though it was not obvious why. Gradually my eyes began to pick up detail. Dust motes kicked up by our feet floated in criss-crossing shafts of light. Rows of dust covered wooden benches spattered with white and grey bird droppings. There was a strong smell of damp wood and dry dust. A stone slab floor, surprisingly smooth and level echoed our footfalls within the church. For a brief second, I imagined the rows of benches filled with people from long ago, their Sunday best clothes worn-out and threadbare, praying to God for survival and prosperity, only to receive neither.

My eyes now adjusted to the light, I turned to the focal point within the church, the altar, and we walked up an aisle towards it. As far as I could make out the altar was flush against the wall. It meant the priest would have had his back to the congregation for most of the mass while he faced the tabernacle. I stepped up the raised platform on which it stood and tapped the dust covered wooden top with a single finger.

"This is a Catholic Church so I guess there must be a relic of a Saint or something under it, unless Father Thomas removed it."

"Well, even if he hasn't it can stay there as far as I am concerned," Andy said adding, "Anyway, how the hell would you know—ah yes—Aunt Mert is a Catholic," he answered his own question.

"So am I," I said in mock indignation.

"Really?" He gave me a funny look and blew a raspberry. "Catholic! You've shagged more women than—than…" he struggled to find a suitable comparison… "Jack Nicholson!" He exclaimed triumphantly.

"Who?" I asked looking puzzled. I had heard of Jack Nicholson and even seen one of his recent films. Was Andy expecting me to believe the old, overweight guy was some kind of stud?

"I may be a lapsed Catholic but I haven't thrown my lot in with the devil yet." My words echoed back and slapped me in the face suddenly it didn't seem to be the right place to be joking along those lines, a twinge of Catholic guilt, just what I needed. I looked at the benches from my new vantage point seeing the church as the priest would have. This time I didn't see the rows of faces of those long ago parishioners but I did sense that something was not right but I couldn't put my finger on what it was.

"The place smells damp and rotten yet when you look around it's as dry as a bone, how do you work that out?" I said, thinking aloud.

"Yeah, maybe it's the bird shit?" Andy suggested.

"Nah," I disagreed, "it's all dry excepting a couple of new ones scattered about. I don't know what it is, but something's not right."

"Yeah, I know what you mean," said Andy as he turned towards the corner at the altar end. "Ah a door!" He said striding towards it.

"That will be the sacristy," I said following, I couldn't see his face but I imagined his eyebrows lifting yet again at this additional proof of my religiousness. Though not locked the door's hinges were stiff and it needed a good push to get it open. It opened on to a dark room that must have been directly behind the altar. The room was almost pitch-black so we left the door open to allow a little of the dim light from the main church in. Andy switched on his torch and focussed the beam on a rough wood trestle table. There were a couple of pot mugs and a water jug covered with dust and cobwebs on top. At one end of the room was a wardrobe with one of its battered doors hanging open to reveal some garments in an advanced state of decay. They looked like old cassocks and surpluses.

"A bit claustrophobic in here," I whispered.

"Why are you whispering?" asked Andy, though in a stage whisper himself.

"Because I don't need to fucking-well SHOUT!" I said, the last word at full volume and the sound bounced in the confined space and rattled our eardrums. As the echoes died down, Andy was suddenly alert, he cocked his head to one side and held up his hand for silence, we both tilted our heads listening. I wondered what noise had caught his attention or even if he was about to play a prank on me, was it the birds on the eaves in the main church perhaps? I strained my ears, trying to separate and make sense of all the sounds I was hearing. We were at the end of the church, the end that pointed towards the sea and I could hear the high tide hitting the rocks at the base of the mount and gurgling through them.

"Yes well—I give up, what am I missing?" I asked.

"Ssh, listen," he said raising his hand. Again I listened and then waited for him to enlighten me. My patience was just turning to frustration there was nothing unusual, no sound that I could make out but then, creeping gently into my consciousness, there was.

The sound of the sea had a different note to it, an echo if you like, as if the sea itself was hitting us from more than one side. Barely noticeable amid the sound of the crashing surf was something else out of sync with the waves faint gurgling noises. These had nothing to do with the open ocean reaching land and crashing in frustration against reef and rock. They were more to do with secret caverns and echoing confined spaces. We looked down at the floor and then at each other.

"Can you hear it too?" I asked.

"I heard it first, mate," said Andy dry as ever. We both lowered our heads towards the floor and walked in a crouch slowly around the room sometimes bumping into each other as we circled. It was not easy trying to find where the sound of the subterranean water noise was loudest. From different sides of the room we both converged on the wardrobe and stood facing it. In front of it lay a rotted coconut fibre mat. I kicked it behind us and walked around to see the side of the wardrobe.

"Pass me the torch a sec," I said reaching out my hand. With the torch I could see the wardrobe was free-standing and not fixed by any screws or nails to the wall. I went to the front again and, crouching shone the torch under the hanging vestments and into the grey cobwebs within. The beam lit a base covered in dirt and some rodent droppings along the back edge but the otherwise wooden fabric of the wardrobe was intact. I was still looking inside the wardrobe when Andy pointed out something on the floor outside it.

"The floor's made of wood here," he said. I stepped back and shone the torch on the floor and saw wooden planks.

"So?" I said standing up straight and shining the torch around the rest of the floor. Then I saw stone flags similar to those in the main church area.

"Yes, you're right," I mumbled, "stranger and stranger."

"You're whispering again," said Andy, but I was too engrossed in the floor to fire back at him. Instead, I scratched my head.

"A stone floor suddenly becomes a wooden floor; what's that all about?"

"Perhaps this wardrobe is hiding something," said Andy.

"Let's shift the bastard," I suggested.

"Don't use language like that in church," said Andy tutting and shaking his head, "or the Pope will excom-circumcise you." I grimaced at this but he just grinned back. We each took a side and walked the wardrobe, corner by corner, away from the planks and on to the stone flags. Then we turned our attention back to the rectangle of planks.

"Where did I leave that jemmy bar?" Andy asked. We both thought back trying to remember.

"You didn't need it to open the padlock," I prompted.

"The altar," he exclaimed. Before I could reply he left the room and I could hear his sandals flip-flopping on the church floor outside, going quieter as he walked away towards the alter and then becoming louder as he returned. The door creaked open and he entered, silhouetted for a second in the open doorway. We crouched at the edge of the planks again Andy with the small jemmy in his hand. If we thought the planks would lift easily with a jemmy disappointment wasn't long in coming. The planks were level with the stone floor and such a close fit to the surrounding stones the point of the jemmy bar could not slip between them. Once again Andy unsheathed his knife and though it could fit between the stone floor and the planks, he decided not to chance snapping the blade of his beloved diving knife by levering back on it.

"These planks are as thick as those on the jetty," he said withdrawing the blade and returning the knife to its sheath.

By now my legs were getting stiff with crouching so I stood up straight and as I was still holding the torch in a sudden flash of inspiration, I started examining the square of planks again. They were black with the amassed dirt of a few centuries that blotted out the joins between the planks themselves. Then I saw what I had been searching for about six inches in from the edge closest to the wall. I stood on the planks and kicked around the area with the toe of my sandal. Andy bent over to see what I what I up to.

"Here, let me get at it with this," he said gouging the jemmy into the area to break up the compacted earth that had disguised the lifting ring recessed into the wood. With the jemmy bar he managed to lift the ring out of its recess. Made of bronze, it had survived the years without corroding. Our elation at this discovery was short-lived, first Andy, and then I grasped the ring tried to lift the hatch door without success. The ring, placed as it was so close to the far wall made it was almost impossible, even for someone with my reach, to gain leverage on the ring to lift the hatch without standing on the hatch itself.

"I'll get some rope from the boat and then we can get both our weights behind it," said Andy.

"I've got a better idea," I said.

"I'll come with you and get a beer from your cool box as well." There was no way I was going to admit that I didn't want to left in that church on my own, not to Andy, not even to myself.

We had to shield our eyes when we stepped back outside the church and I quickly slipped my shades back on. At the boat Andy sorted out some rope while I knocked the tops off a couple of beers.

"Not bad, still cool," I said and let the first mouthful slide down. Andy's eyes were shining.

"This is bloody exciting, don't you think, a deserted church with a secret hatchway. God knows what we are going to find down there?" I was nonchalant but Andy saw straight through it.

"Come on," he chided. "Admit it," I pulled a wry face and took another swig from the bottle; it was already warm. A minute later Andy dropped his empty bottle back into the boat collected up the rope and stood up from the sand where he had been sitting.

"Come on, let's get this lid up then." Together we walked back around the hill, up the stone steps through the graveyard and into the church. Once again it was like stepping into total darkness until our eyes readjusted to the dim light and it was darker still in the sacristy as we entered it. Andy quickly attached one end of the rope to the ring and we each got a grip along the rope as if we were a two-man tug-of-war team. With Andy's strength and my weight, the hatch came up rather easier than I had thought it would. We saw a hinge along the edge closest to us. Picking up the torch Andy advanced and shone it down into the gaping square hole. We'd lost our night sight in the bright sunlight outside so we couldn't see anything beyond the entrance. Andy pointed the torch into the square black hole and at first, we still couldn't see anything. He tipped the torch back to see if it was still working and it was. I stood close behind him and looked down over the top of his head into the hole.

Yes, there were stone steps leading down and the slap of water against rock rose from below. We could feel the coolness of air in the hatchway and the odour rising confirmed the source of the fetid damp odour that had caused us to wrinkle our noses earlier in the main church.

Andy, ever the fearless explorer, slowly and carefully started down the steps. Rings fixed into the wall followed the steps down, like those on the zigzag path leading up to the top of Kasper's Edge, but without the rope. Andy kept his balance with one hand over his head on the rim of the opening as he descended part-way down. My stomach was doing flips and I belched. Only Andy could descend into that black hole of a cellar without showing any apprehension. I placed my foot on the first step and felt that facing a fourth coming of the tsunami would be easier. Andy was close to the bottom when he suddenly stepped into water up to his ankles. He shuffled about extending one foot to probe the ground trying to learn how deep the water was and how far he was off the floor below.

"I think the water only just covers the last step," he reported over his shoulder and I could hear the splash of him stepping off the step and into the water.

"There's some light down here," he said, surprise registering in his voice. That made me curious and I came down a little faster stooping automatically because experience of low ceilings and doors had already dealt my head many bumps in the past. The steps turned slightly around to the left but I could see the light source was coming from the right. A wall of protruding rock at the bottom step and on the right partially blocked it. My feet splashed into the water it was a foot or so deep and the floor itself felt like sand. The flickering beam of Andy's torch moved right and it went dark as he turned around the wall of protruding rock. Being in the dark in that chamber wasn't pleasant and I nearly shouted for Andy to bring the torch back. Instead I felt my way along the side of the cave towards the source of the light and the sound of splashing. It was lighter in this part of the chamber than in the sacristy above and as I rounded the bend, I saw Andy playing the torch beam over the walls. It was clear that we were in a natural cave at the seaward end of the mount. Two shafts of light, one high up and the other coming from two foot up from the water level identified holes in the rock and explained where sea water had entered the chamber. It still gurgled in through the lower hole whenever a wave came against the outer rock face. We backed up and, as we moved away from the two light sources, and around towards the back of the cavern I felt the ground was higher and the water becoming shallower. The light, what there was of it, also became dimmer. We passed the steps and sloshed on towards the darkness beyond. A few strides past the staircase and we were out of the water and on to a damp sandy floor. I stooped lower and raised out an arm in front, expecting my head to crash into a low rock at any moment. I stood aside to let Andy come to the front with his torch and then walked close behind him.

It was fortunate that I had extended my arm in front otherwise my head would have cracked into the rusting metal lamp hanging from a metal hook in the rock overhead. I shook my hand and gasped with pain.

"For God-sake, shine that torch on the ceiling for second before I fucking brain myself," I said, the pain giving an edge to my voice. Andy put the beam over the rough ceiling but there were no more hazards waiting to spoil my looks and we advanced further into the chamber.

"Well, well, well what's all this then?" I moved around to see what Andy had found. The moving beam picked out shelves cut into the rock on either side. The beam flickered over what looked like a bundle of cloth on one. For an awful second, I thought that we had stumbled on a crypt and we were going to see ancient corpses laid out with lolling sightless skulls. The moving torch beam picked out grey circular shapes on the shelves and more of the same scattered around in the sandy floor. There were even some in the sand at our feet. I stooped down and picked one up, it looked like a metal dinner plate.

"A Pewter plate," said Andy.

"A what?"

"A plate made of an alloy of tin, copper and sometimes lead," Andy replied so knowledgeably had it not been so dark he would have seen my mouth gaping with surprise. He took the plate and examined it.

"Poor bastards," he said. I looked at his face in shadow.

"Yes, it was a grim way to die," I agreed but he turned back with a look of mild surprise on his face.

"What are you talking about?" he asked.

"Poor bastards? I presumed you were on about the wave that washed the villagers away."

"Ah," understanding showed on his face. "No, I meant poor bastards for the toughness of the food they had to eat, and I was not talking about the villagers but the sailors who used these plates. Just feel the knife grooves on this plate" he passed the plate to me and I ran my finger across it and I felt deep scoring on the surface.

“So let me work this out,” I mused. “The priest liked to hold his dinner parties in this private little cavern to keep out the riff-raff.” Andy carried on in the same vein.

“Or, the Priest found his Creole congregation were a cut-throat bunch of thieves so he had to hide his best dinner service under the sacristy.”

I have Creole blood, though mixed, so I made a farting noise before adding, “Perhaps it was to protect them from all those rotten toothed pirates coming from England and Cornwall in particular—Hey—what’s that over there?” I asked, changing both the subject and the tone of the conversation. I chafed at not having a torch of my own to point where I wanted. I reached my arm over his shoulder and pointed to a corner of the shelved space. He focused on one of the shelves cut into the rock.

“The stonemason must have been the busiest man in the whole village, the whole Island even. Tombstones, floor flags and now cutting shelves out of solid rock; wasn’t there anything he didn’t do?” I could only agree but it was not the shelf I wanted him to point the torch at.

“Not there, a little further on. Yes there, what is it?” We were looking at a pole of metal or wood we couldn’t tell which, looked to be growing out of the sand. We walked closer, Andy playing the beam up and down the object. “Another lantern,” I said, finally working it out. We looked back across the shelf itself and found more pewter plates, drinking mugs, and bowls and then to our surprise, an ancient firearm in an advanced stage of corrosion.

Andy went to pick up the musket and an orange-red smear of rust covered his fingers and a piece of it crumbled away in his fingers. So if this wasn’t a crypt and we weren’t going to come across any rotting corpses, what was it? I started to get the first tingling of excitement that we may have discovered a treasure trove and I was sure Andy must have been thinking the same. We went through the contents of each shelf thoroughly, even lifting the black and slimy coalesced mass of clothing that at first, I had mistaken for a body. At last Andy summed up what our search had revealed;

“It’s all bloody rubbish not even fit for a car boot sale!” There was genuine disappointment in his voice.

“What’s a car boot sale?” I asked.

“It’s where people sell their old stuff to make more space in their house while making a little money at the same time. You put the junk in the boot of your car and drive to a car park where others are doing the same and sell whatever you can." The lesson over, Andy waved his hand over the shelves. "But stuff like this would never sell."

"Surely these plates are antiques?" I protested.

"Yeah, big deal, a few quid perhaps but they won't get you a new bike or me even a set of spare oars for the boat." He sounded disappointed but added a little more quietly, "If we tried to sell them to tourists, they'd get into a heap of shit with customs. Then we'd get into a heap of shit because the police would trace them to you and me. You'd get to spend time in the town jail with your old mate Henri using you for a punch bag. No thanks, you can keep that." Andy was right, of course and I knew he was still awaiting a permanent stay visa. Any brush with the law could result in him getting thrown off the island under the existing immigration law. The so-called 'clean pair of hands' clause in St Gilberts immigration law that gave officials the power to refuse a permanent stay visa to any applicant under suspicion of wrongdoing. We looked at each other and both shrugged.

I said, "We can talk about it back at the house, but let's get in the fresh air, it stinks down here." The walls and ceiling were still damp and running in the aftermath of the tsunami and a few small dead fish lay beached on the damp sand with the half-buried plates and tankards. I picked up a plate as we went up the stairs and back into the relative darkness of the sacristy. We closed over the hatch removed Andy's rope, walked the wardrobe back over to cover the hatch and even kicked the mat across those few inches of exposed planks that had first aroused our attention and so we left leaving no sign we'd ever been there.

The ride back was easier than the ride in. The tide was still high and though the submerged rocks would have presented a real danger to anything larger, the small Avon inflatable slipped safely over the top of them. The spray and the wind in our faces helped blow away the memory of the cavern's rancid air. It was also easier to load the boat into the shed as the distance to it was shorter with the tide in. We briefly debated having our discussion at Andy's house but in the end decided mine was more comfortable. We clambered on to the Honda only for Andy to clamber off again so as to give me some space to kick-start the damn thing into life.

Eventually, it coughed and held, I revved it hard, more out of frustration than for any practical reason. I had shoved the pewter plate into the waistband of my shorts and put my tee-shirt over the top of it. The route to my house was uphill and I never got above second gear. When I reached my driveway, I kicked it into neutral and switched off the engine so we glided silently up to the front door.

For the second time that day, we sat on the veranda looking down at the sea below. A light breeze had set the small green leaves fluttering on a single strand of Bougainvillea hanging in so the purple flowers quivered as if shaken by an invisible hand. Andy lounged back on the padded wooden chair until he was almost horizontal. Two bottles of beer stood like bookends on the low coffee-table. They were straight from the fridge and misted with condensation which ran down the outside the bottle like tears and on to the glass top of the table.

"Got any grub made up?" asked Andy. Aunt Mert had done her best to make me independent. A key part of that education was to teach me how to cook traditional Creole food. I usually had the remains of something or other in a pan or in the fridge to give me something to snack on after a night on the town.

"I never got much chance for cooking yesterday what with one thing and another," I said. "But I have some bread and tomatoes and some of Aunt Mert's home-made Vegetable Achar." Achar was a spicy vegetable pickle.

"Bring it on, I'm famished," said Andy and so we spent the next thirty minutes or so in silence and dedicated snacking then we washed it down with another chilled beer apiece.

"I've been thinking about that secret chamber," said Andy lounging back with his hands clasped behind his head.

"And?" I prompted.

"Why go to all that trouble to cut a hole in the floor, carve a load of stone steps and shelves only to fill it with junk?" He mused.

"Yeah, it doesn't make sense," I said. "But what struck me as even more strange was that whoever created those steps and shelves couldn't have done it without the whole village being aware of it. You can't do that much hammering of rock and expect people not to hear it. In fact the labour needed to do it would have taken half the village anyway, it's not a one, or even a two-man job."

"Or a one-priest job!" Said Andy adding, "So what you're saying is that our secret chamber wasn't a secret chamber at all?"

"I guess I am," I replied.

"So why go to so much trouble to disguise the entrance?" Andy asked, and again we both sat back in our chairs to think. There we were, two young men with too much time on their hands and a mystery plonked in our laps to provide a welcome puzzle to pass the time with.

"How about this, the priest acts like a banker keeping the villagers valuables safe for them in his secret vault, safe against marauding pirates that must have infested the seas in those days."

"Nice try," I said, "but I don't buy it. Remember, this was just a little village barely scraping a subsistence, having more than one cooking pot would make you well off!"

"So what are you saying?" he asked.

"I don't know, but let's add it up. We have a secret chamber that everyone in the village knows about. Does that mean the chamber was only meant to be a secret from non-villagers?"

"I get you. They were hiding something from the outside world," said Andy leaning forward now, fully switched on.

"Let's see, what would your average isolated village want to hide from the outside world, swinger parties, orgies, satanism, child abuse?" He was speaking out loud and marking each alternative theatrically by raising his finger when he suddenly stopped as if his humour had turned in on itself. I could see that a new idea had just occurred to him. I waited in silence so as not to break his train of thought. When at last he spoke his voice came out quiet, slow, and low as if he was still thinking it through, "They were wreckers. The whole damn village were wreckers and the priest was one of them."

I looked at him, surprised at the change in his manner. "Wreckers?" I repeated.

"Yes. They lured boats close to land so they ran aground and then pillaged them," He explained. "Yeah, it all fits, don't you see?" Andy was still thinking aloud and without a single stammer. "They were all involved because they all stood to benefit. I bet each household was full of stuff—why, even the houses themselves were probably all made of all the timbers from wrecked ships. From those wrecked by accident and from those they lured on to the rocks." I tried to slow him down so I could get a handle on what he was saying.

"Wreckers? But how could a bunch of villagers wreck a bloody great sailing ship?"

Andy answered almost before I'd finished the sentence. He was on a roll.

"They showed false lights!" He saw my look of doubt and incomprehension "Yes, don't you remember that strange lantern we saw in the cavern? Not the one you cracked your head on…"

"Hand," I interjected but Andy swept over my correction; he was speaking so fast but my interruption caused his stammer to surface in one or two words.

"The other one, th-the lantern on a p-pole near the shelves. I thought at the time it looked a bit odd and wondered why it was th-there."

He explained how on a dark night a swinging lantern on the shore looks like a ship's light when you are at sea. When you're at sea, land-based lights are the ones that don't move. Sailors believing they see another boat even closer to the sound of the surf could easily make the fatal error of assuming there was a sufficient depth of water between them and the other 'boat' to continue to sailing in because the moving light causes them to believe they are still a safe distance from land. By swinging a lantern or lanterns on the mount they could lure a ship closer to the shore and thus on to the rocks. "OK then what?" I asked at the end of his explanation.

"They get the ship to pile up on the rocks but what about survivors how do they keep them from telling the authorities what happened?"

"There are no survivors," Andy replied simply. "Villagers drown survivors as they swim to the shore or kill them when they reach the beach." I looked at him to see if he was serious or just having me on, but he was serious all right.

"You see, they had to kill them for the reasons you've just given. You see," he explained, "survivors could put the whole village at risk."

"How do you know all this?" I asked.

"Because it used to happen in England," He replied.

"We used to have a law a few hundred years ago that allowed the owner of wrecked goods to reclaim his property as long as he did so within three months of a wrecking. In an attempt to prevent w-wreckers from s-seizing and destroying salvageable ships they added a clause to the law. This stated that if any man or b-beast escaped alive from the ship then the ship could not be considered a wreck. Of course this clause gave the wreckers even more reason to kill all survivors from a sinking ship because survivors stood in the way of them claiming the loot."

"You seem to be a bit of an expert on wreckers then," I said.

Andy smiled, "Well, it's partly because I had a history teacher at school that was hot on the topic and partly because I am a Cornish man. Parts of Cornwall used to have a reputation for wrecking—mostly unsubstantiated and undeserved if you ask me. But I'm sure there are places along the coastline that saw ships lured onto the rocks and its survivors murdered in the way I've just described. Besides I've read it in respectable history books."

"Well, remind me not to sail anywhere near Cornwall any time soon," I said.

Andy drew his finger across his throat in a cutting gesture and nodded towards me, "You can sail there, Rodney, but if you're wrecked, just make sure you swim out to sea and not to the shore." I had to do a double take just to make sure he was joking. Not totally convinced by his 'village of murderers' theory, I decided to challenge him.

"Well, this isn't England and there's no law like that here. Besides what did they get out of it apart from these shitty plates and a few planks?" I asked. "Obvious isn't it, whatever they could save from the boat and the people on it. Wood, jewellery, pewter plates, goblets and tankards, swords, firearms, clothes, lamps and perhaps most important of all, whatever cargo the ship was carrying."

"Yes, yes, I got all that but it's not as if they could sell to the surplus to the rest of the Island, is it?" I countered.

"Oh I don't know, there's always someone who has the right contacts to shift dodgy stuff—even in those days. It could have been someone with contacts in shipping who could sell it to South Africa or somewhere else. Anyway why would they have to sell it, they could always get the priest to store it in his secret cavern for whenever they needed it. The jewellery and clothes they could wear at home and around the village it was after all a village that kept itself to itself, wasn't it? Isolated from the rest of the Island by that sodding great Kasper's Edge so who's to be any the wiser?" He had a point but whatever theory we came up with, it looked as if the resident Catholic priest must have also been in it up to his dog collared neck. I gave a little inward chuckle at the thought of what Aunt Mert would think of that.

"Jeez if we had a metal detector, we'd probably turn up loads of trinkets from the area below the edge," he said wistfully. We talked around it for a bit longer but Andy believed he had solved the mystery of the secret cavern and since I could offer no alternative, we left our musings at that. However we agreed to pay another visit to the cavern the following morning. This time we'd go prepared with spades and lamps. On our first visit we hadn't been in a position to give the place a good going over and may have missed some hidden treasure. We also agreed that we would keep the secret to ourselves and tell no one else, no one else, apart from Nahil of course.

Gilberts Islanders know how to keep secrets. Secrecy is baked into our culture and forms part of our upbringing. We are brought up to never broadcast private matters outside the family circle. Our Island community is so close and interconnected that people protect and value what little privacy they do have. Financial difficulties, family disputes and sometimes worse, take place behind the closed doors of most homes. The next morning the family members each step out through the door to go to work, school, or to the market, all of them wearing their public faces while the private ones remain hidden. Does this sound cynical? Well, maybe it is, I happen to believe that it's better to make some things public so they can be dealt with. Instead they are hidden and left to fester. Whatever, it is a way of living that we understand and mostly it seems to work.

"I guess you'll be looking for a new girlfriend to land on the island now?" said Andy, and I didn't know if he was asking a question or making a statement.

"Yes," I replied, "but she'll be gone after a couple of days like all the others. She'll promise to text and send emails and probably will, at least for a few months anyway then we'll find that we've run out of things to say to each other, little in common anyway and by then she'll have a new boyfriend, end of story."

"Yeah well, I guess you've been there a few times before," he said, and we both reached for our beer bottles at the same time.

"I always thought that Joelle was at the top of your list anyway," he said and swallowed a few mouthfuls from his bottle without his eyes leaving my face.

"So did I, in fact I still do, but who knows…" I shrugged my shoulders and Andy excused himself to go to the bathroom and I let my mind focus inwards. There was a history of sorts between Joelle and me. We had both lost our parents at around the same age. I lost mine through a plane crash and she lost hers when a bus went off the edge of the road and rolled on to its roof. In my case I was fortunate, my parents had been wealthy and I had Aunt Mert to look after me. Poor Aunt Mert, she spent her late teens and early twenties looking after her invalided mother and so missed most of the freedoms that other young women took for granted, dating, marriage, and kids. Two months after her mother finally died fate lumbered her with me. Her sense of duty relegated her own needs yet again. I was eighteen when my trust fund kicked in and by then my extra curriculum activities with local women had become too much of an embarrassment for her to continue sharing the house with me. She had a good standing in several religious groups she was a member of and never missed the Catholic mass on Sunday. The exploits of her nephew Rodney did not, she believed, reflect well on her efforts in raising me. At eighteen I was out of control and beyond redemption. Shortly after a tearful farewell from the house she started to see more and more of Alfred Stevens, a widower roughly the same age as herself. When I was six months into my eighteenth year Aunt Mert married Alfred and moved into his house. All obligations met she was finally able to live life for herself.

Joelle Kelly, on the other hand had to stay in the hospital after the bus crash for six weeks. Not because she needed treatment of any sort but because it took that long to shame some relatives into owning the responsibilities of taking care of her. If her eventual foster parents were reluctant to take on this new addition to their household and it was perhaps understandable. They were already victims of two of the Island's most widespread problems; too many kids and too little money. The church does not encourage contraception so anyone buying it at the always crowded chemist shop, does so with burning cheeks.

Joelle and I were in the same class at junior school, she was always the scruffy one in tattered out hand-me-downs. She even attracted the cruel nickname of Miss Pissy. In the dry season water supply is always a problem on St Gilberts and the poorer you are the bigger the problem it is. Apart from swimming in the sea the young Joelle could go days or weeks without a shower or a change of ragged clothes. She was a quiet child without a real family and that, coupled with her personal hygiene and tattered clothing led to playground bullies, mainly other girls, picking on her, exclusion and name-calling mostly, but that's bad enough. I never saw her cry so she was tough and I admired her for that and I still do. We were both orphans and outcasts of a sort. My mixed blood showed in my face and blue eyes, softer straighter hair, height, and the fact that my parents had had money caused resentment in some and also set me apart. Joelle on the other hand lived with a family who never accepted her as being a part of it. She was tolerated rather than loved, and even made to feel responsible for dragging the family deeper into poverty. I know because I still remember her telling me how she had heard her foster parents say as much when they argued behind the hanging sheet that acted a makeshift wall screening their bed from the rest of the kids in the room.

We often played together and found we could make each other laugh; we were on the same wavelength and could share the same imaginary world that kids so easily lose themselves in as they play. After junior school it seemed as if Joelle changed. She became more studious and serious. It was as if she found her poverty no longer acceptable and was taking control of her own future. We were still young but Joelle seemed old by comparison and her new-found drive seemed relentless, and to me, even intimidating. As we progressed through Secondary school, well Joelle progressed, I just ambled, we seemed to have less in common and, for a while we hardly had any contact with each other at all. Joelle got a Saturday job in Fleurs, the clothes shop in town, and soon started to come to school in smarter clothes bought with the money she earned. The onset of puberty completed her transformation from scruffy street urchin into the most beautiful girl on St Gilberts. She did well in all her examinations and passed out a creditable third from the top of class. The top two were eggheads anyway. She got a job in a newly opened coffee shop in town and within a year she was managing it. It had been Joelle's idea to turn the coffee shop into the first and only Cyber-café on St Gilberts and she was the one who supplied its name; The Kokonet Café. St Gilberts was then just starting to attract tourists in small but slowly increasing numbers. The younger generation of St Gilberts was keen to embrace the possibilities of contact with the outside world the internet promised. Joelle's timing was perfect and the café thrived.

While Joelle was making her name as a businesswoman, I was also making a name of sorts for myself. When Aunt Mert left the house, I guess everyone expected me to go crazy for a while and I suppose I did. I played the field for just a little too long until my charm wore thin and my approach became predictable. Whatever it was, I came to realise there were no longer any local women who saw me as any sort of marriage prospect, a bit of fun on the side perhaps, especially for the older women, but little else. Word gets around fast on a small island and, besides, it was a limited pool and anyone who would have ever wanted to go with me had already done so, except of course for Joelle.

At around the same time, St Gilberts was beginning to advertise its potential as a tourist destination a little more widely. Billed as the "natural" alternative to other Indian Ocean favourites such as Mauritius, Seychelles, Maldives and Reunion, St Gilberts boasted minimal commercialisation, unspoilt natural beauty, and ticked most of the dedicated eco-tourists boxes. Those opting for St Gilberts unspoilt appeal had a choice of two tourist hotels. Both of the hotels looked impressive to me but I heard tourists describe them as having 'charm and character' and some commented on the 'authentic island experience of staying in them' which I later learnt from other tourists was shorthand for "a basic-to-rough" hotel.

Early on I managed to get a job in one of them but it only lasted for six weeks. The job got off to a great start, yes the work was boring and mundane but I enjoyed joking around with the tourists. At first the manager told me to be more respectful but then he soon started to encourage me when he saw and heard how much they appreciated my light-hearted and informal approach to customer service. The extra money made a noticeable difference and I began to believe that perhaps I had found my—what's the word—niche! Whenever life is going smoothly that's the time to look over your shoulder to see if something is rushing up to clobber you. I guess I never looked. One day six weeks into the job a female customer called me over as I was carrying some small tablets of soap and a pile of towels from the cleaner's store.

She was in one of the larger ground floor rooms that opened on to the square palm garden. She waited on the little veranda with its two deckchairs and wooden table and she was wearing a white towelling robe as if she had just had a shower or returned from the pool. She ushered me inside her room and when I entered to see what she wanted me to do she quickly closed the door behind me. I turned back to see what was going on and there she stood, the robe a fleecy pile at her feet wearing only a smile. She stretched out her arms to embrace me. I will not go into the detail of what happened next except to say the woman's husband entered the room unexpectedly, thirty minutes later. His wife was as surprised as I was but she was certainly not as scared. He had returned unreasonably early from the island boat trip he had booked at the hotel reception. I was lucky to escape the bedroom alive. If not for the wife blocking his way as he lunged towards my semi-naked figure, things might have taken a nasty turn. As I escaped across Palm garden and then up along the beach. The sound of the clamour became fainter the further I ran but I could still hear the couple's 'discussion' thundering around the hotel. It attracted the attention of other residents and then the staff which inevitably included the manager. He went personally to see what had caused the uproar. An hour later, traced to my sanctuary behind the rocks at the end of the beach, one of the security guards, Michel Remacie, told me to get my ass the manager's office. The interview was a study in brevity. I saw immediately as I entered that he was still shaking with rage, so much so that he struggled to speak. As I walked through the door he gulped some air and dropped his chin to his chest.

"Well, did you?" He asked. I pulled a rueful face and spread my arms wide like…like I assumed an innocent man would. But I've never been good at lying and my head was nodding in guilt before I could consciously control it. "Clear your locker and get out," was his second sentence. I spread my arms even wider with open hands as I tried to get some words out.

"But…" I began to plead. His final sentence was shorter still.

"GET OUT NOW!" he roared, cutting me off before I'd even started. After that there was no point in even approaching the other hotel, the news would have reached there before me, even if I'd run straight to it from the manager's office. The incident earned me local notoriety for a few months. When I entered a public place such as the local bars or even St Gilberts only supermarket, I received tuts and frowns from the older ones and giggles and sniggers from the younger ones. The first time I entered the Three-In-One after the incident, I received a standing ovation. Aunt Mert came around to the house to see me and for half an hour, she gave me fire and brimstone as if I were an eight-year-old again. She pointed out that I'd let my parents down, let her down, let St Gilberts down, let the church and hotel down and, worst of all, let myself down. She then went on to check on the state of the house comparing each room with how she used to keep them.

"The place is an absolute disgrace, a pigsty! I worry about you, Rodney, I really do."

My second foray into the job market was in the small fish canning factory on the other side of the island. The cannery was a small scale version of the tuna canning factory on Mahe, the main Island of the Seychelles. Canning is an automated process, so what jobs there are mainly consist of manual work such as cleaning fish, labelling tins and shifting raw fish in, and pallets of tinned fish out. This employment stretched to four months during which time I tried my hand at the full range of available jobs. The work was undemanding and monotonous but it could have been enjoyable if the rest of the workers had been friendlier. It surprises tourists and other outsiders that even on a small island like St Gilberts factions and divisions occur between neighbouring villages. Most of the workforce came from the same village close to the factory. I on the other hand lived close to Port Albert, the name of St Gilberts main town. They saw me as "one of those townies". When word got around that I had inherited a large house and had a private income, my co-workers were resentful and relations with me cooled to open resentment. In their eyes I had taken a job away from someone more needy and deserving. Steady jobs on St Gilberts are few and far between so perhaps they had a point there. I stuck at it for nearly four months then decided there were better ways to spend my life so I left them to ostracise and scowl at someone else.

After that I went back into the tourist industry though this time I decided to stay self-employed. My brief spell in the Hotel had taught me something about myself. Female tourists found me attractive. They seemed to like my height and my face and my aqua-blue eyes seemed to fascinate them, in fact, all the characteristics that had marked me out as an outsider to be picked on and bullied as a child had now, it seemed, finally turned to my advantage. I also believed that visitors were drawn to me because of my genuine interest in them and the lives they lived in their strange and different worlds to mine. Whatever, but that they were drawn to me there was no doubt. Even the woman who had led me astray and got me the sack from my hotel job had not been the first visitor to pursue me. My standing with the St Gilberts women was at an all-time low so why shouldn't I take advantage of the opportunities that dating female tourists could bring?

"Hey! Where have you been?" asked Andy returned from the bathroom and now stood over me as I awoke from my reverie. I shook my head and returned to the present.

"Do you want another beer?" I asked.

"Nah," he answered, but when he saw my shocked expression, he smiled broadly and said loudly, "Of course, I bloody do! I've already asked you twice but you were daydreaming about your beloved Joelle."

"You could always have helped yourself—you know where the fridge is," I countered.

"Just get the bloody beers, for Christ's sake, what kind of a host are you?" I inwardly flinched at his blasphemy, a result of my upbringing rather than religious devotion and showed him a single finger pointing up like I'd seen on American films.

"Wrong finger," Andy jeered as I went into the kitchen for the beers.

Thank god for Andy and Nahil, I thought. I had first met Andy just over a year ago in the Three-In-One. I heard that a white guy had bought up the new bungalow that was close to the beach. Local rumours said he had been a bodyguard to a VIP and had retired early with a large pay-off, after taking a bullet protecting his paymaster. So he had street-cred right from the start. However the first time I met him I took him for a tourist and paid him no attention. Earlier the previous day I had swapped my old watch for a shiny new divers watch. My old watch had been a present from my father's agent in the United States. He came to St Gilberts for my parent's memorial service and a forceful Aunt Mert cornered him in my parent's house after the service.

"You have made a load of money off this boy's father now what about the boy himself? No father, no mother. How am I supposed to raise him alone? AND WITH WHAT?" Aunt Mert had told me the story herself and to cut her longer version short; the shame-faced agent emptied his wallet there and then.

"A few measly bucks!" Mert had snorted. The agent with great reluctance and a great many protestations handed over his watch, the only thing of value left on his body. I imagined Aunt Mert snorting with derision again as she took it from him. Years later when I arrived home from my last day at school she finally took it from the little box she'd kept it in and handed it over to me.

Two days before I met Andy for the first time I had swapped it for another watch on a swap that seemed too good to be true. Just before he'd boarded the small plane to South Africa a fat middle-aged man explained to me that at his age and state of health, he wasn't going swimming any time soon let alone diving and felt a bit stupid with a big flash sports diver's watch on his wrist. However he liked the low-key simplicity of my watch. I remember even been afraid that he was going to change his mind before he left.

The next day I sat in the Three-In-One resting my arm on top of the bar palm down with my newly won gleaming stainless steel watch proudly on show. A white guy was sitting on the stool next to mine at the bar.

"Nice Omega," he said as he leaned over to take a closer look. I was confused for second because I thought he'd said "Amigo" but then I came to realise that he was referring to my watch. He lifted his own arm to reveal an identical doppelganger on his wrist.

"Omega Seamaster 300m Diver Chronometer," he said.

He was obviously something of an authority so I asked, "Is it worth much?"

He held out his hand and I took off the watch and handed it to him to inspect.

"It's genuine all right and you'd pay a couple of hundred over a thousand quid maybe even a couple of grand now for it in the UK."

"Are you serious?" I gasped genuinely shocked and I obviously looked it.

"At least that much for a new one and that looks pretty new to me." I told him that I had swapped my old watch for it the previous day with a tourist.

"I can swim with this one on. I always had to take the other one off first. A real pain."

"So what was your old watch?" He asked.

"Hell, I don't know, black leather strap, simple white dial, black roman numerals, nothing special, I think."

"Did it have a maker's name on it?" He persisted.

"Don't remember, hold on, yes, I think it came from India," I said.

"India, why India?" he asked.

"Er, I think the maker's name was Patak or something like that."

"Patek Philippe?" He asked.

"I don't know, maybe, why?"

He didn't answer but asked another question instead, "What happened to the tourist, is he still around?"

"No he left yesterday. Wouldn't surprise me if he never came back either since he didn't seem to have had a good time here."

"Well, you got a fantastic watch out of him anyway," said the new guy and that was my first meeting with Andy. In a way, that short exchange said so much about his character.

He knew a lot about many things. He obviously knew enough about watches to know that no one swaps a brand new Omega for an old watch unless that old watch is something a bit special. I'd picked up that much from his questions. Once he knew the other guy had gone and wasn't likely to come back, there was little, if anything, that could be done to correct things. He kept quiet and didn't piss me off by telling me how much I'd been duped. For most local guys, that would have been the best part. Andy wasn't one of those guys, he thought before opening his mouth.

He barely came up to my shoulder but I could see that he was fit and had the slim build of one of those deadly welterweight boxers who combine strength, speed, athleticism and stamina. I wouldn't have fancied my chances against him in a fight, but then I would say the same about most of the other guys around my age on the Island. Make love not war was my motto—or run like hell!

Andy left for home about an hour later flagging a bus down on the road outside. I decided to go into town to pick up a few more beers for the fridge though they were a bugger to carry on the bike. The Honda started at the first kick but I just knew it was going to play up on the return journey. Parking the bike close to the market I strolled down the main street and almost immediately bumped into Nahil and her Aunt Josie. Nahil embraced me laughing but her Aunt Josie was more formal, "Hello Rodney how are you?" She spoke in Creole and gave me a stern look.

"I can't complain," I replied and Nahil smiled encouragingly then threw her eyebrows up making sure she was out of Aunt Josie's line of sight first.

"I haven't seen you in church for a long time, Rodney, and Lucy tells me you haven't been sick." Lucy was Aunt Mert's first name and Josie was the only person I knew who used it—apart from Alfred, of course. I think even Aunt Mert found Josie heavy going. I didn't answer straight away and Nahil broke in to get me off the hook.

"What are you doing tomorrow?" I must have looked confused because she quickly added, "It's a public holiday." I immediately remembered the trip to the St Francis Mount cavern that I had planned for tomorrow with Andy but Nahil misread my hesitation for confusion.

"You self-employed people," I knew she meant 'self-unemployed', "lose track of all these little breaks while us in work really look forward them." I didn't want to mention Andy and I going to St Francis Mount with Aunt Josie close by but I didn't want to lie to Nahil either. I countered her question by asking one back.

"What are you planning to do?"

"Guess I'll just spend the day with Andy." I knew then that she'd be joining us on our little adventure. We continued with a few more pleasantries before parting. She and her Aunt walked towards the bus terminus while I went to pick up some groceries from the market. I looked at the fish on the tables it didn't look too fresh so I decided to give it a miss and check if any fishing boats had come in on Tamarind Beach. I could pick some up fresh on the beach if I were there when the boat landed. The Honda did play up and a few people even stood to gawp at me as I struggled to kick-start it. The effort left me soaked in sweat but eventually it fired up and the breeze soon dried me off once I got going. I headed to Tamarind Beach and my luck was in. A small open dingy had just come in and there only a couple of others waiting for it on the sand. I managed to buy two fair-sized Red Snappers enough to turn our little adventure into a picnic as well.

Taking out my pocket knife I gutted the fish and washed out the guts in the sea scrapping off most of the scales as well. I put the fish into a plastic shopping bag and hooked it over handlebars of the Honda and headed back through town and up the hill to my house. I put the bigger of the two Snappers in the fridge and laid the other out on a cutting board. I find cooking helps occupy my hands and my mind and relaxes me. I chopped up some chillies and pounded them in a wooden Pestle and mortar, mixed in some tomato puree I had made earlier and stored in the fridge and added a dash of olive oil. I made several deep cuts on both sides of the fish and rubbed the red paste in adding some to the cavity inside as well. I wrapped it in tinfoil added a drop of water before sealing it up and placed it on a tray in the oven to cook. I made up a small salad and boiled a pan of rice. I had some of the chilli and tomato left so I added it to a pan of spiced tomato sauce, one of my own recipes, the chillies would give it a little kick. When it was ready I sat out on the veranda to eat it. There was a steep drop beyond the thick wooden rail and I credited the up draught of air that always blew up in the evening time with keeping the mosquitoes away. The moon was full and it cast a single silver trail across the surface of the sea. I could hear the surf hitting the beach far below mixed with the sound of the wind rustling the leaves around the veranda. When I'd finished eating I went over and thumbed through my parent's old record collection and pulled out a Marvin Gaye LP and set it turning on the old Bang & Olsen turntable. The player still worked and in its time, my parent's time, it must have been a class piece of kit. Technically it was surely now obsolete but, in my eyes at least it was still was the business. I guessed my mother had loved listening to Marvin Gaye because whenever I played the record it stirred deep childhood memories in a way that nothing else could and that association must have come from somewhere, a deep memory perhaps. I didn't play it often because I was afraid if I overdid it the magic would go and I'd lose this treasured link with the past. I lifted the arm and gently placed the needle on the track I liked best, 'Let's get it on' then I lay on the couch and closed my eyes. The opening bars and then Marvin's voice washed across and around me, a soft tsunami of sound.

In my mind's eye I saw a tall blond woman smiling, her face so close to mine it was difficult to focus on any features. I saw blonde hair, white teeth and blue eyes and, for a fleeting second I felt, as I felt all those years ago, safe and loved. The moment passed and I was back in my lounge lay on the couch looking up at the monochrome photo on the wall. The track was just about finished and at the bit where the sound level drops away and Marvin almost speaks the last few words.

The word 'sanctified' sprang out and jolted me, it took my mind back to that moment earlier in the day when I had stood at the altar in St Francis Mount Church when I'd looked back over the dark and empty pews aligned in front of me. Suddenly our trip the next morning didn't seem such a good idea.

Without my usual night on the town followed by a protracted session of horizontal gymnastics with a tourist, I awoke more refreshed than I have for some time. Whistling between mouthfuls I ate a good breakfast of eggs on toast and a cup of coffee instead of my usual pot of tea. After the third cup I felt wired up.

The grey wolves of doubt from the previous night had receded back into the shadows of the encircling tree line.

I took the second fish out of the fridge. Made more chilli and tomato paste and rubbed it into knife cuts on the fish. I then wrapped it in tinfoil ready for baking and put it in a plastic bag with some salt and pepper. I picked a couple of ripe Breadfruits. By this time my rucksack was heavy but I remembered to squeeze in my lantern style torch at the last minute before setting off for Andy's. I was thankful that they were already awake and up when I got there. I hate disturbing people on the job. With tousled hair styled in the bedroom Nahil answered the door wearing one of Andy's tee-shirts over a pair of orange hot pants but she was otherwise decent for visitors and she invited me in.

"Will you have something to eat with us, we're just finishing but we can soon rustle up some toast," she fussed.

"No I'm fine, honestly, what has Andy told you about our trip today?"

Her eyes opened wide. "Wow, it's really weird and a bit scary," she answered, adding, "One part of me wants to go and see it for myself, but the other half is shitting it."

Pure Nahil, I thought, we both laughed at the same time and I wondered if she had just read my mind. Andy was sitting at the breakfast table filling his mouth with buttered toast and honey.

"What's in the bag, a couple of footballs?" I told him and he laughed.

"You Creoles, every trip's a full-scale party."

"You'd better believe it," said Nahil and Andy held up his hands.

"I do, I do."

We went down to the boat shed again and Andy got a couple of spades, torches and a Hurricane lantern. The lantern he topped up with kerosene before wrapping an old cloth around the glass part and stowing it firmly wedged down in the central locker. Nahil dug out a rusty wire frame from inside an old grill pan that we could cook the fish on and packed a box of matches as well. At last the expedition was ready to roll and once again I held the Inflatable while Andy and Nahil clambered aboard. We would have to sit three in a line with Andy at the wheel, then Nahil and then me. Andy gave me a hand up and we were on our way.

"Let's get this ship on the road!" Nahil exclaimed above the noise of the outboard and Andy smiled over his shoulder at me.

“What?” She complained when she saw the exchange and gave Andy a dig in the ribs.

The tide had just gone out and as we approached Al Solere beach and the St Francis Mount. The underwater spurs of rock that we had passed over the previous day now too close for comfort and Andy weaved in and out until we reached the shore. I had a sudden thought.

“It’s a public holiday today. I know it’s unlikely that anyone would come to spend it here but—”

“Except us,” said Andy. I nodded before continuing.

“Even so, why don’t we pull the boat up and park it to the left of the hill so no one can see it from Kasper’s Edge?”

“Good thinking Batman,” agreed Andy and we dragged it up the beach and into the shade of the hill. Only someone approaching from the sea would be able to see it.

“We’ll go to the church first and then come back for the picnic later,” I suggested and everyone agreed. We gathered all the stuff we’d brought, spades, lamps, torches, and, of course a rope to lift the concealed hatch in the church. As we rounded the front of the mount I looked up and along the line of Kasper’s Edge. We Creoles like to wear bright colours and I knew if anyone was picnicking up there I would have seen them. I saw Nahil looking up as well and could see she was fizzing with excitement and fearful anticipation. She is perhaps the bravest woman I know but there is one area that really scares her. Gris, ghosts and the spirit world.

We went straight up the steps through the graveyard and up to the church door. I’d forgotten about the padlock but Andy hadn’t, he reached in his pocket and brought out what could only be a professional lock pick. It had a flat aluminium handle but the business end was of blued steel. He fitted the toothed end of it into the lock while keeping tension on the barrel with a flat L shaped tension wire, also made of blue gunmetal steel. If he had opened the lock quickly before, now it took him only seconds before he had pulled the lock open. Nahil’s eyes were wide open with surprise then she giggled and hugged him.

“I’ll keep hold of this just so no one can lock us in with it,” said Andy placing the padlock in his pocket. I glanced at Nahil and saw she’d stopped chuckling. Once inside, again it took some time for our eyes to adjust but we didn’t wait. Instead we felt our way up between the benches and straight to the sacristy. Just before we entered, Andy lit the Hurricane lamp and passed it to Nahil. Andy and

I worked together naturally as a team so without any of us needing to speak we lifted the wardrobe away from the hatch and attached the rope through the brass ring on top. Within seconds the black hole of the stone stairway gaped before us. I sensed that this was going to be the make-or-break moment for Nahil so into the silence I dropped.

"It's lighter down there, better than up here." She didn't respond and her eyes glittered through the moving black shadows that played across her face as the lantern swung in her raised hand. Andy pulled out a torch and went down first. Nahil followed and I drew up the rear with a torch in my right-hand. With all the added light in the cavern that we lacked on our first visit the place seemed less threatening; it was also a lot dryer. The tide was out so we stepped on to a sandy floor instead of up to our calves in sea water. Andy let Nahil get her bearings and see the seaward end of the cavern first and pointed out the holes in the rock where both the light and the water entered the cavern. He passed her a spare torch and hung the hurricane lantern from the hook in the ceiling. We gravitated towards the stone shelves and our torch beams crossed and re-crossed the shelves throwing shadows on the wall behind. We played our torches across the objects and looked for lost treasure.

"I was right before, it is a pile of useless crap," said Andy, the disappointment obvious in his voice. We had been rooting about on the shelves for about ten minutes and by then we knew we had seen all there was to see, which didn't amount to much.

"The tsunami must have filled the cavern and washed the stuff off the shelves and on to the floor," I said, but with little enthusiasm.

"OK let's do some digging but I'm not convinced we'll turn anything up," said Andy and he hoisted a spade and dug it into the sand. Clunk!

"Did you hear that?" I said, they had and Andy dug carefully around his first cut and lifted out a pewter plate like the one I had taken home last time. He passed it to Nahil who shrugged her shoulders and passed it back to him he threw it disgustedly onto the nearest shelf. The harsh sound in that confined space made us all jump and, for some reason, we all looked behind us at the same time. I selected my own spot to dig and repeatedly jabbed my spade into the sand moving forward an inch or so every time, Dink!

I crouched down and clawed through the damp sand with my fingers until they closed around what looked like a small section of black metal pipe about an inch and a half long. I could feel that my spade had put a dent in it. I held it up for the others to see but they were too busy with their own prospecting to show any interest so I pocketed it intending to examine it later when we were in the sunshine. We dug around for another fifteen minutes until Nahil, who didn't have a spade to wield said she felt the cavern was a little chilly. We stood up from our digging. All our efforts had produced so far were six more pewter plates' two pewter cups and three jugs also of pewter. In addition Andy had unearthed several small objects that he identified as brass buttons.

"If there is anything in here buried deeper then I for one don't fancy digging for it," announced Andy. He walked over to the strange lantern fixed on a pole planted in the sand against the back wall. The pole was a single rod of heavily rusted metal with a large loop at the top so it looked like a large lollipop. Hanging down from a ring at the top of the loop was a chain holding a rusted broken lantern that I guessed would have held a candle. Andy moved the lantern to show how it would have swung freely just as he had described but only succeeded in causing the corroded chain to snap and drop the rusted lamp on to his exposed sandaled foot.

"Fucking, fucking shit," he repeated as he hopped around the cavern in a war dance. Nahil and I stood back to give him room and watched his shadow flickering about the cavern. We had all had enough and headed back up to the sunshine, struggling to carry our spoils we made our way back up the stairs and closed the hatch behind us. We carefully pushed the wardrobe back over to hide the hatch. I kicked the old rug to cover the wooden boards at the front of the wardrobe thus completing the concealment. Andy replaced the padlock as we left and I scanned the top of Kasper's Edge as we made our way back to the steps leading down to the beach. As far as I could see there was no one there to see us.

Nahil gathered driftwood for the fire and I got together a few stones to rest the rusty grill pan wire on. I used a rough stone to rub the rust off it then walked into the sea a little way to thrust the wire through the water and into the course white sand beneath, working it back and forth. It wasn't perfect but it cleaned up well and would hold the fish nicely over our fire. The breadfruits we'd roast straight in the fire itself. Andy lit the kindling that Nahil had gathered and soon we had a good fire going and a bottle of beer apiece from the cool box in our hands. With the Breadfruits roasting and the Snapper grilling we discussed our mornings work. Andy raised his bottle.

“So we got a few plates and mugs what’s our next step? I mean should we keep our secret a secret or should we tell the rest of the island about the lost village of the wreckers,” asked Andy.

“Well, don’t forget we broke into the church and we have taken these plates and things. Maybe we should just keep it to ourselves, that way we aren’t going to get in any trouble,” said Nahil. I thought of the possibility of having another run-in with Paul Henri and didn’t fancy it either.

I faced Andy. “I don’t think your theory about a village of—what did you call them—‘Wreckers’ and murderers, oh and including the priest, would go down very well on newly tourist friendly St Gilberts. I wouldn’t want to be the one who puts it forward.” Andy disagreed.

“The more bloodthirsty the better. St Gilberts is trying to attract tourists interested in ecology, culture and a genuine Island experience. This lost village, and especially this secret cavern, would go down great guns. Believe me, they’d lap it up.”

“Well, two out of three think the less said about our find the better. So should we agree to keep it to ourselves?” I suggested. Nahil nodded vigorously in agreement. Andy shrugged.

“Suits me,” he conceded. “I don’t want to see St Gilbert overrun with tourists. Besides, you guys are the local experts I’m only an *andover*. But nah, you’re right; we should keep it a secret ’cause once we let the genie out of the bottle there’s no going back.” That said we kicked off our sandals, sat on the sand around the fire and drank our beer waiting for the fish to cook. It was settled; we all agreed the best course of action would be to keep our discovery of Al Solere’s sinister secret to ourselves.

The fish, Breadfruit and beer made us all a bit sleepy and we lay back on the sand and lapsed into a contented silence. Nahil fell asleep and I closed my eyes behind my sunglasses. I must have dozed off for I suddenly started to find Andy shaking my shoulder and telling me we had better head back. We loaded the stuff on to the Avon and set off with a fresh ocean wind in our faces blowing away the last traces of drowsiness. We got back to Andy’s place early in the afternoon. After stowing the inflatable we sat in Andy’s lounge and chatted for a while longer. It was then that I felt the object digging into my side as I relaxed in a chair. I took it out and held up to examine it.

“What’s that?” Asked Andy, and I passed it to him.

"Well, that looks as if it could be the most valuable find we've made today," he said. For a second my spirits rose but Andy quickly tempered them.

"Mind you it's not THAT valuable so don't get your hopes up. It looks like a silver napkin ring probably made for the Captain's table." He examined it more closely scraping at it with his thumbnail.

"There some writing here," he said, and both Nahil and I leaned in closer to see for ourselves.

"It's in a good state of preservation so maybe it has been on the shelf all this time, well at least until the wave washed it off the other day," He said.

"Give it here," said Nahil and she took it from Andy who let it go reluctantly; his examination not complete. She held it up and read aloud the name on the ring.

"Valvaston."

It was my turn to take it from Nahil and, like Andy, she also parted with it reluctantly. The name on the blackened ring was not obvious at first but I continued to examine it and the letters sorted themselves out. "Valvaston," I said at last, enjoying the sound of the name as it left my mouth.

"I think I'll clean it up," I said gently establishing my ownership over the object at the same time.

"That might reduce its value," said Andy.

"Who cares, I'm not going to sell it," I replied and plonked the ring on the middle of the table so they could both examine and play around with it if they wanted to. To be honest I felt a bit disappointed, a bit flat. A silver napkin ring wasn't much to show after we had started out with such high expectations. Andy and I had started to believe we had stumbled on something big. The whole adventure now seemed nothing more than a busted flush. What I missed most was not the hope of discovering treasure, though god knows I missed that, but the sense of purpose I had briefly felt over the last day or so as Andy and I had planned our expedition to the cavern. I was sure that Andy was missing that sense of purpose too. For a couple of days I had a reason to get out of bed in the morning, somewhere to go and something specific to do.

The week that followed contained a series of hellos and goodbyes.

Samy, a slim, fit young woman from Spain came in on an early plane. We met by chance in the Three-In-One on the Monday evening and she left St Gilberts on the Wednesday flight to Madagascar where she picked up an onward flight to Johannesburg, South Africa. Her father was on secondment there and she planned to stay with him for two weeks before returning to Madrid. If we'd reached the airport a little earlier I might have seen the arrival of the plane she was to later fly out on. It was a prop plane, and the new influx of tourists it brought to St Gilberts included Heidi, who was the one hello of the week she was another German and she departed St Gilberts on the Saturday afternoon flight to Mauritius.

I liked both women and I actually bought Heidi a small bottle of local perfume produced from a secret mixture of St Gilberts flora. Of course the Honda wouldn't start and I had to catch a slow bus down to the town and then a slightly faster one along the less hilly coast road to the airport. I thought at first that I must have missed her but then I recognised her straight brown hair amid a crowd of other tourists. We exchanged addresses but the parting seemed flat and soulless and left me feeling uneasy, it was as if she had already left the island in her mind.

I made my way back into town on autopilot and somehow ended up in the Three-In-One. A group of old school acquaintances whom I hadn't drank with for over a year were in there and, after the usual compulsory digs from me about them needing a note from the missus to enter a bar, we settled down for a good session and Samy and Heidi's departure receded into the past as easily as the beer slipped down my throat. As usual I held court recounting stories from the old schooldays even including some of those sat across the table from me on how they used to pick on me at school which raised a few uncomfortable chuckles from those with enough heart to be embarrassed, and I told a few old jokes. We had just reached the stage when each of us had bought a round when two women entered the bar. As the door closed behind them I sensed my group falling silent. There were two more women on the street outside minding prams each with shopping bags hanging from the handles. The women approached our table and I immediately recognised them as wives of two of the friends sat around the table. Both women scowled when they spotted me. I had slept with one of them before she had married and our parting had not been amicable. My lack of commitment to marriage had been the problem yet again. One by one all my newly rediscovered friends reluctantly rose to their feet and, rather sheepishly, I thought, made their excuses and left. The impromptu school reunion was over.

"Excuse me are these seats taken?" The speaker was a woman, good-looking and in her mid-thirties, casually but expensively dressed. She had brown hair cut short and stylish but in a fussy way that was going to take some upkeep in our humid climate. She was with another woman who was younger and slightly prettier in a more natural way but lacking the confidence and poise of her older friend.

"Do you mind if we sit here?" She asked again. I waved an arm towards the padded bench type seats.

"Help yourself there's no need for reservations here." The older woman made sure she sat closest to me on the bench while the other one took a chair on the other side of the table so she could face us both. I knew the older woman was going to start a conversation but she waited a minute to see if I would start it off first. I stayed silent, relaxing on the bench smiling at nothing in particular.

"Are you from St Gilberts yourself?" She asked leaning forward a little so she could look me in the face. I could tell from her accent that she was British. She had blue-grey eyes and a direct, slightly confrontational stare that made me think she might have some of that pushy self-confidence I'd previously seen in an American woman I'd briefly partnered.

"Yep," I replied, still a little deflated after the departure of my drinking party.

"What work do you do?" she asked. Now she was starting to annoy me.

"Is this a job interview or a proposal for marriage because if it's for the latter you'd better be very rich," I replied. She leaned back suddenly as if I'd slapped her face but recovered herself and smiled.

"Well, you are perceptive," she said becoming almost coquettish. "I do interview people as part of my job in HR and I guess I am rich—relatively speaking." I knew the letters HR were short for Human Resources. I'd heard the term on television and knew it was the description of what we on St Gilberts still called Personnel work? How typical of westerners to see people as resources within an organisation like nothing more than cogs and bits of the bigger corporate machine. I looked her in the eye and I noticed hers widen a little as I locked on.

"Rich? What do you mean by relatively rich?" I challenged. She thought for a moment and then looked up under her eyelashes as she said, "Well, maybe relative to you I'm rich." So, she'd weighed me up quite quickly, as I had her. She looked the sort who routinely made mincemeat of wimpy men and preferred men who challenged her. She was right; I didn't look rich. I had a couple of days' stubble, had let my hair grow a little longer over the past few weeks and was dressed in a worn tee-shirt and battered looking surfer's board shorts. But hell, I'd seen millionaires land on St Gilberts looking rougher than I did.

"So you've only been on the Island for, how long, a couple of hours at the most and already you are insulting the locals." Once again she leaned back in her seat as if slipping a punch. She worked in HR and I wondered if she was oversensitive on political correctness and didn't want to be seen as a racist. All of which was outside my life experience, but it's amazing what you pick up from TV, films and, of course, from other tourists. If I'd read the situation correctly then she just as quickly remembered that she was not in an office environment and her bullet-proof self-confidence reasserted itself and she became coquettish again.

"By locals I presume you are referring to yourself?" At that moment I saw Andy enter the bar from the street and I waved him over.

The two women turned briefly to see who I had waved at, saw Andy approach the table and take the seat next to the younger woman across the table from me. The older woman glanced briefly at Andy and then seemed to mentally dismiss him. She returned her 'I'm in charge' stare to me. Female tourists ignoring Andy was something I had witnessed before. Sometimes when he told a joke, they ignored him; if, seconds later, I retold the same joke they would fall about helpless with laughter. I could never work it out. Female tourists just didn't go for him and I wondered if it had been the same for him when he was back in England.

Well, he'd struck gold on St Gilberts. As far as our local women were concerned, he was the main man, steady, quiet, kind, and polite, and, most important of all, obviously loyal to Nahil. Plus he had his own house and money to spend, what more could any girl want? If he hadn't settled with Nahil as quickly as he had, he could have done some serious shagging over the past year.

Andy offered to get a round in but I already had a full bottle and as for the women, well, I didn't even know their names yet. They never looked at Andy in acknowledgement of his offer so he went to the bar and just got his own.

"By the way, my name is Caroline and this is Samantha," said the older woman.

"Pleased to meet you both," I replied and smiled, holding eye contact with the woman across the table for just a fraction longer to take a little wind out of Caroline's sails. Out of the corner of my eye I saw her lean back and take a long pull from her glass. I also leaned back and gave her a smile.

"We only arrived today and would love to see more of the place. Do you know anyone who could act as our guide?" she waited for me to answer. I outwaited her so she added, as if it had just occurred to her, "What about you? Do you have any free time over the next few days?"

I knew then how things were going to pan out. Her need to follow rules would make her reluctant to exchange her holiday money illegally through me until she found out how much better my rates were over the official bank. Then she would go along with it readily enough, I would make a reasonable profit on that. She would also pay for all the meals and drinks giving me the money in advance, it would look better on her if I appeared to be paying. I'd get to keep the change and anything left over. Sooner or later, probably sooner, we would end up in bed. At the end of a week or so the whirlwind holiday romance would be over. She would board a plane home clutching some nice photos to show her colleagues back home of the tropics and tales of her tempestuous romance with an infatuated young handsome lad. She would then show the photo of self-same lothario draping his arm protectively about her.

"Are those contact lens?" She asked, leaning in close to stare into my eyes.

It was both a question and an excuse to lean in and push her breasts against my arm.

"Er… no they're all my own," I replied.

"Did your mother sleep with the milkman?" She asked which confused me completely.

"Milkman?"

"Never mind," she purred ignoring my question but increasing the pressure of her warm soft flesh against my arm. Her forehead was slightly damp in the humid air causing wisps of hair to stick to her temples which I found vaguely erotic.

"I like your eyes, milkman or not," she said. I felt control of the situation was slipping away from me. Unfortunately I also felt the pressure of a full bladder. I had been denying it for the last ten minutes but it now demanded that I take notice.

When she leaned back I seized my chance and stood up heading for the toilet, it occurred to me to excuse myself to the girls. Aunt Mert had always been hot on manners I looked back towards Caroline and said.

"Excuse me, ladies, I'm just off to the little boys room," before walking off again. As I walked I pondered the fleeting expression I had seen on Caroline's face when I had turned back and looked into her face. I could have miss-read it but it looked like the sort of hurt expression of someone familiar with rejection.

Had she thought that I was just going to walk off and leave her? Was her self-esteem really that low? Despite myself I found my attitude softening towards her a little more though I hoped that she wasn't going to be one of those needy clingy ones. They were easier to manipulate according to Dan Meme but only if you had the stomach for those sorts of mind games and scams and I didn't. Just as many men do not like to admit that they are paying for the company of the woman on their arm I have yet to meet a single woman who'd also want to admit as much, even to herself.

Suddenly, I stopped walking as it occurred to me that perhaps I wasn't going to be so good in my new occupation after all, I was far too soft, I always ended up caring too much about the women I went with. Shit! Was this another career path going the way of all the others, another dead end? *Rodney, get a grip*, I told myself. *You provide a service for which you deserve some recompense.* I had stopped walking and Gladys, who ran the small chandler store near the wharf, and was one of Aunt Mert's friends, was looking at me at me as if I had grown two heads. I shook one of them to clear it but with little success and staggered on my way to the little boys' room.

Any misgivings over my new career were forgotten as I exited the toilets. "Rodney!" It was Joelle entering the bar from the side door and I was so surprised that she had actually spoken to me that I just stood and gaped at her open-mouthed.

"Rodney," she repeated. "Are you drunk?"

"Of course not; it's only two in the afternoon," I replied.

"It's four pm actually," she said crisply. "You said you wanted to see how you can download music from the Internet. I've got some free time right now—only if you're free as well of course," and she nodded significantly towards the two women sat waiting for me at the other end of the bar. She must have already seen me sat with them. I found it difficult to reply but simply nodded like a dumb simpleton and followed as she turned and walked out towards her internet café. So, I'd deserted poor Caroline after all.

Together we leant in towards the screen. I wondered if my breath stank like a brewery or if Joelle could see me looking down the front of her V-neck tee-shirt.

"Finish logging in while I get my player," she said and walked towards her office. I moved the mouse on its mat and continued the logging in sequence. The mouse mat was new as was the upright plastic clip board for holding the documents you were typing from. I looked around and saw that each cubicle had the same new additions. That was Joelle, always improving things, always moving forward. Some of the women from abroad I escorted had impressive jobs, at least they sounded impressive to me, so much so I was often left wondering at my own lack of achievement. The same was true of the many tourists, male and female, I came into contact with at the hotels, the world they described as homemade St Gilberts seem small, insignificant and stuck in the past. Joelle on the other hand, I thought, represented a Gilbertise who could stand comparison with any of those high-flyers, and that made me as proud of her accomplishments as I'm sure she was of herself. I was thinking along these lines when I realised she was walking back towards me.

"Put your tongue back in, Rodney, I didn't invite you in to lech." She connected her slim MP3 player to the computer via a cable with a USB plug. Despite my earlier protest that I was sober, it quickly became obvious to both of us that I was several stages drunk. I struggled to understand what she was telling me until she prompted, "Now you try" and for the life of me I didn't know what she had just done or said or what she was now expecting me to 'try'. She sighed and disconnected the MP3 player coiling the attached cable into the palm of her hand.

"Perhaps another time would be better for you, when you haven't drunk half of the Three In One's stock." She raised a quizzical eyebrow adding, "Or maybe you are keen to get back to your new girlfriend?"

"What new girlfriend?" I fired back. "I had a little school reunion party earlier so perhaps I've had a couple of bottles over the odds for this time of day but so what?" Just to support my declaration the woman in bar wasn't my new 'girlfriend', I asked if I could stay on the computer a bit longer.

She simply nodded and started to walk away but then turned back. "I'll book you in for another thirty minutes."

I had the feeling there was something more she wanted to say so I made it easier for her, "And…?" I let the question hang in the air. She looked surprised that I could have picked up any shade in her voice considering my current state and turned back to fully to face me. With both hands planted on the computer table in front of me she leaned forwards, her straight arms compressing her breasts together in a way that I struggled not to stare at. She gave me a look that was in turns contemptuous, regretful and pitying. Well, at least that's what I think I saw but maybe my imagination was reading something that wasn't there.

"We've known each other a long time, Rodney."

“That’s true,” I replied intrigued where this was leading.

“I know you are not dumb.”

“Thanks.” I interjected going for a little levity but her expression remain serious even stern.

“Where are you going Rodney? I mean in life, where are you going? Because it looks to me as if you are just drifting nowhere.”

Stunned into silence I gaped back at her. Joelle had set me a question and was waiting on an answer and for someone who prided himself on never being stuck for an answer—I was stuck for one.

“What brought all this on?” I asked.

“Perhaps because I worry about you sometimes, God knows why,” she replied. “Take this gigolo business, is all that all you think you’re worth?” She looked at me with an eyebrow raised quizzically.

I replied, “Wow, you worry about me sometimes!” I let my voice rise as if in amazement but couldn’t help from adding, “Well, if you want to keep me off the streets won’t you go with me—I, I mean as a girlfriend not…” The question had been asked in all seriousness, in fact, from the depths of my heart, but of course it had come out as a joke. Muddle-headed Rodney had screwed up his chance yet again. Joelle wasn’t laughing and she didn’t take me seriously either. It was not the first time I had asked Joelle out only to be rejected and this was clearly not to be my lucky night either. My latest attempt had descended into farce even before the sentence was half-way through. Joelle’s face confirmed her answer as her full lips went square and she straightened up and turned for the reception desk.

“In your dreams big boy,” she said over her shoulder. Stopping at the desk to write in the internet log.

“You know one day I’ll give up chasing you,” I said lamely after her.

“Thirty minutes,” she shouted back over her shoulder as she left.

“I’ll take that as a maybe then,” I muttered to myself as the door swung shut behind her. The round doughy shape of Noshir Wadia leaned back on a chair from behind one of the low cubicle partitions surprising me; I’d thought I was alone in the café. His broad, round face showed barely a wrinkle despite the grin.

“At last a bird that’s not interested in the great Rodney Leon!” I showed him one straight finger pointing upwards.

“Wrong finger man,” he jeered, just as Andy had, and then he let his chair slam back on to all four legs dropping him behind the cover of the partition. I stared at my extended finger and tried extending another one then gave up. For at least a minute I stared at the screen but my brain was elsewhere. Who the hell did she think she was? Stuck-up cow thinking she's better than me. Who's she to give me the kind of lecture that only Aunt Mert, if anyone, had any right to give me. And, now I came to think of it, why did I find it impossible to swear in her presence?

On dazed autopilot I went to my Hotmail account, there was a message from Tracy telling me that she got back safely and that her sickness had cleared up soon after reaching home. She said she missed me and of course St Gilberts to. But the typed words somehow lacked conviction and in them I read instead that she had moved on. She was back in a different world, her world, and I was just a pleasant but fading memory. I replied with a brief thanks and good luck for the future type note, sent it, and then deleted both files from my mailbox. I had no idea of how to make the best use of what remained of my free internet session so I opened Google. I could hardly visit any porn sites as Joelle would surely find it logged somewhere and I couldn't escape the fact that I cared what she thought of me. In the search box I found myself typing in the name

"Valvaston"

I positioned the moving cursor arrow over the search button and clicked the left mouse button. The result was disappointing. The screen contained a question; 'Did you mean:

"*Galveston*"

Below the question were on-line dictionaries one of which featured mistypes. No luck there. I tried again but replaced Valvaston with "Indian ocean shipwrecks".

This threw up twenty-seven sites some were scientific and concerned with the degradation of the wood in old shipwrecks in the Indian Ocean but when I went to the sites and tried to find out more my way was blocked awaiting payment of a subscription. "Stuff that," I said and moved on through all the remaining sites. They were merely a collection of more of the same with a few small variations. I thought for a moment and changed my search to "Shipwreck" this time with the quotes to focus the search and this time I got over two million hits. I had no time to start scanning through all of them but I did look over page one and then, at the start of the second page I saw the Wikipedia had a list of shipwrecks. I knew Wikipedia was a free on-line encyclopaedia written by volunteers around the world and I had used it before and found it helpful as well as being easy to navigate and follow. There was a list of shipwrecks arranged by country.

When you are born and live on a small island like St Gilberts it's easy to start life thinking it is the centre of the universe. A little later in life it comes as a shock to realise that most people on the planet have never even heard of the country where you live. In fact, only those living close by on equally small neighbouring islands know where St Gilberts is. This realisation shook me badly when it first hit—I was aged eleven years at the time.

There were two wrecks listed specifically against the Indian Ocean but they were recent and I was looking for something a few hundred years back. I checked the wrecks for East Africa but again there were not many and all were still too recent to be of any interest to my search. I then checked South Africa and the Eastern Cape. This listed one wreck in the seventeenth century but it was not the Valvaston. My time was nearly up and though I could have extended my session I was beginning to think it wasn't going to go anywhere anyway, and perhaps Caroline was still in the Three-In-One. I decided to go for one more throw of the dice and typed in 'shipwreck registry' again without the quotes and got over one hundred and thirty thousand hits the first one being; The Worldwide Database of Shipwreck. "Bingo!" I exclaimed and leaned in closer to look at the screen and I sensed Noshir leaning out again to see what I was up to. I scanned the first page of the site and quickly learnt that some information was available free and some was available only if you paid for it. Based in the UK the company running the site also mentioned treasure, and treasure ships, which got my attention straight away. I burned up minutes scrolling through the pages. The site was full of interesting information though I soon realised that I would have to contact the organisation direct by e-mail or phone to find out if they had details of the Valvaston on their database. Maybe that's one for next time, I promised myself. I clicked back to the Google page listing the hits for 'Shipwreck Registry' and, was just about to escape out of it, when I saw a site titled; Free—Instant ship and shipwreck checker—find details of ships and shipwrecks free of charge.

I clicked on the link and entered the site. It was not a flash site at all. In fact it was downright plain with no adverts either. Obviously not selling anything I thought and read the menu of choices in a box down the left-hand side of the screen, one jumped out at me. "Tell me more about this ship". I clicked the option and a white oblong box appeared on the screen into which I was instructed to type the name of the ship I wanted to find out more about. Aware of time I quickly typed in Valvaston. I hesitated, mentally checking my spelling of Valvaston against what I remembered seeing on the silver napkin ring and, sure I had it exactly right, I placed the cursor over the search button and left-clicked the mouse.

Philippe Ronnier walked out of the bathroom followed by a cloud of steam. Even with the white towelling robe wrapped about him he still felt the drop in temperature as he entered the lounge and then carried on through to the smaller room he used as an office. Two hours previous had had left the apartment to go to the residents gym which was on the seventh floor and, as always before leaving his apartment he had logged out and switched off his computer as a security measure. On returning he had switched the computer on before taking his shower. He never used the showers provided at the gym ever since he had picked up a verruca virus on his left foot there. He knew the computer should be ready for use when he'd finished his shower. The new computer security suite he had downloaded the previous week to update his existing firewall and antivirus software had slowed the computer down so it was now running maddeningly slow. It was as if someone had poured treacle into the top of the damn thing. Perhaps he needed to upgrade the computer itself—after all it was a year old! He typed in a password and waited tapping his finger on the desk top. Determined not to waste his time he went into his small, but expensively fitted kitchen, and set a kettle to boil. He spooned some freshly ground coffee in to a cafetière and, just as the water in the kettle was starting to boil he heard a distinctive 'ping' from the computer in the office. He felt a sudden frisson of excitement but his face remained passive as he continued with what he was doing. He filled the cafetière and carried both it, and a cup, back into the home office with him. Phillippe Ronnier did not believe in displaying his emotions because he believed it let others know too much about him and might leave him all the weaker for that. That the website had received an interesting hit needing investigation excited him since it was the first such hit it he had had.

He clicked on the tracker software toolbar at the top of the screen and had to wait again, "damn computer," he muttered but at last the screen he had been waiting for appeared. He looked for the information he wanted contained in the three small white oblong boxes. In the first box was the single word 'Valvaston' the second box gave a time and a date '16.58. February 1st 2008 he looked at the third white box which contained the identifying Internet Protocol number of the computer used to contact the website. In the box were the letters I.P. followed by a series of numbers;

303.327.275.56.

He reached for a pen and a pad and jotted down the contents of each box before scrolling the cursor down to a bar along the bottom of the screen. He clicked on the button labelled 'TRACE'. Nothing happened for a few seconds and again he cursed the computer under his breath. In the top drawer of his desk was a small black moleskin notebook and he removed it and turned to the inside back page and looked down the list of names written there. He didn't have to look far down the list in fact it was at the top of the page and had three asterisks alongside it, one of only three names that had that distinction. The rest had either two or only one asterisk alongside.

He looked back at the computer screen again, but now there was intensity in his eyes and, for a microsecond, a muscle twitched under his left eye. The computer now presented a split-screen with a basic map of the world filling the left half of the screen and to the right an empty box waiting to be filled. At the top of the screen was the instruction

"Enter the address or IP to trace."

To the right of this was a white box into which he quickly entered

"IP 303.327.275.56."

He then clicked on the green horizontal arrow to the right of the box and had to wait yet again. This time his impatience with the speed of the computer was edged with his excitement to see the result, it made him curse the computer for the third time that day. After what seemed like an age text started to fill the box on the right of the screen but his eyes stayed locked on the map to the left. Two red lines, one vertical, the other horizontal moved across and down the map. They converged forming a cross somewhere over the Indian Ocean and a white lozenge shaped box popped up and overlaid the intersection containing the address 'St Gilberts GZ'. He'd never heard of St Gilberts before but a quick look down a sheet of paper headed 'ISO 3166 Country Codes' showed that St Gilberts, in the Indian Ocean, had the two letter internet code of GZ. He turned to read the text in the boxes on the right of the screen. He started at the top which read;

Running Services

*An **SMTP** service is running, the port is open.*

*An **HTTP** service is running, the port is open. The system is running Apache/2.0.54 (Unix). To view this service click here.*

An FTP service is running, the port is open.

***Location verification**:*

*The system is almost certainly located in **St Gilberts GZ**, it was an exact match in the database.*

#	***Hop Name***	***Location***
1	*(Unnamed)*	
2	*11.ar20.gst.dst.pipex*	*Belgium. BE*
3	*ge.-1-0-3.cr01.gst.dst.pipxr.net*	*Belgium. BE*
4	*ae.0-0.co02.gsl.dsl.pipex.net*	*S.Africa.ZA*
5	*pc9.cr05,tn5.bb.pipex.net*	*S.Africa.ZA*
6	*cr02.ldr01.pccwbtn.net*	*S.Africa.ZA*
7	*dltg.ge10.2 br02. ash01.pccw*	*S.Africa.ZA*
8	*coloba.iad.keepitsecure.net*	*Madagascar.MG*
9	*Mailserver Airtalk.com*	*St Gilberts.GZ*

The computer language meant little to him but he knew enough to be able to follow the trail that had led back to the source in St Gilberts. He had found the haystack, perhaps, but where was the needle?

There were other things he could do to refine the search but first he had to make a call. The three asterisks marking against the name Valvaston signalled that any enquiry connected to that name should prompt a call to Mr Denver regardless of the time of day. Valvaston must be something of incredible importance. Richard Denver was one of the richest men in the world and access to him for most mortals, including senior politicians, was through several layers of his management team who acted as human filters protecting him, and his precious time, from those who would waste it. Taking the moleskin notebook again he turned to a marked page and looked down a list of international phone numbers, his finger went down over each number and stopped underneath one, he reached for the phone.

Richard Denver felt like he was rising from the ocean floor. He knew that he mustn't rise faster than the bubbles of air he was breathing out or he risked getting the bends. His air supply was failing fast and he could feel the demand valve dragging reluctantly with every breath. The mother ship above was sounding an alarm. Confused, why could he hear an alarm under water? He looked up and saw a lamp hanging from the ceiling and despite his momentary confusion he realised that it was the phone by his bed that was ringing. His hand groped around until it closed around the handset and he had to juggle it around some more before he could put it to his right ear.

"Denver, who's calling?" He growled into the mouthpiece.

"Philippe Ronnier Mr Denver, I thought you might like to know that someone has made an online enquiry about the Valvaston."

"You thought I might like to know?" Repeated Denver and Ronnier sensed an edge in the other's voice.

"Someone's keyed Valvaston, the full name into the site and…"

"From where?" Cut in Denver.

"St Gilberts," said Ronnier annoyed at not being allowed to finish his sentence.

"Where?"

"St Gilberts, it's a group of Islands in the Indian Ocean north of Madagascar and the Comoros Islands. Well, that's what it says on the tracker map."

"Hmm, Indian Ocean, how sure are you of the location?"

"I have no reason to think that I'm wrong at this stage," said Ronnier but Denver seized on the hesitation in his voice.

"What the hell does that mean? You're sure or you're not sure, which is it?" Denver's voice was loud down the phone line and Ronnier's eye muscle twitched again.

"Well, several factors can influence the reliability of a trace…" Ronnier had to stop in mid-sentence as Denver cut in yet again.

"What factors?"

"Well, the use of a fake IP address, or the use of an internet proxy could show a wrong location. Also, if the contact had used a dial-up connection over a long-distance telephone call from another country, and even the use of certain firewalls by the individual or the internet service provider…"

His flow came to an abrupt stop as Denver roared down the line, "What the fuck are you talking about, Ronnier? All I want to know is, does someone in St Gilberts—wherever that is—know something about the Valvaston?" Denver's voice dropped slightly as he hissed, "Even if it's only the fucking name, and that they logged on to your site to find out more?"

Ronnier managed to keep a lid on his annoyance and his voice was a study in calm authority when he replied, "Yes, that is what I believe. The contact never registered on to the site but the trace result is straightforward enough." There was silence down the line and Ronnier waited.

When Denver finally spoke, his voice was also calm, even reasonable, "OK good work. Now I want you to trace whoever made that enquiry and find out what they know, all of it. Most of all I want a location. Of course no one else is to hear about this, no flags and no markers, nothing to alert the competition and, it's most important that you never mention the name Valvaston to anyone. Is that understood?" Before Ronnier could respond, Denver's voiced thundered down the line again, "I said; is that understood?"

Ronnier replied with deliberate control and calm, "Of course, no one will hear that name from me."

Apparently mollified, Denver turned to the practicalities. "Call Amanda and get her to make the travel arrangements, Of course I'll want regular updates of any developments and, do you need a cover?"

"I'll go as a tourist; it'll avoid any visa issues and provide a valid enough excuse as to why I am there," replied Ronnier and Denver grunted his approval.

"OK. Oh, and Ronnier, if a wreck location exists and you bring it to me, you'll never need to work again."

Ronnier smiled, but then asked, "Is there anything I should, or I need to know about the Valvaston or what it contains?"

Denver's voice was hard again and Ronnier had to move the phone away from his ear.

"Stop fishing, Ronnier, you know the name of the boat and that's all you need to know. Just do what I'm paying you to do and find me a location." Ronnier heard the connection break and the line went dead. He reached for the moleskin notebook again and looked down the list of telephone numbers again, memorising one he dialled it and waited. He smiled when he heard a click at the other end and the sound of a woman's brief cough down the line.

"Good day Amanda, it's Philippe Ronnier, I'd like you to make some travel arrangements for me."

When Richard Denver had returned the phone to its cradle, he let himself fall back on to the bed. The young woman in the bed with him was only twenty years old. He had met her the previous night and he couldn't for the life of him remember her name. She had not been woken by the call and continued to breathe heavily as she lay on her side with her back to him. Attractive young women were, as he saw it, one of the many perks of having more money than you could spend in several lifetimes. Such wealth gave you power and it was the power that mattered most to him. He now headed several multinational organisations but still kept the salvage organisation from which it had all begun fifteen years earlier. Yet, he thought, what good was power unless it brought you contentment and a measure of happiness?

As his wealth had grown, Denver had also come to realise that contentment for him was a moving target. When you could have whatever you wanted your palette became jaded by excess. Denver's appetite for life in general seemed to be waning. The young woman sleeping next to him moved her position slightly. He glanced at her and then, In line with his train of thought, his gaze drifted towards the small cardboard box partly hidden behind the clock on the bedside table. Inside the box were tablets that promised to be more effective than Viagra. Now, Ronnier's call had re-energised him. It had clarified what he already knew about himself, that it was in his nature to be content only when he was striving, taking on some new challenge, reaching for something just beyond his grasps.

It had been Denver's own idea to set Ronnier up with the tracker software so he could monitor the website for interesting hits. He knew that Ronnier was no computer wizard but also knew that once the software produced a lead, Ronnier was the man who could follow it up on the ground. Denver thought a moment, was Ronnier really the man to trust with something so important? He had only met the man on a handful of occasions and hadn't taken to him. Ronnier had struck Denver as a bit odd, fussy and pedantic to the point of being anal. He was obviously one of life's loners, but then he did get results and he was discreet.

Ronnier was Belgian, to Denver being Belgian meant you had a national identity, but only by subtraction. You weren't French, or Dutch, and you were certainly not German, so you had to be Belgian. You were the citizen of a country of coalitions. Ronnier was not connected to any of Denver's companies; also not on any of Denver's official payrolls, and certainly not on any personnel file either. Denver had once used a specialist agency to check Ronnier's past but the report they finally presented to him was meagre and told him next to nothing. Ronnier, it appeared, had no family, no girlfriend, no boyfriend, no hobbies apart from the gym, nothing! His asexual and sterile life made Ronnier the ultimate expendable man. If he disappeared, no one would notice he was missing and no one would care.

Denver's own security chief and long-time friend George Kirkham had met Ronnier on a couple of occasions and had suggested there could have been a stint in the French Foreign Legion in Ronnier's past. When Denver had asked Kirkham on what evidence he had based his suggestion the Security Chief had replied that it was just a guess based on nothing more than his personal intuition. All of this was perversely reassuring to Denver who saw Ronnier as a secretive man who knew how to keep secrets. Ronnier may have lacked the sophistication and the smooth expertise of the ex-secret service personnel Denver also employed but Denver knew from experience that Ronnier was precise and meticulous.

That Ronnier preferred working alone and could deal with the more brutal side of business that sometimes cropped up and deal with it in a low-key but effective way. Apart from Denver's PA, Amanda, who arranged some of Ronnier's travel, Ronnier communicated directly with Denver and it was Denver who arranged payment of his fee into one of Ronnier's offshore company accounts.

Denver half smiled as, distracted for a second, he tried to imagine Ronnier masquerading as a tourist, but then realised he couldn't.

Philippe Ronnier stood looking into the open suitcase on his bed. He had slowly and fastidiously folded all his summer clothes and now he started to pack them in to the case. He needed a few more items but would be able to buy them at Brussels National Airport. The travel documents had arrived by courier service the previous day and he had spent a few hours trawling the internet for information on St Gilberts and the small group of Islands that fell within its jurisdiction. There were twenty-one Islands in total but only nine of those had the size and natural resources to sustain human habitation. St Gilberts was one of the largest of the group and was also the main Island housing the government and administration, such as it was. He had quickly scrolled through the statistics picking out salient details from the CIA World Fact Book website. The website grouped the information under nine main headings some of which had sub-headings below them. The main headings were; Introduction, Geography, People, Government, Economy, Communications, Transportation, Military, Transnational Issues.

"Back shit-kicking little village," muttered Ronnier as he scrolled through the information on the screen. He focused on the Introduction and then went straight to the Communications section.

Total population 24,000

Total Area 490 square kilometres

Languages: Creole 91.8%, English 4.9% (official), other 3.1%, unspecified 0.2% (2006 census)

Currency: St Gilberts Rupee. Tight controls on exchange rates and the scarcity of foreign exchange have impaired short-term economic prospects. The black market value of the St Gilberts Is rupee is twenty-five per cent less than the official exchange rate. Without a devaluation of the currency, the developing tourist sector will remain sluggish as vacationers seek cheaper destinations in the area such as Comoros, Mauritius, Seychelles and Madagascar.

Communications St Gilberts

Telephones main lines in use:	*15,700 (2007)*
Telephones._.mobile cellular:	*17,100 (2006)*
Telephone system:	*general assessment: effective system domestic: radio-telephone communications between islands in the archipelago international: country code—897; direct radio-telephone communications with adjacent island countries and African coastal countries; satellite earth station—1 Intelsat (Indian Ocean) Mail Server Airtalk.*
Radio broadcast stations:	*AM 1, FM 1, short wave 2 (2003)*
Television broadcast stations:	*1 (plus 9 repeaters) (2000)*
Internet country code:	*gz*
Internet hosts:	*1 (2006)*
Internet users:	*1,600 (2006)*

He decided to print off all the sections and read through them during the several flights it would take to get to this speck in the Indian Ocean.

It was a typical early February day in Brussels, grey with a drizzle that soaked your clothes in minutes if you had no umbrella, or, like Ronnier, had too much luggage to be able to carry one. He had caught a taxi to the Grand Central rail station alighting at the entrance across the road from cream fronted Meridien hotel. He bought a ticket for the twenty minute journey to the airport and descended the steps to the platform where other travellers with luggage were also waiting. A family stood to his left, the two parents trying to control their excited offspring consisting of two small boys and one girl, their ages ranging between six and ten years old. The larger of the two boys snatched a comic from the smaller boy who shrieked and, having got his mother's attention, started to whimper. Ronnier closed his eyes, the total expected duration of the flights was 28 hours and 55mins it was going to be a long journey. The flight to Zurich was uneventful. Service from the cabin staff deteriorated from half-hearted to surly during the flight. From Zurich he flew to Dar es Salaam in Tanzania. By then he just wanted to get to his destination and begin his assignment. The airport processed him through to a small Twin Otter, a great plane for short runways and high payloads. As he settled himself into his seat, he felt for the first time in what seemed like a lifetime, that he was finally nearing the end of his journey.

I had not seen Andy and Nahil for a while because I'd been spending nearly all of my time with Caroline who had now returned back to England. After I'd left the Kokonet Café following Joelle's little training session and my fruitless internet search for info on Valvaston, I had returned to the Three In One only to find Caroline and her mate had already gone. However I caught up with her later the next day since it's not exactly difficult to find people on a place like St Gilberts.

Caroline had turned out to be something of a revelation. She was excellent company and knew instinctively how our relationship should work. She always gave me ample funds before we went for a meal or drink or day trip anywhere. What's more she never asked for change but continued with further kitty top-ups as we went along, always without any prompting from me. I changed money for her and she was as delighted with the rate of exchange I gave her as I was with the commission I paid myself for the service. Taking my cue from her I also rose to the challenge of playing my part in her holiday romance. When we were together I gave her one hundred per cent of my attention and took her to places that as a tourist she would never have found. With her money we hired one of the small mini-mokes for a day and she let me drive her to all my favourite spots. We watched a sunset off Memory Hill on a weekday when the usual local lovers weren't there. We took a small picnic and, as the colours in the evening sky became fiery, we made our own memory together right there on the hill. We even reached our climax in time to see the bright red sun sink below the horizon. With the torch I'd brought we still struggled to walk back down the steep slope to Lolas beach. Giggling like teenagers we tripped and supported each other down the rocks until our feet hit the sand.

Away from her own environment, her work and area of expertise, she softened with each passing day becoming calm and gentle in outlook. I guessed back home her work was not only stressful but that it was a part of her identity. Away from it another Caroline was gradually able to emerge, an identity that was more vulnerable maybe even fragile. It was as if she was desperately afraid I would let her down if she became too attached, maybe something had happened in the past. Our love making was also a revelation. With that direct and challenging stare of hers I'd assumed she was the sort who would want to take charge, go on top, set the pace and call the shots. Instead she was a true romantic at heart and liked her love making gentle and slow, more inclined towards quality rather than athletic quantity which suited me just fine. However I think I really started to feel close to Caroline when she first rode pillion on my old Honda. Her sense of fun and enjoyment was so open, obvious, and childlike I couldn't help but find it infectious and her ever more endearing. At times like those I wanted to gather her in my arms in a big protective hug and, in fact, I often did just that, and felt surprised how natural it felt to do it. Over the days that we were together we packed a lot in and grew to understand each other. Our differing backgrounds, cultures and life experience were revealed layer by layer. Each of us shared a growing understanding of the subtle yet complex part each of us played in the short but intense romance. It was a collaboration where we each had our own version of reality yet the two separate pieces seemed to fit together.

Would or could it have ever come to something more? If, for example, Caroline had bought a house and stayed on St Gilberts or, I had moved to live in England with her, would it have worked? I doubt it, in fact I am almost sure it wouldn't, and yet I am not sure why. I was really fond of her and totally enjoyed her company, but I had difficulty in separating my true feelings and true self from the part that I was playing and deep down I knew it was affection not love that I felt towards her and maybe that's why she never visited, or even saw my house, and I never intended that she would. No doubt she imagined I lived in basic circumstances and so would have been surprised to see where I lived. It would probably have dislodged one of those cards on which the delicate balance of our relationship rested.

Nevertheless, there were tears at the airport when we parted and they were genuine tears on both sides. She promised to write and e-mail, the usual stuff, and I wondered if she would. On one level I hoped she did because knew I was going to miss her. On another, I thought that the days we spent together that we had filled with so much, had been enough. I was not sure I could have continued the charade of our romance much longer no matter how pleasant and rewarding it had been for me and how pleasant and therapeutic for her. I don't like to analyse what I do too much. Occasionally a stinging comment from the Aunt Mert, or Joelle, does make me feel bad, that I'm a leech preying on hapless lonely female tourists. They believe tourists give me money because of my looks and because I somehow trick them into thinking me something I'm not, namely a poor native in need of financial aid. Joelle used the word 'gigolo', others, sneered that I was 'a male prostitute, having his shag-a-thon paid for'. I disagreed. They underestimate the awareness and intelligence of women like Caroline who know the score. But how could I ever begin to explain that to Joelle? I knew I was good at what I did and that the women I went with always wanted much more than just sex. I have come to understand that the way they experience St Gilberts is so much different to the way that I do. To me, St Gilberts is just the familiar home that I grew up in and have always known but to them, it has a sort of exotic, romantic, magic and of course a nice romance helps to consolidate the illusion. I am sure that New Yorkers, Parisians, Londoners view their cities in a much different way than how I would see and experience them. If my tourist girlfriends had dreams and fantasies of how romance should be, then I just assist them to imagine that maybe reality could actually match the dream. They had come to St Gilberts in search of paradise and romance; I just helped out on the romance side. Is that putting what I do too high? What I mean is that I am in the business of escapism; sun, sea, romance and sex, all provided without long-term emotional commitment (well at least on my part). All they need to bring is the script and their wallets and I'll do the rest. Caroline had gone home with some lovely memories. I was left with a little extra spending money in my pocket for being her banker, tour guide and lover. Her memories would last longer than the cash, but I had my memories too. I was sure that a memory bank full of happy memories was just as valuable, in its own way, as a bank full of cash.

After I'd seen Caroline off at the airport Andy and Nahil had dragged me off to the Katcholo Club to cheer me up.

To be honest, I didn't feel much like going to the Katcholo or the possibility of the long walk home from it afterwards. The three of us started the evening off in the Three-In-One and then two hours later shared a taxi to the Katcholo Club a large wood built barn of a place where the sea facing wall is open with a large veranda so clubbers can cool down and then warm up again as they coupled-up and got close. *God help us all if a dropped cigarette butt takes hold* I thought, and then wondered at myself for thinking it, was it a sign I was getting old? The club already had a big hand-painted banner over the door with "Tsunami Party" in broad blue writing and a childish drawing of waves book-ending the legend. Crowded, hot and sticky inside, we all took a deep breath and dived in. At least I could see over the mass of heads but for Andy and Nahil it must have been like walking through a living jungle. It took Andy twenty minutes to get served and by then Nahil had gone to the dance floor to join the entire population of the Island under the age of fifty, or so it seemed.

We fought our way back through the crowd trying not to spill our drinks and I could see Nahil dancing in and out of the seething mass on the dance floor. The high overhead ceiling fans slogged sullenly round and round defeated by the heat and smoke and my shirt was starting to stick to my sweating back. The bottle in my hand was no longer chilled, in fact, barely even cold, but I drank on, and alternating turns with Andy to go to the bar. If I had been alone with Caroline then she would have paid for all the drinks now, Andy and I had to dip into our limited weekly budgets to pay for the drinks and I was already spending through the little I'd made during my time with Caroline. The dim overhead lights streaked like comets every time I turned my head so I knew the drink was taking effect. I fell back a step only to feel the back of my shirt and jeans drenched with by cold liquid. I turned to find I'd knocked a full beer glass held by my old school rival Thomas Azemia. He was a tall handsome guy who, like me, had played the St Gilberts women recklessly, and for too long, got a bad name and then run out of local women who were still willing to succumb to his charms. We had never been friends. He had been the school athletics champion and was competitive in everything he did, a real alpha-male type. I was not competitive at all but I envied and resented the fact that he had once dated Joelle Kelly, albeit very briefly. Joelle had always resisted my advances but one day, I promised myself, I'd work out how to win her round.

Above the noise in the club I tried to apologise but Thomas simply sneered and rushed in towards me so I, in an instinctive and defensive reflex action, shoved him back as hard as I could. He reeled into the circle of dancers who had stopped to watch with relish the unfolding events of which I was unfortunately at the centre.

The circle of clubbers prevented Thomas from going down and they pushed him back to the upright. His eyes were flashing in anger and I could see that adrenaline was gearing him up to fight. I on the other hand wanted to put as much distance between us as possible. What rooted me to the spot however, was the crowd which now encircled us both. Well, that, and some vestige of self-respect, St Gilberts is a small place and what happened in the next few minutes would be news on the street tomorrow morning. I think few on St Gilberts including me, would have given much for my chances at that moment. Thomas couldn't match me for height but he was more than a match for me in all other respects and he knew it. Most of the guys who had been in my class at school had beaten me up at one time or another in those friendly, and not so friendly, playground tussles that boys engage in to establish their status. I had no doubt that most of them could still repeat their earlier success over me today if it came to it. As a fighter my status had been low whereas Thomas's had been frighteningly high. As well as my height I have wide shoulders that apparently make me look shorter when I'm seen from a distance but close-up add to the illusion that I am larger and bulkier than I am. But there was no hope that I was going to intimidate Thomas with them now as we squared up to each other.

"Come on you fucking coconut," He yelled in Creole. Though the swear word was in English.

"Or are you going to hide behind that faggoty white bumboy mate of yours?" He was still yelling in Creole but Andy would have had no difficulty understanding everything said so far and I wondered if he was going to intervene. I would have welcomed the backup of an ex-bodyguard but when I gave a quick look around there was no sign of Andy.

"You're the only effing batty boy around here," I yelled back, getting into my stride, "you can't even pull a bird these days, so fuck off, and go and pull yourself off."

I was aware of the effect this would have on Thomas and what his likely response would be. At that moment I didn't care. Perhaps it was the drink or his "coconut" reference to my mixed parentage and the company I kept, but my blood was up.

In that second I felt up to anything he could throw at me and crouched as he rushed in head down like a charging bull. I took a swing but my fist bounced ineffectually off the top of his forehead and I felt a sharp pain shoot through my hand. Even as I winced and shook my hand out his right fist came towards my chin and I barely moved my head in time. I wrapped both arms around him pinioning his arms in the way I had seen heavyweight boxers do when they needed a rest or needed to smother an opponent's attack. To some extent it worked, but not for long for he was as strong as an ox and twisted in my grip. I knew it would not be long before he started to use his head, feet and knees so I worked around to one side of him while struggling to contain his arms. To some generous souls it may have looked as if I was controlling him for his own good while trying not to hurt him too much. In fact nothing could have been further from the truth if, at that moment, I had been able to knock his brains out all over the floor I would have done so, but I was more intent on stopping him knocking mine out. I became aware the music had stopped and somewhere in the club a whistle sounded and the circling crowd fell back a little.

Paul Henri was easily St Gilberts most unpopular policeman and that's saying something because, off-hand, I am not sure if there is a single popular one. I had been a friend of his son, Christopher at junior school but we had had little to do with each other after that. It was well-known that Paul Henri regularly beat both his wife and son Christopher especially after a night on the booze, which was every night he wasn't on duty and even most of those that he was. Maybe that explained and almost excused the bitterness that soured young Christopher's attitude to life as he grew up. Our friendship petered out soon after junior school and, though I pitied him his home life, he was starting to show signs of having inherited his dad's temper and use violence as a means of expressing it. In the end I just didn't enjoy being around him anymore.

My other connection with the Henri family came in the form a school romance with Christopher's older sister who was in the year above me. I was still only fourteen and she fifteen. We had a few tumbles on Memory Hill at Lolas Beach and later, after I said I wanted to split up with her, she pretended to be pregnant. In a moment of vindictiveness she told her dad that I was the one who had taken advantage of his little daughter and he had stormed around to my house. In those days Aunt Mert was still at the house bringing me up in place of my parents. Henri had burst into the house bellowing like a bull, tiny Aunt Mert had stood fore square in front of him with hands on hips. She was wearing an apron and that look she always used on me when I'd got a bad report from school. Cowering behind her while at the same time towering over her, I thought Henri was going to tear me limb from limb but Aunt Mert proved to be more than a match for him. A few long minutes of staring and muttered threats, curses, and an excess of heavy breathing from Henri and he eventually caved in under Aunt Mert's frosty stare and calm authority.

Paul Henri had never made any secret of his contempt for my mixed parentage. My mother was a Swede but my father was a Creole and. as a top league basketball player in the United States, he probably earned more in season than Henri would earn in his whole life. When Christopher reached twenty years old he left St Gilberts. Shortly afterwards Paul Henri proudly told everyone after church one Sunday that his son had an important management job in Mumbai, though he called it Bombay back then. Eleven months later Paul Henri had to fly to India to identify his son's dead body. It later leaked out through foreign news reports that packages of heroin had disintegrated in Christopher's stomach as he got ready to smuggle them to the UK. Clearly he had been a regular drugs mule from the moment he had left St Gilberts and, several long-haul trips later his luck had finally run out. When Henri returned to St Gilberts he started to drink even more and became even more angry and vicious than before. His wife left him and went to live with her brother's family on Rainier, a neighbouring island. Henri remained to vent his anger on those poor sods that came within his sphere of power the power given to him through a combination of Police uniform, badge, and sheer physical presence. Until I had grown a few inches past him Henri had been the strongest and tallest man on St Gilberts and proud of the fact. I certainly wasn't any stronger but I was taller and he didn't like it. He had a habit of walking with a slow measured stride and always paused for a second in any open doorway before entering a room of people. It was as if he expected it to fall silent just because it was he that was walking in. He took it for granted that everyone should be in awe of him. In fact most saw him as a sad drunken loser, behind his back of course, because he was still a big, barrel-chested mean-spirited bully with the power to make a person's life a misery if he chose to.

Henri dwarfed Thomas as he stepped between us with his shining drinker's face tilted back a little. That was another of his little mannerisms, looking down his nose at people as if he was wearing a peaked cap that prevented him looking straight ahead. It was as if he was making a point that he had to look down at lesser mortals because he was so much higher than everyone else. My height made that impossible but Henri, determined not to have to look up to anyone, especially me, tilted his chin up at a ridiculous angle and sighted me down the barrel of his bulbous boozer's nose. I guessed with growing unease that I might have to pay for the effort that this adjustment was costing him. He stepped towards me and his hand reached behind his back for something, handcuffs perhaps or was it a nightstick? At that moment the fire alarm went off and there was general mayhem as people shrieked and rushed about and out of the various open doorways. Caught in the sudden melee and I found myself separated from both Henri and Thomas and steered outside to the veranda at the back.

"Down here," hissed Nahil who took her arm from around my waist and jumped down to join Andy on the sandy beach six foot below. I jumped down behind her to join them. It was dark away from the lights and it was easy for us to melt away in the shadows and make our way back to the road.

As we reached the point on the road where Andy and Nahil turned off to head down to Andy's house Andy asked, "Do you think Henri is going to let it go at that?"

"Sure," I replied. "What did I do wrong anyway? Nothing, that's what."

Nahil threw her ten rupees worth with a contemptuous, "Who gives a fuck what Henri thinks or does?"

I do, I thought, because I knew that Henri could make life difficult for me if he wanted to.

"Thomas's head is bloody hard," I said shaking my aching right hand, "I'm lucky I didn't break my fist."

"Join the club," said Nahil and she showed me the cut and bloodied knuckles of her right hand.

"Who got on your wrong side tonight then?" I asked. She didn't answer but Andy answered for her.

"The glass fire alarm cover."

The next day my hand still twinged a little now and then as I wandered around the house. I was listless and bored. So I ventured down to town and had a single beer in the Three-In-One hoping to see Andy and Nahil there. As I've said before, on St Gilberts it's almost impossible not to bump into people and especially those you want to avoid and, speaking of those you want to avoid; as I left the Three-In-One I walked straight into Paul Henri. I made to walk around him but he stretched out a straight arm to block my way. Resignedly I stood still and faced him. He adopted his usual posture of looking down the barrel of his nose and, because I was taller than him, tilting his head back to meet my eye. We both faced each other like this for a few moments. I could compare it to a stand-off between two wild west gunslingers but in reality it had more in common with school playground posturing. Unfortunately, to complete the analogy I defaulted to moving my jaw as if I were chewing gum and staring sullenly back at him. It was an affectation from my rebellious teenage years as a silent way of showing defiance to teachers and other authority figures attempting to discipline me, no doubt with just cause. I never used it on Aunt Mert of course she would have clouted me across the ear if I had dared to show such defiance. It was also a mistake to try it with Henri who reacted as if I had spit full in his face. His features contorted into a nasty grimace.

"You think you're clever Leon but you're not." I leaned back slightly to avoid the spittle spraying from his mouth but he hadn't finished, in fact he was only just getting into his stride.

"I haven't forgotten about that incident in the club last night when you attacked Thomas." I started to protest but he halted me in mid-sentence by suddenly leaning in and dropping the volume of his voice, to increase his menace.

"I know all about your little gigolo money changing scams." I gaped back at him consciously arranging my features to register innocent surprise. If I had had a knob of butter to hand I would have popped it on my tongue and we both could have waited in vain for it to melt. Money changing was a national pastime on St Gilberts so I wasn't unduly alarmed as Henri leaned in closer towards me, except when I smelt his sour breath. His head was no longer tilted back as he continued.

"The men in Parliament House are looking for their biennial scapegoat and you're in the frame son and I'm going to give you to them served up on a plate with an apple in your gob. You're going down Leon and that's a promise, trust me." I didn't like the way this was going, illegal money changing is endemic throughout the St Gilberts group but I knew he was telling the truth. Every two years or so, the authorities make an example of some poor sap by sending them to prison for illegal money changing. It's meant to act a message across the island group, a reminder to the general populace that money changing is illegal and punishable. The penalties were in fact draconian; up to two years on the small outlying prison island of Raynauld.

We were still facing each other out but Henri's head was dead level now, his eyes looking up into mine, I wasn't chewing imaginary gum any more. Henri gave a nasty little snort of laughter at finally getting the reaction he wanted. Normally I would have responded with a smart-arse comment but instead composed my features into a 'have you finished yet' expression. Henri smiled made his finger like a gun barrel and aimed it at my head then turned and walked away with even more of a swagger than usual. He was still looking back over his shoulder at me when within two strides he nearly knocked over Nahil's aunt, Josie, who was walking towards him. Henri was a model of politeness. With both of his huge hands on her shoulders to steady her from falling he checked she was OK asked if she needed to sit down or even have a cup of coffee to recover from the shock.

"Don't make such a fuss young man I'm not a doddering old woman yet," she said brushing imaginary dust from her jacket with her hands. But I could see that she was appreciating the attention and when she finally freed herself from him and came towards me, she commented as she passed, "He's not as bad as everyone makes out, quite nice in fact, not like some." She lowered her chin at that and looked pointedly at me as she walked by. Henri was still looking after her as if to confirm she was still OK and none the worse for their little collision. Then his eyes slid sideways to meet mine and he gave me that nasty little smile of his again.

The approach had been dramatic, first sight being suds of cloud on the horizon, with just a sense of green haze beneath. Then there was the emerald of the Island, encircled by a turquoise lagoon and separated in parts from the ocean by only a pencil thin line of surf crashing on to the reef. The plane came in low over the crystalline clear blue sea and the coral beneath the surface broke up the dazzling aquamarine with swirls of darker shades below the surface. The runway was close by the sea and, as the plane came into land, Philippe Ronnier looked through the window towards the landside and saw spiky green heights, ridges and glens, shaded tints of green. The shore was verdant with coconut palms, feathery Casuarinas trees, and flowers everywhere. Through the window across the aisle he could see the sun glittering on the surface of the sea far out to the white line of surf he had seen on the approach. Ronnier wondered how soon it would be before he left this dot in the middle of no-where and then compressed his mouth as he wondered how brutal were things going to get.

The cabin doors opened and Ronnier descended the staircase on to the runway where the heat and humidity hit him as if a giant oven door had swung open the hot air filled the legs of his trousers. He sniffed and caught the scent of the flowers he had seen on their approach to the landing strip. A heady perfume carried on the air even through the acrid airport smells of hot tarmac, oil, aviation fuel, and burnt rubber.

The single story building that handled the new arrivals terminal seemed little more than a shed to Ronnier. In contrast, the taxi he climbed into thirty minutes later, after clearing through what passed as immigration control on St Gilberts was surprisingly new and clean.

"Tourist," Asked the driver shouting over his shoulder as they set off from the airport.

"What else," Ronnier replied.

"Exactly, what else is there to come to St Gilberts for—except to relax," roared the driver over his shoulder but it was obviously a rhetorical statement and they both lapsed into silence. This suited Ronnier who, although he realised that he was missing an opportunity to pump the man for local information, decided to wait until his head was clear. Besides, for a taxi-driver, the man, despite his initial bluff hearty manner, seemed surprisingly reluctant to get into a conversation, and Ronnier wondered if the man's spoken English was limited. As they drove along the coast road he noticed the steep gradients of the inland roads as they snaked upwards towards the villages set high on the green peaks. He realised why the taxi was new, only a vehicle in good condition could cope with those roads. In wet conditions even with a new car you'd need prayers as well. There was a mish-mash of house styles from wooden shacks to dazzling white and turquoise villas with colonial style verandas and filigree detail carved into the wood around the windows, roof eaves and red terracotta tiled roofs. Against the backcloth of dappled green foliage there were colourful flowers; reds, yellows, orange, pinks and white. To his right the sun still reflected off the sea with a brightness that forced him to squint against it. High palms on the beachside of the road momentarily blocked the sun as the taxi passed so the bright light strobed into the cab in a series of blinding flashes. At last the road widened and there was a little more traffic. There were also more buildings and he mused if it was a village or a small town perhaps?

"Ah welcome to the capital of St Gilberts, where all the action is."

The taxi-driver shouted back over his shoulder. *The capital? Action?* Ronnier looked at the sleepy backwater they were entering and then quickly at the driver's face reflected in the rear-view mirror. He expected to see humour in the driver's eyes confirming the irony behind his last statement, but there was none. To the driver, this really was the capital—the place where all the action on St Gilberts happened. It was the centre of this man's universe. Ronnier's mouth compressed in contempt again as he looked out of the window to his left and then at a modern glass fronted building set back from the main road. It seemed busy with islanders both entering and leaving through the revolving doors at the front, but it was the name running just below the flat roof in large, three foot lettering that had caught his eye, "AIRTALK" a name he remembered from the trace report. Ronnier sat back in his seat and smiled for the first time in days the underused facial muscles managing only a ghastly rearrangement of his usually impassive features. So, the hunt was off to a good start. He was tracing the user of an IP address and what he, or she, using that address knew about a boat called Valvaston, only he wasn't supposed to mention the name. His smile slowly faded as he wondered how he was going to manage any of that.

Amanda had booked Ronnier into the Reef Sands Hotel on the edge of town. The hotel was basic and the staff appeared so relaxed that he wondered if he would ever clear reception. It was after lunch local time and, though he had adjusted his watch to St Gilberts local time on the plane, he compared his watch against the hotel clock on the wall just to make sure. He checked in and then exchanged some Euros into St Gilberts Rupees and frowned at the poor exchange rate. He hoped the local prices were going to be low. His room was basic and clean and, tempted though he was to lie on the bed and sleep for a while he made do with splashing cold water into his face. After all it had been roughly thirty-three hours and several time zones since he had left his apartment in Brussels. He had managed to get a little sleep on the final leg of his journey but he still felt a little light-headed and slightly disorientated. He showered, changed clothes and went down to the hotel bar. The bar was dark in contrast to the brightness of the light outside and Ronnier confined himself to an orange juice before heading out on foot to cover the short distance to the centre of the town.

He noticed there was a harbour with several yachts moored in the natural bay formed by the curved coastline. He could see an office and marine chandlers store with a small café, toilets and laundry room attached. There was also a refuelling depot and several capstans spaced along the wharf. Ronnier turned in towards the cafe. The café contained only one customer apart from himself and, after ordering a bottle of beer he sat leafing through the menu he found on the table. Albert Raguin was sixty and had worked at the harbour since he'd left school at the age of fourteen, from his position behind the bar he had seen the white man enter the café and had taken his order for a beer. St Gilberts wasn't anywhere near overrun with tourists but Albert had still seen plenty over the last few years, well it seemed like plenty to him, but this one was different again. The newcomer was a big solid looking man about six foot tall and not carrying any fat either. He looked well dressed like a man on his way to church on a Sunday. Tan coloured trousers with a shiny brown leather belt that matched polished brown shoes. He wore a flowery shirt cut differently from the usual island style that tourists liked these days. Made with a discreet pocket on the front and all the seams hidden, Albert wished that he had a shirt like that. In fact he wished he had the trousers, belt and shoes as well. They sure didn't make clothes like that on St Gilberts and you couldn't get them in any of the shops that sold imports either. Was the man in his forties or early fifties, it was difficult to say, but Albert guessed that some of the local girls would see him as a bit of a catch. From his clothes he looked well off and that wouldn't do his pulling power any harm either. It was strange though, that he wasn't with a wife and family and he didn't carry a camera, wear shorts, or even a baseball hat, he was different in every other respect from the usual relaxed backpacker brigade who carried their packs and rubber roll mats on their backs and wandered, smiling like innocents, into the town looking for cheap digs only to be directed back to the only two hotels that would take them.

The man raised his hand and Albert picked up a pencil and pad and walked over to his table.

"Good afternoon," said the man beating Albert to the punch adding, "Lovely day isn't it?" In fact Albert thought that it was about time that St Gilberts had some rain to fill the water tanks, quench the fruit trees, and keep the dust down, but he nodded noncommittally to the customer.

"Yes it is, are you here on holiday?" Albert asked.

The stranger replied with an easy smile, "Yes. I've just arrived and was walking into the town when I spotted this café and felt a snack and a drink would be just the ticket. What's the club sandwich like?"

"It's good, I make them myself."

"Do you run this Marina?" asked Ronnier. He never suspected for a minute the old man was anything other than a low paid hireling, but hoped the question would work like a subliminal compliment.

"Yep," the man replied.

"Do you own it as well?" asked Ronnier unsure if the old man had understood his first question correctly.

"Yep," the man replied. In fact Albert shared ownership of the business with his wife. His two sons and two daughters helped in the day-to-day running of the Marina in fact they more than helped—they virtually ran it for him.

"Do you run the office next door as well," asked Ronnier now struggling to keep disbelief out of his voice?

"Yep—that to," Confirmed the man. Ronnier looked suitably impressed but held back from asking more questions. There was something about the man's terse responses and defensiveness that was preventing the conversation flow in the way Ronnier wanted it to. Instead he looked at the menu and then up at the man.

"A club sandwich it is then, oh, and another beer to help it down. thanks." The man didn't bother to make any note in the pad in his hand but set off for the bar and soon Ronnier saw him duck down to rescue ingredients from a small fridge placed behind the bar. Fifteen minutes later Albert brought the sandwich and the beer over to Ronnier's table. The sandwich had many layers and there were a pile of crisps around the plate, the beer bottle was misted with condensation that pooled and ran down the side of the bottle in small rivulets. Ronnier turned to thank the man but he had already turned back for the bar. Ronnier sensed a faint under current of resentment from the man but couldn't for the life of him understand why he should have directed at him.

Albert stood behind the bar clearing the wooden chopping board he had used to prepare the stranger's sandwich. A small sink was at the end of the bar and it was out of line of sight of the man who was at the table near the window, the one that looked out over the jetty and the sea. When Albert was sure the stranger could not see him reflected in mirror behind the bar or in the window he was sat near, he watched him covertly. As he watched the stranger Albert began to construct a new theory about the stranger's reason for visiting St Gilberts. The man wasn't a tourist but a businessman on a fact-finding mission to choose a location for yet another hotel. Perhaps he was checking out the marina because he worked for a shipping line that wanted to include St Gilberts as one of its regular ports of call. Albert nodded to himself as he replaced the wooden board to its place in the drying rack. Why couldn't they leave St Gilberts alone and just the way it was? Surely it had already gone through enough change over the past ten years? The stranger had raised his hand for the bill and Jean went to him with the bill already made out. As Albert handed him the bill the man asked;

"Is this the main harbour for St Gilberts?"

"Yep and it's just about the only one worthy of the description as well, it's plenty deep."

"Do many boats stop by here?" Asked Ronnier.

"Plenty."

"How long do they usually stop?"

“A few days, sometimes a week.”

“As well as the other excellent facilities I can see, have you got Wi Fi available at this marina?” Ronnier’s tiredness was causing his patience to wear thin and he decided to shelve the stealth approach and ask direct questions. It would save a little time and would still be low risk. After all he wasn’t giving anything away. Albert screwed up his weathered face.

“Why what?”

“WI FI. Wireless fidelity—it’s just something that some, he was tempted to say ‘most’, marinas have. It allows their visitors to use the Internet on their yachts.” Albert’s face now registered outright anger, “The Internet—that’s computers and stuff, isn’t it?” His voice rose both in volume and pitch.

“Sailors and yacht owners stop here to refuel and relax, if any of them want to spend time messing about on a computer then they can get themselves to the Kokonet Café in town.” He said it in such a way to leave Ronnier in no doubt what he felt about the use of computers on boats. He took the notes that Ronnier handed him and produced a fist full of coins from a pocket in the front of his apron. Ronnier waved away the change but that still didn’t bring a smile to the old man’s face. Ronnier sensed the old man’s eyes on his back as he left the café and carried on up the road towards the cluster of shops ahead.

How many notes he had passed to the old man? Ronnier did a quick mental calculation to convert the cost of the meal and drinks into Euros. *Merde!* he thought, *I could have a decent meal in Grand Place for what I just paid for that plate of crap*, and then realised that he had nearly said it out loud. He stopped by a small general store and bought a packet of peppermints and had to break into another high denomination note, he cursed himself for not having kept some of the change from the café. He chewed on two of the peppermints and hoped they’d cover the smell of lager on his breath. The main street was busy with locals dressed in bright colours and wearing styles varying from the modern western style clothes worn by the younger islanders to the more conservative clothes worn by the older members of the population. He stopped walking for a second when a sudden dizziness came over him, the cumulative effect of those thirty hours of air travel, lack of sleep, time zones and the beer were catching up on him. The dizziness quickly passed and he considered returning to his room and leaving his investigation to the following day. Sorely tempted though he was, Ronnier shook his head clear and walked on. Denver would want an update of progress and since he was in town he would check at AirTalk before he went back to the hotel to rest. He rounded a curve on the street and saw the glass-fronted building he'd noticed from the taxi on his arrival. He noted the locals eyeing him as they passed him in the street and realised that it would be almost impossible for a stranger to blend into this small village-cum-capital of St Gilberts.

As the revolving glass door swept him into the building the cool, almost chilly air, of the lobby settled over him like the first draught of cold on an autumn morning as he stepped out of his Brussels apartment. The conditioned air, scented with what he guessed was cardamom, smelt pleasant and refreshing. The lobby looked modern; its interior arranged much like a bank with a row of counters able to serve several people at once. Ronnier could see that all the counters were currently occupied and there was one man waiting ahead of him in the queue. Even as Ronnier took in the layout of the place two counter spaces became available simultaneously and as the waiting man took one of the places Ronnier walked to the other. The young woman behind the counter was strikingly attractive with flawless light brown skin and long hair worn loose over her shoulders. She had a brightly patterned blouse that competed with Ronnier's shirt for loudness but with hers just falling short. A plastic name badge on front of her blouse gave her name 'Patricia'.

"Can I help you, sir?" she asked. Her voice was soft and pleasantly accented. Ronnier thought he detected a teasing undercurrent in it but wasn't sure it may have been his imagination. He brought his cell phone out and placed it on the counter between them.

"I'd like to buy a local sim card for my phone please."

"Certainly sir, have you just arrived on St Gilberts?" she asked conversationally.

"Yes, is it so obvious?" Ronnier smiled and their eyes met briefly.

"It's a small town and everybody knows everybody else," she replied.

"So far the place looks gorgeous to me from what I've seen I'd sure love to have a house here."

"Well, why not buy one and move in. I bet our houses are cheaper to buy than they are in…?" She looked at Ronnier and he answered the unspoken question.

"Belgium, I live in Brussels—the capital." Her brows drew together and then down as she searched her memory banks for any morsel of knowledge she knew about Belgium obviously drawing a blank. Suddenly her face lifted and she gave him a wonderful smile.

"It must be exciting to live in a big city," she sighed wistfully. Ronnier thought she must have time to spare or that she didn't get much opportunity to speak to foreigners and so was making the most of the opportunity now that she had one. Either way it suited his purpose well. "Oh you're not missing much Patricia, the novelty soon wears off, believe me," he lied, he was a city man to his core and the thought of spending more than a week on a small island like St Gilberts had no appeal for him at all. The young woman looked momentarily surprised when she heard her name used but her expression quickly changed to one of pleasure and she beamed back at him. Ronnier brought his hand to his mouth as if he had just had a thought.

"I suppose if I moved here I could work from home."

"What do you do for work?" she asked.

"Oh I deal in shares, buying and selling," Ronnier replied offhand as if he was trying to downplay it. The young woman raised her eyebrows and looked impressed. Ronnier added as if an afterthought, "I'd need to have access to the Internet though."

"I—I think it could be arranged," the young woman said, but sounded unsure. Ronnier picked up on the note of doubt in her voice.

"Do many houses have internet access?" he asked.

"Not really," she admitted as if embarrassed by the fact. "The airport, and some of the businesses close to it, have the internet and so has the Kokonet Café just up the road if you need personal access. Otherwise it would depend on where your new house was situated. If it was in town or near the airport you would have a better chance than if you were high up on the mountains. But of course you would need to speak to our contracts manager for more information on that." She nodded to herself as if the problem of Ronnier's need to access the internet after his move to St Gilberts was now resolved.

"If I moved here perhaps I'd be the first individual to get a home connection. I could have a big party to celebrate," he joked and the young woman giggled delightedly, Patricia loved parties.

"Where do you recommend that I visit while I'm here," he asked to distract her from the previous topic, the main object of his interest.

"Lolas Beach," she said without hesitation.

“All the tourists say it is beautiful, they say it is the most beautiful beach they have ever seen.” So much for the cultural highlights of St Gilberts thought Ronnier but he smiled back at the girl who was also smiling, her teeth several shades whiter than Ronnier’s. She reached behind her and produced a colourful cardboard wallet.

“This contains your new AirTalk prepaid SIM card and a phone voucher, we call them phonecards, and it’s worth two hundred rupees. The SIM card is free so you are only paying for the call card. All the instructions are with it but if you need help putting the card into your phone we,—I can arrange to have someone do it for you free. So the total cost is two hundred rupees.” Ronnier paid with another note and said that he would be able to install the new SIM card into his phone without help and thanked the young woman for her help.

“No problem sir I was happy to be of help.” She said it in a sing-song voice as if it was a mantra from a customer care course. However when he thanked her again and said goodbye she replied in a quieter voice and he had no doubt she was openly flirting with him now.

“So long, I hope to see you around very soon.”

“Er, yes, you never know and thanks. See yah,” he added a wink for good measure and hoped he hadn’t over played it, having a contact inside AirTalk could be useful. He turned and walked through the revolving doors and into the hot humid air outside.

The moment Ronnier exited AirTalk the young women at the counter on either side of Patricia burst into shrieks of laughter. They mimicked their friend's voice, "Hope to see you very soooon," drawing out the 'soon' in a parody of Patricia who put up her hands to cover her face and then giggled behind them.

"But Patricia, surely you don't fancy HIM," asked one, reverting to Creole.

"Why not?" Patricia shouted back. "He's not bad looking and he's thinking about buying a house here."

"Yeah sure," sneered one of the young women who then burst into giggles herself.

"Because he's old enough to be your dad," said the girl who was in the counter second along to her right.

"Yeah, old enough to be my sugar daddy," retorted Patricia and they all laughed together.

A tall slim man wearing a white shirt with a red polyester tie came through the door of the office behind the counter and looked in mock surprise at the commotion. His bland features rearranged themselves into an obvious, almost stage frown of disapproval. He swept his hand across his lank thinning hair and coughed loudly to get the girls attention. "Now girls let's get some work done, chop-chop," he said clapping his hands together in time with the "chop-chop" bit.

One of the girls, called Barbara, replied in English with a bored sounding "Go and stuff a pineapple up your arse." The others laughed so hard some of them had to brace themselves over their counters as they, most in vain, tried to catch their breath. One nearly wet herself. The slim man who was the new focus of the women's mirth had been brought in by head office from Port Louis in Mauritius, his mission was to get the St Gilberts Island office up and running and in line with Mauritian standards.

Being a Mauritian, he understood the local Creole which was little different to his own. But knowing the language had opened no local doors for him, or at least none he cared to enter through. The secondment had been sold as a promotion but it was, as he had come to realise, the worst professional move he had ever made, it was a poison chalice of a job. The local labour that was available, employable, and suitably qualified, did not amount to a great number of people so employers could not afford to be choosy. That, coupled with the clannish way they closed ranks against '*andovers*' or outsiders, of which he was one, gave employees considerable clout, if he sacked one it was highly possible that he'd have an all-out strike on his hands. He found the locals displayed a degree of tribal solidarity that would have been the envy of any workers' union. His managerial authority didn't amount to very much at all. Clenching his jaw he dropped the file he had been carrying into an in-tray and walked back through the door into the bunkered sanctuary of his office.

Ronnier's body was screaming at him that it was time for sleep regardless of what time it was locally. He headed back towards the hotel where he ordered some food on room service. He had to wait another forty minutes before the food arrived and he used the time to exchange the SIM card in his mobile for the new one he had bought. He switched the phone on once the card was in place and a message on the screen asked him to enter a PIN number. He typed the four digit number printed on the SIM certificate into the phone followed by the # key as directed. Taking the call credit voucher he scratched off the silver panel on the reverse of it. He had to refer to the back of the voucher again for directions to the next step in the process. Having read the instructions he dialled 110 listened to automated voice instructions that were thankfully in English, and then keyed in the number from under the scratch off silver strip followed by the # key again. His phone was now ready to use and he considered calling Denver to give him a progress report but decided to wait until the food had arrived to avoid any interruption to his call. Twenty minutes later there was a knock on the door and a rickety trolley wheeled in by a stout middle-aged woman in a white uniform that could have had her mistaken for a nurse or nursing home carer back home in Brussels. Ronnier gave her a tip and she gave him a dazzling smile in return as she left the room. He lifted the lid off the plate and checked the paper at the side of the tray just to remind himself of what he'd ordered. "Jack Fruit and Pork Curry." Ronnier tipped some of the boiled rice on to a plate and then spooned the contents of the stainless steel bowl over the top of the rice. After checking the contents first he added a spoonful of the tomato chutney from the small cruet on to the side of his plate. He put a serviette over his lap, took a deep breath, exhaled slowly, and then lifted his fork to the plate.

The food did have an interesting spicy taste to it but Ronnier decided the chef had added too much salt for his palette and left a third of it uneaten. Putting down his knife and fork he walked over to the bed and sat on the edge of it. He reached for the phone, thought about what he would report to Denver and how best to phrase it. He had little and nothing of substance to report and knew that Denver would seize on that with his usual belligerence. He felt dull with fatigue and the light-headedness he had felt earlier in town overtook him again.

He let himself fall backwards so he lay flat in the middle bed. The arm holding the phone also flopped down loosely at his side so it bounced on the bed causing the phone to slip out of his relaxing handgrip. Ronnier smiled, the bed felt good, he knew where he had to visit the next day and Denver was going to have to wait till after he had been there for his first progress report.

He woke at 5.30am. His body clock was still on Belgium time and sunlight was beginning to flood into his room through the thin curtains. It confused him into believing it was much later in the day than it was. Besides, he had slept well and felt strong and refreshed as he pushed the covers aside and went to the window. Drawing the curtains aside he looked out. There were a few people moving about even then though mainly hotel staff. He looked over at the sea, the sun was still too low to give the water the aquiline blue colour it had had on his arrival the previous day. He could see a thin string of seaweed twenty metres out parallel to the shore. He looked across to the edge of the hotel grounds and noticed four low beachfront villas with white plastic sun loungers and patio furniture outside. Closed curtains on all the villas and the lack of any towels or swimwear drying outside led Ronnier to believe they were all unoccupied. He needed to be able to move freely about the island, to come and go, whether night or day, without hotel staff being aware of his every move. Still wearing the same clothes as he had the previous day he went to the pool front dining area. It was early and the kitchens had not even started to prepare breakfast. He enquired at the reception desk about the villas. The receptionist told him they were vacant and, if he wanted, he could exchange his room for one of the villas for an extra payment of four hundred and fifty Rupees a night. Ronnier paid the extra and the receptionist told him that the current morning's breakfast was already paid for under the hotel room charge for the previous night.

"Feel free to continue using the hotel dining facilities sir. Each villa is self-contained so any meals you have in our restaurant we simply add to your bill." The receptionist called a member of staff over then told Ronnier that a cleaner would prepare a villa for him to move in and that it would take another hour. Ronnier returned to his room and had a leisurely shower and changed into some fresh clothes from his suitcase. Since Ronnier had not yet unpacked his luggage it was a straightforward matter for him to transfer. At eight am he dropped off the key to his hotel room at reception and collected the keys for the villa. A porter offered to carry his luggage but he shook his head and walked the relatively short distance to the villa furthest away from the hotel. The sun was still low in the sky and he managed the transfer without breaking into a sweat. The villas, newly built were all ceramic tiles and white painted walls, and contained two bedrooms, a small kitchen with a stove, fridge, kettle and a toast maker and an assortment of cutlery, crockery and pots and pans. Ronnier placed his luggage inside a built in wardrobe in the larger of the two bedrooms and made his way back to the dining area of the hotel in time for the breakfast service which was now underway.

He ordered coffee, toast and, what was listed as a traditional Gilbert Island breakfast. Ten minutes later a waiter brought a plate of egg, bacon and grilled tomatoes. He returned to the villa to answer a call of nature and went into his bedroom to change. He slung a camera on a strap around his neck and placed a white Panama hat on his head. He felt the hat transformed his appearance into that of the quintessential western tourist in the tropics, however when he stepped out of the bedroom he noticed for the first time how dark it had become. At the veranda he watched as hotel staff scurried around the pool snatching the thin padded mattresses off the sun loungers before running for the shelter of the hotel. Seconds later the rain came in heavy droplets increasing in volume and force until he felt closed in by falling grey walls of water. He threw the hat on to a table in the villa and sat on a chair on the veranda. He was out of the rain itself, but it was still close enough to feel the light touch of spray on his face drifted in by the down draught of the storm. An hour later it was still raining. Ronnier could see through the deluge that a solitary tourist had decided to brave the storm and was swimming from one end of the pool to the other. The poolside bar was closed for business and a line of hotel staff mingled with tourists stood under the eaves of the hotel and watched in silence as the lawns turned into green puddles. Ronnier remembered the large striped umbrellas in the reception area for residents use but just walking the short distance to the hotel would have left him as drenched as if he had jumped fully clothed into the pool. He walked back into the villa and switched on the television. The local news was on and the presenters were speaking in Creole. He recognised many French words in the broadcast but it took too much effort and concentration so he gave up and went back to the bedroom where he lay down to think. He had slept well the previous night yet for some reason he felt tired and weary. Was this the result of jet lag or was it the celebrated island fever in which the sufferer always put off to tomorrow what should be done today? No, that wouldn't happen to him he'd find the wreck site, if it existed, and earn the promised reward. Afterwards Denver and he would part company forever. With that happy thought he lay back and was soon in a sleep that stole away the rest of the daylight hours.

When he awoke his limbs felt heavy and uncoordinated. He staggered like a drunk as he left the bed making his way to the light switch and from there to the bathroom. It took another fifteen minutes before the torpor wore off. By then the rain had stopped and pool and garden lights reflected in the wet glistening leaves like fireflies amid the dark foliage. He walked across to the hotel and ate dinner in the hotel restaurant then drank at the bar late into the night. He had lost a day and his head still felt heavy and his mind dull. The alcohol didn't help and he knew that he would have to make up ground the next day because he needed to report something to Denver. He found it difficult to sleep when he later returned to his villa and lay in bed but eventually sleep came.

I stood at the end of my steep garden path where it met the road and looked across towards the low cloud covering the jagged green hilltops. At the top of my driveway the road rises steeply going to the left, but going right the road drops equally steeply downwards towards the town. I looked left and up at the bright red flowers on the Flamboyant tree startling in contrast to the dark grey of the gunmetal sky behind.

I could smell the unmistakable scent of rain on dry sun-baked earth and parched vegetation and noticed the drop in temperature on the moist breeze. Seconds later a grey wall of rain swept across the peaks hiding them as it came towards me. I walked inside took off my tee-shirt and returned to my doorstep just-in time to meet the advance droplets of the rain as it moved across the island like a vast army its advance droplets raising the dust from the parched ground. Tourists like to describe St Gilberts rainstorms as real tropical storms. I don't know any other kind of storm but I do know the Island had been waiting for this one for almost a week. Those in the town struggled to manage on the restricted water supply and many had not flushed toilets for days having to make do with pouring strong scented toilet cleaner over after each visit. Those in the outlying villages with pit latrines fared better. Thanks to my parents foresight my house had rain storage tanks to fall back on if the mains water supply gave out but even they were now almost empty.

The rain was falling heavily and I walked out into it feeling it cool on my skin. I let it fall for a few minutes to give the rain chance to clear all the dead leaves and bird shit off the roof and wash the gutters clear of all the piled up dust and muck. Then I walked around to the front water tank and diverted the water from the gutter downspout and directed it, with the aid of a flexible coupling, straight into the top of the tank. I then went around to the other side of the house and did the same with the other tank. It would not take long, with this volume of rain, to fill both tanks and then I would redirect the downspouts back into the drains and fix the lids back on the tanks. I had once left the lid off one of the tanks and a small animal, a mouse I think, fell in and drowned making the water stink. Without the lids Mosquitoes and other insects also found their way in and I could do without that. The island had reasonable rainfall but lacked the capacity to capture and store enough of it to meet its current needs. Its reservoirs were small and there were not enough of them. Created before the two tourist hotels existed the reservoirs could no longer meet the new demands placed on them. Hotel laundry, tourists having several showers a day, sprinklers keeping the gardens and lawns green, the swimming pools the flush toilets and so on. I smiled here I was blaming everything on the tourists like a typical local—which of course I was—well almost.

I checked if the tanks were full and had to wait another ten minutes before I could redirect the downspouts and place the lids back on the tanks. I went back inside, towelled myself dry and went to sit on the veranda looking through grey mist of rain at the equally grey sea. No aquamarine and turquoise colours today. All the tourists would be stuck in their hotels and I toyed with the idea of going down to see what Andy and Nahil were up to. I had almost made up mind to go when for some reason I decided against. I might catch them at it which would probably embarrass me more than them. There was always the Three-In-One, but in this weather I'd be sat at the bar dripping on Bengy's floor like a drowned rat. The Kokonet Café was a possibility, perhaps I'd even see Joelle, but then there was the same problem of getting soaked wet through as soon as I left the house and then having Joelle complain that I was wetting and marking her precious chairs. There was nothing else for it but to kill time in the house for a while. Boredom is, in its own way, a great motivator and after a desultory look through my CD collection and even my parent's old collection of vinyl I foraged restlessly in the kitchen until I finally had an idea. What I needed was company, and for a change, a rugged male environment would be a good antidote to the past few weeks of romancing Caroline and I knew just the place to get it along with a cheap drink. A little way up the road from my driveway there was a dirt track that led inland towards the main peak on St Gilberts. No more than a hundred yards along it you reached a wooden house belonging to old Jean Marguerite, one of Nahil's many uncles. At the side of the house was a large low barn, open at the sides, but with a pretty decent corrugated iron roof that kept out the rain. Jean brewed the local jungle juice known as Kalou made from fermented coconut sap and he sold it for two rupees a glass. As I approached I could see a long ladder stretching up one of the palms behind the barn. There were at least six men sat on the wooden picnic chairs under the barn roof, their glasses on the table in front of them. A row of slumped shoulders led me to guess I was joining at the end of a heavy session. Mostly they were older men in their late fifties and sixties and I knew all of them by name and they knew me. They nodded towards me as I sat down on a vacant chair. Jean brought me a glass of Kalou and I passed him two rupees.

"Not seen you around here for a while Rodney," he said.

"What?" I yelled above the racket of the rain on the metal roof above. Jean repeated himself.

"Yeah I've bit a bit busy recently," I replied only to hear what sounded like a snort coming from the old man sat on my right. I turned and saw the leathery and deeply lined face of Patrick Volcere cracked into a slack mouthed grin that revealed a pink gap where his upper front teeth should have been. From the end of the table John added, as if continuing a conversation that had started before my arrival;

"At least Rodney won't mind another Hotel being built on St Gilberts." I was surprised at that. I hadn't heard anything about the building of another hotel.

"Another hotel? But they can't even fill the ones we got already!" I exclaimed.

"No but you can fill the women in those," Patrick slurred and then chuckled at his own wit.

"Who said there is going to be another one anyway?" I asked just to kill off the direction Patrick's aside was likely to lead and to keep some sort of conversation going.

"Dan said that he heard it from Albert when they were drinking at Toffies yesterday," John answered. Well, at least the source was good, Dan Meme was a friend of mine and one of St Gilberts genuine characters. Struck down by Polio in infancy it had left him with a bobbing limp which he had never let slow him down. He was two or three years older than me and had spent two of those years in jail for various crimes, illegal money exchange being just one of them.

Despite not being considered a 'looker', Dan did as well, if not better with the women than I did. In fact if the two of us ever came to chase the same woman I'd lose out to him for sure. Dan's sheer exuberance, confidence, obvious fearlessness, and humour seemed to make him irresistible to a wide range of women few of whom could resist him when he was on form. He had that one of those booming voices that you could hear across a crowded bar even with the music playing high and this gave him presence and made him appear much larger than he was. As well as Creole, English and French, he could converse in booming tones in German and Italian and even a little bit of Japanese. He could work a scam out of anything and always knew before anyone else if something was going down on the Island. He could be an intimidating character to those who crossed him but he also had barrels of charm and a quick wit. His resonant voice was his greatest asset and he could switch from loud and commanding into beguiling, soothing and seductive, in an instant.

You could say that he and I were in the same business, the tourist business, but compared to him I was 'junior school' while he was 'premier league'. He would always be far more successful than me because he had that voice and the streak of ruthlessness that made the difference. Besides, pulling off a scam successfully actually meant something to him beyond the money. Just knowing that he could run rings around better educated and richer visitors was important to him, it gave him pride in what he did and, I guessed, self-esteem too. Besides, he needed the money more than I did. He often drank the locally made Kalou at Toffies on the far side of town. Though it was not against the law to brew alcohol for domestic consumption it was, strictly speaking, illegal to sell it on to others for profit. There were several local brews but the main three were Kalou, baka and Lupire.

Kalou, sometimes called Toddy, was made from quickly fermenting coconut sap, Baka was made from fermented sugar cane juice, and lupire made from anything that fermented when mixed with sugar. Pineapple was usually a favourite, but even potatoes worked O.K. No one in living memory had ever been arrested, let alone jailed, for selling, not surprising really considering almost the entire police force including, and especially Paul Henri, derived most of their daily calorie intake from drinking the stuff, usually at Toffies. I knew Albert at the marina well enough, though I knew his two daughters much better, I found it difficult to credit Albert as being the source of breaking news on something as big as a new hotel. Had some big wheel developer arrived in a luxury yacht, parked up at the marina, and confided in Albert? It seemed unlikely.

It was too much of an effort to continue any conversation under the din of the rain hammering on the tin roof overhead so we fell silent. Jean produced a wooden box of dominoes and we settled into a series of games and drank steadily throughout. Jean's Kalou is much better than the average version you come across on the island and he takes pride in the fact. Not a big drinker of his own brew Jean nevertheless is fussy with the ingredients and fermentation timings and the proof is in the taste. At least a couple of hours passed before we realised the rain had stopped and we could hear ourselves speak—not that anyone was in a state to converse much by then. When the last round of dominoes finished each of us began to push away from the table and attempt to stand and then to stay upright.

I agreed to help Patrick home as he lived on the same side of the road as me only further down towards the town. I was still reasonably in control of my limbs but Patrick needed some serious support and I ended wrapping my arm around his shoulders and together we zigzagged back up the path towards the road. First our trousers and then our shirts became soaked as we brushed against, and staggered into, the tall rain laden grass on either side of the narrow footpath. Before we reached the road I could hear the sound of the bus from town grinding up the hill in first gear. It passed just as we were approaching the road. By then Patrick was making heavy work of it and kept falling against me causing us both to stagger one way and then, as I overcompensated in pushing him back to the upright, to stagger back in the other direction. We were tacking in this fashion as the bus drove past and all the passengers on the right-hand side looked down at us their faces registering various expressions ranging from surprise, pity, disgust, amusement, contempt and indifference. One beautiful face, almost ghostly, looked out through a rain spattered window at the back of the bus. It was Joelle, and, for a brief second our eyes met, then she deliberately turned her head to look straight ahead, her face expressionless. With my arm still around Patrick we sagged into each other like exhausted lovers and stood and watched it continue up the hill. He turned his leathery face up towards me and gave me that toothless grin of his. He mumbled something and I ducked my head down to hear better and asked,

"What's that old man."

"Your place or mine?" he growled and then shook with cackling laughter.

When Ronnier opened his eyes next the sun was once again flooding through the thin curtains and he could hear birdsong as well. Something told him it was going to be a good day and he felt confident he could catch up on the lost day. He was halfway into the town before the sun had risen in the sky, it was then, with the temperature creeping higher, that he was glad of the shade the Panama provided over his eyes. First on his list was the Kokonet Café, twice mentioned by the locals in his conversations the day before. As he approached the main street he saw the café almost immediately. A sign over the door said 'Kokonet Café' and he could see the café part arranged at the front of the premises overlooking the street. The furniture inside was of light-coloured wood and from what he could see it was modern and clean inside. He walked past and decided to explore the town a little before entering the café. He needed time to think ahead to clear his mind and not lose sight of his main objective: namely to get the site of a wrecked ship. The first lead was to trace the computer the enquiry had been sent from, then the person who had sent it. He had noted the computer IP number and the date and time of the enquiry which he had obtained from his trace software on to a card now safely tucked into his wallet. Whoever had made the enquiry would have some knowledge that could point the way towards a wreck site. If it turned out the Valvaston had wrecked off St Gilberts then he would drive around the coast and check the shoreline. If he had a site he would try to corroborate it as best he could against information as sea approaches, currents, natural hazards such as submerged reefs and rock outcrops. It was clear that he would need to hire a car and to get a better map than the one he had brought out with him. He turned right up a side street that was busier than the main street itself. As he walked up the slight incline of the street there were small stores on either side. Some were clothes shops selling a sad selection of stock that looked like seconds from a charity shop in the rougher suburbs of Brussels. Another store sold music compact discs and had speakers placed outside on the pedestrian-way so the whole street could either benefit, or suffer from, depending on each shopper's taste in music. It was playing soukous music perhaps a local band Ronnier guessed. To his ear the music was simply a din and he quickly walked past relieved when the volume diminished as he carried on up the street. Sixty metres further up the street widened out and he saw a large covered area to his right. It was the local market and as he entered the covered area which was roughly thirty metres wide by forty-five long. A wide variety of fish stared up with unmoving eyes from the polished stone trestles and the stores tried without success to whisk away the flies that tried to settle on them. In the middle of the market were wooden trestle tables containing colourful displays of fruit and vegetables. He wandered about and, remembering his camera, took some photos of the colourful scenes from various perspectives as he imagined a typical tourist might. On one of the fruit stalls oranges arranged in neat piles of four made up of three laid together to form a triangle and the fourth on top to complete the pile. They caught his eye and reminded him he was thirsty. He selected a pile and the stall owner smiled then tut-tutted when he saw the large denomination note Ronnier produced from his wallet. The stall owner sent a small boy to one of the stores down the street to return a few minutes later with change. With the oranges in a brown paper bag Ronnier left the market the same way he had entered and headed back down the street clutching his purchase. It was midmorning and he felt it time to check out the Kokonet Café.

He pushed open the door with his free hand and felt the cool of an air-conditioned room and smelt ground coffee. The café part was served by a glass fronted counter which had a display of biscuits and what looked like banana cake on plates under a clear plastic cover on a steel shelf. The control desk for the internet part was a wooden counter curved around a small office space. The counter formed a desktop and there was a phone and what looked like a large open diary with a pen lying on top. Behind the desktop were some small wooden pigeon-holes containing stationery and small pieces of computer equipment. Ronnier had taken all this in as he walked up to the food counter and stood looking around the café. A young woman wearing a pinafore with the logo 'Kokonet Café' embroidered discreetly on the front greeted him.

"Can I help you sir?" For a second his eye rested on the brightly coloured depictions of Hibiscus flowers on her pinafore. She waited patiently and looked at him expectantly as he raised his eyes.

"Er yes, thanks, I'd like a cup of coffee, an expresso please, and I think I'll try a bit of that Banana Cake; it looks delicious." The girl smiled and, using a spatula transferred a section of the cake on to a clean plate and set to working the coffee making machine against the wall behind her. Ronnier spoke to her back.

"I'd like to use one the computers to check my mail if that's OK. What's the procedure? Do I need to book in?"

"Yes," she replied over her shoulder. "Could I ask that you finish your coffee and cake in the café area before going on the computer to avoid any accidental spillages and for reasons of hygiene?" She smiled to soften the instruction and added, "Some of our customers have spilt drinks over the keyboards and others left crumbs between the keys so Joelle has said that all food must be eaten here away from the computers." The girl waved her hand towards the chairs and tables arranged near the window.

"Joelle, sounds like a sensible woman to me, is she the manager?" asked Ronnier.

"Yes she's not only the manager but the owner as well," said the girl and Ronnier detected a note of respect in her voice as if she was proud to be working for such a successful person.

"Sounds impressive," said Ronnier.

"Yes, she is the youngest businesswomen on St Gilberts. I sometimes wish I could be more like her," said the girl her tone wistful.

"There's time," said Ronnier not wanting to patronise her and not interested in her either. He looked down at the tray she was passing to him with the cake and espresso coffee on it, and she noticed the brown paper bag in his hand and realised he might struggle to carry the tray as well. Quickly she came around the counter and carried the tray to a place near the window. Ronnier approved of her customer service and of the place she had selected for him, from it he could both watch the comings and goings on the street outside and any who came into the café. The girl spoke to him again over the counter, "When you're ready, I'll book you on a computer for as long as you want."

"Thanks," said Ronnier, who just managed to get the word out before he placed a piece of banana cake into his mouth. As he ate he glanced across the room and over the top of the screens that provided a measure of privacy for the computer users. There were a couple of young girls who, from their appearance, were obviously locals and of school-age. They huddled together over one of the computers and every so often they emitted suppressed giggles as they looked at something on the screen. A studious looking young man wearing spectacles, also a local, guessed Ronnier, occupied a corner cubicle. Apart those three people and himself, the café was empty. Ronnier wondered if there were any colleges in St Gilberts that had access to the internet and his optimism for a speedy conclusion dropped a little as he imagined his field of search widening.

The coffee was far superior to that of the hotel and the cake was fresh and not as heavy as he had feared it would be. Placing the empty cup and plate back on to the tray he returned it to the counter. The girl, unused to anyone returning their trays to the counter, thanked him for the gesture and asked;

"Would you like to use a computer now?"

"Yes why not," he replied. As he stood and started towards the desk he heard the door open behind him followed by a draught of warm air. A short stocky woman with grizzled grey hair bustled into the café and started speaking loudly in Creole before she had even properly entered the café. There was enough French in the Creole for Ronnier to understand the woman was asking for a cappuccino. From her familiar manner Ronnier guessed she may be a relation to the girl behind the counter. The girl looked helplessly towards Ronnier who nodded and signalled with a gesture of his hand that she should go ahead and serve the woman first.

The older woman looked at Ronnier, seeing him for the first time and spoke directly to him in English, "Oh I'm sorry sir I didn't see you there."

Ronnier smiled and quickly replied, "No please go ahead I'm on holiday and I've got all the time in the world and not much to do." The woman went as if to protest but Ronnier forestalled her protest, "No, really, I insist," and he gave a little bow ushering her towards the counter while moving towards the desk area of the counter himself.

"You are a gentleman sir and believe me there are not many of them around here," she said in loud voice and looked defiantly towards the computer area as if expecting a challenge, but none came. Placing her shopping bags on the floor in front of the counter she stood hands-on hips waiting for her cappuccino. The woman's arrival was providential as it gave Ronnier the opportunity to see if there was anything of interest at, or around, the desk itself.

The large open book that had he had taken at first taken for a diary was in fact a hard backed ruled exercise book. More than three-quarters of the pages already filled in and Ronnier could see that it was a log of all the users. Each page entry started with the date on the left-hand side followed by a number, presumably the assigned cubicle number, the name of the person using the computer followed and then the time in and the time they left. Ronnier quickly looked across to see how much time he had before the girl came to the desk she was still wrestling with the coffee making machine, so he had time. He was just about to riffle back through the log book when he let his gaze wander to the space behind the counter. There was a chair which he hadn't noticed before and stationery on the flat writing surface formed by a shelf of wood inside. Pinned to the side of a cupboard was a clipboard holding a sheet of paper containing typed information in nine squares on the page Ronnier gasped when he realised what he was looking at. In a breath-taking piece of luck he had stumbled across a sheet of paper with the details of each of computer listed on it. The boxes numbered one to nine, obviously corresponded to the nine computers in the café. Each section contained technical information on the individual computers including the serial numbers of the computer and screen in each of the nine cubicles and the IP number of each computer as well. Ronnier reached for his wallet and, with fingers that were almost fumbling with excitement he removed the card he had placed there in Brussels. Glancing at the row of numbers on the card and then quickly down the clipboard and the typed list on the paper, his eyes flicked between the two. One set of the numbers matched. He went back and checked more slowly. This time he went down the information on the paper stopping when he got to the information against the data for cubicle six. He took up the pen that was lying on the counter and wrote on the bottom edge of his card the IP number as he read it off the paper, silently mouthing the numbers as he did so.

303.327.275.56.

He looked down at the numbers he had just written and checked them against the IP number higher up that he had written on the card in Brussels. The two sets of numbers were identical. He now needed to check who was in cubicle six on February 1st 2008 at 16.58. The information would be in the log.

"Sorry about that but my Aunt does like her cappuccino." The girl took hold of the log and turning it on the counter to face her she wrote in the date and looking across at the cubicles said, "How about cubicle two?"

"Fine," replied Ronnier, sorely tempted to ask for number six instead. But he now knew the information he wanted was in the log and the right time would come for him to get it.

"What's your name please?" Asked the girl.

"Philippe Ronnier," he replied and he helped her to spell it correctly in the log.

"How long would you like?"

"Let me start off with thirty minutes," said Ronnier and the girl looked at the clock on the wall and noted the time on the page.

"Why isn't all this done on a computer?" Asked Ronnier.

"Oh it is," replied the girl. "Joelle does it herself. We have lost data in the past, computers crashing and viruses and such, so Joelle likes to have this log as a backup. She says it's quicker as well and she can get certain people to sign in on the page personally if she needs to."

"Why would she need to do that?" asked Ronnier genuinely interested now.

"She has an arrangement with the local college to allow a certain number of students to use the computers during the week days and the log acts as a register of their attendance, so they have to sign in." The girl turned back a page and pointed out a column with signatures alongside hand printed names.

"So the college doesn't have computers of its own?" asked Ronnier.

"Oh yes, it has its own computers—but the college isn't connected to the internet, they haven't got broadband yet. They use their computers in a stand-alone capacity for number crunching, word processing and that sort of stuff."

This is just too easy, thought Ronnier, the information keeps presenting itself to me without any effort on my part.

The girl was talking to him again, "Anyway, Mr Ronnier, if you'd like to take your hat and your paper bag I'll show you the computer I've booked you on." He followed her to a cubicle and settled himself in the swivel chair and faced the screen.

"Are you OK with everything then?" She nodded towards the computer and Ronnier simply thanked her and said that he was. As the girl returned to the counter his eyes followed her and then came to rest longingly on the log on the counter. He toyed with the idea of simply walking over to the counter and looking through the log to get the information he wanted. He could always make up some excuse for his actions if the girl asked what he was doing. The more he thought about it the more it seemed the best course of action to take, and yet? He tried to think ahead.

Once he had a name from the log he still had to get the information he wanted out of that person and god knows what he would need to do to achieve that. He sat back on his chair and looked at the screen. Yes, he decided, he would do nothing that would draw any undue attention to him. He may have to rely on keeping a low-profile in these early stages to avoid falling under suspicion for anything he had to do later on. Less than five minutes later the option of interrogating the log was taken away, literally!

Ronnier heard the door open he looked up in time to see a young girl in her mid-twenties enter the café. She was breathtakingly attractive and Ronnier; surprised at the effect her beauty had had on him, gaped as he gazed secretively at her over the screen. He realised that she was not only stunningly beautiful but that she oozed class, class and poise despite the ridiculously short skirt she was wearing. Everything about her from her shoes to her long tousled hair seemed perfect. She could have worn sackcloth and still looked stylish. There was something else about her and he searched his mind for the words to describe it: clean—that was it—clean and fresh. Something stirred deep inside Ronnier, feelings that had long been dormant, and he found himself unable to take his eyes from the girl and furtively watched her. He took in her beauty, her poise, her dark smooth clear skin, and her youth, suddenly he felt old and strangely intimidated.

The girl behind the counter moved swiftly to meet the new entrant. From her deferential and eager-to-please manner, Ronnier guessed the girl who had entered was in fact Joelle, the manager, of whom the girl who had served him coffee had spoken of in such glowing terms. The two exchanged a few pleasantries and the young girl behind the counter addressed the other by name, "What should I do with the till float, Joelle?"

Ronnier could not catch the short conversation that followed as the screens around the computers were obviously effective sound suppressors. Joelle looked briefly at the computers and Ronnier looked down. When he raised them again Joelle had picked up the log and replaced it with a few sheets of ruled paper and then she walked through a door towards the rear of the computer section presumably to where she had her office. Ronnier shook his head in a vain attempt to clear it, his opportunity to check through the log had gone. Now he would need to return another time when the log was back on the counter or break into the café in the small hours of the morning.

He decided he would return the next day. He now felt no urge to leave the Island and, though he couldn't admit as much to himself, it was the promise of seeing Joelle again that had influenced him. He also needed to call Denver and give him a progress report it promised to be a thankless task that he wasn't looking forward to. Ten minutes later Joelle emerged from the office without the log and conversed with the girl at the counter. Together they counted out some money from the till then ran off a long till receipt presumably giving sum of the takings. Placing the money in a cloth bag Joelle left the café.

Ronnier checked his emails and when his thirty minutes were up he thanked the girl and left the café into the street. He was unsure of which way to walk and was just toying with the idea of returning to his hotel when his eyes settled on a large white colonial style building. From where he was standing he could just read the words over the door 'Museum and Library' yes, he thought, what better place to get a feel for St Gilberts history and any famous wrecks on the island. Clutching his paper bag of oranges and with his hat back on his head he crossed the road and entered the cool shade of the museum. A man, whom Ronnier guessed to be in his mid-sixties, sat at a desk just inside the entrance, he looked up at Ronnier.

"The entrance fee is forty rupees, sir." Ronnier watched as two locals walked in unchallenged and wondered whether they worked in the museum or if the entrance charge applied only to tourists. He suspected the latter but paid the man without comment. He entered through another door into a large drably decorated open hall filled with glass cabinets mostly containing various species of fish mounted on display plinths. The cabinets went around the edges of the room and in a grid formation in the centre and spaced to form aisles so the visitor could walk around each of the cabinets and view the displays up close. There was nothing of much interest to Ronnier in the large hall but he noticed a door leading to another room and he went through it. This time there were books, documents and old sepia photographs on display, his spirits lifted.

However, twenty minutes later he had still not read anything of interest that remotely referred to shipwrecks so he strode out again. The only thing he had learnt was that the name of the island came as a result of a visit from a catholic missionary in 1555. The missionary, a certain Father Gildea had been a member of the Gilbertine Order in Sempringham Lincolnshire England. The Gilbertines were, according to the faded page that Ronnier read the one truly English order of Monks consisting of twenty-six houses of Gilbertines and founded by St Gilbert himself in 1130. The Gilbertine Order closed down during the dissolution of the monasteries introduced by the King of England Henry V111 in 1538 and its closure was permanent. Apparently, Father Gildea had left England for India and had somehow landed on this Island. He had set up a church and converted most of the population. He then rather arrogantly and imperialistically, named the Island St Gilberts in memory of his old Order. Ronnier pondered the nature of the priest and wondered at the physical resilience he must have needed in order to achieve what he had done in those far-off days when life was hard and life-spans short. Also, how the hell had he stumbled on this small dot of an island in the Indian Ocean when it had taken him a good three days of plane travel and airports to reach it?

There was a section of the room devoted to the great catastrophe of 1706 when a wave of vast proportions had wiped out a whole village in a single night leaving only one survivor. Ronnier remembered recent television news reports of a tsunami sweeping across the Indian Ocean about a month ago and he wondered if it had struck St Gilberts. He checked out the cabinets and visited two more rooms but they focused almost exclusively on the Island's flora and fauna with no mention at all of dangerous reefs, currents, or, of shipwrecks. It was a minor disappointment and Ronnier hoped it did not signal the end of his current run of good luck of information simply presenting itself to him.

If there had been even the slightest mention of a wreck he could have done some additional research, asked a few questions and discovered more. As it was he still had nothing more to go on than the internet café.

He left the museum into painfully bright sunshine and the shimmering tropical heat. There was an empty bench under the shade of a magnificent Flamboyant tree in full bloom like some giant bright red umbrella with its clusters of flowers each with five red petals. He placed the bag of oranges on the bench beside him and took one out and started to peel it. When he had finished eating it he looked at his watch thought for a moment and then took out his cell phone. He'd installed Denver's number the previous day so he flipped the phone open, brought up the number and pressed to call.

Richard Denver looked at the team of lawyers sat across the table from him. All of them looked too young to be working let alone lawyers. Denver's own two lawyers, there to support him against this team of young guns, looked old by comparison. In contrast to the opposition they had grey hair on their heads and lines on their faces which told of decades of late nights spent working through pages of detailed clauses. Denver should have felt confident and in control but he didn't. The young guns had the fearlessness of youth and by god they were sharp. The negotiations were for a land deal for Carr's latest project to build a thirty story building in Dubai, something Carr would normally have done himself but he had yet to add the superhuman ability of bi-location to his already formidable list of talents.

The young guns had already scored a minor victory over Denver on exchange rates but it was the way they had blind-sided his team that worried Denver. These kids were showing him no respect, lounging back in the leather swivel chairs grinning at each other and so relaxed it was clear that they were enjoying the whole process. He wasn't. It would have been easy to say their behaviour was gauche and unprofessional if they had not been so damn good, so quick. They hardly needed to refer to their notes the information being instantly accessible to them from their quick brains. Denver wanted to do something that would effectively slap them down and show them who they were dealing with, especially the cocky baby-faced one second from the middle across the table and to his right. He looked at his team engrossed in the documents open on the table in front of them. He saw their faces creased in frowns of concentration that did little to allay Denver's fear the kids across the table were getting the better of him. At that moment sound of his cell phone ringing broke the silence in the meeting room. He took it out of his pocket and checked the number but did not recognise it, it was, however, an international call.

"Let's break for a moment gentlemen." Outside the room he answered the call and when he realised it was Ronnier calling. He could scarcely contain the hope in his voice.

"Ah Ronnier please god give me some good news," he said catching Ronnier a little off guard.

"You asked for a regular update of progress, Mr Denver," said Ronnier formally.

Denver waited for Ronnier to continue and when he didn't, he shouted into his phone, "Well, come on give me the bloody progress report then."

Ronnier responded almost immediately, realising he had Denver's full attention. "I've traced the source of the enquiry to an internet café."

Denver frowned and held his phone a little away from his face to look at it then his features hardened with anger.

"Traced it to an internet café? I thought the software I set you up with had already done that?"

"No Mr Denver it only traced it to St Gilberts—the Island—and to an internet service provider," Ronnier explained as patiently as he could.

"Well, have you got me a wreck site?"

"No but—"

Denver cut in and talking over him. "Have you found the person who made the enquiry then?"

"Er no not yet, Mr Denver, but I'm—"

"Wasting my time, Ronnier, that's what you're doing, wasting my fucking time. Look, ring me when you've got some news right. I don't need to know when you've gone to the toilet for a shit or when you've found what must be the only internet café on the island. What I want is for you to find whoever made that enquiry and get me a map reference or a wreck site! Is that clear?" Denver's face was red with shouting into his phone but Ronnier's reply was so calm it bordered on impudence.

"Yes I understand, Mr Denver. I will contact you again when I have the information you seek."

Denver held the phone away from his face and looked at it again, was Ronnier taking the piss with that 'there-there calm down' patronising tone of voice? And, as he frowned down at his phone, he heard the line click and go dead. Ronnier had ended the call! Ronnier had cut him off! Denver fumbled with the keys on his phone, his hands shaking in anger; he brought back the number

Ronnier had just called him from and was halfway through the keystrokes to call him back, and by God he would verbally roast him, when for some reason his finger stopped short over the keypad. *All in good-time*, he thought; *let Ronnier find the wreck site first and then we'll see about Mr Smart-Arse from Brussels. What a day, openly disrespected twice in the space of fifteen minutes, what a crappy day. Am I losing my grip or is the world going to hell in a fucking handcart?*

The next day I had a hangover. The good news was that the rain had brought my garden back to its former glory and my water barrels were both full to the brim. Even better news was that my allowance for the month would be in the bank and the sun was shining again. A trip into town to collect a little pocket money and do some shopping would be the ideal way to spend the day. As I stepped out of the house and locked the door I remembered that I had forgotten to cover my Honda from the rain the previous day and so it was unlikely to start easily if at all. There was also a tear in the vinyl seat that would release the rainwater captured in the foam beneath into the backside of my shorts. It would continue to do that for the next few days every time I sat on the bike.

At that moment I heard the distant rumble of the bus its engine popping and grinding and its brakes hissing as it tried to control its descent down the steep road. Buses on St Gilberts rarely get the opportunity to get above second gear. I ran out and managed to flag it down just in time. Ten minutes later I stepped out of the bus and into the market. After a quick visit to the bank I stopped and tried to recall the vague list at the back of my mind of the supplies I knew I wanted to buy in town, milk, bread, rice and a few bottles of beer. I was just walking up the main road towards the store when a booming voice ran out across the street noise.

"Rodney my man." The voice came from behind me and even before I turned I knew to whom that voice belonged. There was only one person on the island with a voice of that volume and force, Dan Meme. He was standing in the open door of the Three In One, shaven headed, bull-necked and wearing a black tee-shirt that contrasted well with the chunky gold necklace around that thick neck of his. He waved me over. So much for shopping I thought as I stepped inside.

"What do you want to drink?" he asked and I looked at him in surprise.

"Are you buying?" I asked, unable to hide the disbelief in my voice.

"Of course and don't sound so surprised my old mucker," he roared and slapped me on the back hard enough to propel me forward a step or two.

"I'm in shock," I said and I wasn't joking. Dan's tourist scams were effective mainly because he had been perfecting variations of them on his fellow islanders for years. Although he did buy rounds of drinks from time to time on principle he always made sure he got two back in return.

"Wasn't that rain fantastic yesterday? The water's running again. I had my first shower in seven days and I finally flushed four days of shit down the toilet." Several people in the bar turned, pruning their faces.

"Glad to hear it, especially as you're standing so close," I said. It was when we were halfway into our first beer when, from the back of my mind, out popped the memory of my drink at Jean's place the previous day and how Dan's name had cropped up.

"Hey, what's all this about a new hotel going up?" I asked.

"What new hotel? Who's spreading that story?"

"You are," I said, and recounted what I'd heard at Jean's place. Dan's brow furrowed in concentration as he thought back.

"I've drunk a bit since then, oh, yes, Albert did say something about a rich looking man at his marina asking a lot of questions like he was sizing the place up."

"What do you think?" I asked.

"I think Albert doesn't know his arse from his elbow but if you really want to know why don't you ask the guy himself—he's sat behind you."

I resisted the urge to spin round. "Who's behind me, Albert?" I asked in a low whisper. Albert and I weren't close buddies, well not since he had discovered that I had had carnal knowledge of one of his daughters, just as well he hadn't discovered that it had actually been with both of them.

"No, the mystery rich man," replied Dan continuing to boom, but as we were speaking in Creole, I took comfort from the belief that it was unlikely a white visitor would be able to follow.

"I'll check him out on my way to the John," I said and waited for a couple of minutes before I turned and passed by the man sat at the bar. He was a white guy wearing a loud shirt and, what I could only properly describe as slacks. It was one of Aunt Mert's favourite English words when describing formal trousers. His shirt, a bright flowery affair, looked at first glance as if it might be silk but I changed my mind as got closer. It certainly wasn't what we'd describe as 'island style' it just looked too neat and fussy. Church-going wear for the older man I thought. That was it; he was out of his time, a throwback to an earlier era when visitors to St Gilberts left Aunt Mert and her age group feeling like scruffy savages by comparison. Not any more, my contact with tourists has given me some insight and clues of what to look for when I assess a visitor's financial worth. It is more about social class and status. On this I consider myself more knowledgeable than the average St Gilbertise. I am fairly confident of my ability to assess a tourist's wealth by what they wear; it is my job after all. I've learnt for example, that it has little to do with the sharpness of the creases in trousers or, if you like, slacks. Neither is it much to do with the prissy smartness of shirts or blouses. I guessed this guy was reasonably well off but I wouldn't put him down as rich. He was just a guy with little or no taste, a fashion sense stuck in a bygone era. I meant to get a good look at him as I walked past and I hoped to do so without him noticing it, but as I approached his head turned and we ended eyeballing each other for an uncomfortable second. As I entered the toilet I wondered at that. Why had it been uncomfortable? As I stood at the urinal the answer came to me; the guy had been just too alert. For someone sat at a bar relaxing on holiday he seemed wired. He had turned to look at me it was as if he was half expecting me to attack him and, what was even more unsettling, he looked ready to deal me with if I had. I returned past him again and although he never turned to look at me again I sensed there was a charge of readiness about him, a tension in his back and the way he was sitting. Was I suffering from an overactive imagination? I have learnt to trust my intuition and instincts over the years and they were telling me there was something not quite right with this one.

I returned to join Dan and stood with my back to the man as before.

"Are you going to try any money changing with him?" I asked. Dan replied but did so in a volume that didn't blow my hair back.

"Nah I'll wait and see which way the shit blows with this one. I'm not sure about him."

"You sense it too?" I asked.

"Yeah something fishy going on and I don't know what it is," he said, and his thick links of his silver bracelet clattered on the bar as he reached for his glass. I told Dan about Paul Henri stopping me in the street and at first he shrugged it off as the empty threats of a "Pisshead". Then, after a pause he undermined what little reassurance he had just given me by advising me to watch my back. Again, in what was for him was almost a whisper, he said, "I'll tell you how they got me for it, Rodney. They picked up this blond bird, one that I had been showing around the island. You know the usual stuff, Lolas Beach, Memory

Hill," he sniggered and moved his hips suggestively, "and of course, a little side-line in money changing where she got a little more than money for her money if you know what I mean?" He repeated the hip movements, "and I got a little commission. All harmless stuff no one hurt and everybody happy except for those Government wankers—and pu-rlease—someone tell me—what have they ever done for the tourist business anyway? Nothing; that's what they've done—except price St Gilberts out of the fucking market?" I felt a twinge of depression as I realised how, in those few careless words of his, Dan had just described Caroline's short romance with me. With a handful of words, what I had considered a little bit special, he'd managed to reduce to an island cliché. But Dan was still speaking and, noticing that I was not with him attention-wise, prodded my arm till I was looking him in the eye again.

"Next thing the police drag her off the street in the middle of town and into the police station, not got the balls to go straight to the hotel for her as the hotel's owned by that politician Paul what's-his-fucking-name. They question her in a cell and threaten to keep her locked up and then charge her. Years in a stinking gaol and all that stuff until she's shitting in her knickers. Then they tell her that she has a chance of getting off free and clear if she helps the police by giving a statement telling how I tricked her into changing money. One hour later she is back sunning her little white backside on a lounger by the pool and it's me that's in the cell. Only difference is I don't get out and next thing I know I'm digging holes on Raynauld Island." He pointed a thick stubby finger into my chest.

"Rodney you better make sure those girls of yours aren't going to shop you if Henri get tough and puts the screws on them."

"Yeah and how am I going to do that?" I asked.

"With this," he thundered and pointed to his crotch roaring with laughter then slapping me on the back until my teeth rattled and the beer that had been halfway down my throat came up and out of my mouth in a frothy spray causing me to double up coughing and gagging.

"It's incredible to think the kids in class used to call her smelly and Miss Pissy Pants at school," said Dan adding with a leer, "I bet she sure smells sweet now." I followed his line of sight through the open door and saw Joelle about to cross over the road away from the Kokonet Café. She looked back and I wondered if she could see me and Dan watching her and hoped she couldn't. I felt relieved when Dan just as unexpectedly changed the subject again.

"Where's your bike?" he asked.

"Left it at the house," I replied.

"Good man; that means you are not driving let's have another drink, and..." he fixed me with those slightly bulging eyes of his, "...it's your round." This last bit said in a tone that sounded like a serious threat.

"Jeez, the tourists must really love you," I mumbled, as I turned to try to catch Bengy's attention behind the bar.

We eventually left the Three-In-One together. I needed to make a return visit to the bank having just gone through more money than I had planned or could afford to and also to pick up a few groceries. My head was slightly muzzy with the drink and as I went first towards the store to pick up the staples, we heard the fast clip-clapping of sandals on the pavement behind us getting louder and louder as they drew closer.

"What the hell!" roared Dan. "Are we being run out of fucking town?"

We both turned to see two young locals girls close behind and giggling at us. Dan gave me a nudge in the ribs that nearly sent me off into the road.

"Hey come on, Dan, they've barely left school," I hissed, though I knew one of them was at least eighteen. In reply he held up both his wrists as if they were handcuffed.

"Don't put the cuffs on me, officer, put them on her and I'll share her with you." His voice boomed across the street. I shook my head and gave him a look somewhere between despair and horror; several pedestrians also turned, scowled and shook their heads. The two girls giggled all the louder and, as they passed us, one turned and gave me a flirtatious wink while Dan slapped the ample buttocks of the other. *Was this the way things were going?* I thought. No longer considered eligible among local women of my own age group, was I now to start all over again with the upcoming generations? Dan clapped me hard on the back as I ducked into the store and he continued on behind the two girls.

I was picking a bottle of milk off the refrigerated shelf when a stiff hand prodded into my back like a gun barrel. I jumped in surprise and turned to see Nahil's and Andy's smiling faces. They had several full bags and told me they were just on their way back home.

"We had to get out of the house, got so fed up stuck in all day because of that rain yesterday," Nahil said. At my suggestion they readily agreed to come back to mine so we could all cook and have dinner together. We got some extra rice plus a few more beers and all piled on the next bus going up past my house.

Andy sat out on the veranda with a bottle of beer smiling in amusement as Nahil argued with me over what should be the correct quantity of the ingredients to go into the Creole sauce to go over the fish. It was after we had all eaten and were all sat back in the easy chairs on the veranda that I brought up the rumour about a new hotel. Neither Andy nor Nahil had heard anything so I filled them in on what I had heard at Jean's place and then from Dan himself.

"Albert's full of shit," said Nahil succinctly. For a while we discussed St Gilberts, and our own, love-hate relationship with tourism. On the one hand it brought the Island income in foreign exchange and provided work for some of the population. The tourists themselves lent a vitality and energy to our otherwise quiet island and showed us many advances, if you could call them that. They had a different way of behaving; of dressing, dancing, and speaking, and in the way they used their hands when speaking. They showed us new fashions, music and so many other gadgets that we couldn't help but be impressed by them and even feel poor in comparison with them as well. I am sure this exposure was subtly changing the way we thought about ourselves and, in small increments, was altering the way we behaved and lived. We now wanted goods our parents had never needed and we aimed for a standard of living that was based more on goods and appliances than the old traditional values of nature and community. Well, at least that was the view of many of my older neighbours. The younger generation, of which I was still a member, saw it as progress. Tourism was St Gilberts connection to the outside world. We learnt of technological advances, medical breakthroughs and the like through news channels like CNN, Al Jazeera, and the BBC. We saw the wealth and education of the visitors who visited us evident in the way they dressed and the knowledge they displayed in their conversation. In response many locals would hold up our own island lifestyle and culture and the beauty of our environment as something to not only feel proud of—which we were—but also as a proof of some moral superiority. But the truth for many of us was that the visitors made us realise that we were, in comparison with them, still part of the so-called 'developing world.' It was an uncomfortable truth and added to our individual and collective inferiority complexes.

However, and as is usually the case on St Gilberts, such talk always comes down to a discussion about people and then becomes mired in local gossip. Andy cut across the tourism debate with,

"Where did Albert get his information from?" He'd reached the nub of the issue in a single sentence.

“From a new guy that’s going around town at the moment,” I said and went on to tell them about the stranger and of my experience in the Three In One.

“We’ve seen him already,” exclaimed Nahil and Andy in unison.

“He passed us on the main street this morning and went into the Kokonet. Very smart man,” said Nahil. Andy followed up with more detail.

“Yeah, dressed just as you described, coordinated and fairly expensive but not modern, a bit like Roger Moore as James Bond.”

“But I like Roger Moore,” protested Nahil. “He was the first James Bond I ever saw so he’ll always be THE James Bond to me.” Andy snorted and Nahil frowned and punched him on the shoulder causing him to wince in pain, even a playful punch off Nahil was something best avoided.

Andy stroked his chin intrigued by my impression that the stranger seemed hyper-alert.

“Well, I’d trust your instincts mate and steer clear,” He advised. “Despite the poncey outfit, he looked a bit of a handful to me.”

Now I was interested. Andy rarely commented on anything to do with assessing someone as a risk or how dangerous in a fight they were likely to be, which was, I suppose, strange considering he used to be a VIP bodyguard. In fact, come to think of it, I had never seen Andy raise his hand in anger at anyone despite being severely provoked in the Three-In-One bar a couple of times and once on the main street by one of St Gilberts celebrated hard nuts. Each time he had tried to calm the aggressor and had simply made his excuses and left. Sure, he had to keep ‘a clean pair of hands’ to stay on St Gilbert but I must admit that I also secretly wondered if fighting wasn’t Andy’s thing at all but, even if it wasn’t, I would never have thought any less of him for that. VIP bodyguarding must be more about anticipating, defusing, and avoiding trouble than it is about getting involved in it and, if you have a gun then why bother yourself with all that hand-to-hand combat stuff?

“I never noticed how big ‘Roger Moore’ was as he was sitting on a bar stool,” I said.

“Well, take it from me, he’s not someone to spill your beer over,” said Andy.

“Well, if I had spilt my beer over his shirt, you’d never see the stain in that pattern,” I said, and Nahil raised her bottle in agreement and burped.

Ronnier returned the phone to his pocket and leaned back on the bench. The dappled shade of the tree was a cool oasis in the sun bleached street. Despite

Denver's rudeness he felt good and even better now that he knew he only needed to contact Denver when he had something of significance to report. He opened the paper bag and unpeeled another orange. When he had finished eating it he stood and walked back up the street. He passed at the Kokonet Café going back and looked in through the window towards the counter that had held the log. There was no log and the sheets of loose paper still lay in its place. He would return the next morning and check for it then.

After deciding to return to the villa he noticed there was a bar a little way up the street from the Kokonet Café. A sign over the door proclaimed the 'Three-In-One Bar' almost without thinking he entered and, as he smelt the cigarette smoke and alcohol he felt himself beginning to relax for the first time that day. Taking a stool at the bar he ordered a cold lager and looked around the busy room. He could see there was a beer garden at the back of the bar and the bar room itself was filled almost exclusively with locals, perhaps he could find out some useful information in here after all. Ten minutes later, just as he was about to ask for another lager, he heard a burst of laughter to his right. He turned to check the source and noticed that someone new had entered the bar because if they had been in the bar before Ronnier was certain he would have spotted him. The new man stood with his back to him at the other end of the bar and was a giant in comparison with those around him. Ronnier guessed the man to be over six and a half feet tall with wide shoulders a slim athletic build and tousled hair. When he turned his head slightly to one side Ronnier could see the outline of a high angular cheekbone. The man's scruffy appearance hinted that perhaps he was a labourer or a fisherman but then most of the others in the bar were not smart either. A fisherman might just be the best source of information on dangerous currents, submerged rocks, reefs and likely wreck sites. Ronnier ran through an idea in his mind, if he chartered a local fishing boat to give him a tour around the island he could get a good idea of any possible, or likely locations of any wrecks. Besides a day cruise would be just the thing a tourist would do. His mind snapped back to the present when the tall man turned around to face him and Ronnier saw that despite the stubble and tousled hair, the man had one of those sorts of faces that stare out at you from the glossy magazines in airport duty-free stores and in-flight airline magazines. It was the sort of face that sold expensive designer colognes for men. Ronnier could also see the man was little more than a boy, early to mid-twenties tops and with the weirdest light blue eyes. The young man walked past him to the toilet and for the briefest fraction of a second their eyes met and locked until each broke the contact simultaneously. The relaxation Ronnier had felt minutes earlier suddenly evaporated like a drop of water on desert sand. It was not the shock of staring into those vivid aqua-blue eyes set in a dark-brown face that had alerted Ronnier's survival instinct, though god knows that was an unsettling experience in itself. Ronnier had felt his own eyes unable to focus under the piercing gaze of the other, but no, it was something else. The man had turned deliberately to check him out for some reason and had done so under the pretext of going to the toilet. Ronnier's instinct told him that what he had just witnessed was not the casual interest that you would expect an islander to show towards an outsider visiting his bar. He re-ran the events in his mind's eye starting before the man had turned and walked past him. There had been laughter he remembered that, some loud exchanges in Creole as well, and then… nothing for a while, though maybe they had been talking quietly. Then the man had turned with deliberate casualness and carefully checked him out as he passed. Ronnier took another sip of his beer, was he imagining things? Was he being sized up for a mugging or a con?

Ronnier smiled at that, he would have relished a little workout teaching a couple of bumpkins a lesson in manners, though that would only draw attention to him and he could do without that. A new thought struck him, had Denver sent anyone else to check around for information or even to keep a check on him? He thought about but then dismissed it as unlikely, besides the man had surely been a local despite his eye colouring. The young man returned past him and took up his place at the end of bar with his back to him again as before. Some of the other locals in the same group glanced at Ronnier but it was no more than you would expect being a stranger in a close-knit community.

In the end Ronnier dismissed the incident and after another beer left and returned to his villa. On his way he passed a small store and went inside. Within the store organised chaos reigned. Goods shelved haphazardly looked in danger of avalanching over him but Ronnier managed to find some groceries, a bottle of Gin, two bottles of tonic water and one bottle of mineral water. At the check-out the man ignored Ronnier's cheery hello and instead of placing Ronnier's change in his offered hand slapped it down hard on the steel top of the check-out counter. Ronnier wondered if this was some archaic cultural tradition but a quick look at the man's surly face suggested it was more likely down to piss-poor manners. Ronnier swallowed back a sudden flare of anger. His right-hand itched to grab the man's throat and lift him from his stool and teach him how to respect his customers with a lesson he'd never forget—provided he survived it. Instead he gathered the coins and shopping and walked out into the bright sunlight. The heat had sapped his strength so when he had reached his villa he had to resist the urge to relax. Instead he changed and went across to the hotel. As he passed the reception desk he noticed the older man was on duty and so took the opportunity to ask if the man knew any local fishermen who knew the Island waters well.

"And any prepared to take me on a cruise around the island?" The old man became enthusiastic at the idea and said he had a few friends who themselves were fishermen. He promised to ask them what they thought of the idea. Ronnier stressed he wanted to experience a little genuine island life. Comfort and luxury were not on his agenda, it was knowledge of the local water conditions, history, and wildlife that he was looking for. He threw the wildlife bit in because it sounded right. The old man delighted to be able to help promised to get back to him early the next day. Ronnier returned to his villa changed into shorts and went to manoeuvre one of the sun loungers on the patio under the shade of a young palm tree. He lay back gratefully. His mind drifted over the day so far. The Kokonet café, the name contained in the log book. The breathtakingly beautiful girl who managed it, a busy local bar, a tall young man with unusual blue eyes that looked at him and through him and assessed him for some reason he couldn't fathom. In his fatigue was he reading too much into that last one? Had his instinct, always so reliable up to now, let him down? With these questions swirling around inside his head he closed his eyes and surrendered himself to the sleep his body craved. A shadow falling across his face caused him to open his eyes. He half expected to see someone looming over him but there was no one, only the sun disappearing behind a cloud and a cooler breeze blowing in from the sea. He wondered if the weather, and his luck, was about to change again.

Ronnier walked briskly up the main street. It was eight thirty in the morning and he felt good. He had slept well the previous night and the old man on the hotel reception told him he had arranged the boat trip. Ronnier was to be at the marina ready for departure at ten thirty am. When Ronnier had asked how he would recognise his skipper for the day the old man had told him the skipper would find and recognise him and Ronnier had noticed the little smile on the other's face.

Fortunately the weather had not taken a turn for the worse as he had thought it might the previous evening. He had time to visit the Kokonet Café and check if the log was back in place. As he passed the front of the café he looked through the window and saw the log opened at the end of the counter. The young girl was behind the counter and there was no sign of the manager Joelle which suited his plan just fine. He walked straight in and said a cheery hello and good morning to the girl behind the counter who smiled in recognition as he entered. He engaged her in small talk and then asked for a cappuccino adding that he would like to book thirty minutes on a computer. As he said it, he walked to the log.

"I'll start filling in my name, should I?"

"Yes, if you would," replied the girl who was busying herself with the coffee milk steamer. Ronnier took the log and flicked back through the pages to the first February 2008 and scanned the side of the page for the times shown. The log showed only two people in the café at 16.58, the time of the Valvaston enquiry, and they were Noshir Wadia and Rodney Leon. Rodney Leon booked into cubicle six the computer from which the enquiry originated. Noshir Wadia booked into cubicle three.

"Your coffee will be ready in a moment," the girl said and she walked towards him smiling. Ronnier made a show of riffling through the pages of the log.

"This café really is a popular place; it's amazing how many people use it in the course of the week."

"Yes it gets too busy sometimes," said the girl.

“I was just flicking the pages when the name of an old friend of mine from Brussels sprang out at me, Rodney Leon. I haven’t seen him for years and I don’t suppose for a moment that it’s the same Rodney. About medium height, hair greying a little at the temples, wears frameless spectacles.” Ronnier had touched his temples to show were the hair was greying and had made spectacles with his fingers to embellish his description of his imaginary friend. The girl smiled, patiently waiting for him to finish before setting him straight.

“Well, that’s certainly not our Rodney. He’s too young to show any grey hair and he’s this tall.” She reached her hand high above her head and then stood on tiptoes to make the point that the Rodney she knew was very tall indeed. Then she added, “Besides, our Rodney has blue eyes and no specs.”

Ronnier felt a frisson of excitement which he hid with a chuckle. “Sounds like your Rodney and my Rodney are not from the same family.”

The girl was suddenly serious. “Rodney doesn’t have a family anymore.”

“I’m assuming he’s a local boy so where on earth did he get those blue eyes from?” asked Ronnier.

“God knows,” replied the girl starting to smile again. “But his mother was a blond Swede with blue eyes and his grandmother, on his father’s side, was also blond blue-eyed Swede might have something to do with it. All the men in the family seem to have a thing for blue-eyed blondes.” At that moment another customer walked in and the girl went back to the counter to greet a young studious looking teenager. A moment later she called him to say the cappuccino was ready and to save her walking around from the counter he picked it up from the counter himself and took it to a window seat. So he not only now had a name but he also had a face.

Ronnier frowned at the realisation that he had no plan for what he should do next. He needed to find out what this Rodney Leon lived and what he knew about the Valvaston. He recalled Denver’s warning that he should not under any circumstance mention the name Valvaston to anyone but how the hell can you find out anything about something you cannot even mention by name? Did Denver think he was going to go about St Gilberts doing a version of charades?

It was clear that he needed to get Leon alone and somewhere private and then somehow find out what he knew even if at some stage that meant asking ask him directly. If Leon was reluctant, or even refused to talk, then Ronnier would have to persuade him. Finding out where he lived would be a good starting point. Ronnier wondered if the run of luck he had enjoyed so far was about to end.

Would he find that Leon lived in a hut in the middle of a bustling close-knit shanty surrounded by nosey relatives, a wife, and half a dozen kids? Getting the information he needed out of the blue-eyed giant might well prove to be the most difficult part of the whole assignment.

After spending a desultory fifteen minutes on the internet, Ronnier left the café to saunter down to the marina. A young teenage girl was working behind the counter and there was no sign of the sour old man who had served him on his first day on the Island. He ordered a beer and sat at a table that allowed him a view of the boats in the marina. The heat was starting to build up as the sun rose higher in the sky and Ronnier was glad that he had covered his face arms and neck in high factor sun cream before leaving the villa. He also had his hat. A few hours on a boat under this sun promised to be a severe test of his UV precautions.

He didn't have long to wait. A wooden, blued painted fishing boat chugged into the marina and a slim wiry man, with long grey hair and a black baseball cap, tied it off and walked with a slight limp towards the café. From the stern set of the man's face Ronnier guessed that he was not in for a chat filled day. The man looked around the half-empty café and, seeing Ronnier, walked straight towards him with his hand outstretched.

"Mr Ronnier?" He asked and his handshake was firm. Ronnier felt hard calloused skin on the other's hand.

"Yes pleased to meet you, Mr…?"

"Call me Joseph," said the man and sat down across the table from him adding, "Don't rush your beer."

"How about you, can you manage one?" asked Ronnier.

"Well, I suppose one wouldn't do any harm," the man replied. He had a heavy accent but his English was understandable. Ronnier waved the girl over and after ordering another beer he faced Joseph and smiled.

"How long will it take us to go around the island?" Ronnier asked.

The other man looked surprised. "Around the island?" he exclaimed. "There's no chance we could get around the island today, Thomas told me that you wanted a bit of a cruise offshore to get a better view of the island, its beaches and its wildlife."

"Er yes that's right," agreed Ronnier, adding, "Is it really so far around the island?"

"It's far enough and, as you may have seen, there are plenty of reefs and rocks out there to stove in even a small boat like mine. Sail too close in on the

North coast and we'd be holed good and proper. If you want to go there we'd need to sail far out to sea which will extend the journey. I take it you are not a sailor then?"

"Er no, no I'm not," admitted Ronnier.

"Well, tell me what you want to see and we'll aim for that first."

Ronnier frowned in thought for a few seconds before replying, "You mentioned reefs and submerged rocks. Do many ships wreck off St Gilberts?"

Joseph rubbed his chin at this sudden change of tack.

"Not that I can think of, nobody visits us hardly except the odd supply ship to drop off goods and stuff and none of them have ever run aground, at least not that I know of."

"Then what about in the past?" asked Ronnier.

"Again I can't recall any, anyway, why are you interested? Did you want to go looking for wreck sites or something?" Joseph fixed Ronnier with a level gaze.

Ronnier answered as breezily as he could, "Not particularly, but then who doesn't have some interest in sunken ships and all that?"

Joseph was still looking straight at him. "As long as it's not my boat that sunken then I can't say that I do."

Ronnier was starting to get a strong impression that Joseph wasn't going to put himself out to make polite conversation or perhaps any conversation at all.

They set off in the little boat heading north. A fresh sea breeze mercifully kept the boats strong fish smell at bay. At first they hardly appeared to be making any headway at all and Ronnier realised that a trip right around the island would be a hellish long trip even in a speedboat. Joseph was a man's man, one of those strong silent types that have no time for pleasantries. He was however a professional and if he had accepted a charter to give a tourist a natural history cruise then that's what he was going to do. He pointed out the various beaches by name and showed he was knowledgeable on the flora and fauna. He gave Ronnier a running commentary as they chugged on the engine out and away from the shoreline. Once out into clear water Joseph asked Ronnier to hold the tiller while he set up a small sail then took back the tiller and switched the engine off. All at once the more peaceful sounds of the water lapping the sides of the boat replaced the noise of the engine. The wind fluttered the edges of the sail and the creak of rope on wood and wood against wood as the mast strained in its housing and the boat leaned into the wind.

Ronnier began to enjoy his little cruise. The wide open space and cooling breeze cleared and opened his mind. He nodded in feigned interest as Joseph continued with his natural history narration and, to give Joseph his due, he did know an impressive amount about the islands habitat. However Ronnier needed a different sort of local knowledge and so he decided to try to steer the skipper's flow in a different direction.

"That's an impressive villa up there," he said conversationally and pointing up to a villa set on the limestone rock hillside overlooking the beach. The villa was built so it blended into its natural surroundings and he could see the rail of a large open veranda perched right on the edge of the rocks high over the beach facing out the sea and framed by trailing bougainvillea in pinks, whites, and orange. Ronnier could imagine that it must afford excellent views of both. Joseph turned on the bench type seat at the rear of the boat where he held the long wooden tiller, to look at Ronnier and where he was pointing.

"That place up there? That's young Rodney's place."

Rodney? Ronnier felt a jolt of surprise run through him as he heard the name and found himself repeating the name out loud as an implied question, "Rodney…?"

"Yes. Young Rodney Leon's got the place to himself now that Mert's gone and got married."

"Must have cost him quite a packet?" said Ronnier but Joseph wasn't the type of man to indulge in gossip, idle or otherwise, and he was already beginning to think that he had said more than he should have about Rodney's private life to this nosey stranger.

"It's not my place to go talking about what others pay or don't pay for their houses. If you want to know that then you should ask him yourself," said Joseph.

"Fair comment," said Ronnier, but he thought the opposite, what the hell was the problem with having a little harmless conversation. Ronnier smiled back at Joseph who simply returned a deadpan stare and Ronnier felt his frustration growing into outright anger at his surly tour guide. As much as he longed to teach the oaf a little civility he turned his back on him instead. He looked back up at the villa and tried to spot some marker that would help him find the place again from the vantage point of an inland road. Just to the left of the villa there was a tall flamboyant tree and, close by that another taller tree with a distinctive whitish bark.

Leon's villa had been the first thing that Ronnier had pointed out for his guide to elaborate on and it had turned out to be the house of the man he needed to locate. He now also knew from his guide that Leon lived alone. Yes, it was all too easy and though Ronnier was not a superstitious man he was beginning to find it strange how pieces of information continued to present themselves to him. It was as easy as following a laid paper trail. But even so the next piece was always tantalisingly held back for a little longer. For example the log book in the Kokonet Cafe and now the information about how a scruffy young local man could afford a villa overlooking the sea. Not just any villa but a villa that would be the envy of many a millionaire. Whatever and wherever Valvaston was, maybe Rodney Leon had already found it.

Engrossed in his thoughts it was sometime before Ronnier noticed their change of direction. The boat had started to wallow and pitch, Joseph asked Ronnier to hold the tiller while he collapsed the sail. With the sail down and the engine running again Joseph swung out to sea as if to steer around the long buttress of rock that reached out at right angles from the land like a giant outstretched arm. The boat started to rise and fall as it met the larger swells and Joseph steered to give the rocks a wide berth. They were heading directly away from the land out towards the open sea. Only when they had cleared the furthest extremity of those rocks showing above the waterline, by a good one hundred metres did Joseph turn again so they were again parallel to the shore but now much further out. Ronnier could see that beyond the outreach of rock was the northernmost point of the island. Ronnier stared at a vast deserted sandy beach stretching inland and becoming rough arable ground that came to an abrupt stop when it reached the base of an almost vertical limestone cliff close on one hundred feet high. Meeting the sea at one edge of the beach was a large hill also of limestone, with a white stone church on the top of it.

"St Francis Mount Church," said his tour guide and skipper who had obviously been following his line of sight.

"A church," exclaimed Ronnier, "but does anyone live here?"

"Not anymore. Long time ago a big wave came and everybody vanished." Joseph made a whooshing noise to suggest the rush of a giant wave and made a cutting motion with his hand held like a scythe. "All gone in a single night. Nobody lives there anymore."

Ronnier gathered that he was not referring to the recent tsunami that he had heard about but one that had visited the island maybe hundreds of years ago.

Strangely the beach still showed signs of the after effect of a large wave or violent storm. There were fallen trees strewn across the open ground and dried seaweed far inland and well beyond the normal high tidemark.

"You said you were interested in wrecks, mister. If there was any place around this island likely to wreck a ship then this place is it," Joseph was shouting over his shoulder as he pushed the tiller away from him to turn the boat in a tight arc. Ronnier realised that they were returning on a reciprocal course back to the marina, it looked as if his tour had gone as far as it was going to.

The day after Andy and Nahil had come around to eat I spent the whole morning and afternoon doing minor repairs around the house and a little pruning back in the garden. Normally I wouldn't have bothered with such domestic chores preferring instead to cruise the beaches of the tourist hotels drumming up business. But Henri's threat had unsettled me more than I cared to admit and so I kept a low profile. The following day however, I was itching to get out and meet people. After a titanic battle with the Honda, which didn't want to start, I eventually prevailed and, placing a plastic bag over the tear in the seat to keep my shorts dry I went down to town. I parked on the front near the Three In One. The sun was already up and beating down and I was glad I had my shades on. I walked up towards the fish market and, almost immediately met Nahil walking down towards me heavily laden with a large sisal bag obviously full of shopping.

"Where's Andy?" I asked and she told me that he was out fishing. I knew Andy was managing to make some money on the side by selling the fish he caught to the tourist hotels. The hotels were always eager to buy good quality fresh fish it helped them meet their customers' insatiable appetite for locally prepared seafood.

"We were thinking of having a picnic this afternoon and we were going to ask if you wanted to come along. We would have given you a call but you must have been out and you don't have a mobile these days," said Nahil.

"Yeah it was old and the battery couldn't hold its charge longer than a couple of hours so I binned it. But I'm up for a picnic," I replied. This was just what I wanted to hear and it pleasantly solved my problem of what to do with the rest of the day.

"Which beach?" I asked.

"Well, the beach below your place, Raffin, is always quiet and it's nicer than the beach at Andy's, though don't tell him that I said that," she giggled. We both knew she wasn't afraid to say anything to anyone.

“Tell you what, Nahil, I’ve got a few things I need to get in town but why don’t you leave this bag for me to bring up on my bike later while you go ahead on the bus. Go to my place and get some stuff ready from the fridge. There is a wire rack from an old grill pan leaning against the wall around the back. A little scrub with some wire wool and we could put the fish on that.”

“Good idea,” she said glad to be offloading the sisal bag on me. “I’ll knock some Breadfruits down as well.”

Using her ancient BlackBerry phone, she rang Andy who was still out at sea on the Avon inflatable.

“Hi it’s me. I’m with that horrible Rodney man and we’re going to meet at his place to get the food ready and carry it down to Anse Raffin. Yes, the beach below his house.”

“OK then don’t be too long, see-yah.” She ended the call. “He’s on his way to the Reef Sands Hotel then he’ll go home, drop the boat off and come and join us at your place,” she said.

I gave Nahil the key to my front door and watched as she made her way towards the bus terminal then I hefted the bag over my shoulder. I went into Denis’s sports shop to leave it behind the counter down near the little wooden draws containing fish-hooks until I returned. I walked towards the bank intending to get some money out and as I walked I straightened my shoulders back and felt good, it was going to be a great day after all.

On his return from the cruise Ronnier organised the hire of a Toyota four-wheel drive and, after filling in a series of forms, was able to take possession of the car the same day. Glad to be mobile he would make full use of it the next day. He slept well and after a hearty breakfast in the hotel restaurant he returned to his villa to get ready to carry out the next stage of his task. He swapped his shoes for some black training shoes and then went into the kitchen to check through the cutlery draw. Air travel after September eleventh made transporting weapons in personal luggage not worth the risk. Eventually he chose the vegetable paring knife because its blade was strong and formed an integral part of the handle it was also sharp with a wicked looking point. Next he cut a section of the cereal box and folded it around the blade several times to form a crude sheath then wrapped tape around the card to keep it in place. He took a roll of Elastoplast from his medical kit and after first running a razor over the calf of his right leg to remove the hair he strapped the knife in its sheath to his lower leg. He checked to make sure the trouser leg covered the knife and then crouched and practised extracting the knife a couple of times just to check that it was secure and easily accessible. Next he took several plastic cable ties from his suitcase and rolled them together into his pocket. Finally, he pocketed the set of lock picks stored behind the tweezers, scissors and nail clippers in the gentleman's vanity set he'd brought.

He drove into the little village the locals called the capital and parked across the road from the Three-In-One the bar he'd visited the day after the rain. He quickly confirmed Leon was not inside the bar then returned to sit inside the Toyota. He had a newspaper from the hotel and stretched it over the steering wheel he glanced through the pages while keeping an eye on both sides of the main street. He tried to decide his most effective way forward and eventually it seemed to boil down to one of three approaches. Plan A, to visit Rodney Leon at his house and say he was from the firm that ran the website Leon had contacted. He just happened to be in the area and thought he'd take the opportunity to call in for a chat? Even thinking through it Ronnier felt that it sounded thin and unconvincing and would give away the fact that he'd tracked Leon down. The advantage of the plan was that he could witness Leon's reaction. Plan B was to get into conversation with Leon probably in The Three-In-One bar and draw out the information in casual conversation using elicitation techniques. Plan C was to wait until Leon was out of his house and then go and have a look inside it to see what he could find.

As Ronnier sat in the increasingly warm cab of the Toyota he ruled out Plan A but remained undecided whether to go for B or C. Both plans needed Leon to be in town and that was what Ronnier was now waiting for. The first sight of Leon would be the moment to decide between plan B or C. He was sure something would happen, a sign that would make the choice clear. After an hour he had to get out of the stifling heat of the car. He walked over to a nearby bench under the shade of a Geiger tree, its large oval leaves and clusters of orange flowers breaking the rays of the sun into a cool dappled shade. He didn't want to enter the bar and start drinking before his target was in there. Ronnier was used to surveillance work but he wondered how long he might have to wait. Leon might not visit the bar or town for days. Ronnier knew he could hardly sit all day every day on this town bench without attracting unwelcome attention. He looked up and down the street and back towards the road that led up to Leon's place and then back down to his newspaper. He'd already read it from cover to cover thirty minutes ago. It seemed as if only a few seconds passed before he glanced up again just in time to see the tall figure of Leon himself dismounting from an old motorcycle. He parked the bike outside the Three In One and Ronnier decided that it was going to be plan B, get Leon into a conversation and elicit the information over several drinks. At that moment a petite local girl struggling under the weight of a large bag stopped in front of Leon and the two of them engaged in friendly conversation leaving the other pedestrians using the pavement to walk around them. They were obviously friends as they both smiled and laughed a lot and used plenty of expressive hand and arm gestures. The girl was roughly five foot in height and barely came up to Leon's chest but she was extremely attractive with a neat figure and long dark hair. Her jeans showed off a pert backside that would have brought her many admirers in Brussels. After a few minutes the girl took out a cell phone and made a call while Leon stood and waited, she then passed the heavy bag to Leon who hoisted it over his shoulder. The two waved goodbye to each other and went their separate ways. Leon did not go into the bar but went instead to a nearby sports shop emerging seconds later but without the bag. Ronnier watched as Leon walked up the little side road that headed towards the market. In that second Ronnier decided that it was going to be plan C break into Leon's house and see what he could find. He moved quickly not wasting a second of time. He got back into the Toyota turned the ignition and moved into the sparse traffic, turning and taking the road that led up towards the villa he had seen from the boat the previous day.

The road became steep but the Toyota made short work of it. After a mile or so Ronnier slowed to look out for the trees he had assigned as markers the previous day. The hillside was verdant with vegetation and heavily wooded and, as he drove, he fretted that from his current and different perspective the markers were not going to be visible. At times the green closed in on either side of the road and then at other points it was low and sunlight streamed in through the windscreen. He also caught tantalising glimpses of the sea to his left-hand side. The road was steep and he had to concentrate to stay on it. The thick vegetation and slope of the land obscured his view of the coastline and the possibility of him being able to use it to orient himself by. The road wound on and up with the steep peak forming a green wall on his right-hand side. Ronnier wondered if he had already past the villa when, as he rounded a corner out of dark-green shade and back into the sunlight, he saw a large tree silhouetted against the perfect blue of the sky. He was already driving slowly in second gear but he slowed a little more as he drew closer and recognised the bright red flowers of a Flamboyant tree growing at the side of the road a little way ahead. From what he remembered he should have passed the tree with the white bark slightly before the Flamboyant. He brought the Toyota to a stop and switched off the engine but left the car in gear with the handbrake. He climbed out and looked around him. There must be hundreds of Flamboyant trees on St Gilbert but something told him he was close to the villa. He looked down over the left-hand side of the road and found himself looking through the upper branches of a tall tree on to the red roof tiles of a beautiful colonial style house with an ornately carved triangular porch roof. He walked closer to the edge to get a better look at the house and saw a steep gravelled driveway leading from the house and to the road joining it a short way back from where he stood. He had passed it on his way up. From his new vantage point he could also see the tree, through whose upper branches he had just viewed the house, had a whitish bark. Feeling a frisson of excitement he quickly got back in the Toyota and reversed it down the road so he could turn left off the road and down the gravel drive to the house. The track extended beyond the back of the house allowing him to park the vehicle out of sight around the side of the house. Anyone coming down the driveway would not see it unless they walked around the house instead of entering through the door under the porch at the rear.

Ronnier walked back to the door and hammered on it. There was always a possibility that someone with a house like this would also have a housekeeper or a cleaner but no one came and he could hear no sound from within. First he tried the door before taking out his set of lock picks and setting to work on the lock. It was a simple lock of the Yale type and age and use had worn some play in the barrel making it ridiculously easy for him to pick. He carefully opened the door and stepped inside closing it again behind him.

Ronnier gaped at the interior he had not expected anything so beautiful. Everywhere he looked he saw exquisitely grained wood in the cool airy room. The décor was a blend of modern and traditional and whoever had designed it had balanced the two perfectly. Overhead was a high cathedral style ceiling from which hung punkah fans. Over to the right the room opened out through glass doors on to a broad veranda overlooking the sea. He saw tumbling multicoloured tresses of Bougainvillea forming a natural frame for the view.

Ronnier knew he could not afford to lose a single moment if Leon returned there was no way he come up with a story to justify his presence in the house. He paused, and looked around trying to orient himself to the layout of the house. To his left he could see an open door leading to what looked like the kitchen. A large poster size monochrome portrait photo hung in a frame on the wall which, because of its position, formed the main focus of the room. The portrait was of a young couple with a baby. The woman was blonde and the man black, the child was black though a lighter shade than the father. Even though the photograph was monochrome Ronnier could see the eyes of the child were unusually light and in a sudden flash of insight realised he was looking at a very young Rodney Leon.

There was an old-style turntable and a collection vinyl records. A large wooden dining table that could seat more than half a dozen with room to spare and some quality furniture placed around the large open-plan room, easy chairs, couches and the like. Ronnier strode down some steps and into the room and his eyes darting around the room taking in the ornaments and on the various polished wood shelves and table tops. He checked each of the doors hoping to find a study or an office but found only bedrooms and bathrooms. Only one of the bedrooms looked to be in regular use with the sheets on the bed still crumpled from the previous night. Ronnier quickly and expertly went through each of the draws in the room and then the contents of all the cupboards and finally the wardrobe top to bottom. He was sweating when he had finished and quickly strode through each of the other bedrooms checking each in turn. The kitchen had plenty of cupboard space but after an almost frantic search of each he had to wipe the sweat from his forehead that was pouring down his face and into his eyes. He looked at his watch he'd already taken too much time in his search and, feeling his heart pounding in his chest, he walked back into the large main room. Something was nagging him, something he'd seen and yet not seen. He stood in the middle of the room and slowly turned around concentrating on looking at everything carefully. He stopped at the portrait on the wall and carefully lifted the bottom of the frame away from the wall so he could see what was behind it but there was no secret compartment no safe. He continued to turn looking for papers, a locked drawer, a cupboard, some clue. He blinked forcing his eyes to register every detail turning like a human lighthouse. He stopped without knowing why and his eyes went back to a collection of ornaments grouped on a low cupboard top as if drawn by a magnet. He walked over to the cupboard, which he had passed earlier on his way to one of the bedrooms, and looked more closely at the objects. There was a small stack of grey pewter plates obviously of ancient origin and what looked like an old napkin ring it all looked out of place in the room.

The ring, bent out of shape, and with a dent in it showed a bright flash of silver where the patina of oxidation had been scraped away, caught his eye. Ronnier's heart began beating even faster, he held his breath and his hand shook as he lifted the small band and read the engraved name running around it; Valvaston. At that moment Ronnier heard the faint noise of what sounded like a lorry or a bus engine as it struggled up the steep road above the house outside. He stood still his mouth slightly open so he could hear all the better. It must be a bus and its engine was idling, it had obviously stopped to allow passengers to either alight or get off. Ronnier listened waiting then heard the roar of the bus engine as it continued its journey uphill. He was not expecting Leon to arrive on a bus after seeing him in town on a motorbike. Nevertheless Ronnier remained stock-still his ears straining to listen through the lengthening silence that followed the departure of the bus. Nothing broke the silence and he relaxed, breathed out and then drew in a deep lung full of air. It was then that he heard the crunch of gravel on the path outside and the sound of a woman's voice singing, still in the distance, but getting louder as she drew closer. Without thinking Ronnier pocketed the ring and drew back into the kitchen, seconds later he heard a key scraping in the lock and the hinges squeak as the door opened.

The girl was still singing quietly to herself as she entered and Ronnier stood behind the open kitchen door watching through the crack between the door and the jamb. It was the girl who he had seen speaking to Leon in the town earlier, the one who had passed Leon the bag. As he watched she walked straight towards the kitchen and through the door. Ronnier waited until she had walked past him and into the kitchen before stepping out behind her and placing his left-hand over her mouth. He forced her head back against his shoulder holding her as if in a vice. His right hand reached up and around to the side of her face and his thumb pressed into the point just below her left ear where the jaw met the skull. Within seconds, her body went limp and he lowered her to the tiled floor. She would be unconscious for about an hour, maybe longer, possibly shorter.

"Merde," he exclaimed to himself, "why did she have to turn up?" He reached in his pocket for a cable tie and then changed his mind, perhaps they didn't sell cable ties on St Gilbert and it was important that he did not direct attention towards visitors such as himself. He had not planned for this to happen but the situation was still retrievable. The girl had not seen him and it was still possible for him to leave the house and drive off without anyone else seeing him either. Then there would be nothing to stop him waiting a little while before adopting plan B instead. He could go to the bar in town and just strike up a conversation with Leon next time he met him in there.

Ronnier went to the cupboard near the pedal bin which he had searched earlier remembering that it had contained some small hand tools garden stuff and other similar items. He pulled open the door and rooted inside until he eventually found what he was looking for, a coil of plastic coated washing line. He quickly turned the girl over so she was face down and tied her hands behind her back. He took a knife out of the nearby knife block and cut off the surplus line. He was still stooping over the girl when he heard a noise in the main room and looked up and into Leon's shocked face and piercing blue eyes.

"What the…?" Leon said but Ronnier cut him short.

"Just stay where you are, son, unless you want me to hurt your girlfriend."

"Hurt… what's going on?"

"Just stay calm and no one gets hurt," said Ronnier, Leon walked forward a step towards the girl but Ronnier showed him the knife and held it against the girl's neck.

"What you do in the next few seconds will decide whether I cut through this girl's throat or not. What I want you to do is lie face down on the floor, just there where you are, and put your hands behind your back. Do it now."

Leon looked confused as if his mind couldn't take in the information his eyes and ears were supplying to him. Ronnier knew from experience that he would have to get the kid switched on to get his compliance.

"GET FACE DOWN ON THE FLOOR OR I'LL CUT HER FUCKING THROAT OUT!" he roared and had the satisfaction of seeing the young man lie face down on the floor. He sighed and reached in his pocket for a cable tie. Standing over Leon, he placed one foot between the young man's shoulder blades allowing enough weight to bear down to force the breath out of Leon as he fixed the cable tie around his wrists. He checked it was secure and noticed the expensive watch on the man's wrist, it looked like an Omega.

"Don't move, stay just as you are," he ordered and, picking up the washing line he used it to tie a length of line connecting both Leon's ankles leaving just enough spare line to allow the boy to hobble with short steps when he was standing.

"What have you done to Nahil?" asked Leon but Ronnier ignored the question and instead picked up a chair placing it just back from Leon's head so he could sit and face him.

"Right son, this hasn't worked out how I planned it to but there's still no reason for anyone to get hurt. If you're sensible and answer a few questions things will be just fine."

Leon just looked back his eyes boring into Ronnier's.

"Where did you get this from?" Asked Ronnier taking out the napkin ring from his pocket and holding it where Leon could see it.

"I found it," said Leon.

"You found it where?" said Ronnier patiently.

"On the beach."

"Listen son, you're starting to piss me off and I haven't got time for it. I'm going to ask you again one last time, where did you get this ring?"

"I found it on Al Solere Beach."

Ronnier wondered if he had heard that name before, but couldn't recall when or where.

"How far away is it?"

"Not so far," replied Leon.

"OK let's all go on a drive and you can show me exactly where you found it," said Ronnier who was still holding the napkin ring in his left hand and the knife in his right. He had to put the ring back in his pocket and the knife down to help the trussed Leon to his feet.

"The cars around the side of the house, if you walk slowly you won't fall and I won't cut the girl." Ronnier stooped and lifted the girl hoisting her over his shoulder. He reached awkwardly for the knife and then followed close behind Leon as they made their way to the Toyota. Ronnier had left it unlocked and managed to open a rear door and then lay the girl along the back seat.

"Get in," he ordered and held the front passenger seat open for Leon and helping to push him up and into the seat. With the knife point held against Leon's throat Ronnier reached around Leon and grasping the buckle of the seatbelt pulled it across the other's chest.

"Lean back," commanded Ronnier.

"I can't my arms are behind my back remember?" Leon complained but Ronnier pushed him roughly back and snapped the belt buckle into place.

"When I get to the top of your driveway is it left or right to Al Solere?" Ronnier asked.

"Left," replied Leon.

"OK, here's how it goes son, you try to shout out to anyone and I'll ram this knife up to the hilt in your leg." Ronnier let Leon feel the point of the knife on his inner thigh.

"You have a major artery around there and there's every chance I'll hit it then most probably you'll die or, if you're lucky, never get to use that leg again. Stay quiet and you'll get through this in one piece." Leon nodded towards the prone girl on the backseat.

"What have you done to her?"

"She's asleep, that's all," said Ronnier as he started the engine and drove slowly up the driveway turning left when he reached the road. There was no one at the bus-stop or indeed anywhere along the road. *So far so good,* thought Ronnier and wondered why they were going uphill if they were going to a beach. Perhaps the beach was on the other side of the island and they were climbing to travel across to the other side?

"How come a kid like you has a house like that?" Ronnier asked.

"My parents left it to me."

"Did they leave you that watch as well?"

"No I swopped my old watch for it, with a tourist."

"Yeah sure he did, a tourist gave you his new Omega for your old watch? You're full of shit, kid," snarled Ronnier. "Anyway, how busy with people is this beach likely to be?" Ronnier asked glancing across at Leon.

"It'll be empty," said Leon and regretted the words as soon as they had left his mouth.

"Good," said Ronnier and Leon felt his stomach turn over with fear. They drove on in silence for a while, Ronnier's eyes constantly moving, checking Leon, the road ahead and the rear-view mirror—the girl stretched out on the back seat.

"How far now?" he asked.

"There's a turn off on the left about half a mile up the road," said Leon.

"This one?" asked Ronnier as they approached a break in the wall of trees. Leon nodded and Ronnier turned off the road on to a broad dirt track that passed between a dark wood of tall trees. The track had a slight gradient downwards. Further into the wood the track narrowed and at times it seemed as if the trees might be too close together for the Toyota to pass through. But Ronnier could see sunlight ahead then the trees gave way to open ground and soon they were driving slowly out into an open grassy expanse dotted lightly with trees. A small hill rose ahead of them a little to the left with only a narrow footpath leading up it the rest was grassy open ground that ended abruptly fifty metres or so ahead of the Toyota. Ronnier could see and hear the sea and realised they were on a cliff and quite a high one at that.

"Stop here," said Leon and Ronnier brought the vehicle to a gradual stop, frowning in confusion because he had not been led to a beach.

"So where's the beach?"

"Down there," said Leon. Ronnier got out of the vehicle and walked over to the edge and looked down. Immediately he recognised where he was. He remembered the white church on the hill close by the sea the very one he had seen the day before on his cruise. He recalled the old man's words, "You said you were interested in wrecks, mister; if there was any place around this island likely to wreck a ship then this place is it."

He walked back to the Toyota and opened the passenger side door.

"Get out," he commanded. "And don't try anything or I'll cut the girl."

He then pulled the girl out of the back. She moaned and looked to be regaining consciousness. He half supported her and as they moved away from the Toyota he found to his surprise that her legs were taking her weight and, though she was still very groggy, she could stand without assistance, albeit unsteadily.

"Right show me exactly where you found that ring."

Nahil felt as she was going to vomit, her head ached and when she opened her eyes what she saw only increased her sense of confusion and nausea. She saw the back of someone's legs and shoe heels rising and falling and the ground moving away from her. Her mind tried to make sense of the jumble of fractured images that flashed behind her eyes blending confusingly with those seen with her open eyes. Memory and present blurred into one. She was entering the kitchen then…?

She had a vague recollection of blood rushing to her head, of movement and then lying on a car seat. A wave of nausea rushed through her again and she felt the sudden chill sweat that precedes a bout of vomiting. Before she retched voices distracted her and, in concentrating on them, she forget her own condition.

"Lean back," commanded a voice she didn't recognise followed almost immediately by a voice she did—Rodney's.

"I can't my arms are tied behind my back remember?" Rodney was saying. Nahil wanted to shout out to him that her arms were also tied behind her back, but some instinct kept her still and silent where she lay. She must be on the back seat her knees together and drawn up with her face towards the driver's seat in front.

The stranger's voice spoke again, "When I get to the top of your driveway, is it left or right to Al Solere?"

"Left," replied Rodney.

The stranger spoke again, "OK here's how it goes son, you try to shout out to anyone and I'll ram this knife up to the hilt in your leg. You have a major artery around there and there's every chance I'll hit it then most probably you'll die or maybe never get to use that leg again. Stay quiet and you'll all get through this in one piece."

"What have you done to her?" she heard Rodney ask, and realised with shock he was talking about her.

"She's asleep, that's all," the man replied and Nahil knew with certainty the only man who could help her now was Andy because something very bad was going to happen to both her and Rodney. Nahil closed her eyes in concentration and pain. The movement of the car caused her body to rock gently; she tested the tightness of the binding around her wrists. There was a little play in the binding and her though her hands were almost against the back cushion of the seat she knew her body hid them from the driver's view. Her fingers moved imperceptibly towards the phone in her back pocket.

Nahil's fingers pulled the battered BlackBerry from her pocket.

It is common to see people in the Katcholo Club simultaneously, holding conversation with a friend while dancing to the music, holding and sipping a drink with one hand while sending a text on their cell phone with the other. They have no need to look at the phone while typing or sending the message either. Nahil's dexterity with her phone was therefore more than up to the task it now faced. She concentrated hard to visualise how the keyboard would look relative to her thumb. Rodney and the man were talking again but Nahil concentrated her mind's eye on her thumb moving over the keypad of the phone. The message she sent to Andy was short and succinct:

'HELP-Kaspers E'.

Then she felt the car turn and her body sway against the seat as the suspension tried to absorb and dampen the bumps from the uneven road surface underneath. The slight downward slope combined with the rocking motion worked to move her towards the edge of the seat but soon the path levelled out and light streamed into the car. She heard Rodney say, "Stop here" and felt the vehicle come to a gradual stop.

"So where's the beach?" The man asked.

"Down there," Rodney replied and she knew they were at Kasper's Edge. The cold hand of fear turned her guts over and she almost gasped when the driver side door suddenly opened and the car rocked as someone got out. Seconds later the passenger side door opened.

"Get out and don't try anything or I'll cut the girl," the man said. Nahil was too terrified to pretend unconsciousness when the door near her head opened and she felt a pair of strong hands under her arms dragging her out and lifting her on to her feet. She was unsteady but through her lowered eyes she saw for the first time the owner of the voice she had been listening to, it was the man she and Andy had seen in town a day or so ago and who they had all talked about at Rodney's house. In his hand he held a kitchen knife.

"Right show me exactly where you found that ring," he commanded and Nahil looked up to see Rodney standing with both arms behind his back and his legs hobbled by several turns of shiny rope running from ankle to ankle. She almost fainted but instead staggered and only just managed to stay upright, at least her legs were not tied and that gave her a little hope.

Everything had happened so fast for me almost from the moment I had switched off the bike's engine and freewheeled down the driveway. I had let the bike run past the rear of the house as usual and it was only then that I had noticed the Toyota parked at the side of the house. I was confused I didn't know anyone with a Toyota four by four. The back door of the house was already open and, as I entered the house not sure what to expect, I heard a noise in the kitchen and second later the nightmare began.

Now I was at Kasper's Edge. Nahil half unconscious and barely able to stand and a mentally unstable and dangerous stranger waving what looked like one of my kitchen knives at me. It was the 'hotel developer' Roger Moore dress-a-like from the Three-In-One and he wanted to know where I had found the small silver napkin ring with Valvaston engraved around it. I would be happy, even eager, to tell him where I found the sodding thing if I thought that would make him go away. But that was the big question, what would he do to me and Nahil once he knew? It seemed there was only one answer to that question he would have to kill us, that is if he wanted to stop us from telling everyone how he'd behaved like a gangster. I needed to get my arms and legs free and I had to play for more time to think of a way out of the deadly fix we were in.

"The place where I found it is down there on the beach over near the church." It was difficult to refer to a nearby location without being able to use my hands to point at it as well so I found myself pointing with my chin instead.

"I'd show you but I'll never make it down tied up like this," I added.

"Show me from here," he said and together we walked a little closer to the edge, Nahil looked as if she was sleepwalking but she had moved forward and closer to us.

"Describe where on the beach you found it," he demanded. I nodded and looked towards the beach but my attention was elsewhere. In the distance I could hear the beautiful sound of a Honda's four-stroke engine protesting at being driven too hard uphill.

"Look at me you fucking freak, I asked you where you found the ring," screamed the man moving his face closer and pointing the knife towards my face.

"Tell me before I cut those blue eyes out of your fucking head."

The note of the engine changed as it turned off the road and was heading through the woods towards us. I was sure I still had the keys in my pocket but when had a lack of keys ever stopped Andy? The man's attention was also now on the noise of the approaching motorcycle. He stepped back a little from me and looked towards the trail leading out of the woods and at that moment Andy on my Honda roared out of the dark shadow of the tunnel of vegetation and came straight towards us. He swerved around the Toyota and braked hard to a stop about thirty feet away. He reached forward and under the headlight and fiddled with some wires that were dangling from the casing until the engine died then flicked out the bike rest and dismounted. He strode purposefully towards us. At that moment Nahil surprised us all and especially the madman. She had edged closer to the stranger when Andy's dramatic arrival distracted his attention. Now she moved closer still and suddenly kicked up hard at the outstretched hand which held the knife. The element of surprise coupled with the force of the kick from her strong hillwalking leg, was enough to knock the knife out of his hand sending it spinning in an arc to land on the grass a good ten feet away. In shocked surprise he gave Nahil an angry backhand slap but I could see her ride the blow even though she had to fall back on to the ground to do it.

The man's eyes narrowed as he calculated the odds, should he make for the knife or not. Seeing Nahil knocked down spurred Andy into a sprint, not for the knife lying on the grass but straight towards the man. I looked at the man's face and I saw him reach a decision, turning to me he quickly placed a leg behind me and pushed hard on my chest sending me tumbling to the ground backwards. I jack-knifed forward so as to land on my buttocks instead of my tied hands and arms. So now it was just the madman and Andy. Having never seen Andy in a brawl I wasn't sure how, or even if he could, deal with this lunatic. The man was a good two or three stone heavier than him and had a height advantage of five or six inches. I could only watch helplessly from my new position on the ground as events unfolded.

"You're going to get hurt son," said the man.

"You-you reckon," stammered Andy and when the madman heard it I could see his little smile of contempt and a 'this is going to easier than I thought' sneer as he adopted a fighting crouch and lunged towards Andy. In a blur of movement

Andy flicked out his right-hand with the fingers extended towards the man's eyes, they never made contact but the move stopped the man in his tracks who instinctively jerked his head back to save his eyes. In the same instant Andy's foot stomped down hard the side, or front, of the man's leading knee, I couldn't see which, there was an awful popping sound and the man stumbled forward off balance. As Andy's stomping foot came down he used the forward momentum to move into his opponent and swing a truly vicious elbow spike at the man's face connecting with his lower left jaw line and I heard the crack of bone and cartilage, and saw blood starting to flow from the corners of the man's mouth. Andy then rammed the heel of his hand up and under the man's chin ramming his head backward causing more crunching noises as the broken jawbone grated horribly. A yelp followed by an animal-like moan came from the man's throat.

No ballet style martial arts for our Andy then I thought, in just a few seconds he had reduced what had looked to be a formidable opponent into a broken, bloody and whimpering wreck of a man. With a flash of insight I realised why Andy never involved himself in local punch-ups, he was way too brutal and destructive for a drunken late Saturday night disagreement. Perhaps, I wondered, he only had one fighting gear 'total annihilation'. The man was half kneeling with one foot forward and the other trailing behind. He tried to speak but couldn't make his broken jaw work and only mumbling gurgling noises and blood came out. We watched frozen in fascination as he started to fumble about his ankle underneath his trouser leg. As his hands scrabbled at the leg he lifted his misshapen face and looked up, focusing on Andy with dark eyes like those of a desperate cornered animal, a dog's resentful stare when it realises its master is about to put it down. Suddenly he rose up on his one good leg and his right arm swung up gripping a knife. With a gurgling roar he launched himself at Andy trying to catch him with a surprise knife thrust but the knee Andy had kicked earlier gave way on him and he stumbled, caught his footing, and then stumbled again his momentum carrying him forward in a lurching stagger. Andy stepped to one side out of the man's line of attack but man was beyond correcting his charge, he was just trying to stay on his feet and his many corrections had spun him so he was lurching towards the cliff edge. I think we all realised at the same moment what was about to happen but by then it was too late. Andy sprang forward to try to catch the back of the man's shirt but I could see that he was never going to reach him in time. For long seconds we looked at the sea through the empty space the man had just filled before going over the edge.

We heard a series of thuds that suddenly stopped, two seconds of silence then a deep slapping thud then more silence, save for the pounding of blood in my ears and surf falling on the distant beach. Andy looked over the edge in silence then looked at Nahil and then me before walking over to where the kitchen knife lay on the grass, the one that Nahil had kicked out of the man's hand. He used it to cut first my hands, and then my legs free, and then did the same for Nahil. Not one of us spoke we simply looked at one another and then walked over to the edge to look down. The angle of the man's head and the way his body was twisted way left us in no doubt that the man was dead, but we continued to look down as the seconds gathered and drew into a long silent minute.

Nahil abruptly broke the silence, leaning over the cliff edge she shook her fist down towards the body, "That'll teach the bastard!"

Maybe if Andy or I had spoken first or if Nahil had said something different our response to the situation might have been different. But that's what she said and at that moment it acted as a slap, it reminded us that the man who lay dead at the foot of the cliff had attacked each of us. Nahil was stating her support of Andy. She wasn't going to let a broken dead body spoil things for them. To remain on St Gilberts Andy needed a 'clean pair of hands' which less than ten minutes previous he had had, but now he hadn't. I also had no wish to place myself at the mercy of the law—and Henri in particular. I could imagine how that interaction and subsequent interrogation would go;

"So what you're telling us Leon is that a respectable looking tourist decided to break into your house. Your house, local gigolo and foreign exchange crook. He takes you and a local girl, who happens to drop by captive. Drives you to Kasper's Edge threatens you with your own kitchen knife. Luckily you are both miraculously saved by our resident Englishman. Oh, and the tourist is so scared by the arrival of the short-arse white man, he runs and jumps off the edge of a cliff?"

Andy broke into my thoughts by raising the question that concerned us all.

"So do we tell the police or not?"

"They'll find out anyway won't they?" I said but Andy shook his head.

"Why would they assume anything had happened apart from a tourist having an accident by falling off the edge of a dangerous cliff?"

"But we haven't done anything wrong here," I protested.

"I know that and Na-Nahil knows it as well but how can we explain it in a w-way that makes sense?" asked Andy echoing my thoughts of the moment before.

"But none of it makes sense," said Nahil with a wail in her voice.

"Where did that man come from and why did he know about that effing ring, the one Rodney found under the church?"

"Yeah what is it about that ring? The bastard was ready to kill us all for it," I added.

"P-police or not?" Andy prompted.

"No police," said Nahil immediately and they both looked towards me.

Deep down I wanted the police, well, maybe not so much the police, but the rest of the island to know everything. I wanted absolution and freedom from the guilt for a man's death. It wasn't my-our fault but I felt responsible nevertheless. But then I also knew how island gossip takes any happening or calamity and twists the facts to create new and more scandalous versions of the 'truth'.

"No police," I said finally. So far Andy had held back I guessed he wanted the final decision to be Nahil's and mine. Perhaps he felt he had played a bigger part in it, and was therefore more responsible for the man's death than either Nahil or me. I don't know but as soon as I had said "no police" he knew what we needed to do next.

"Ga-gather up all the bits of rope and those bits of cable tie," he ordered.

"I'm go-going down to check that he is really dead," his stammer surfacing as his mind calculated the angles. He went to the edge and started down the narrow zigzag path that lead down to the beach, the one we had all started down and then had to run back up when the tsunami had come in what seemed like a life time ago.

He was gone for what seemed ages and eventually I walked over to the edge to look where he was only to see him already on his way back up the path. He was carrying something wrapped in tissues in his left hand while his right hovered over the rope handrail. As he got closer I could see that he was holding a knife in the tissues but otherwise the body looked undisturbed from the position it had been before. When he reached the top he placed the knife on the ground still wrapped in the tissue and looked back down at the path. The ground was hard and he had left no footprints.

"I don't know whether to pull one of these rings out to make it look more like an accident," said Andy and I noticed that his stammer had gone. Perhaps the physical effort of the climb had burned off some of his nervous energy.

"I think we should just leave it as it is," I said, he nodded and climbed the last few feet on to the top.

"I checked in his wallet and his name is Philippe Ronnier and he's from Belgium. He had some credit cards and he was carrying quite a bit of cash in Euros and US dollars, some local money as well. I didn't touch any of it so I cannot see any reason the police should suspect anything other than he fell off the path." He paused for a moment and then said, "I did find this though," he produced a piece of white card from his pocket that at first looked like a business card. It was not a printed card but was blank apart from some writing in pen on one side only. Andy's face was serious as he presented the card face up towards me and Nahil. Written neatly in black ink were the numbers:

'303.327.275.56.'

Below these was a date and time.

'February 1 2008 16.58.'

Below both of these and written less neatly this time in blue biro ink was my name—'Rodney Leon'.

I stared at it and my vision blurred and my stomach churned with fear.

"Oh and this," Andy was saying and he reached into his pocket again and produced the napkin ring and held it out to me. I was reluctant to take it from him but Andy held it out until I did. He said as I finally took it from him, "This means something even if we don't know what that something is. One thing I do know is that it must be something bloody significant. Anyway, let's think about it later," said Andy. "We can't afford for anyone to see us here right now so let's get the hell out of it while we still can."

I did a quick check in the Toyota for evidence that could link us to it and found nothing incriminating. The only thing of interest was the car hire's papers which told me the Toyota was on hire from Reef Car Hire and was due for return the next day. It was booked to a Mr Philippe Ronnier from Belgium his temporary address in St Gilberts, The Reef Sands Villas, Apartment 1. Andy gave a low hiss suggesting that we should get a move on so I put the documents carefully back under the dash and joined the others.

We checked around on the grass and especially at the spot where Andy had demolished the stranger in their short one-sided encounter. We found some drops of blood on several blades of grass and wiped it off. There was blood on the soil underneath but we left it, even close up I had a job to see it. The police on St Gilberts are nothing like the CSI crime scene investigators I had seen on American TV shows and I always suspected that the ones in America weren't either. In Paul Henri's normal half-cut state, his main concern would be to prevent himself from staggering over the edge as well. Henri wasn't the only cop on St Gilberts but the pay was so piss-poor that a job in the police force held no attraction for anyone with the wits to do better.

Andy picked up the knife, still wrapped in tissue paper and placed it on the seat. He started fiddling with the Honda's electric wires which he had dragged from behind the headlight. A minute later he replaced them and announced the bike should start OK if I used the ignition key. It was already in my hand and we took our usual positions on the bike. Me forward and half on the petrol tank, Andy perched on the back of the pillion with Nahil wedged between the two of us. Nahil had the job of carrying the two knives, mine and the other still wrapped in tissue paper. If we crashed on the way down they'd find us all skewered like a kebab. The Honda struggled up the dirt track but once on the road it burbled happily downhill to my house with only the worn-out gears and brakes preventing us from hurtling all the way down into the town. I turned right off the road and down my driveway but this time I did not switch off the engine at the top as usual but drove all the way down to the door. We dismounted in reverse order starting with Andy.

"Hey why's my arse wet?" Nahil was feeling her bum and staring at the tear in the vinyl.

"Did you see anyone on the road just now?" Andy asked.

"Not a soul," I replied entering the comforting surroundings of my own home. I felt a glimmer of hope that all three of us may just manage to keep a 'clean pair of hands' after all.

We slumped on the easy chairs on the veranda. Nahil suggested we needed a drink and then pulled a face when I produced three bottles of beer but her smile came back when I also produced a bottle of Rum and some Coke to go with it. Andy and I stuck to the beers. The large bag I had carried up from town for Nahil was still by the door where I had dropped it earlier in the day seconds before coming face to face with the Belgium. There were several columns of small black ants crossing the tiles to the base of it so I carried the bag outside to give it a shake. When I returned I laid out the contents on the low table between us.

"Let's make something to eat and then try to work out what the hell just happened," I suggested and they both agreed. The work of preparing the food and cooking it was a great diversion and the routine normality of it distracted us, albeit temporarily, from the events of the day. We made a curry and ate it with boiled rice washed down with more beers. We hadn't held back when adding the chillies and Nahil was making fun of Andy's red face and the beads of sweat running from his forehead. It was strange, for minutes at a time we could push the memory of the day to one side as if nothing had happened and everything was back to normal again, then a horrible feeling would come, like a heavy stone in my chest, and I knew things would never be the same again.

When we had finished eating we left the table and moved back to the easy chairs on the veranda carrying our beers. Andy threw the white card on to the low table with the numbers, time and date, and my name on it and looked at each of us.

"So what was the sequence of events today?" asked Andy and the question forced us to try to put some order to the events of the day. Nahil told her story beginning from when she had met me earlier in town and then caught the bus up to my place. From then on she could not remember much at all. She remembered walking into the kitchen after which everything was vague. Sometimes she felt that she was half awake or felt a build-up of pressure in her face.

"Perhaps that was when he carried you to the car," I suggested. She remembered feeling as if she was going to puke up but then hadn't. She recalled snippets of the conversation she'd heard in the car and shuddered when she described how the man had threatened to stab me and cut her up. She told how she had sent the text message to Andy which had no doubt saved both our lives. I then told my story, much of which overlapped with Nahil's except the bits where she was unconscious. I told them about the man's insistence on knowing where I found the napkin ring. Andy didn't need to recount his part in the saga since we had all been there and it was not something we were keen to recall anyway—at least not the bit at the end.

"So what's all this about?" asked Andy pointing to the card. I took the napkin ring from my pocket and placed it on the table alongside the card.

"And this?" We sat in silence staring at the two exhibits until I set the ball rolling with a question.

"What's special about that date and that time? What happened on the first of February at two minutes to five in the afternoon? Where were we on that date?" There was an even longer silence as we cast our minds back. We rubbed our chins, tilted our heads back, stared blankly into the middle distance, and then finally shook our heads. Not one of us had a clue what we had been doing on that day or at that time.

"Was it the day of the tsunami?" Nahil suddenly offered, again we thought back in silence.

"No that was definitely in January," I said suddenly recalling the month because the tsunami had coincided with something else in January—though I couldn't remember what that was either.

"OK then what about those numbers?" Andy leaned over and read them out aloud, "Three zero three, three two seven, two seven five, five six." I could only stare blankly back at him and Nahil the same. We weren't getting far at all so I asked Andy a question I had meant to ask earlier.

"What's the idea behind wrapping that knife in tissue?" Nahil turned to hear his answer too.

"Well, the knife, your knife, the one that is now back in your kitchen has his fingerprints, my fingerprints, your fingerprints and now possibly, Nahil's fingerprints on it. The other knife, the one he brought stuck down his sock or something has his fingerprints on it but none of ours. If it comes down to a police thing then that might help us prove that he was the aggressor and not us."

"Good thinking Batman," said Nahil with a small grin, obviously proud of her man's ability to think ahead.

"Then we should put it in a plastic bag and keep it somewhere safe," I added and they both agreed.

"Anyway, back to that card," I said. "Who's saying that those numbers and that time and date have anything to do with me and what happened today? For a start my name's written in a different colour of ink and it looks a bit scrawled compared with the rest which looks to have been written using a ruler."

"Good point," agreed Andy adding, "I don't think it's just the napkin ring that interested him because he could have just taken it and you would probably have been none the wiser."

"True," I conceded.

"I think his main interest was the Valvaston itself for some reason," said Andy.

"Yeah but as he's dead I guess we'll never know now," said Nahil.

"Don't be too sure," said Andy cryptically.

"What do you mean?" Nahil and I asked simultaneously.

Andy leaned back on his chair. "Well, so far we have assumed that this Ronny what's his name, was acting under his own steam, but how do we know he wasn't working for, and sent by someone else?"

"What else don't we know about him?" I asked. "Everyone else on the island assumed he was a hotel developer."

"He was a bloody nutcase that's what he was," pronounced Nahil.

"You're not wrong there," said Andy and Nahil frowned as she tried to work out the meaning of Andy's reply and whether he had agreed with her or not. The Brits and their double negatives.

"We need to find out what's so special about this Valvaston," insisted Andy.

"I've already tried," I said remembering my Google searches at the Kokonet Café and I went on to describe to them how I had searched the internet for information and found none.

"Perhaps that's something that I can help with," said Andy.

"I have a friend, Josh, who joined the Marines at the same time as me. He's a real geek on maritime history."

"I didn't know you were in the Marines," I said, genuinely surprised and I saw Nahil nodding to show that she already knew.

"Well, I might as tell you it all now," said Andy fully relaxed in his chair and stammer free. "I joined the Marines from school and a year or so later passed the physicals and tests and transferred into the Special Boat Service the SBS."

"SBS. Is that like the SAS I've heard about on films and stuff?" I asked.

"Yes very similar and in fact we often work together on combined operations. In the SBS we specialise in operations at sea, along coastlines and on river networks and we also had a team on standby for maritime counter-terrorism operations. It wasn't just water-based operations though. We also did our fair share on dry land. The last job I had was in Afghanistan after that I signed out and went into the security business."

"Why did you leave?" I asked and Andy didn't answer at first and, after a while, I began to think he wasn't going to then he looked up and grinned.

"Time for a change I guess, it was great in many ways, great mates, you knew you were in with the very best there was—bar none. It was never about Queen and country for me, the risks I took, we took, were all about looking after each other's backs, look after your mates and they looked after you. Trouble was, my mates kept getting killed in action. As they go, one by one, you try not to let it get to you but in the end it does—well it got to me. To stay alive is the beat the clock, that's what we used to say in the SBS. It was great at first, always challenging, we were young, invincible, fit as hell and all hooked on adrenalin. What made me leave? I guess I began to feel the law of averages was about to catch up with me."

"What do you mean?" I asked.

"That my luck was about to run out," he replied then paused, thinking, "Sometimes being good, even being the best—not that I was ever that—isn't enough to guarantee it won't be your turn next."

"So that's why you left?"

"Sort of, but losing my mates was the main reason, I guess."

"That's when you became a bodyguard then?"

"Yes the world of international security—the Circuit, as it's known—was a natural place for someone leaving from either the SAS or the SBS. My first year was spent working for an American billionaire and during that time the most serious threat I had to deal with was flat tyre on a hire car I was driving when chauffeuring him and his family on the Amalfi coast. When he moved back to the states I decided not to accompany him but to move on elsewhere. After 9/11 and the start of the war in Iraq the Circuit expanded into a multi-billion-pound industry. Eventually demand outstripped supply; standards went into freefall, a military background was no longer an essential requirement—shit—they were even taking on bouncers! Inevitably, as supply caught up with demand the bubble burst and security firms slashed wages and cut back on equipment and training." Andy stopped and looked around to see if I was still listening, still interested, I was. He took another swig of his drink.

"I decided I didn't want to work with a team of amateurs. I always applied the same SBS ground rules to my security work: plan ahead, blend in, and respect the local population. Many of the new guys on the Circuit in Iraq were strutting about pumped on steroids, wearing shades, full body armour over their clothes and carrying an arsenal of weapons in full view. Looks great in Hollywood but in places like Iraq it just draws attention, gets you noticed, and almost guarantees sooner or later you'll get hit. Luckily I got offered a job in Oman protecting a prince and the team I worked with were all ex-special forces like me. But if I thought the Oman job was going to be safe and dull much the same as working for the American I couldn't have been more wrong. Six months into the job someone pulled a handgun on my man and I got in the way. Luckily the Kevlar vest and a ceramic tile insert stopped the bullet but I got a nasty bruise close to the edge of the vest. Another inch up and I'd have been stone-dead but I'd saved the Prince's life and he knew it. He rewarded me with enough dosh to retire—well—as long as I didn't go on any mad spending sprees," he looked pointedly at Nahil as he said this last bit and she pulled her tongue out at him.

"OK. So why St Gilberts?" I asked still fascinated, I never heard Andy say so much in a single sitting and, I suspected, probably never would again. Finding out that your best friend was in one of those special service military units that send men down ropes from helicopters into the world's trouble spots has to be on par with finding out that your neighbour is James Bond. Conjuring the image of James Bond caused my mind to link with Nahil's comment about Roger Moore and then the stranger. In my mind's eye I could see the fussily dressed broken dead body at the foot of Kasper's Edge. I blinked the image away and listened to Andy's answer.

"Well, I'd visited the place with the prince in early 2006. I was one of his bodyguards and where he went I went. I fell in love with the place. You must have heard how we took over The Planters Club Hotel for two days even though we mostly stayed on his yacht, yacht, more of a cruise liner really?"

"Yeah that's right I remember, never guessed you were in with that lot though," I said remembering the complaints and moans about the visit from the Three-In-One crowd. They'd turned Dan Meme away at door and not very politely either according to him.

"When I left his service, the Prince himself put in a good word for me to some top politician here and so getting to stay wasn't too much trouble, though I guess that I still need to keep—"

"—A clean pair of hands!" Nahil and I finished the sentence for him and when all three of us held up our hands at the same time to show our clean palms we all spontaneously burst into laughter. It was the only laugh of the day and it released the tension and sense of foreboding that I felt whenever the conversation lapsed into silence or my eyes had drifted towards the sound of the sea and the dark beyond the veranda rail.

"What I can't understand is how that man connected Rodney with the name on that ring," said Nahil, after our giggling had died down and we became serious again thinking about what she had just said.

"OK he found the ring when he broke into my house but what made him break into my house in the first place?" I asked.

"That's what I'm getting at," exclaimed Nahil who added, "I never told anyone about our little St Francis Mount Church trip or that ring or anything. In fact until I heard that man asking about Valvaston, I'd forgotten all about the name anyway."

"I haven't told anyone either. I mean, who could I tell?" Said Andy and then they both looked towards me.

"Well, don't look at me!" I exclaimed. "I wouldn't tell anyone would I?" The way they continued to look at me made me frown and I thought back. I have been known to get talkative when I've had a few drinks, but no, after a few minutes I shook my head.

"I never even mentioned it; not even to Caroline and since she never visited my house, there was no way she could have seen that ring."

"I think we're missing an important point," said Andy and we turned towards him and waited while he took a swig from his bottle before continuing, "That guy came all the way from Belgium to St Gilberts and aims straight for you like a guided missile wanting to know where you found up that ring. No offence, but St Gilberts is not very well known outside of this part of the world, I mean it's hardly even a regular tourist destination. His arriving here is unlikely to be a coincidence, which means that he must have known something before he left Europe. Something pointed him in this direction and towards you." Now they were both looking at me and, as Andy's words sank in, I felt another cold chill run up my spine.

"So you're saying someone came all the way from Europe just looking for me?" Saying it made me shudder again, I was getting the creeps.

"Not quite what I said," corrected Andy. "It seems to me that he was looking for the source of the napkin ring. That was his objective and he thought you knew the answer. What I can't understand is how he came to identify you as a possible source of the information he was looking for." I had to take a few deep breaths.

"Jeez, I'm beginning to feel like someone's put a contract on my head," I said hoping to hear them pooh-pooh my suggestion, instead Andy sent my stress levels even higher with his next observation.

"And what we still don't know," he mused aloud, "is whether he was working alone or whether he was sent as part of a team working for an organisation." I sprang to my feet and paced about the veranda to try to burn off some of the tension building up inside me.

"Turn it in, Andy, you'll have me a nervous wreck." He nodded in understanding and went past me to get me another bottle.

"Perhaps we should have gone to the police after all, do you really think we've done the right thing not telling them?" I asked.

Nahil had no doubt and replied immediately, "For sure."

Andy thought about it a little longer before giving his response, "Again, no offence, but in most other places I would have involved the police from the start but here I'm not sure it wouldn't cause us all sorts of problems. We'd get questions that we can't answer simply because we literally don't know the answers. It's always twice as difficult to prove a negative. In fact we'd have difficulty proving anything. Besides I'm guessing that St Gilberts tourist board, with its hopes of the island becoming a tourist destination would prefer the cause of death to be an unfortunate accident, death by misadventure rather than the result of something a bit dodgy."

"That's true," agreed Nahil.

"OK," said Andy. "Let's all agree on where we were this afternoon."

"We spent the whole day here from midday onwards," I suggested and they unanimously agreed.

Eventually we turned our attention to the rum bottle and it was late into the night before we decided to turn in. It was too late for them to return home so they crashed out in the tidiest of my spare rooms. I was glad they stayed, even though the drink had numbed and befuddled my senses, deep down I still felt that heavy ball of apprehension in my guts.

I slept badly, I often do when I finish the night on spirits. I dreamed, but kept drifting in and out of sleep so the dreams blurred with those times I was awake. They were uncomfortable dreams and when I awoke during the night I felt a sense of unease and dread. At one point I drew the sheet over me so there must have been a temperature drop. I heard the wind rise outside and a minute later, the drumming of heavy drops of rain on the roof and then the splash of water pouring down drainpipes and dripping off the broad leaves all around the house. I listened until I fell back into sleep again.

We were a house of zombies when the morning sun finally lit up the house. We converged on the kitchen and I made both tea and coffee, and several slices of toast. All three of us drank a couple of glasses of water straight off which effectively killed off our appetites for anything else. Nahil had survived the excesses of the night better than either Andy or me and she sat munching her way through the toast putting large dollops of Aunt Mert's guava jam on each slice. I confined myself to drinking tea and the letting out the occasional moan as each new wave of nausea swept over me. We went to the veranda and slumped on to the chairs shielding our eyes against the low sunlight glittering off the turquoise sea below. Roundabout eleven a.m. Andy and Nahil headed off home. I offered Andy the keys to the Honda and even volunteered to drive them myself, but they refused, both preferring to walk off the alcohol instead. I agreed to drive down to their place later in the day so we could share any news we might have heard about the Belgian man. I walked up the drive with them and left them at the road, watching as they walked down together. I pottered about towards the top of the driveway within sight of the road half expecting to see one the islands four police cars drive past towards Kasper's Edge. The road remained as quiet as usual. I returned to the house and forced some toast down and felt better almost immediately. As an afterthought I checked all the doors were locked and bolted, thinking the house was too quiet now Nahil and Andy had left.

We met up that afternoon as planned. I had no news to give them as I had not left the house all day and they hadn't heard anything either. We cooked and ate out in Andy's garden. We all went easy on the alcohol and confined ourselves to beer. Andy tried to persuade me to stay at his place overnight and, to be truthful I nearly accepted, but for some reason I refused and returned home. I think I was testing myself it would have been too easy to become reliant on Andy and Nahil to keep the sense of gnawing apprehension at bay. But I knew eventually I would have to face it alone and it may as well be sooner rather than later. I slept badly again and yet felt unable to lie in bed beyond eight a.m. Once again I felt the need to be around normal people and thought of an early start at the Three-In-One but it was late opening on Sunday. On an impulse I decided to go to morning mass instead, I couldn't remember the last time I had been. If I were to face the ghosts of Al Solere, both old and new, every night, then it wouldn't do any harm to have some spiritual credit in the bank—would it? However, despite my good intentions I arrived late to the church, when the service had already started, so I went into arrears immediately. The back door had one of those damned springs on it and it banged shut behind me before I could catch it. Josie, Nahil's Aunt, turned to give me a disapproving stare and dug her elbow into Aunt Mert at her side. If I'd been expecting Aunt to show delight at seeing the prodigal Rodney's return to the Catholic fold her expression left me in no doubt that she felt none. She dropped her chin and looked at me sternly over the top of her reading glasses before turning back to her missal.

After the mass finished I waited outside, it was customary that all the parishioners meet outside to show off their church finery and to catch up on local gossip. Aunt Mert took hold of my elbow and led me to a space away from the rest of the milling congregation. She cautiously looked about her to make sure no one was within ear shot before facing me.

"Is there something that you should be telling me Rodney?" It was asked in that stern school mistressy voice she had always used when my behaviour fell below the standard she demanded. To my embarrassment it still has the same effect on me now as when I was at junior school. What did she know I wondered? And, how had she found out? I gaped back at her for what must have seemed an age as she waited for me to confess. Confess what, had they found the Belgian's body?

"Rodney?" her intonation reminding me that I still had a question to answer. I had difficulty meeting Aunt Mert's stare and might have given myself away had Aunt Mert not broken the silence first.

"Rodney, seeing you sneaking into church just tells me that you have something on your mind that needs the Lord's forgiveness. Come on and tell me, which poor young girl you've have led astray, is she pregnant?" It was not easy convincing her that I'd made no girl pregnant, as far as I knew, and when I eventually managed to convince her she seemed a little disappointed. She still gave me another one of those funny looks that said she knew I was guilty of something.

"Anyway Rodney I trust we will see more of you in church from now on, now that you have remembered where it is." She pushed a few strands of grizzled grey hair back over her ear and back under her best hat, the one she only wore on Sundays. She touched me on the arm and wandered back to join Josie and her husband Alfred. I was out of place and slunk away like a sinner who had neither repented, nor received absolution.

It was still too early for the Three-in-One to open its doors so I got my Honda started and set off back up the hill back towards the house. Half a mile up and I heard a car toiling up the hill behind me. I moved towards the side of the road to let it pass. My Honda is well past its prime but the car behind was no sports car either and it only managed to overtake me as I slowed and turned off the road down on to my driveway. I stopped and watched it go past and upwards. It had the Reef Car Hire logo on the side and at the wheel sat Simon Marengo who worked for the car hire firm connected the Reef Sands Hotel. Robert Boudane, a mechanic for the same car hire firm, rode shotgun alongside him. Intuitively I knew they were the search party sent to find the Toyota four-wheel drive, the one booked for return yesterday. There are a limited number of roads on St Gilberts that can take a car and it was easily possible to check them all inside a day and I guessed that's what they were doing now.

I freewheeled down the rest of the driveway parked the bike and walked back up the driveway with some garden tools. I stopped part-way up with my head level with the road. I had chosen a spot lower than the road level so I could see a passing car without its occupants seeing me. I set about turning over soil and doing some pruning and soon became engrossed in what I was doing. I had neglected the garden over the past few weeks, so it could have been almost an hour and a half before I heard the noise of a car in low gear coming up the hill. I parted a cluster of pink flowers on the Rangoon Creeper and, like a spy in a B-movie I scanned the road through the gap I'd made in the vegetation. I got that feeling of dread again, but wasn't surprised, when I saw the approaching car was a police car. Sod that nutter going over the cliff I thought bitterly. But now I knew the real waiting game was about to begin. Would the police see death by misadventure or would they suspect foul play?

No one could ever accuse Richard Denver of being charming though he had once being popular among his circle of friends and even his crew when he had skippered his own marine salvage ship. His lack of charm did not prevent him from being a powerful and wealthy man by his mid-thirties. As his wealth and power had grown Denver found he became less concerned with qualities such as charm, or indeed, what others felt about him. It was an attitude that many thought defined his approach to business, and to life, and which explained his success in the former and his increasing isolation in the latter. Others looked to his tough Northern roots to explain to his lack of social grace. Denver had few close friends but on the other hand, there were plenty who looked forward to the day when Richard Denver got his come-uppance. A few, in his inner circle of business colleagues had begun to think, and even hope, that day might just be sooner rather than later.

Richard Denver made his name and had his first taste of wealth, as a marine salvage engineer. In free time snatched whenever his regular marine salvage work allowed, he did historical detective work to trace a sunken treasure ship, the Levia. He spent hours at a time and even days sifting through ships log books, diaries, ships' plans, records of official inquiries, insurance records, tidal movements, analysing the direction of currents, old weather reports, and hearsay. He charted his findings as he went along, and compared his findings with the disparate research of others. Until one summer, off the coast of Scotland, his determination and perseverance paid off. A blip on the sonar and an exploratory dive confirmed he had indeed found his prize, the Levia. A Spanish Galleass, a longer and narrower version of the larger Spanish Galleon. The legendary Levia held the massed valuables of its passengers and also those of four other Armada ships. The valuables recovered belonged to many of the leading figures of Spain's aristocracy. Of course he had to negotiate his way through the legal complexities of salvage. Establish ownership of the hull and the cargo. Explore the cultural heritage implications of the find and the fact that the wreck sank in British territorial waters. He came out of it with much less than he had found but still a considerable fortune and an overnight reputation in the popular press as the man with the golden touch.

Richard Denver knew the chances finding another sunken treasure were slim and he was forced to confront the possibility that he had hit, and passed, the high point of his life and the realisation depressed him. Regular marine salvage work now depressed him to—not that he needed to continue doing it anymore. As his life began to drift uncomfortably towards a treadmill of city based social functions, a chance meeting with an old friend from Manchester, his home town, was to take his career in a different direction and change the course of his life. Like Denver, Gerald Carr had worked his way out of the tough side of Salford. He was a few years older than Denver, a Chartered accountant by profession, and working for a research firm that provided intelligence to the business community and to investors in particular. During their meeting they realised that their knowledge, experience and contrasting personalities had the potential, when combined, to create a powerful moneymaking partnership. Denver's nerve, new-found wealth and reputation as one of life's winners when combined with Carr's business experience, inside knowledge, contacts and analytical mind made for a formidable pairing. Both realised that together they could go further than either of them could alone. They formed a company together. Their strategy was to disrupt markets that had been allowed to become too cosy for the existing dominant companies. Carr applied the business "Rule of Thirds" which decreed that an acceptable result was for one-third of their start-ups to fly, one-third to tread water and one-third to fail. In fact their successes usually outperformed the rule of thirds so their wealth and power gradually increased into an empire.

By then, the contrast in their personalities that had made them so effective and successful at the start was beginning to tear the union apart. A common history of having grown up in Salford's Moss Side may have brought them together but it was never going to be enough to bridge the yawning chasm between their temperaments; Denver, unashamedly single-minded and relentless, Carr suave, open to influence, and pragmatic. Denver, when dealing with business contacts tended towards the arrogant and brusque even to the point of rudeness while Carr was socially adroit and had a talent for diplomacy and building useful webs of contacts. When their goals aligned and they were moving in the same direction they made a formidable team but when they were not, the gulf between them seemed unbridgeable.

The meltdown in the US sub-prime mortgage market in the third quarter of 2007 predicted by many, including Carr, began to unfold into the so called "credit crunch" of 2008. Back in 2006 they had watched as large businesses and banks built and serviced sub-prime mortgages, along with firms who specialised in creating asset-backed securities. They saw them begin to suffer heavy cutbacks. Slavic Village in Cleveland, Ohio, was seen by many as the epicentre of America's sub-prime mortgage catastrophe, and thus of the whole 'credit crunch' crisis that spread to paralyse the world's financial markets. In fact it was simply the first surfacing of a widespread cancer. The thirty-four thousand inhabitants of Slavic Village, many descended from the community's hard-working Eastern European founders, watched in horror and then despair, as house after house was re-possessed and boarded up. Picket fenced houses that had once epitomised apple-pie American charm lovingly cared for by their owners were left empty to the mercy of vandals, squatters and graffiti artists and a rapid decline into dereliction. As the property market collapsed many other firms were already feeling the heat. In particular property firms were facing funding difficulties and began to sell an array of tempting securities to raise funds to meet the demands of their prime brokers. The markets continued to tighten and creditors became less willing to refinance wobbling companies and so the companies themselves became attractive to 'Vulture Funders', those who buy up or buy into firms that have become the equivalent of corporate carrion.

Denver and Carr's organisation had surplus cash and so were able to move in along with the other predators. The irony was not lost on Denver who had started his career searching for wrecks on the seabed but who now found himself trawling for companies foundering, or wrecked, on a reef of debt. The reality, however, was that Denver's experience in marine salvage was irrelevant to this line of work; it was Carr's skill and judgement that steered them to success. He had an uncanny knack of being able to spot the gems amid the rubble. He also had exquisite timing. He knew when to swoop and when to hold off on those firms whose stock value had still further to fall before reaching their nadir. Denver and Carr made spectacular returns but as their already considerable fortunes grew Denver became increasingly detached from the business itself. When they had first gone into business Denver had been the dominant character in the partnership, not only did he have the more forceful personality but he was already an established celebrity, the man with the golden touch. He was also the one supplying the start-up capital. He saw himself as decisive and bold, as a man who always liked to advance, but being decisive is only an advantage if you make the right decisions.

Carr on the other hand was prudent and cautious and often delayed before committing himself to a business decision. Denver came to realise, as he watched Carr grow their combined fortunes, that a cautious, prudent approach was the right approach in vulture funding. Denver also lacked the skill and finesse needed for this type of work while Carr had it in abundance. Denver found himself increasingly, and unwillingly, relegated to the role of nominal figurehead. The sheer diversity of their business organisations left him struggling to absorb the mass of information he needed to fully engage and contribute in the many meetings he attended. Denver was great at historical research and a respected skipper at the helm of his salvage vessel, but in Carr's world the sheer speed and volume of incoming information defeated him. There was never enough time for him to catch up and then keep up. He looked back with nostalgia on the long nights he had spent searching for and then poring over documents as he looked for the Levia. In those days he had been his own master doing what he did best. He could lock on to a single objective and then pursue it relentlessly. That's what he needed now, another Levia. He fished his cell phone out of his pocket and brought back the last number Ronnier had used to contact him and dialled it—nothing. He tried again, twice, and then brought back Ronnier's old number—again nothing.

So, on his last call Ronnier had cut him off and now he had gone AWOL. He picked up his office phone and called George Kirkham his security chief.

"George I want you to use whatever contacts you have in South Africa and the Indian Ocean and find out if Philippe Ronnier is still on St Gilberts and what he's up to. He was travelling under his own name." George Kirkham, the one whose intuition had put Ronnier in the French Foreign Legion, nodded and left. Two hours later he returned to Denver's office.

"I contacted a friend of mine who's living on Madagascar he says reports in the local press say a tourist called Philippe Ronnier died in an accident on the island. The local police do not suspect foul play." Denver stood open-mouthed, stunned by the news.

"Killed, by whom?" He asked after he had recovered his wits.

The security man's reply was laconic, "No one apparently, he just fell off the edge of a cliff."

Denver thought for a moment and then said in a distracted voice, "Send someone to Ronnier's place in Brussels to clean it up. The usual thing, laptop, discs, notebooks, diaries, anything at all that might have information belonging to me, concerning me, and bring it here." Minutes after the other man had left his office, Denver continued to stare with unfocussed eyes trying to think through the various scenarios that might lead to a man like Ronnier to falling off the edge of a cliff. Denver frowned he could think of none. Ronnier slipped off the edge of a cliff? He wasn't that kind of man. A third party was playing hardball and they had just raised the stakes. His shock at hearing of Ronnier's death was under pinned with a frisson of excitement.

He had sent Ronnier to St Gilberts to follow up a possible lead that could lead to the finding of a wreck, the Valvaston—to see if a wreck even existed. He had only half-hoped for a genuine lead and was equally half-resigned to it leading to nowhere. On his last phone call to Denver, Ronnier had actually cut him off suddenly at the end of it. This new development suggested that perhaps there was something worth following up after all. For a brief second, he thought about Ronnier and felt a twinge of guilt at his death. He realised that apart from the travel arrangements that he had paid for and expenses advance, Ronnier had gone without any other payment.

He remembered his promise to Ronnier, *Find me the wreck site and you'll never need to work again*, a promise he would now never need to keep. Ronnier himself or, more likely, someone else, had taken Ronnier off the job market permanently.

Later that evening Denver walked into the steel and concrete strongroom he had had built into his house. When he walked out he carried a box containing a bundle of letters, some papers, a journal and a book. He placed the box on to a table and spread the contents out in front of him. In an age of computerisation and digital records he found the weight of the ancient documents reassuring. It had been a few years since he had read through them, but now, because of Ronnier's death, he felt he needed to refresh his memory and to justify his continuing search for the Valvaston.

Just holding the documents brought back memories. Denver remembered the circumstances that led to his ownership of each of them. The documents contained everything he knew about the Valvaston and what it may have carried when it left India hundreds of years before. Each of the documents' represented a piece of evidence and the acquisition of each had provided him with a moment of intense excitement and satisfaction. He placed the artefacts into five separate piles across the desk top; first there was the book; Travels in India by Jean-Baptiste Tavernier. The second was a large leather bound journal. The third was a bundle of letters. The fourth, two photocopied sheets and the fifth, was a single sheet of A4 paper with a few lines of type on it.

Denver knew from experience that the first clue or potential clues often went unnoticed simply because nobody was looking for something that they didn't even know existed and so they lay unrecognised as anything other than just an interesting footnote in a historical journal. But Denver had a talent for filing such nuggets of information in a corner of his subconscious. Later, sometimes years later, he would come across a related fact or snippet of information and was able to connect it with the footnote he'd earlier filed away in his head. When viewed in conjunction with the new information the relevance of the footnote was revealed. That is how it was with Levia and now the Valvaston's chain of evidence was going the same way. Denver had always taken a keen interest in history and was widely read in that field. Another of his interests was precious stones and it was in relation to this interest that he had first read the book; Travels in India by Jean-Baptiste Tavernier. The book in his possession was a translation from the original French edition of 1676 and so it appealed to his love of history as well. His interest stirred, he had also read more recent literature on the celebrated traveller, jeweller and chronicler.

Jean-Baptiste Tavernier, is still regarded by many as the most important authority on historic Indian diamonds. Between 1631 and 1668 Tavernier made six voyages to Persia and India, buying and selling jewels as he travelled. In the December of 1668 he returned to France and Louis XIV ordered him to attend court. Tavernier took with him a large quantity of diamonds comprising forty-four large diamonds and a collection of smaller ones numbering some 1,122. The king, delighted with the display, bought all the diamonds for a total price of 897,831 livres around 180,000 dollars. Roughly a quarter of the total sum went towards the cost of a large blue diamond weighing a little over 112 carats it was named the Tavernier Blue after Tavernier himself. The beautiful blue diamond was more impressive for its size than its cut. In India back then the size of a stone took precedence over its brilliance. This resulted in large stones undergoing only slight faceting work to remove surface flaws to keep the stone as large a size as possible. The trouble with this approach is that it left the stones lacking in shape, clarity, cut and brilliance. Louis XIV had the diamond cutter Sieur Pitau recut the gem and the finished result was a heart or drop-shaped diamond of just over 67 carats which the King later had set in a piece of jewellery known as the Order of the Golden Fleece with a red spinal stone known as the Cote de Bretagne. This new newly faceted version was called the French Blue. This blue diamond effectively disappeared during the French Revolution in 1792 when thieves stole it from the Garde-Mouble.

Twenty years later in 1812 a slightly different blue diamond appeared in London. This new blue diamond weighed 45.52 carats and was a mixed cut, non-symmetrical with fifty-eight facets. Diamond dealer, Daniel Eliason, sold it to Henry Philip Hope in 1830 and was called the Hope Diamond. Few doubted this new diamond had been cut from the French Blue.

The fame, or notoriety, of the Hope diamond, came only partly from its unusual colour, size and quality; it was its history and the misfortune that seems to accompany its various owner's right from the time of its discovery to the present-day. Tavernier himself, according to some reports, lost his fortune and travelled to Russia to try to recoup his losses but instead got his throat torn out and his body ripped apart by wild dogs. Well, it made good copy to say the diamond had a curse and then link it to a series of human misfortunes ranging from the downfall and execution of French royalty to ruination and death of its subsequent wealthy owners. Denver knew that his detailed and careful studies reveal little, if any, foundation to the supposed curse of the Hope diamond. He uncovered that Tavernier was not ripped to shreds by wild dogs but in fact lived on to a ripe old age. All the other mishaps that befell its later owners were events that seem likely to have happened anyway. For its current owner, the National Museum of National History of the Smithsonian Institute based in Washington DC, the Hope Diamond has brought only good luck. It remains their most popular exhibit and attracts millions of visitors every year. Denver himself had gazed through the glass casing surrounding the gem in the Harry Winston Gallery, named after the man who donated the diamond to the institute. He recalled the large bluestone, big as a walnut, turning round and round on its plinth driven by a mechanical wheel underneath the display.

Denver pushed the book to one side and stood up. He walked over to a drinks cabinet and poured himself a brandy but, just as he reached it, the phone rang. He checked the caller display it was a female friend and he left the phone call unanswered. He took the brandy and returned to his seat at the table.

The Hope Diamond and the book by Jean-Baptiste Tavernier were both in the public domain and, apart from invoking the same curiosity in him as it had in many others, Denver's study of the Hope diamond would have ended there. However a footnote had lodged in the back of Denver's mind and that footnote was the absence of information that normally should have been there, the details of provenance of the Tavernier Blue that Tavernier had omitted in his book.

His professional interest stirred, Denver began to notice, and collect information about Tavernier and the Hope diamond. He wondered why Tavernier had been uncharacteristically vague when it came to recording the origin of the Tavernier Blue. Where it had come from? Who had he bought it from? How much had he paid for it? He failed to answer these questions with regard to the Tavernier Blue and yet had meticulously answered them in some detail on all the other gems he collected. How strange then, that when it came to his most celebrated find there was nothing. This omission has prompted some gem historians to assume that Tavernier had been trying to hide something shameful about his acquisition of the stone. It also provided fuel for pulp theorists who churned out the lurid stories that further added to the myths that surrounded the Hope Diamond.

Andy's head broke the surface of the water and he held aloft a fish on the prongs of his trident spear. The fish had speckled hexagonal markings and I groaned inwardly. Treading water, with his other hand Andy pushed the diving mask back on his head and let the snorkel dangle free on its strap.

"It's some sort of G-Grouper," he shouted spitting salt water out at the same time. He was smiling triumphantly so I gave him a little cheer and clapped a few times. Nahil was not so diplomatic, or two-faced. Her true feelings showed on her face and it wasn't a happy one. Andy saw it to and wailed, "W-What's up now?" In a frustrated voice that rose in pitch towards the end of the question.

"Oh no, it's one of those Honeycomb types, like chewing rubber!" She snorted.

"Not with our master chef here," Andy replied nodding towards me. I shrugged my shoulders.

"Still like chewing rubber but I could try to make it into tasty rubber." Andy's smile was starting to droop but he still tossed the fish aboard and scrambled in after it over the side of the boat. We had borrowed a wooden sailing dingy off Nahil's uncle. He was a fisherman but Sunday was his day of rest, if two and a half-hours singing, clapping, and waving your arms about in a Pentecostal church could be regarded as a rest. The dingy was roomier than Andy's inflatable and its sail provided shade from the sun and meant that we could save on fuel and take our time. We also didn't need to worry about fish-hooks and knife blades putting holes in anything. We had spent the previous hour fishing with a line close by the reef but failed to catch anything worthwhile. Action man Andy slipped on his mask and snorkel, grabbed his trident went over the side and caught something almost straight away. Unfortunately, as Nahil and I were concerned, he'd caught the wrong fish.

"I'll get another," he offered and though Nahil was all for letting him go, I convinced them both we had enough to cook up already and I passed them both a beer from the cool box. We all took a few swigs in one of those contented silences that happen between friends until Nahil spoke.

"I saw you with Dan last week. What does he know about the police investigation?" The way she pronounced 'investigation' with a sneer gave us no doubt what she thought of the ability of the local police to carry out any sort of criminal investigation. She was looking directly at me and I cast my mind back to see when she could have seen me with Dan.

"Ah, yes, I saw in him the Three-In-One last Tuesday," I said remembering.

Nahil nodded and said, "He drinks Kalou at Toffies, the cop hangout, so he must have picked something up off blabbermouth Henri." Her question set me remembering something I had all but forgotten in the alcoholic haze of that meeting with Dan Meme came to mind.

"Yes he did say something now I think back, something about…" I had a blurry memory of seeing Dan's mouth moving as he bellowed, in his usual fashion, straight into my face and then some of his words forcing me to try to pay more attention.

"Well, go on," Nahil and Andy shouted in exasperation.

"Hold on I'm thinking, it-it's coming back to me now, the police contacted the authorities in Belgium but no one knew anything about him." As I spoke, more of what Dan had told me loosed from my memory banks. "The police found some items on the body that made them suspicious about the man's background, some cardboard thing taped to his leg they couldn't explain; oh—and they found a professional lockpick on him too."

This was clearly of news of paramount importance to all of us and so should have been at the forefront of my mind whether obtained when I was drunk or not. Was it selective amnesia and a hefty dose of denial which had determined that it wasn't?

"I must have missed those when I checked through his stuff," said Andy and as he started to speak Nahil joined in as well so they spoke as one.

"So what are they going to do about it?"

"Dan reckons they are going to go for death by misadventure. If nothing else it'll save them from admitting they've got a case they can't explain or solve."

"Sounds good to me," said Andy.

"Yes," I agreed. "Exactly what we wanted to hear."

Andy tempered our optimism with his next comment, "So who's coming next to look for the Valvaston?"

Nahil punched him on the shoulder and frowned.

"Don't be so looking on the bad side," she said and Andy smiled at her with affection and, for a second, I felt as if I was intruding.

Our lives were slowly, and tentatively, returning to some sort of 'normal'.

Denver was still looking at the documents, the glass of brandy in his hand. He took a sip and replaced the glass on the table and reached across the table to pick up the journal, perhaps the key link in the chain of historical evidence. The journal had been in the public domain until Denver had bought it at an auction, partly to store it away from other treasure hunters who may possibly have been following the same trail. As a result, few living historians have read the personal journal of Thomas Pitt who was Governor of Madras from 1698 to September of 1709. In his own way Thomas Pitt led a life equal in terms of adventure to that of Tavernier. Pitt's life is irrevocably connected to the history of the British East India Company of which Denver had a particular interest given his passion for maritime history to the extent that he had become something of an authority on the Company and its ships.

The English East India Company was set up in 1599 to rival the Dutch influence on trade. English merchants outraged by the price of pepper rising from three to eight shillings a pound, set up the English East India Company with £70,000 contributed by two hundred investors. In January 1600, Queen Elizabeth first granted the new company a charter, giving them the sole right to trade in:

The East Indies, in the countries and Parts of Asia and Africa, and into and from all the islands, Ports, Havens, Cities, Creeks, Towns and Places in Asia, Africa, and America, or any of them beyond the Cape of Bona Esperanza (Good Hope).

With this monopoly on trade came the right to own and dispose of land in any of the areas which the Company occupied, and to impose and raise taxes in them too. There was an attempt by the Dutch to undermine the power of the British East India Company by persuading the spice growers of Indonesia to stop selling to the British. In response the British East India Company concentrated on India and broadened it interests to cottons and silks. It was trade in these that eventually provided the reason they stayed, rather than the spices that had been their initial interest. The British East India Company soon became the largest single organisation and employer in the empire's history. It had its own administration, legal system and army.

However, despite its size, power, and the extent of its reach, the Company did not have everything its own way. The Dutch East India Company continued with its hostile rivalry. Closer to home, some independent traders continued to run the risk of defying the Company's monopoly on trade by conducting unauthorised trade with the nations covered by the Charter. These trader's ships, known as 'interlopers', continued to trade illegally. Denver discovered that the term 'interloper' was derived from Latin and Dutch, the language of the Company's great trade rival. Inter, borrowed from Latin, meaning between and among. Loper, derived from the Dutch word lopen meaning to run and leap. The Dutch also use it in their word landloper meaning vagabond, someone constantly on the move across the land. In the 17th Century the word interloper used in the extended sense came to mean "busybody". One of the most famous 'interlopers' was Thomas Pitt who, on the one hand undermined and trespassed on the Company's trade while on the other, was one of its most prominent employees.

Born of a religious Cornish family Pitt left England in 1673 to take up a post in the East India Company in India. It wasn't long before he was trading on his own behalf. Pitt ruthlessly exploited the Company's accounting system and its supplies to broker private deals with local traders enabling him to buy cheap and then send the goods back to England for sale. It was only a question of time before the Company discovered what Pitt was doing and, once they had, they quickly moved to have him dismissed. However Pitt pulled off a masterstroke outwitting them. He did a deal with the Company's chief executive in Madras, Matthias Vincent, and then married Vincent's niece. Thwarted, but unappeased, the Company continued to hound Pitt until he bought them off with an out-of-court settlement of £400. At that time £400 represented a huge sum of money to most people but to Pitt it was a mere fraction of what his wheeler-dealing was bringing in. After the payoff Pitt became increasingly wealthy and soon merited the locals describing him as a 'Nabob' an anglicised version of the Indian word for an Indian prince 'Nawab'. The anglicised term Nabob also described those English entrepreneurs who had become rich through their dealings in India. Pitt liked to flaunt his wealth which resulted in less well-paid employees who lived in the same neighbourhood, facing rising prices for the local commodities they needed. Pitt ploughed much of his money into buying properties in England including the Boconnoc estate in Cornwall.

Pitt's most famous purchase, however, was the Pitt Diamond. A four hundred and ten carat gem cut from the Mogul's mine and valued at the time at £125,000, a figure that would make it priceless by today's standards. Pitt later sold the diamond for a profit to the French Duke of New Orleans. The Pitt diamond went on to become a part of the gem collection of the French crown and, even later still, was set in the hilt of one of Napoleon's ceremonial swords.

Denver's interest in Thomas Pitt stemmed initially from his interest in The English East India Company. It was that interest that prompted him to buy Pitt's journal at an auction of antiquities. He outbid several museums to buy the journal and its purchase ensured the journal was out of circulation thus preventing others from discovering the connection that he was about to.

The journal certainly made interesting reading for Denver and gave him an even greater insight into 17th Century India and, more importantly, into the character of Pitt himself. The entries in the journal confirmed that Pitt was a chancer and daring to the point of reckless but he was also shrewd and intelligent. He had boundless energy and he channelled it into extracurricular interests outside his role as the Governor of Fort St George in Madras. He was a natural entrepreneur and his journal entries showed the wide and varied nature of his interests. An entry in the journal made by Pitt described one of his frequent trips to the city of Galconda.

Most if not all of India's diamonds passed through Galconda at some stage. Many went on from Galconda and then onward to the international market. In his journal Pitt recalled how, in a side street café placed under the brooding presence of Galconda's ancient fort, Pitt had spent an evening with an India acquaintance of his, a jeweller who dealt at the high-quality end of the market. They had been discussing the unique quality of the large gems found in India, including his own, the Pitt Diamond, when the conversation turned to a discussion of the Tavernier Blue. Pitt noted in the journal how he had commented on Tavernier's failure to reveal where, and how, he had acquired the gem. To Pitt's surprise the jeweller told Pitt of a story that he had picked up from a local source, another jeweller. Pitt prided himself on having his finger firmly on the pulse of India but the story his friend related to him of how Tavernier had acquired his Tavernier Blue was completely new to him. Pitt rated the jeweller as a reliable informant, and not one for passing on unfounded gossip and this confidence was reflected in Pitt's journal entry on the subject. If a smart operator like Pitt believed the jeweller's tale, then why, thought Denver, should he not? Other historical references written in Pitt's time alluded to rumours about Tavernier and the bluestone. One told how Tavernier had arranged for the theft of the stone from a temple statute. The paid thief prised it from the forehead of a statute of Shiva the Destroyer where it had been functioning as an eye. Other variations existed along the same theme some even involving bribery and murder, but Pitt was shrewd enough not to take them too seriously. He realised that Tavernier himself was largely responsible for the rumours because of his reticence to give away any true information about the diamond's origin.

The Jeweller told Pitt that when Tavernier discovered the stone he'd been travelling with an English man, a rich nobleman called Stillwood-Hamilton. From the journal notes it was clear that Pitt already knew the Englishman and identified him in the journal as Rupert Stillwood-Hamilton.

Away from Pitt's Journal Denver researched into Rupert Stillwood-Hamiltons. They were a family who had once boasted an impressive family estate. 17th Century England had several such families, families whose wealth was dissipated by a wayward son. For example, the Verneys of Claydon had their Sir Francis Verney, who became a Muslim convert and a pirate. Francis really was a wayward son, he brawled and gambled away his family's wealth and then went to Tunis to join a North African pirate fleet but instead ended up as a galley slave himself. A friendly Sicilian warship eventually freed the hapless adventurer. When his short life ended at thirty-one years of age all he left behind was a turban, a couple of silk tunics, and a pair of Ottoman slippers.

Rupert Stillwood-Hamilton was surely cut from the same cloth as Sir Francis. Rupert aside, the Stillwood-Hamiltons appeared to lead respectable, if somewhat impoverished lives, probably due to Rupert's obsessive gambling, drinking, and ill-founded business ventures. In 1641 Rupert travelled to India intent on making enough money to cancel the family debt and restore the Shropshire Stillwood-Hamilton estate to its former glory.

Denver knew this particular fact from the collection of letters on the table in front of him. Denver also believed that Rupert's concern for his family and the family estate said more about the depth of Rupert's fondness towards his younger sister Emily. It was a fondness that, after he had read all of the correspondence between the two siblings contained in the letters, Denver felt leaned towards an incestuous relationship between brother and sister.

Denver returned his interest back to Pitt's journal and carefully turned the page taking care so as not to tear the fragile paper. Pitt appeared surprised at the alliance between Tavernier and Stillwood-Hamilton. Pitt himself described Stillwood-Hamilton as a scoundrel of the first water listing some of Stillwood-Hamilton's exploits which, as Pitt explained, went counter to Britain's interests in India. Pitt's condemnation of Rupert was, Denver thought, a bit rich coming from a notoriously self-motivated wheeler-dealer like Pitt. Tavernier obviously valued Stillwood-Hamilton both for his insight into the British administration in India, which had been growing in power and influence during Tavernier's time there, and also Stillwood-Hamilton's natural facility with languages. He was a gifted linguist who spoke, in addition to his native English, fluent French and passable Hindi and some Tamil. This must have helped the pair during their travels across India. Hindi was spoken in the North of India and Tamil was the main Dravidian language of Southern India in the South. What did Stillwood-Hamilton get out of his association with Tavernier? Pitt suggested that Tavernier's reputation and his access to India's various Royal courts and to the top jewel merchants made the allegiance worthwhile for Rupert Stillwood-Hamilton.

The two men were travelling in Galconda when a small-time local jeweller had approached their party. Camped at the time in a rural district some way from the town of Galconda Tavernier did not know the Jeweller but the Jeweller had heard of Tavernier and recognised him immediately. He had a strange stone and thought an expert like Tavernier would be interested in viewing it. This struck Pitt as odd since Galconda was full of expert jewellers, many of whom were far more expert and experienced than even Tavernier himself. Nevertheless, the two travellers followed the jeweller to a small hut a mile distant and once there the jeweller offered them tea and some small spiced cakes. He then produced a large dark glassy stone and passed it to Tavernier. The stone, the jeweller explained, came from a shallow gravel pit shortly after the monsoon rains and he had never seen anything like it before. Tavernier examined the stone and recognised almost immediately that it was a large blue diamond but he had skilfully hidden his surprise and excitement. However, the jeweller had far too many years' experience of reading customers faces to be fooled. Tavernier produced his field scales and the stone weighed in at 397 carats. It was clear the jeweller knew it was a diamond all along despite the dark colour of the stone and the fact it was so large. In fact the diamond, at a casual glance, could have passed as a piece of obsidian.

Pitt made it clear in his journal entry that he thought the jeweller had approached Tavernier specifically because he knew Tavernier had an interest in large gems and reputedly had the means to pay for them. Tavernier's feigned doubt about the nature or value of the stone was a familiar bargaining strategy but the jeweller was patient and Tavernier eventually acknowledged the stone was indeed a diamond but a diamond unlike any he had seen before.

It soon became clear to Tavernier why the jeweller had chosen him for a second opinion; the jeweller had chosen Tavernier specifically in the hope that he would make him an offer for the stone. The stone was well above ten carats in weight and any stone that exceeded ten carats in weight automatically became the property of the king of Galconda. Large gemstones decorated the King's elephant's and royal robes or were used by the king as a medium of exchange with other royals for goods or services. The jeweller clearly stood to gain more by selling the diamond secretly to this foreigner even for much less than its intrinsic value than he would by simply declaring his find to the authorities.

Denver paused from reading to rest his eyes and take another sip of brandy. He sat back and imagined himself inside that dusty hut with the three men and he felt something of their greed and excitement in his own quickening pulse. Denver knew the jeweller would have had another reason for thinking he could get a good price from Tavernier. Coloured gemstones were popular and valued in Europe whereas in India the clear transparent stones were far more highly prized and only high caste Brahmins were allowed to wear them. The stone the jeweller held before Tavernier was dark and only showed any sign of blue when put against a light. It was so dark that it was close to the colour of those stones allocated to the warrior caste of the Kshatriya.

The jeweller knew the stone's size would guarantee it would have value in its own right. Perhaps he could sell it to some wealthy Indian buyer prepared to risk the wrath of the King but he guessed correctly that it was worth far more to Tavernier. Tavernier must have been aware of the risk that the jeweller was taking himself and also inviting him to take. Balanced against that risk was ownership of a gem the like of which he had only ever seen in his dreams. The temptation led him to weigh the risk and decide to take it. Apart from the three men present in the hut the jeweller confirmed only one other man had seen the stone and that was the labourer in the gravel pit who had discovered the stone. The jeweller was confident the labourer had not been aware of the value of his find. The jeweller told Tavernier and Stillwood-Hamilton that he had made a convincing show of annoyance when the labourer had presented the stone to him and had even cast it disparagingly on to the floor. Nevertheless he had made sure the labourer had not subsequently stooped to reclaim it on his way out by a well-timed distraction.

Tavernier realised that he had to have the stone there and then. There was simply too much risk involved in leaving it any longer, in his experience the existence of a gem of that size would not stay secret for long. Tavernier took the Englishman to one side and, speaking in French to exclude the jeweller, outlined the situation to Stillwood-Hamilton. Unfortunately for Tavernier he had limited funds on his person because he'd recently made several large purchases of diamonds. Stillwood-Hamilton, on the other hand for once in his life, had had a successful run of card games with a party of Indian businessmen and nearly held enough gold to meet the jeweller's price. Denver wondered if the two men considered the possibility of simply taking the gem then threatening the jeweller into silence or even killing him. In the end, according to Pitt's journal entry, Stillwood-Hamilton negotiated with Tavernier. Stillwood-Hamilton would buy the stone from the jeweller and Tavernier would later repay Stillwood-Hamilton half of the total amount as soon as he had access to more funds. Each would then own an equal share of the gem. Denver frowned, as he had frowned the first time he'd read the journal, wondering how the storyteller had found this out, Pitt himself must have wondered at the source of the story too. Denver couldn't see either Tavernier or Stillwood-Hamilton leaking the story, even an over-long session on the pop wouldn't have got that out of them. Denver doubted the local jeweller would have risked an unpleasant and life-threatening punishment by telling someone else of his secret transaction with the two foreigners either. There were no additional journal entries mentioning Tavernier and Stillwood-Hamilton suggesting that Pitt's contact had anything more to add to this story and so, no more information on what the two travellers actually did with the large bluestone they had acquired.

The identity of the jeweller remains a mystery. Pitt was a resourceful man so he must have made it his business to find out more. He knew the rough bluestone Tavernier had presented to Louis X1V weighed around 112 carats. If it was from the same stone that he and Stillwood-Hamilton had purchased in that hut on that day so what had become of the other 285 carats?

Denver leaned back in his chair and scratched his scalp. He knew that if a stone was badly cleaved large amounts of it are lost but he doubted someone of Tavernier's experience would allow that to happen. Perhaps another large blue diamond lay in a private collection unknown to the rest of the world? Denver scrutinised Pitt's journal repeatedly but found no further mention of the two men or of the Tavernier blue or the original diamond from which it was cut.

Nahil and I were right about the fish, it was like chewing rubber, but as we sat on the sand around the fire and washed it down with beer and then some more beer, it didn't matter. Life was good after all. I was glad that Nahil had questioned me about Dan and what I'd learnt from him about the police case on the dead Belgian. Dan's belief that the police were likely to treat the Belgian's death as a self-inflicted accident was great news. The axe poised to fall on our heads had been removed and we could all breathe a sigh of relief, release the pause button, and get on with our lives. Dan told me the police had checked with the authorities in Belgium and found no one who knew the man who had attacked us. If there was no one to miss him maybe no one would follow him out here and stir up trouble for us. I for one didn't want to share Andy's belief there must be more nutters already on their way to take over where he had left off.

On the tour-guide tourist-companion front I had escorted a couple of female tourists over the past three weeks and even managed to charm a little spending money out of them. The first, was a blonde named Vicky, she came from somewhere in the UK, a place called Newcastle and, though I struggled to understand her strong accent she turned out to be a fun easy-going girl a couple of years younger than me. When she met Nahil the two of them got on like a house on fire though it was clear that Nahil could barely understand a word she was saying. Vicky liked drink, dance, and sex and usually in that order to. She soon worked out how things were to work between us when we were together and complied without any fuss. She covered the cost of drinks and meals and let me exchange her money, in return I played my part to the hilt and between us we had a barrel full of laughs. It's a pity the same couldn't be said about Helen, the French woman that followed her.

As girlfriends go Helen was another net of fish altogether, the complete opposite of party girl Vicky. I literally stumbled across Helen as she lay stretched out on a towel on the beach area of the Reef Sands hotel. Why she was on a towel and not one of the white sun loungers the hotel provided remains a mystery. At the time I had been wearing my shades against the fierce overhead sun and my attention had been out to sea as I walked along the sand. My foot caught her outstretched ankle causing me to lurch forward and her to shriek and sit up suddenly. After the usual round of apologising on both our parts I squatted down beside her and we chatted. I took off my shades, saw her eyes widened a little, and I knew I had another one on the hook. Her name was Helen and I offered to buy her a drink hoping it would be the last drink I would be paying for. In a bikini Helen scrubbed up well and her specs gave her an air of intelligence. She was tall for a girl but also thin and gangling. Her skin was the whitest that I had ever seen on any tourist. I could even see the blue veins beneath the skin on those parts of her breasts that weren't covered by her bikini top and, when I got to know her a little better, under the other parts as well. Nevertheless everything was in the right place and she seemed keen on me to the point of enthusiastic. Despite English being her second language she was much easier to understand than Vicky though Nahil never took to Helen at all. I soon came to realise that she did not have much experience in the dating game and what little she had had, had not been good and her view of men in general was understandably tempered by that. She was tall and confessed that my height was the key reason that she was attracted to me. I have heard something along these lines before from female tourists, and in fact only from tourists, and I have to confess that it is no more flattering to me to be told I have been chosen for my inches of leg bone as it must be for a woman to be told by a man that their attractiveness lies in the fact that they've got big tits. Compared to Vicky, who was upbeat, knew how to dress and have a good time, Helen's dress sense was casual and conservatively stylish. It was all well-made and looked too expensive and posh to have designer labels. Almost immediately she began to nag me as if we'd been married for years. For example, she'd complain if we went to a café or restaurant, "You shouldn't eat so much meat" and "You drink too much…" and so on, until it started to drive me nuts. Meat: in fact I hardly ate it at all. Perhaps she hadn't noticed that St Gilberts had neither the space nor the landscape for cows and sheep so meat was expensive and the only time I ever got to eat a steak was when someone like Helen bought me one. *Lucky for her, or me, that I didn't smoke as well.* Helen, I soon found, out was very new-age an eco-holistic therapy warrior. All good stuff in Paris but we were already living that stuff every day of our lives. She was two years older than me and obviously felt that I was in need of some heavy-handed life advice which she doled out liberally.

"You should be more positive Rodney, and you should definitely take a more pro-active approach to life." Once she advised me, "live each day as if it is your last day on earth."

And then got justifiably annoyed at my flippant reply. "What? Lie in bed all day slipping in and out of consciousness?" I'd joked.

She'd given me one of those 'I'm staring at a lost cause' looks and busied her hands with the string of local beads she had bought that day. Island made beads, the ones that only tourists ever buy and wear.

I'd once heard a tourist say something that interested me so much I asked him what it meant when he'd used the expression, 'Gallows humour'

The meaning of 'Gallows Humour' as he explained it to me pretty much summed up St Gilberts Island humour, in fact, I'd say we've taken the concept to an art form. It is our default setting and if looking on the negative side of things in an ironic and humorous way helps us joke our way through adversity then what's the harm in that? Apparently quite a lot according to Helen who warned me how negativity could drain away my energy and that of everyone around me. "Some people are radiators who warm you up and others are drains who bleed your resources away," she preached, but it was her preaching that was draining my energy away.

I knew Helen was an intelligent person but, to me at least, she often came across as smug, and condescending. Once she remarked, "I envy you islanders and your simple life." I knew she meant it as a compliment but it left me feeling—well—simple. Another of her pearls of wisdom went, "Anyway, Rodney, you…me, islanders…Europeans…we're all humans; we're all the same under the skin." I'm sure I'm being unfair but it came across like she was granting me, and the rest of St Gilberts, the honour of being like her, of being like a European!

"Under the skin?" I asked, just to wind her up. "What's the matter with over the skin?"

"Nothing," she had said defensively. "We're all still just the same."

"But I'm black and you're white," I said.

"I never really noticed it, Rodney, anyway skin colour doesn't make any difference to me."

"Are you colour blind or something?" I asked, but she just sniffed and gave me a sidelong glance.

"It seems to me, Rodney, that colour is more of an issue for you than it is for me. Besides, you're hardly 'black'; you have mixed blood that's all."

"OK, so I'm white then?"

"Er, no, I didn't say that but…"

She shrugged, shook her head and looked at me as if it was my fault I couldn't follow her thinking. I nearly replied that she was not exactly white herself but pinkish but then, damn it, she was white, as white as anyone could be short of being an albino! I took her to the Love Nut beach bar and to the restaurant under the Takamaka trees on Anse Allamanda. We had stuffed ourselves on the As Much As You Can Eat Sunday Special and she tried a little small talk with the woman who brought us some more beers and then sat back beaming.

"See Rodney, I can fit in anywhere in the world by just being myself." The truth was she wasn't fitting in anywhere and certainly not into St Gilberts. We don't go in for public shows of affection on St Gilberts. I don't mind a woman hanging around my neck and kissing me in private or on Lolas Beach and Memory Hill, but not out on the street and in the hotel bars. It makes you stand out in a close-knit community like ours. Whenever we were in town, I dreaded bumping into Aunt Mert, my old schoolmates and, most of all, Joelle.

Dan Meme once saw us together on Main Street as he stood in the doorway of the Three-In-One. He roared across the street at me causing everyone within earshot, to turn and look, first at him, and then, following the direction of his gaze at us, to see what he was shouting and grinning at. When we turned towards him, he grinned wider and shot his arms out straight in front of him, both thumbs pointing up from the fists. Others around didn't join in his hearty encouragement. I saw their mouths turn down in disapproval.

In short, the relationship did not work as it should, well, at least not as far as I was concerned, and I was both glad and even slightly out-of-pocket when I finally put her on her plane home. My time with Helen had triggered some nagging questions, Joelle style questions, what exactly was I doing with my life?

Her questions echoed in my head, was I really cut out for the tourist industry or, as she put it, being a "Gigolo?" I could empathise with people well enough, maybe too much, but I was too soft to use it against them. The problem was I couldn't see anything else that I could turn my hand to and there was no vacancy where there wasn't already a queue of more competent people waiting to fill it. I'd ruled myself out of hotel work by being caught humping the wife of a hotel guest while on duty. The tuna factory job hadn't worked out for me either.

Fishing and farming work tended to run in families and they weren't known for their generosity in sharing their expertise or jobs outside of family circles, believe me I've tried. I did have an uncle on St Gilberts, Jean Claude, who had a boat and did a bit of fishing but my life would be easier in the French Foreign Legion than working for him, dour sod that he was. I knew I could stretch my trust fund allowance further by turning over more of my garden to vegetables and fruit and by catching fish as opposed to buying it. Helen would have approved, but I didn't see it as a step forwards it was simply; keeping your head above the water stuff. Anyway these were things I was doing already to some extent but they were the sort of measures I expected to be resorting to in retirement—if I ever reached that age—not at twenty-six years old. There had to be something a guy like me could turn his hand to. I found myself thinking about that damned silver napkin ring again. Everything connected to it had been bad news, the nerve jangling descent into the secret chamber under the church, the bloody business on Kasper's Edge with that lunatic Belgian. Looking back however, I knew I had never felt more alive in my whole life than in those two moments of intense excitement and fear. The more I thought about it the more I wanted to experience those feelings again. That was it, I needed a bit of excitement and adventure, an adrenalin rush—something to scare me and shake me out of the directionless rut I was stuck in.

Denver's brandy glass was nearly empty. The journal of Thomas Pitt lay close to hand on the table. Denver leaned forward and pushed it to one side and drew a packet of letters closer. He smiled as he looked down at them remembering. He had arrived at back in England from an extended business trip to Seattle. A chauffeured car had driven him to his country home in Somerset his current partner, Sara, sat beside him. While he was in meetings she had spent his money on clothes and jewellery in the boutiques. Once home he showered and changed and then flopped on to the large white sofa alongside Sara and reached for the television remote. He flipped through the terrestrial channels and stopped when he recognised 'Home Treasures'. He liked the antiques programme as it appealed to his interest in history and valuable objects. The format of the show was simple, each week a group of antique experts converged on a town in the UK inviting the residents of the town to bring their old family heirlooms for the experts to examine. The experts gave an expert opinion on the family heirlooms, provided interesting historical background and finished by giving an estimate of what the object or objects could fetch should they ever make it into an auction room. In fact the appeal of the show had little to do with antiques.

The programme attracted millions of viewers some like Denver who had a genuine interest in antiques but many were watching because Home Treasures was about other people, and more importantly, other people's stuff. It was about the drama of one man's trash becoming another man's treasure and about people's greed, their surprise, credulity, nosiness, carelessness, and their past and it was all conducted in the most civilised and polite language.

The young woman beside Denver pulled a face and let out a moan, "You're not going to watch this are you? It's so boring my mum always watches this." Denver smiled as he recalled Sara's moan but remembered that at the time her comment had raised a sensitive issue. Denver had in fact been a couple of years older than Sara's mother.

"Well, I happen to like it too," he had snarled at her. "Look, go in the other room if you want another channel," he added in a slightly softer tone. It was at that moment when he heard the name "Stillwood-Hamilton". Denver scrabbled for the remote to increase the volume. Sara had not noticed his sudden interest in the television and started to say something about a new dress she had bought in Seattle. Denver had leaned forward to catch what the expert was saying, raising his hand to Sara for silence as he did so. Denver pulled a rueful face as he remembered how Sara had either not seen his gesture or had chosen to ignore it and had continued to speak across the expert on the television.

"Wait till you see what I—"

Denver remembered how he had interrupted her, "Hold on Sara please be quiet a moment."

But she had carried on, "Richard, I was just telling you—"

"Shut the fuck up, will you?" He'd snapped at her and now he winced as he remembered how she had slumped back against the back of the sofa, her lower lip pushed out in a silent sulk.

On the screen was a couple, both in their mid-fifties, they were sat across a table from a dark suited man with unruly hair who was wearing a pair of dark framed spectacles. Denver knew, having watched the show before, that the man wearing spectacles was one of the team of antique experts. He was rearranging a packet of age darkened envelopes, which he had lifted out of a battered looking silver casket. From what he could see of the background behind the seated figures they were in a large municipal hall. "So what can you tell about these?" enquired the expert and the camera focused on the smiling couple who were obviously enjoying their brief moment in the spotlight. Guessing they were husband and wife, Denver had watched as the husband gave a brief smile and opened his mouth to start speaking.

His wife began a split-second before him, "Well, these were sent to—"

Her husband simply talked over the top of her, "These letters were sent by one of my wife's ancestors from India…" His wife fell silent, seeming to shrink in on herself as she did so. The expert halted the husband's flow with a rhetorical question.

"That ancestor being Rupert Stillwood-Hamilton?" The husband simply nodded and continued with scarcely a pause. He had mentally rehearsed his little piece and he didn't want to lose his train of thought.

"The letters are all from abroad mainly India and they are from Rupert to his sister Elizabeth, all dated, and sent, in the seventeenth century." The expert was Julian Hatton; his area of expertise was scientific instruments, weapons and war memorabilia. He had joined the Home Treasures team as an expert aged thirty-five years, now ten years later he was an experienced and a seasoned television presenter. Previously, he had worked as an auctioneer at Sotheby's. He had obviously had sight of the letters before and had had time do a little preparation before the filming began.

"What we have here is an intriguing glimpse into seventeenth century life through the eyes of one of its more colourful characters. I guess you have read these letters so what can you tell me about your distant uncle?" The expert aimed the question directly towards the wife and the camera zoomed in on her face so the husband's face no longer appeared on the screen. The woman gave a nervous little giggle and looked at her hands as she spoke.

"Well, he was a bit of a lad I gather. He was the one who brought the family to ruin with his gambling and drinking and then ran off to India. He was obviously close to his younger sister Emily and the letters show that he hoped to make his fortune in India and then return home and put everything straight again."

The expert smiled encouragingly, her answer had given the broad outline without stealing his thunder. As far as he was concerned she had given the perfect answer.

"But that never happened did it? Rupert never made his fortune, he never returned home from India and the family estate in Shropshire was eventually sold to meet the debts Rupert had run up."

"Yes that's right." The woman nodded ruefully pulling a 'that's life' sort of face but then suddenly smiled and said, "Otherwise I could be the lady of the manor today instead of—"

Julian Hatton smoothly interrupted and finished the sentence, "Instead we are here with this fascinating collection of letters."

The expert had seen the husband's face darken at where his wife's last statement appeared to be heading and his instinct warned him that she was in danger of revealing some negative personal details that neither he nor the show's producers wanted. Having smoothly taken over the woman's sentence, he now attempted to turn it into something more positive.

The wife however, was not going to be cut off so easily. "But I think he had found his fortune, the last few letters clearly show that he was onto something, if only he had made it back to England then—who knows?" Her voice trailed off again.

Julian Hatton picked up the thread, "Yes maybe history would have judged Rupert Stillwood-Hamilton more kindly had he returned and saved the family estate. As it was he appears never to have left India. Or, if he did, then he died on the six month sea voyage back to England..." He let his words trail into silence as if expressing some regret or sympathy for the couple's loss before continuing in a lighter, more upbeat tone of voice.

"So what would this intriguing collection of letters be worth if they ever came to auction? Not, I'm sure, that you could ever bring yourself to part with such a family treasure." The couple both shook their heads in silent agreement.

"Well, there is a niche market for this sort of historical correspondence and I saw a similar collection fetch £600 about a month ago at Sotheby's but, who knows what this particular collection could bring, you've kept them in excellent condition and they do give a glimpse into an interesting human story involving one of the more colourful characters of the seventeenth century, a century that already had more than its fair share of characters..."

Denver could see that Hatton was flannelling and knew less about Stillwood-Hamilton than he did. Denver also knew he had to get hold of those letters. From what he had heard, they seemed to confirm Pitt's journal entries and could contain more clues as to what had happened to the blue diamond.

He'd watched the programme to its conclusion and learnt at the end, that the show had been filmed in Shrewsbury, the birthplace of Charles Darwin, and the county town of Shropshire. He checked the television listings and saw the programme would be repeated on a sister channel the following night. Denver had then checked his network of British 'freelance consultants' and singled out one of them as being perfect for what he had in mind. Denver had looked around and saw that Sara was in the kitchen presumably in a sulk. He picked up the phone and then put it down again. He scrabbled inside a cupboard until he found a telephone address book, it he opened on 'H' and, looked down the page and began to dial.

Denver had not been aware that when Julian Haverston put down the phone after their brief conversation Haverston's expression had been a troubled one. Julian Haverston was always glad of the income that usually followed a call from Richard Denver. Nevertheless he found speaking to the man unpleasant. Haverston checked the television listings and set his V-Box to record Home Treasures the following day. Though not a regular viewer of the programme he found himself enjoying the show as he watched it the next day. Tracing the couple who had brought along the box of letters that Denver was so eager to get his hands on was simplicity itself. He simply accessed a free web-site that gave information on births, marriages and deaths and checked for the surname Stillwood-Hamilton. He quickly narrowed the short list down by the searching on marriage date, age, and geographic location. Margaret Stillwood-Hamilton married Eric Stanley Newbold in a marriage registered in Shrewsbury. There were several entries under the surname Newbold in the on-line telephone directory for Shrewsbury but only one for E. S. Newbold and he copied down the address, 33, Mansfield Close, Shrewsbury, Shropshire, he copied down the telephone number as a backup.

Denver took a final sip to clear the brandy glass and reflected on the differences between Julian Haverston and Philippe Ronnier. Where Ronnier had led a secretive and solitary life, Haverston was sociable, outgoing and possessed of considerable charm. A boarding school education had given him an accent that spoke of privilege and wealth though in reality he had neither. His early private schooling had given him the right accent and though his parents had paid for the education they had done so simply to get the child off their hands leaving them free to continue their hedonistic lifestyle and love of recreational drugs. Unfortunately for them their money ran out and young Julian had to leave the private school while the invoice for his final months schooling fees remained unpaid. The young boy then experienced a traumatic culture shock when he was dropped instead into an inner-city comprehensive school. He had no friends but he did have an accent and manners that marked him out as a prime target for every bully in the school, both male and female. Julian lacked the physicality to ward off either. He left the comprehensive with a rudimentary academic education of sorts but an ability to survive second to none forged in the scores of playground confrontations he had endured and survived.

Margaret Newbold was more annoyed than surprised to see a man's silhouette behind the frosted glass door panel. It was the second caller she had had that day and as she opened the door she took a breath ready to launch into her "not today thank you very much" spiel. Something in the stranger's appearance stopped her and instead she stood gaping at the man who was clearly not selling anything. In fact she was soon to realise that he wanted her to sell something to him. She looked at the man afresh and reassessed her first assumption that she was looking at just another doorstepping nuisance. Here was someone who really was 'someone'. The man was tallish and ascetically thin. He had thinning blond hair swept back off a high intellectual forehead and he spoke in a beautifully modulated voice. Haverston's refined accent, manners and easy charm made sure that his tweed suit and well-worn waxed Barbour overcoat gave an impression of nonchalant old money. He's obviously one of those with little interest in the vagaries of modern fashions thought Margaret approvingly. She never considered the possibility that he was a man living close to his means with a lifestyle habits that frequently took him beyond them.

"I'm awfully sorry to disturb you, Mrs Er, Newbold?" Haverston checked her face for confirmation though he had instantly recognised her as the woman in the TV show the moment she had opened the door.

"I wonder if you could spare a moment of your time, I am calling with respect to your appearance on the programme *Home Treasures*..." He waited a second before continuing, "I have been asked to contact you regarding the package of letters you brought along to share with us on the show." Margaret had smiled at the mention of the show and now her eyebrows lifted in interest as she waited to hear what the man was going to say.

"I am representing a client, who wishes to remain anonymous, but who is interested in making you a financial offer for the letters." The woman, obviously taken by surprise, was stuck for something to say, and then, looking behind her she opened the door wider and invited the man into the house. The interior was tidy to the point of being Spartan, not hoarders, thought Haverston and wondered how the letters had survived the many clear-outs.

An hour and a half later Haverston left the house with the letters but without the silver casket they had been presented in on the TV show. It had been fortunate that Eric Newbold had been at home enabling him to get a decision to sell there and then, he had joined them when he came in from the garden, where he had been doing some weeding, Haverston gave them his pitch.

Denver had told Haverston that he was prepared to pay up to a thousand pounds for the letters but that he should negotiate the best price he could for them and keep the balance himself along with the fee that Denver was paying him. To pay a high price would be to invite unwanted interest in both the letters, and in him. With this instruction in mind Haverston began slowly, and listened patiently to the couple as they explained how the letters formed a part of their family history and were invaluable heirlooms. However, after some gentle haggling at which Eric Newbold displayed an affectation of sucking in and then puffing out the fleshy cheeks at each new offer, the 'invaluable' was eventually valued at £560. Haverston asked if they had any other family memorabilia connected to the letters but they shook their heads. He wound the negotiations up deliberately making sure he left the couple with the impression that they had bargained hard and skilfully, and had driven him to pay well above what he had intended. His client, he confided with them, was a historian and academic, who made a special study of the seventeenth century. He reassured them the letters would be well cared for, even cherished. His policy was to leave the Newbolds happy so they would have few regrets and nothing to complain to others about at a later date. As Haverston drove away from the Newbolds' house he smiled, perhaps he would put a little something on Whistlers Fortune in the 2.30 at Kempton, after all.

Julian Haverston had sent the packet of letters to him a little over two years ago. Now Denver sat and looked at the collection of letters on the table in front of him. He remembered how eagerly he had studied the contents of the parchment like letters, jotting notes as he deciphered Rupert's spidery handwriting. It had not taken long before he found himself drawn into the strange self-obsessed world of Rupert Stillwood-Hamilton. All the letters were from Rupert to his sister, presumably the sister's replies disappeared with Rupert. The tone of the brother's letters supported Denver's earlier guess the brother-sister relationship between the two had crossed over into something darker. Incest. However the constant theme throughout the brother's correspondence was Rupert's paranoia, his belief the world was against him. The lack of any of the sister's letters forced Denver to guess what had been said in reply to previous letters to make sense of the brother's inferences. However, after repeated readings of the letters they gave him two key pieces of information for his outlay of a thousand pounds plus the eight hundred pounds he had paid directly to Haverston. The first was that Rupert Stillwood-Hamilton was in possession of something of such value that he believed he could settle all the family debts and restore the family estate to its former glory and still have money to spare. The second, and most exciting piece of information, was a sentence in the final letter Rupert sent to his sister. Denver remembered how his hand shook as he read the letter for the second, third and fourth time.

"I am bound for England on the 25th May this year."

Rupert Stillwood-Hamilton had given the departure date though frustratingly not the name of the ship. The letter was dated 1669 and had been posted from Surat. From his studies of the British East India Company, Denver knew that the town of Surat was north of Bombay and under British Governorship at the time.

Denver had wondered at that, according to East India records Rupert Stillwood-Hamilton was wanted by the Honourable Company on several charges of "interloping and other nefarious deeds." The only way that Rupert could have travelled on East Indiaman ship would be in leg irons. There was, according to Denver's research into the East India Company records, no mention of that happening. Rupert must have booked his passage on a foreign vessel or a British interloper masquerading as a foreign vessel. After another visit to East India House to check for any record of Rupert Stillwood-Hamilton's transportation back to England, Denver turned his attention to the port of Surat and scoured all the records he could find relating to it. His search confirmed Surat had been the main headquarters of the English along the West Indian coast. However in 1668, a year before Rupert's departure date, the East India Company had relocated its head office to Bombay. Later, in 1703, Surat itself fell under Bombay's Governorship. Denver meticulously searched through the British East India archives but it was in the cloistral silence of the reading library that he finally had an amazing stroke of luck a true breakthrough. Lost in an obscure batch of notes was the journal of Gerald Aungier.

Denver pushed the packet of letters across the table to rest alongside Jean-Baptiste Tavernier's book, and the journal of Thomas Pitt. Only two sets of papers remained. Denver reached for one of them and drew three A4 pages to the table in front of him. The pages were photocopies he'd made in East India House from the journal of Gerald Aungier. At the time Denver had been tempted to cut the pages from the journal with the small pocket knife he always carried. It was his love and respect of history and historical artefacts, rather than any moral imperative that stayed his hand and sent him to the photo-copier instead. Just before Denver had come upon the journal, he had read with interest how in 1669 the Governorship of Surat changed. Sir George Oxenden, who had been in post since 1662, returned to England and his replacement was Gerald Aungier. Aungier exemplified the 'new broom' of the old adage, the one that 'always sweeps cleanest'. Whereas his predecessor, Sir George Oxenden, had watched helplessly as his power inexorably trickled away towards the new headquarters in Bombay. Aungier, who had never tasted those heady days of power when Surat was the main Governorship along the coast, saw his posting to Surat as an exciting and prestigious promotion. He applied himself energetically to his new empire. From the first page of the Journal Denver saw a high level of detail in Aungier's reports and was impressed. In contrast to that of his predecessor Sir George Oxenden, Aungier's energy was fuelled rather than diminished, by India's dusty heat. Aungier took his role seriously and used what power he had to pursue interlopers with conscientious zeal. It was in relation to one of his entries on this that Denver had had another of those spine-tingling moments.

The journal entry in question described how a midsized Frigate flying foreign colours had been seen leaving from a small dock south of Surat's main port. Denver had slowed his reading speed to concentrate on each word so as not to miss a single detail. Aungier reported that a well-dressed gentleman had been seen boarding the ship in question moments before it cast off. The well-dressed gentleman in question was identified by a Company employee as none other than Rupert Stillwood-Hamilton. Aungier knew Stillwood-Hamilton had several charges of felony levelled at him and so sent word for all Company ships to be on the lookout for an interloper outward bound from Surat 25 May 1669. The ship's name was 'Valvaston' and any able Company vessel coming across it was instructed to intercept it, check and impound its cargo, and then to arrest and return Stillwood-Hamilton to England for trial. Denver read and re-read the page before sliding it to join the others to one side of the table. Only one sheet of paper remained, the one that Philippe Ronnier had sent to him in a plain envelope marked 'Personal: Addressee only' posting it from Zaventem International Airport Brussels at the start of his one way journey to St Gilberts. The folds in the paper caused the sheet to concertina on the table but even without leaning forward Denver could read Ronnier's heavy hand written note below the computer-speak information provided by the tracker software.

Enquiry on Valvaston 16.58. February 1st 2008
Internet Protocol number—303.327.275.56.
Source—St Gilberts (GZ) Indian Ocean

Denver knew that a May departure would have set the Valvaston into the south-east trade winds blowing across the Indian Ocean west to east. If the Easterlies were constant and the Atlantic trades favourable then the Valvaston's voyage to England would have taken roughly six months. He also knew that it is wrong to assume that the trade winds blow consistent and true to the extent that they carry sailing ships back and forth between England and India as if they are on rails. The trade winds can, and do, vary greatly from their general direction. The change of direction may be only temporary but when added to the many tropical storms that occur in the Indian Ocean, accurately plotting the course of a ship that sailed over three hundred years ago is impossible. Besides, Denver wondered if the Valvaston had intended to off load its cargo of spices, tea and fabrics on mainland England. Surely it would have made for one of the Channel Islands to avoid the authorities. Denver sat back in his chair and closed his eyes as his mind trying to consolidate what he knew so far. The documents hinted that a large blue diamond, the other half of the Hope diamond, existed and had been acquired by Rupert Stillwood-Hamilton. He had boarded a ship called the Valvaston bound for England from the port of Surat on the 25 May 1669. No further record of the ship was found despite Denver's extensive searches. Recently a person, or persons unknown, based on St Gilberts Island in the Indian Ocean had entered a web-site and typed in an enquiry specifically naming the Valvaston. One of his operatives had visited the island to investigate the enquiry and now that person was dead. The trail of evidence was sparse, insubstantial, and mostly based on heresy, scattered journal notes, and old letters. Denver smiled, if treasure trails were obvious then no treasure would be hidden or lie undiscovered. He liked a challenge, the greater the odds the greater the victory but…? The Indian Ocean covered twenty per cent of the earth's surface, if—and it was a big if—he located a wreck it would all hinge on its location and condition of the wreck. If it was anywhere near the surface it would have been ingested by coral and close to impossible to find. On the other hand, if the ship had run aground and smashed pieces on a reef its contents scattered across the ocean floor what chance would there be of finding a solitary dark blue stone? Under water it would look like a black pebble rather than a diamond, if it wasn't already buried under a mile of sand. Logic told him it was a fool's errand and that he should quit, but-but, Denver was not a quitter and this quest was important to him in other ways, it gave him something to dream about, it gave him hope. Also, what was going on in St Gilberts? Denver promised himself if St Gilberts turned out to be a dead-end he would throw in the towel. He walked to a desk drawer and took out a file. He checked down the list of names noting one with a line through it; Philippe Ronnier, glancing further down the list he checked the other names and the geographic location given alongside each one. Denver pencilled an asterisk next to seven of the names, they were the 'possibles', and then he picked up the phone and began to dial.

Keith and Jeanette Ryder were holding hands and laughing as they left the Hotel Le Sterne Protea. They veered left and up Boulevard Hubert-Delisle walking the short distance to their yacht. They were in St-Pierre, Reunion Island's third largest commune after its capital St Denis and St Paul. However, at little more than fifty-five thousand inhabitants it was hardly New York. The restaurant had pampered them and the roomy lobby of the three star hotel leading to the restaurant had made a welcome change from the confines of their yacht, luxurious though it was. They had chosen from the French menu and washed it down, not with wine, but with bottle after bottle of Biere Bourbon, the locally brewed beer. Reunion's sultry weather had given them both a raging thirst. Their yacht, a Hallberg Rassey sixty-two footer drew long admiring glances from other yacht owners in the small harbour and from knowledgeable locals on the quayside. Once onboard they threw off their clothes and lay naked side by side on the bed in the large aft cabin. They felt bloated and drowsy and their bodies glistened with sweat. Both had finally drifted off into sleep when the ring tone of the satellite phone woke them up. Keith reached out for his cell phone at the side of the bed and then dropped it down again when he realised it was not the right phone. Jeanette was already out of the bed and he watched the muscles move under the skin of her naked buttocks as she bent to pick up the phone. He turned his head to lift his ear clear of the pillow to hear the conversation. He saw his wife straighten her shoulders back and compose her face into the friendly yet professional look, the one she used with those clients she considered worth the effort.

"Well, hello Mr Denver, long time no hears, and what can we do for you this time?"

The Ryders were both born and raised in Johannesburg. In their twenties they had worked as paralegals, but for different companies only properly meeting when the separate companies they worked for were involved on the same case. Much of their work involved travel outside the city and living out of a suitcase in a series of different hotels. One night, by chance, they had both booked into the same hotel and each recognised the other from across the court room earlier in the day. Their paths had already crossed many times during their work in and around the courts. Now, delighted to see a familiar face, even if they only knew each other by sight, they welcomed the opportunity to avoid another lonely night in a strange hotel. They introduced themselves and agreed to share dinner together in the hotel restaurant. They soon found that they shared more in common than just their line of employment. Intelligent and independent minded they shared with each other how they felt capable of taking on greater challenges than their current work provided. Over the meal they also learnt they shared a love of sailing, both being experienced sailors who took every opportunity to go out on the water. They began by regaling each other with amusing sailing mishaps but then went on to share their personal feelings about sailing and why it meant so much to them. Later that same night, they also discovered another thing they shared. As they writhed together in bed, the sexual chemistry between them was intense and intoxicating. Keith Ryder was forty-five years old, medium height with black wiry hair going grey at the temples. Neither ugly nor handsome he had the sort of face that you would struggle to pick out of a line-up. Jeanette Sanders was forty-one years old with mousey hair she'd coloured to a honey blond. Usually she wore contact lens but replaced them with spectacles for a few days each month when her eyes became too sore for the lens. Her figure was slim and athletic and would have made a woman ten years younger proud and, most men could have picked her out of a line-up.

Six months after that first dinner together they were married. Both left their current employment as paralegals to set up in partnership. They opened their own private investigation company. In South Africa, private investigators are in high demand because of poor police work and a high crime rate so Ryder Investigators Limited did well financially. They were discreet, shrewd, astute, and had enough business savvy to survive the difficult start-up years as they established the business. Their legal backgrounds, contact expertise, and sheer drive ensured their business's continued growth. Three years in they decided to change their business strategy. They decided to become more discerning about the work they were prepared to accept and began to target high-income high status clients only. Their accountant and other business colleagues advised against the change but they were proved wrong when the Ryders success story rose to a higher level. Soon they were raising their fees considerably in line with the fact that they were dealing exclusively at the top end of the market. As their business partnership flourished their sex life also became more adventurous. They entered the Joburg swinger's scene where Jeanette could indulge her voracious sexual appetite and she began to develop a previously unexplored attraction for women as well as men. Comfortable in the knowledge that husband Keith gained as much satisfaction from his passive role of voyeuristically watching her in action as he did from taking part in the three and foursomes they often enjoyed with other swingers. At Jeanette's insistence they progressed, if you could call it that, into the world of sadomasochism. They met others in the BDSM scene and engaged in role-plays involving chains, handcuffs and whips. Keith noted how Jeanette seemed as much at home in bondage rooms, rooms made to look like medieval dungeon torture chambers in gothic B-movies, as she was in the palatial surroundings of her client's luxury offices and homes.

The death of Jeanette's eighty-five year old mother left them with a well-placed city centre property to sell. It added a considerable sum of money to their already swollen coffers. Life was good for the Ryders but they both believed that it could even be better. After many long discussions often well into the night they began a series of consultations with their accountant, lawyer, and their bank manager, and those clients whose business they intended to retain. Once the decision was made they closed their premises in the city, put their city centre house up for let and bought Wave Ryder, the yacht of their dreams, a Swedish made Hallberg-Rassey 62. Fortunately for them they found the yacht available for sale in South Africa but then had to wait three months for it to be delivered. The yacht was worth every long minute of that wait. A large chunk of their now dwindling capital went on fitting the extra accessories and modifications to the boat to meet their own requirements for its use as both an office and a home. The yacht's specification was already comprehensive and luxurious but they needed additional communication equipment so clients would be able to contact them easily, and vice versa, wherever their location. Socially, their new peripatetic lifestyle suited them both. Their love of sailing grew deeper as they gained a thorough and intimate knowledge of the yacht and, despite the fact they were now spending twenty-four hours together, their relationship remained surprisingly free from strain. They both had the constant distraction of sailing to occupy them and they soon worked together as a team communicating with almost telepathic ease. Their libidos if anything became more rapacious amid the enclosed confines of the yacht and the isolation of the ocean. They continued to spice up their sex life with mild S&M role-plays and, though they initially thought that they would miss the swinger's scene of Johannesburg, they soon replaced it with something that provided even greater sexual piquancy.

When they visited the less developed islands of the Indian Ocean they would invite local prostitutes back to their yacht and then use them to satisfy their increasing range of sexual predilections. Over time these sessions began to take on a darker tone becoming less role-play and more real and pain laced with genuine fear and terror, at least for their guests. The young women who boarded the yacht, giggling and a little drunk, usually left the following morning quiet and sullen. As they walked painfully away from the yacht maybe they reflected on the nature of wealth and power and how those without it were prey to those who had. The roll of notes they carried in their pocket was payment, not only for their services, but also for their silence. The amount was always more than generous by local standards yet it didn't prevent them from feeling cheap, used, and abused. The two white people on the yacht living in the most beautiful floating house imaginable were at first polite and friendly and had made them feel special. Then suddenly, it was if they turned into animals—especially the blond woman. Even the most callous of local punters would have treated them better. At least the local punters had the excuse they led tough, sometimes brutal lives themselves, but those two? What excuse did they have for behaving like that—apart from the fact that they could and that was no excuse at all?

It was in this aspect of their new life that cracks began to appear in the couple's otherwise idyllic lifestyle. Keith had always been a willing participant in his wife's sadomasochistic fantasies, even if his participation veered towards the passive and voyeuristic rather than the active. She had moved on from the S&M fantasies she used to enjoy so much. Now she was at the stage where harmless role-plays and acting no longer gave her the sexual frisson she craved. Keith found he now had to pay any girl his wife brought on to the yacht a considerable amount of money to compensate them for the marks his wife left across their backs and buttocks. It was just a question of time before one of the girls brought back the police, or a pimp, to the yacht to exact a higher price than they could afford. Not only that, he found himself repelled by this new and unattractive side of his wife. Her indifference to the fear so obvious in the faces of the girls she had brought on board and their subsequent discomfiture and pain, it all gave him a queasy uncomfortable feeling. It was illegal, cruel and wrong—

a viewpoint his wife would probably have agreed with—but then, she would probably have explained, "But that's why I like doing it dear."

On a professional level the Ryders developed another specialisation that fitted perfectly with their new lifestyle. It involved tracing stolen yachts and making a visual identification on location. Most quality yachts are fitted with tracking devices so if stolen the yacht's movements can be tracked around the globe. The authorities once alerted move into seize the boat and all those on board. This arrangement suits most boat owners but not all. There are those who, for their own reasons, have no wish for the police to gain access to, and inspect their boat. The Ryders asked few questions and promised the utmost discretion. Their role was invariably to trace the stolen vessel and report to the owners when they found it. As part of this service they also sent photographic evidence showing the current condition of the boat and a detailed report of its movements along with descriptions and photographs of those on board and anyone visiting the yacht whether at sea or at mooring would also go in the report. Once they'd beamed the information back to the owner they would await further instructions. Occasionally the instruction was to continue surveillance until instructed to stop. However, the more usual instruction was to cease surveillance altogether, leave the location and report their new location within a given period, usually a matter of hours. They guessed this last was to confirm they had followed instructions. This new line of work was lucrative and went some way towards providing the funds for them to continue what they enjoyed doing anyway—sailing their yacht around exotic locations. However the tracking work had its drawbacks. It was unfulfilling to not be able to take an assignment through to resolution. The work left them with no feeling of having completed a job well done. In addition, there was the uneasiness they felt at their involvement in something possibly unpleasant and probably illegal. Although the Ryders carried firearms onboard they knew they would be no match for most pirates, who often worked from small open boats in groups of eight and armed with Kalashnikov rifles and rocket propelled grenades. The Ryders therefore had to turn down assignments where both the yacht and its owners had been seized and ransoms demanded. That was a job for commandos and Special Forces and they were welcome to it. Two of the yachts they had been asked to track headed towards the Gulf of Aden and later put in at the lawless port of Eyl on the Somalia Coast. There was no way that the Ryders were going to sail within 1000 miles of the Somali coast, or the

Yemeni coast for that matter, they immediately reported back and refused to continue with the surveillance.

There were other new avenues of work the Ryders found they were now starting to attract which stemmed from the positive referrals from previous satisfied clients. Richard Denver had heard about the Ryders at an informal discussion over drinks he was having with friends in a private yacht club in Sydney. He had subsequently contacted, and employed them himself to check conditions around some alleged wreck sites in the Indian Ocean. The Ryders enjoyed this type of work for it drew on their ability to sail in challenging waters. It also required them to spend time ashore on remote islands checking local knowledge regarding the coastline while trying to unearth any other historical information that could confirm the likely location and condition of a wreck. Denver, like all their clients, demanded the utmost discretion and the Ryders made sure that he got it. When Jeanette had put down the satellite phone a beaming smile had lit up her face.

"We're off to St Gilberts," she announced. Neither of them knew exactly where it was. Later, standing at the chart table, Keith plotted a course north that would take them along the east coast of Madagascar and then out to sea beyond its northernmost point. They had enjoyed Reunion and would no doubt get the opportunity to call there again, perhaps when this latest assignment was complete.

Joelle picked a cake from under the glass counter and placed it in the middle of a clean plate which she then carried to a table near the window giving her a clear view overlooking the street. She was in the Kokonet Café—her café. Julie her assistant was out on lunch, no doubt meeting her boyfriend near the market as usual. Business was slow and only three of the computers were currently in use by customers. She had time to think and that was not always a welcome luxury these days.

Joelle was not a person who liked to spend much time in introspective thought preferring activity instead and making progress by doing things. New ideas for her business often came to her when she was in the shower, washing her clothes or walking through the market. The bit she enjoyed was turning the ideas into reality. She enjoyed planning and then implementing the plans. Sitting and thinking about the so-called big questions in life was something she avoided if at all possible by making sure she was always too busy to have time to do it.

But sometimes, no matter how much you push things to the back of your mind, they have a habit of creeping back uninvited to ambush you when you least expect it and are least prepared to deal with it. Questions like; where am I going in life, what do I really want for myself and why am I so unhappy?

Joelle recalled all too vividly the childhood she had endured, rather than enjoyed; the conflicting feelings she felt towards the uncle and aunt who had been her surrogate parents. Conflicting because the passage of time had softened her view of her of them allowing her to appreciate the sacrifice they made in taking her into their family after the death of her own parents. She knew the difficulties they must have faced to take on the responsibility of yet another child when they were already on, or below, the poverty line. For that she owed them a debt that she could never repay and yet… How and why had she always known right from the start that she was tolerated rather than loved?

Her uncle and aunt argued with each other regularly and resentful words aimed at her had come through the thin sheets they'd hung from the ceiling around the bed to give them some privacy. Even now she recalled how the words had hissed out through the thin cotton walls like a foul gas during their many rows. Especially on those evenings when her uncle had returned home late after frittering away what little money he made on toddy. Throughout her childhood they had remained 'uncle and aunt' never encouraging or letting her regard them as mother and father. The couple's resentment of Joelle trickled through to their own children so they to also came to resent Joelle's presence as well, and to blame her for the many problems the family faced. She grew up in no doubt of her lack of status in the family; she was made to feel different and apart from them. The children at school treated her no better. They ganged up against her and shouted names in her face, "Miss Pissy" and "Pissy Pants." Even now she could see the circle of girls around her holding their noses and jeering. Worst of all was the leaden feeling of isolation she still experienced, like a stone in her chest, of being an outsider looking in through an unbreakable glass window at the closeness of the family that was St Gilberts. It was a family she was beginning to believe she would never join or feel a part of.

Without the distractions of playground and other group loyalties she had been able to focus on her studies and soon realised that getting an education and some skills could provide her with the means to make money and gain independence. Life with her uncle and aunt had taught her a lack of money was the root of most problems. Even from a young age she knew it was up to her, and her alone, to make a way out of her current life and into a shiny new one. This goal became her driving force and soon took her in a different direction from her playground tormentors. Slowly, and with reservation at first, people began to respect her for her hard work and commitment. She worked hard and progressed. When she took over the Café, her standing in the community grew. Other business owners respected her as a person of energy, drive and substance, on an island where those qualities marked her out as exceptional. She had money, not a lot perhaps, but still more than she had ever thought she could have back in those days of wearing rags. More importantly she knew the formula to create wealth, she had cultivated an almost an instinctive understanding of it, and she intended to use it.

She collected a wardrobe of smart new clothes, many from abroad that she'd ordered on the internet. She was fastidious, bordering on obsessive, about her personal hygiene sometimes showering several times a day and washed her hands frequently between times. She used the most expensive perfume she could afford, again from abroad, and, as she walked through the market often the other women would stop, behind her back and inhale the air as she passed theatrically wafting the air up to their noses and sighing as if in rapture. In the space of a few short years she had, through her own talents and effort, transformed her life. Yet, despite having good reason to be proud of her achievements, questions as hard to face as any ring of jeering schoolchildren on a dirt playground crowded her when she lay in her bed at night waiting for sleep. Those same questions crowded her now as she gazed through the window of her café at the heat haze shimmering just above road outside. The town traffic had thinned, not that it was ever heavy, and what few cars remained seemed to have slowed in the heat of the midday sun. One question in particular unsettled her now because it tainted her enjoyment of all the success she had built in her life so far. Why didn't success also bring happiness? She had her own business, posh clothes, and money to spare, but the feeling was, *so what*, is this all that success amounts to? She knew she had won respect for her success in business and for how she had overcome her upbringing, but she still felt like that little girl on the outside looking in.

The street outside was also emptying as people sought the refuge of cool restaurants and bars. Lunchtime was when everyone else had people, friends and lovers to meet and things to do that were not work related but everything to do with love, life and living. Sitting looking out at through the window Joelle realised a part of her life had remained unchanged and that she would gladly have traded some of that business success and respect she enjoyed for some love and affection.

She pondered, not for the first time of late, if her mood had anything to do with her so-called 'biological clock.' It was an expression she had heard on the television a few times but recently she had heard a woman use it in conversation in the café to. Joelle was twenty-five going on twenty-six and most other women her age on St Gilberts were already married with kids, though the usual order was kids then marriage. Some had even started their families when they were only fifteen or sixteen years old, yet another fact that caused Joelle to feel as if she was outside normal island life. But kids need a father and she didn't see anyone on St Gilberts that she wanted to start a family with and none of the visitors to the island she had seen so far interested her either. Once she had thought that Rodney Leon could, and would, be the one. As children they had been close, both orphans, both on the outside looking in even though their circumstances were quite different. Rodney's mixed parentage was written large in his face in those unusual blue eyes of his and hair texture being slightly straighter and softer than everyone else's. His height and fluency in English trust fund and house also set him apart and thus marked him as a target. Rodney, like her, had never really fit in and she suspected that beneath the surface civility of those around, that was still true today. His parent's wealth and celebrity status marked him out for special attention on the playground and though Rodney was no fighter, he was outgoing with enough charm and wit to win over the mob. She, on the other hand, had been poor, unwashed and unwanted but when she and Rodney were together none of that had mattered. Their friendship stood out as the only bright oasis of happiness in her young life.

A year or so ago she had dreamed about them getting back together and taking their childhood friendship into something more. The trouble was, Rodney seemed stuck, instead of growing and developing into a man, he was going backwards. He had lost his way and the gigolo stuff he was doing these days turned her stomach and made her wonder if he was worth thinking and worrying about any more. She had seen him with three different blonde women over the past few months and wondered if he had would finally settle down with a blond white woman like his father and his father's father before that. The thought saddened and depressed her. Her mind had wandered through her life options and pulled up short. Someone on the street outside wearing dark clothes walked past the window and for a fleeting second turned the glass into a mirror, Joelle caught a reflection of her own face in the window-pane she looked into her own eyes. Something had faded in them. It was as if any hope in the future had died in her eyes.

Julie returned from her lunchbreak hot and sweaty. She had run from the other side of the market to get back to the café in time. She had been with her boyfriend and Joelle wondered if running was only part of the reason her assistant was so hot but made no comment. Anyway, Joelle was not openly strict on timekeeping preferring instead to lead by example thus giving Julie the opportunity to follow without being told. Julie had soon picked up on the unspoken vibe that her boss valued those who were punctual. She respected Joelle and followed suite despite the effort it cost her. Punctuality was a rare quality on St Gilberts in fact it was generally regarded with suspicion and seen as more the sign of a character defect than anything else.

Joelle stood up and told Julie to take charge of the café. She set off up the street towards the stationers who supplied the Kokonet Café with paper and cartridges for its printers. She set off at a brisk pace but soon slowed to a gentle island stroll as the heat from the sun above, and bouncing up from the pavement, hit her.

Julie was crouched down behind the counter rearranging the biscuits and cake selection in the refrigerated display cabinet when she heard the door ooze open. She lifted her head and looked through the glass to see who it was. She knew all the local customers by name but saw immediately that the newcomers were tourists and obviously a couple by the way they were together. She stood up to greet them and both the man and women immediately burst into laughter and continued laughing until they doubled up holding aching stomachs. Nonplussed Julie stood awkwardly waiting for them to calm down. Her experience in the café had taught her that even older tourists could behave like children but now she felt uncomfortable because she wasn't sure if they were laughing at her. Gasping to catch their breath one of the tourists, a blond woman in her late thirties or early forties eventually straightened up and, with an effort, tried to compose herself.

"I'm sorry we must look very rude just walking in and then starting to behave like a couple of school kids. We are not laughing at you it's just that we have been onboard a boat for the last few days and we always get a bit giddy when we finally get back on land."

“Especially after a few gin and tonics as well…” the man added. Julie sensed he was quieter than the woman and a little older. His looks were average whereas the woman was slim and attractive.

The woman was speaking again, “When we came in, you just seemed to rise up out of the floor like a genie…” she broke off and the two of them began to laugh and double up again. This time, Julie laughed with them.

Keith and Jeanette Ryder were in cubicle five in the Kokonet Cafe staring at the computer screen. Denver had told them how his previous operative had traced the initial internet enquiry to this café. When Denver's security team had examined Ronnier's computer the tracker software had also provided the computer internet protocol number as well –

IP 303.327.275.56.

The data summary from the search also gave the name of the internet service provider which linked the computer to the internet the provider was AirTalk. Finally Ronnier's computer also supplied a date and for the first enquiry as,

February 1st 2016. 16.58

When Julie booked the Ryders internet session in the log book, checking with them for the correct spelling of Jeanette, the significance of the log book to their assignment did not go unnoticed by the couple. They saw the current log was new and only went back two weeks they would need the previous log book to trace who was on the computers at two minutes to five on February the first. But first they would check the IP numbers of the computers in each of the cubicles so when they gained access to the log they would know which cubicle booking to check for a name. As Julie completed the booking she discovered the couple were married and their family name was Smith. From the way they were together she guessed the woman wore the trousers in the marriage. Finding the IP address of the computers was simplicity itself, they merely logged to an internet website that checked the source of whoever placed an enquiry and provided the information instantaneously and without charge. The website invited then to click on a link which immediately showed on screen the IP address of the computer from which the request had been sent. The number now showing on the screen did not match the one they were looking for. The Ryders looked at each other and then at the other eight computer cubicles in the café. Jeanette Ryder rose and walked up to the counter Julie left the food counter to see what she wanted.

"Listen Julie can I book my own computer, that nosey lump there keeps reading my personal emails?" Jeanette Ryder pointed towards her husband who replied by putting his tongue out at her and then smiling.

"Try cubicle six it looks to be free and he won't be able to see your screen from where he's sat," said Julie conspiratorially nodding towards the husband who now pulled a mock sulky face. Minutes later Julie was amused to see the woman call her husband over to her cubicle then the couple started chuckling like teenagers. Julie liked this couple they were happy and they made her feel happy just being around them. They were living proof you didn't have to go all dull and boring when you got older they were proof that couples could still have fun together even after years of each other's company, well, she guessed, they'd been together some time because they seemed so close.

Julie hoped that when she eventually married her boyfriend—if he ever got around to popping the question—a big if—that they would be like this couple. They were the sort of people she envied in life, the ones who just need to be themselves for it all to come good. Jeanette Ryder returned to the desk interrupting her thoughts. "Excuse me but we think a friend of ours may have visited this café a few months back, probably in February I think?" Julie asked for a description of the friend.

"His name was Tom Wilson, average height, average build, dark-brown hair. Not much to go on, I'm afraid," Jeanette apologised. Julie frowned in concentration.

"I don't remember anyone of that name or description but then he may have been in when I was out on lunch or off for the day."

"Who takes over then?" Asked Jeanette.

"Joelle, she's the manager," answered Julie.

"Hmm, this logbook doesn't go back far enough, have you got the one before this one," asked Jeanette and Julie hesitated for only a moment before going to the office. It was a good five minutes before she emerged again and she was not carrying a logbook, instead she was shaking her head.

"No sign of it, maybe Joelle took it home or something."

Jeanette Ryder hid her disappointment behind a smile. "Well, it was a good try perhaps we'll ask er, Joelle when we see her." Jeanette smiled again and returned to her cubicle. Ten minutes later, the couple got up from their cubicles stopped to chat with Julie for a few minutes and left the café. As they headed back towards the marina and their yacht, they felt their spirits buoyed. Matching the IP number to cubicle six so quickly had been a spot of genuine luck; they now had the excitement of the hunt coursing through their bodies. They diverted up a side street towards the market to collect some fresh fruit and vegetables. Twenty minutes later and staggering under the weight of several bulging brown paper bags they returned to their yacht.

"Why don't we get the boat refuelled, top up with water and then plan how we are going to get a sight of that logbook," suggested Keith. His wife nodded in agreement but warned, "I'm not going anywhere without a shower and a long cool drink first."

Three hours later they were back in the Kokonet Café sitting side-by-side in cubicle one, their heads ducked in towards the screen. When they entered the café they had chatted with Julie before booking another thirty minutes on a computer. During the conversation they learned that Joelle, the manager, had returned to the café just moments after they had left earlier but had slipped out again not saying how long she was likely to be gone. They settled down to surf through the South African and world news sites and quickly became engrossed in catching up on what had been happening around the world while they had been sailing the Indian Ocean. A sudden rush of outside noise into the café alerted them the door to the street had opened. Jeanette Ryder leaned back a little turning to see who had entered the café. The side panel of the cubicle obscured the door itself but seconds later a young woman came into view and stood at the counter talking to Julie. Jeanette stare became steady and predatory she whispered under her breath, "I must have her." Her husband Keith had not heard what she said but he looked at his wife and recognised the alert set of her head. He followed her line of sight to the counter and saw a young woman stood at the counter speaking to Julie. This island girl was more than just pretty; she was breathtakingly beautiful with large long brown eyes. She wore a short yellow miniskirt and tight black top that showed off her figure to perfection. Her brown skin glistened from her walk in the heat of the late afternoon sun. Long wavy hair with natural highlights fell in a cascade down her back, some loose strands of it sticking to the bare skin of her shoulders and backs of her arms where the skin was damp. Jeanette turned to her husband and he recognised the hungry gleam in his wife's eyes.

"I—we must have her," she said again in a low urgent voice, he met her eyes, and nodded.

The girl in the yellow mini skirt suddenly turned, looked in their direction, and started walking straight towards them. They had to resist their instinct to duck back and make out as if they had not been ogling her for the past minute.

"Hi there, my name is Joelle and Julie tells me that you want to check the previous log book to see if your friend visited here?" The Ryders nodded, momentarily struck dumb by the young woman's unexpected approach and her striking looks. Jeanette noted the young woman's voice and manner was pleasant but without a trace of deference towards them, her poise and quiet authority only added to her appeal.

My god, she is absolutely fucking stunning, thought Jeanette, Keith closed his gaping mouth but continued to gaze, almost in wonder, at the young woman. "If it's any trouble then please don't..."

"No trouble," interrupted Joelle and disappeared into the office only to appear a moment later with the logbook in her hand.

"Where was that?" asked Julie from the desk.

"In the bottom desk drawer—the locked one," Joelle replied and flashed a smile of dazzling white teeth.

"I never looked there," said Julie apologetically.

"When do you think your friend might have visited St Gilberts?" Joelle asked and the Ryders looked at each other for a moment before the man replied.

"Late January or early February we think." She placed the logbook on the desktop in front of them pushing the computer keyboard back towards the screen and they leaned in to read the entries on the page.

Joelle opened the book to where the date at the top of the page read tenth of January and placed it where the couple could both see it. Slowly she turned the pages whenever the Ryders signalled for the next page to be turned. When the first of February came up their eyes moved through the time entries up 1600 hours to see who logged in then and then to the column showing the log out time. At 16.58 there were only two people still on the computers. The person logged in cubicle six was Rodney Leon. His session had started at five minutes past four and finished at five pm. The other person was Noshir Wadia, he or she was on the computer in cubicle three.

"Have you seen your friend's name?" asked Joelle who had noticed their increased concentration.

"No just struggling to read some of the writing; let's try the next page," Keith Ryder lied. They sat through all the pages up to May pretending to scan each page just as carefully before declaring that their friend's name wasn't in the log in as far as they could see.

"Well, it was a long shot anyway, we're sorry to have put you to any trouble," said Jeanette.

"No trouble at all; I'm glad to help," replied Joelle closing the log. "Is there anything else I can do for you while I am here?"

"No—er—well yes, if you don't mind," said Jeanette. "We've only just arrived on St Gilberts and don't know anywhere. Could you give us some advice on what there is to do around here on a Friday night?"

"Depends on what kind of thing you want to do," replied Joelle. "You just tell me and I'll tell you if we have it and where to find it. As you must have noticed, St Gilberts is not very big."

"How about somewhere nice to eat and a good place to drink?"

"Well," said Joelle, "there's an Italian restaurant at the top end of town, just turn right out of the door, walk up to the top of the road and there is a little place that does Creole dishes. It's up near the Marina, in fact you probably passed it on your way here."

"Do you mean the pretty little place set lower than the walkway with the tables and chairs outside and the hanging baskets?" Asked Jeanette.

"Yes that's the place," agreed Joelle.

"What about you," asked Jeanette, "where do you usually go on a Friday night, in fact what are you doing tonight?" Joelle looked surprised at the question but hesitated for only a second before answering, "It's going to be a quiet night for me. Once I've locked up here I'll go home."

"What; no clubbing, no boyfriend?" asked Jeanette shaking her head and pulling a face of mock horror. "Well, that does it! You must join us for dinner, I insist!" Jeanette exclaimed.

Joelle appeared nonplussed at the invitation, and for a second it looked as if she would lose her poise.

"No…I couldn't—really, but thank you for the offer; it was very kind." Realising she had spoken a little too formally she stood awkwardly for a second before Keith Ryder spoke to her for the first time.

"You'll have to forgive my wife for being so direct, she's always like that with people she likes. Besides, I'm sure that you have lots of better things to do than spending your Friday evening with a couple of old fogies like us. However, if you were free then we would love to have your company and learn a little more about this lovely island of yours."

"Besides," Jeanette interrupted, "I want to know all about how you set up this fantastic business all by yourself. The meal would of course be our treat." She watched Joelle's face intently and saw the other's beautiful brown eyes defocus as she gave their offer serious consideration.

Normally, Joelle would have turned down the couple's offer but then she thought, what else had she got lined up for the night, or any other night for that matter? Her social life was non-existent surely being invited to a restaurant by this friendly couple had to be better than eating alone in her apartment. She had never learnt to cook as a young girl as her foster family had never had enough in the way of food for her to learn with. Julie shouted to her from the counter snapping her back to the present, "Joelle, is it OK if I go off now?" Joelle looked at her watch and smiled.

"Yes go on and have a good-time, I'll lock up," she shouted back and turned back to the couple again, "Yes I'd love to join you but I'd need to shower and change before we go."

Jeanette shook her head slowly and emphatically. "No need for all that. When you've locked up, we'll just go straight there. It's only up the road isn't it? Anyway, you already look a million dollars and put me to shame, doesn't she, Keith?" Keith nodded enthusiastically, "She sure does—she looks fantastic." His wife pulled a face and jabbed him in the ribs with her elbow. Out of the corner of her mouth, she growled, "Thanks for your support, hubby."

"I mean you both look great," he mumbled ruefully putting his lower lip out in a parody of a repentant little boy. They all laughed together.

Joelle approved of the food in Bab's Café, basic island dishes but well-presented and spicy, the way she liked it. Jeanette asked her to choose between red or white wine to go with the meal but Joelle had replied, "Pink."

"Ah Rose, a great choice," said Keith and they had kept her glass topped up throughout the meal. Now she had lost count of how many glasses she had drunk. They were attentive hosts and listened to her as if she was the most important person in the world. They were interested in everything and asked questions about the island, the café, and then about her. Why hadn't she married, did she have a boyfriend? Mostly it was the wife Jeanette who asked the questions but the husband, Keith, asked her what she hoped was going to happen in her life over the next few years. The questions were uncomfortably similar to the ones that had depressed her earlier that day when she had eaten alone in the café but now she felt relaxed. No one ever asked her questions like that before, there was no one with whom she could talk things through, and share her concerns for the future, no one was bothered about her, not until now.

The couple would sail off soon, maybe even tomorrow, it was possible she'd never see them again and that made it all the easier to talk openly with them. They ran their own business, just like she did, what was it they did? Marine insurance claims or something like that. But they were older and wiser and obviously knew more of the world than she did, somehow it felt right to be telling them personal, and up to now, secret things about herself. They were people who could give her a different perspective, maybe even advise her on which direction her life could, or should go. Jeanette leaned in towards her and spoke earnestly.

"Look Joelle, I know St Gilberts is a stunning island, I know it's stunning because I have visited islands all over the Indian Ocean, the Caribbean and the South Pacific; Tahiti, Bora Bora, Rarotonga, St Lucia, Cayman Islands, Seychelles, Bali, you name it I've been there, but I can tell you St Gilberts is special it really is the prettiest of them all by miles, no contest." Keith nodded in agreement. His wife continued, but speaking low so other diners would not hear.

"But after saying that, what can island life offer a young woman with your drive and ambition? With your energy, brains and looks you'd be welcome anywhere in the world. Have you never thought of travelling, of living abroad?" Joelle blinked at the question, she could feel the effect of the wine throughout her body and in her head, and it felt good. She thought before answering, "Yes I've thought about doing that a lot but I don't know anyone abroad. I've only ever seen other countries on TV and in films and I'm not sure it's for me."

"What makes you say that?" asked the man also leaning in towards her.

"Well, I'd have to leave the café and I don't want to. I'm proud of what I've done with it and I know I can grow it even more."

"But you could open another café somewhere else, somewhere with lots more customers where they'd really appreciated you. Besides, what will you do when families on St Gilberts get their own computers and Internet connections? It can only be a matter of time."

"I've already thought about that," replied Joelle, more sure of her ground now. "I'll run computer courses in the Café. Getting a computer and a connection doesn't mean a person can actually use a computer, most wouldn't even know where to begin."

"Good point and well made," said the husband, and Joelle thought she heard a slight note of patronisation in his voice, he was humouring her.

"Abroad, you'd get paid a lot more," added the woman.

"Maybe, but I want to be successful here on St Gilberts first."

"But you already are," Keith reassured her.

"Not yet I'm not," said Joelle and here was a note of stubborn defiance in her voice that surprised the other two. Jeanette sensed an inner conflict within the young woman and it intrigued her.

"Is there another reason why you don't want to leave here?" she asked quietly.

"If I ever leave it will be when everything is going well and I'm happy. Then I'd know that I was leaving because I wanted to travel rather than just leaving because I was unhappy or because I'd failed in some way and wanted to escape."

Surprised and a little confused by what Joelle had just said, the other two sat in silence until Keith coughed and suggested, "Sometimes when you have taken things as far as you can and no effort on your part seems to improve what you are doing any further, then surely that's a good time to seek a new challenge somewhere else?"

Joelle shook her head. "I read in a book once that you shouldn't travel to escape unsolved problems as they will only follow you, because maybe the problems are really to do with yourself. Best to sort everything out before moving on otherwise you could travel and travel and yet stay right where you are."

Jeanette sighed in frustration. "God! What sort of self-help stuff have you been reading, Joelle? And what problems could an absolute darling like you possibly have?" As she spoke, she reached across the table and gently laid her hand on Joelle's forearm. It was the gesture of a mother to a teenage daughter.

Joelle didn't answer but her free arm reached for the wine glass. Despite the alcohol, an internal alarm had gone off in a deep recess of Joelle's brain. She may have been drunk but she still knew when she was being patronised and when her heartfelt beliefs and ideas were being belittled and dismissed. It was the cavalier way the woman had dismissed her views, Joelle now knew she would not trust any further advice from this woman she was no longer an ‘ally’ but an outsider whose motives she didn’t trust.

“Hell! Where the hell are we?” asked Keith when they finally left the restaurant into the comparative dark of an almost empty street.

“I’ve completely lost my bearing, which way is the Marina?”

“Don’t worry, dear. I’m sure that Joelle won’t desert us just yet, not until we have found our way back. You won’t desert us, will you, Joelle?” Jeanette asked turning to Joelle who then somehow found herself promising to walk them to the marina. They were all tipsy but Joelle, less used to alcohol than the other two, was the only one who staggered. Out of her line of sight, the Ryders exchanged quick glances. When they reached the yacht, it seemed the most natural thing in the world for Joelle to accept the couple’s invitation to join them on board for a nightcap.

She had been on-board yachts before and they always impressed her by how cosy and comfortable they were inside. This yacht was something else again bigger and more luxurious than all the other ones she had seen. She wobbled across the passerelle and again down the steps into the main saloon where she found herself gasping at the beautifully polished teak wood trim, the white covered couches and bench seats trimmed with blue it was so sophisticated and expensive looking. Jeanette steered her to one of the long bench-type seats and sat next to her so close their bodies touched.

“I just can’t believe a stunner like you has not got a boyfriend,” said Jeanette her voice soft and soothing. Then she rested her hand palm downwards on Joelle’s leg just above the knee.

“I just don’t understand it at all. Don’t you like men, Joelle?” Joelle’s eyes were half asleep but they opened slightly at the question and the touch of the other’s hand, appearing to notice for the first time the closeness of Jeanette’s body leaning in towards her. Then she felt the other woman’s breasts pushing against hers and the warm hand moving slowly up her thigh. Joelle had grown up in a small, overcrowded one-room apartment, being in close physical proximity with others was normal to her. She had slept with her cousins packed like sardines on mats on the floor. Nevertheless, she had always been separate and apart at an emotional level so physical intimacy and contact of sexual nature was something she had only limited experience of.

Now, through her dulled senses, she felt something not quite right and she instinctively drew away from the other woman. She placed a hand on the seat between them so her arm acted as a barrier and then leaned against the other's arm, forcing it from her leg. Jeanette felt a sudden surge of annoyance but kept her face impassive and her voice reassuring. When the younger woman made to stand and mumbled, "I s-think I have to go now" slurring only slightly, Jeanette even managed a little smile.

"Of course you do and we will make sure that you get home safely, though you could of course stay overnight on the yacht with us. We'll take you back first thing in the morning—which would make more sense if you ask me. While you're thinking about it, let's have just one last drink, a little one, to round off the night. I'll get them, Keith?" she said and Keith nodded towards her back as she moved towards the galley area.

A few minutes later, she returned. "Guests first," she said holding out a single glass containing a twist of lemon swirling in a generous measure of Gin. She placed it on the table in front of Joelle then took a full bottle of Indian tonic and topped up the Joelle's glass. She went back to the galley and returned with two more glasses of Gin and set one in front of her husband and the other in front of herself.

"Let me propose a toast," said Jeanette and Joelle found her hand closing around the glass in front of her.

"To new friends, may they become ever closer," and the three raised glasses clinked together over the table and seconds later all returned to the table empty. The free flowing conversation they had enjoyed earlier in the evening had dried up. Keith Ryder, only slightly light-headed himself, watched the young woman with eyes that were both covetous and protective. Her openness in the restaurant had struck a paternal chord in him. The way she kept her dignified poise that, coupled with her underlying vulnerability, attracted him as much, if not more, than her exquisite face and lush young body. She was clearly not used to drink yet she still had poise and maintained a level of command over herself—or she had been up to now.

Keith studied her more closely and felt growing concern at the way the girl's head had begun to loll on her shoulders and at the glassy look in her eyes. He turned to his wife who was also watching the girl intently though with a calculating predatory stare. Keith Ryder suddenly stood and walked to the galley, seconds later called for his wife to join him. She entered the galley to find her husband's face contorted with rage. In his hand, he held a white cardboard tablet box with 'Rohypnol flunitrazepam' printed on the side. The box and the tablets it contained were counterfeit.

"When and where the hell did you get these?" He demanded. Jeanette Ryder closed the door behind her so the girl wouldn't hear.

"Picked them up on our last visit to Joburg," she mumbled. "Thought they might come in useful."

"Useful!" Keith snapped. "Yeah useful if you're going to fucking rape someone! Besides these are counterfeit; god knows what's in them, you could kill someone—her—seriously!" He shook his head in disgust. "I hope no harm comes to that girl, for your sake, our sake!" At first Jeanette would not meet his eye but then her chin came up and she stared coldly back at him until it was he that backed down.

"She'll be fine," Jeanette said her voice soft and soothing. "They are good counterfeits, exactly the same as the real thing. The only difference is they don't contain that chemical that turns blue in alcohol leaving a nasty residue on the surface of the drink."

"Yeah, and why did the manufacturers put that chemical in the genuine tablets I wonder?" Sneered the husband. "Nothing to do with warning young women that their drink's been spiked with the date-rapist's drug of choice then? What the hell do you think you're playing at, Jeanette? Joelle isn't some backstreet whore you can just use and push off the boat in the morning with a few dollars in her handbag. She's a respected businesswoman, for god sake, and we are on an assignment in case you'd forgotten."

"Keep your voice down, will you?" his wife hissed back at him at the same time she leaned back to open the door a crack and check if the girl was listening. Joelle had slumped over in the seat, her head lolling on one side and her body looked as relaxed as jelly.

"Look, she was already three-quarters pissed when she came onboard; how the hell could she have got home anyway? Surely it's better for us to put her up for the night?"

"Oh and it's safe here then?" Keith challenged, but his voice had lost its resolve and his wife heard it.

"Look Keith. It's not as if I'm going to hurt or mark her; when she wakes in the morning, all she'll remember is having too much to drink and passing out. She'll see us as her saviours."

Her husband gave a little snort, "huh, saviours" obviously still unconvinced, he grunted his acquiescence before falling silent. His wife had always been able to argue a logical case for doing exactly what she wanted to do. They had never drugged anyone before, well not that he knew of anyway. Up to now they had only brought working girls back to the yacht, complete strangers anonymous and remaining so. Joelle was different, she was not a prostitute, in fact she was clearly rather innocent in sexual matters. In addition she had shared with them so much of her life history and future aspirations that Keith at least, felt a concern for her that overrode his desire to possess her physically. It was obvious that the same restraint did not apply to his wife.

"OK. Help me get her to the cabin," she said in voice tone just short of a command. "In the morning we'll just tell her that she fell asleep and that we helped her to the spare cabin." Her husband nodded, lifted the girl up and carried her to the side cabin they had had converted especially to accommodate their sexual adventures. The bunk beds replaced by one large bed with enough space around it to walk comfortably. The bed itself had points at each of the four corners to which restraints could be attached and the polished teak at each of the points already showed signs of friction wear. Apart from a basic toilet and a small sink, the cabin contained nothing else and the ventilation and windows were too small for anyone to either enter through or escape out of. The door itself was solid and could only be locked and unlocked by someone outside the cabin.

Any 'guests' were thus prevented from leaving the cabin while the Ryders slept and gaining access to the rest of the yacht and the valuable equipment it contained. Once the soundproofed cabin door was shut and locked, anyone inside would not be going anywhere.

Jeanette eyes gleamed with anticipation as she stood at the door cabin looking to where the girl lay. "Well, are you coming in or not?" she demanded.

"Not tonight, Jeany, it just doesn't seem right with this one," he replied, using her pet name to soften the rejection and to try to persuade his wife to leave the girl be.

"Well, suit yourself," she sneered, "I don't know what your problem is; you've never gone all prudish like this before." But her words and the tone she used to deliver them only made him even more determined to have no part of what was to follow. Their values, once so aligned, now seemed to be diverging with each passing week.

"What? You're not losing your sex drive, are you?" she mocked, and he picked up the note of chiding contempt in her voice. His face hardened as he turned without answering and walked aft towards the master cabin.

Sometime later in the night he woke from his sleep when his wife returned to their cabin and climbed into bed beside him. Her arm reached across him but got no acknowledgement, no response. Was he asleep, she wondered, then looked at the dark silhouette of his body she heard the slow regular breathing of a person sleeping but she sensed a tension in his neck and shoulders that made her think otherwise.

Fuck him, she thought removing her arm turning over to face away from him. With her back to him she quickly fell into a deep and satisfying sleep. The sun had already been up for two hours when she awoke to find herself in the bed alone. She waited for the mug of coffee Keith usually brought to start her day. When none came and she could hear no sound, save the lapping of the sea against the hull, she got up and shuffled into the saloon. There was a yellow post-it note stuck in the middle of the main table. On it her husband had written:

"Gone ashore to trace R.L—back soon—Keith."

She silently unlocked the door of the cabin with the girl and looked inside. Joelle was still out cold and Jeanette wasn't sure if it was from the drug, the drink, or a combination of both. Quietly, she locked the door again and moved to the galley to make the coffee she had waited in vain for earlier. After her first cup, she opened the fridge, took out some eggs and bacon, and began to cook.

Her husband surprised her by returning while she was still eating, she had expected him to be away for considerably longer.

"How's the girl?" He asked after they had exchanged restrained greetings.

"Fast asleep."

"Too soon to move her yet?" he asked.

"Well, I don't think it would be very good for her or us for that matter, if she were to go staggering away from the yacht—do you?" She asked.

"No, I suppose not, the main street is rather busy, must be market day or something," he agreed. "By the way, I now know where this Leon guy lives, if we cast off and go up along the coast a bit we should be able to get a view of his house. From there we can plan our next move. Agreed?"

"Sure." His wife said, pleased there was no bad vibe between them.

"Don't worry about the girl she'll not be a problem. She won't even remember a thing about last night. Probably just put it down to drink and her lack of experience in handling it."

Ten minutes later they were making steady progress up the coast and way from the main town towards Anse Raffin as shown on their nautical map of St Gilberts. They were on the engine and the Perkins six cylinders were so well sound insulated that the noise of its working was almost undetectable outside the engine room.

"That's it there," Keith Ryder pointed up the rock face at a house designed to blend in with the rock and trees surrounding it. Cascades of different hued bougainvillea trailed down around a roofed veranda cum balcony overlooking the beach below. Jeanette put the binoculars to her eyes and focused on the veranda. She saw a tall figure moving in the shadows of the house behind the veranda and watched until he had moved out of view. She kept the glasses on the house admiring the way it blended in with its environment.

"Jee-zus, that's some house!" She exclaimed. "It would almost be worth living ashore again if we had a house like that."

"You're not serious are you?" Keith asked a note of disbelief tinged with concern in his voice.

"No I guess not," she replied, "but if I HAD to live back on land then that's got to be THE place to be."

"Hold on, someone's coming into view," she refocussed the binoculars on to the figure who had just walked on to the veranda and up to the rail and who was now looking out to sea, or, more likely, directly at their yacht.

"Is that Rodney Leon?" She murmured to herself. "Looks like a bloody film star from here." Keith took the binoculars from his wife, refocussed them to suit his eyes and then looked at the figure at the rail.

"Well, I'd guess he's local, looks young, slim, good build, longish hair and tall though it's difficult to tell from here. Dressed—erm—scruffy, casual. Thing is we don't know if that's Leon or whether it's just a hired hand."

"I don't think he's Rodney Leon," said Jeanette Ryder. "For one thing he looks a bit young and down at heel to own a house like that."

"You could have just described any number of millionaires," countered her husband, she took the binoculars back readjusted them and put them to her eyes again.

“Nope I still think I’m right, I can usually spot money whether it’s dressed up scruffy or not and this guy ain’t money,” she said. “If I had to guess, I’d say he’s Leon’s heavy, he looks big enough, or maybe he’s simply the gardener.”

Keith Ryder didn’t reply as he reached over to push a button on the steering pedestal to lower the anchor, he reversed the boat and then went forward trying to get the anchor to bite but without success. He tried again and again, several times until at last it found purchase then he dropped extra chain just to make sure, his eyes checking all the while that there was no chance that they’d drift onto the reef.

Andy had given me another yet another fish a Titan Triggerfish. I thanked him enthusiastically enough at the time not wanting to be ungrateful, but secretly wished he'd given me a Red Snapper or at least something that I could actually get the bloody scales off. I stood outside in the yard scratching the sides of the damned thing with the prongs of a fork, which normally does the trick without any bother, but this fish wasn't having any of it. As I scrapped I let my mind drift and, for some reason, the Internet and the Kokonet Café came to mind.

I'd visited the Café two days earlier when I'd opened my Hotmail account to find a message from Caroline. She'd obviously been in a reminiscing mood when she wrote the message because she'd picked out the highlights of our time together. The message went over a few screens and recalling each of our landmark moments together, it had brought a warm smile to my face as I read it. Meticulous as ever, she had obviously been keeping a diary of her holiday because she included details of the dates and the times of those moments starting with our first meeting in the Three-In-One on 1 February 2016 at 3 pm-ish right through to our tearful goodbyes at the airport.

I was still smiling to myself when I remembered with a jarring realisation that on the afternoon I'd met Caroline I had deserted her to follow Joelle into the Kokonet Café. That was the day I searched the Internet for information on the Valvaston. I couldn't remember how many web sites I'd checked but it must have been quite a few. I stopped scrapping at the fish because a new memory, a connection, flashed before my mind's eye; a small white card with the date 1st February 2016 written on it, the small white card that Andy took from a dead man's wallet at the foot of Kasper's Edge. Had it been that internet search which had brought the Belgium man to St Gilberts looking for me? He must have somehow traced my enquiry back to the Café and then to me? I went inside, dropped the fish into the sink and sat down to think.

I needed someone who knew the techy computer stuff and only one name came to mind—Joelle. I got the Honda fired up and set off down to town and the

Café. I put the bike on its stand just outside the door of the Café. The smell of coffee and freshly baked cakes hit me as I opened the door and a welcome draught of cool air from the aircon. Julie was behind the glass counter and she gave a brief smile when she saw me, too brief in fact.

"Hi Julie, is everything all right?" I asked.

"Yes," she replied then added, "I don't know where Joelle is, she was due in at eight thirty and she's never late." I picked up the concern in her voice but unlike Joelle and Julie, I was a typical Islander in my disregard for time and schedules of any sort.

"Perhaps she had a late-night or a headache or something," I suggested but Julie shook her head.

"She would have rung in to tell me, and besides, she's not at home I've tried ringing her number and got no reply."

"Where do think she is?" I asked.

She thought for a moment before replying, "Well, there was this white couple in yesterday. All very friendly and smiley and I introduced them to Joelle because they wanted to check in the log to see if their friend had visited the café in January or February this year. We've just started a new log so Joelle had to get the old log out of the office for them." I felt a sudden chill run up my spine and an awful sense of foreboding.

"Where is the couple now?" I asked. She looked sharply at me picking up on the note of urgency in my voice.

"I'm not sure but my boyfriend said that a couple sounding like them arrived at Albert's marina a day or so ago in a big beautiful yacht. Everyone was standing looking at it."

I pushed the Honda hard the short way to the marina and skidded to a stop outside the café. There were a couple of yachts moored up against the side but nothing that would attract a crowd so I went into the café. I approached the counter and gave silent thanks that it was the daughter on duty and not her miserable father who would rather shoot me than help me.

"The couple with the big boat; have they gone?" I asked without going through the usual pleasantries compulsory in polite island conversation.

"Earlier this morning they set off up the coast without saying goodbye. Maybe they'll come back, who knows." She raised both hands and shrugged her shoulders, "Anyway they have booked their mooring spot for the week."

"Have they paid for it yet?" I asked.

"Er, yes, but anyway what's the problem?"

I didn't answer but asked another question instead, "Have you seen Joelle Kelly anywhere today?"

"No, but my brother saw them leaving Bab's Café last night; looked like they had been drinking loads." Joelle drinking loads… didn't sound like any Joelle I knew.

"So she was in Bab's Café last night with the couple who sailed off this morning?" I asked.

"Er yes that's right; is something wrong?"

I turned to jog back to my bike and found myself saying, "I hope to god not", more to myself than in answer to Albert's daughter. After several kicks I got the Honda started, it must have sensed I wasn't in any mood to be messed about with. Then I just sat there with the engine ticking over not sure of where I should go next; too Joelle's place? No, she hadn't answered Julie's call, back to the Café then? I was about to head back to the café when I remembered the yacht I had studied from my veranda earlier that morning, stationary, just off the reef. I felt my guts turn in cold fear as the trail of events started to fall into place.

I thrashed the Honda's old four-stroke engine all the way back up the steep road and only eased back when I had reached the driveway to my house and even then I drove down on the engine instead of coasting as usual. Once inside the house I ran to the veranda and saw straight away the yacht was still there. I tried to plan my next move but it was difficult to think straight and I found myself taking large gulps of air as I paced around the house driven by the adrenalin coursing through my body. Whatever trouble I'd visited on myself by finding that damned Valvaston ring I'd now brought it onto Joelle as well. I had to know if Joelle was on that yacht and if the couple sailing it had come to St Gilberts to find me. I could only think of one way to find out for sure. I left the house and walked through the garden heading for the path that would take me down to the beach below.

I was breathing hard when I reached the soft white sand of Anse Raffin but at least I had managed to burn up some of the adrenalin that had wired me up back at the house. The yacht looked further away from my new vantage point on the beach and I knew that just to reach it would be a hell of an achievement for someone of my modest swimming ability. The hardest part would be staying on course to reach the gap in the reef that would allow me to swim through to the yacht on the other side. I experienced a moment of indecision as I looked across the lagoon and I stood for a few seconds taking deep breaths.

Fuck it I thought and, stooping, removed my cargo shorts rolled them up and hid them behind a small Sea Hibiscus tree. I was wearing trunk style underwear underneath and they would be easier to swim in than the shorts with all those pockets catching water. I waded out to sea and took a bearing on the gap in the reef. There was an exposed pinnacle of coral to the left of the gap which pretty much lined up with the yacht behind it. If I swam using that pinnacle as a marker I might just make the gap in the reef, whether I'd get through it one piece was another matter.

Jeanette turned to her husband.

"So what's the plan we can't wait here forever, for one thing we're a bit close to the reef and that swell is getting high."

"Well, things would be more straightforward if we didn't have the girl to sort out as well," he retorted and she took the note of bitterness in his tone as the intended rebuke it was.

"Now don't start off on that again, we'll put her ashore later today when she comes round. Meanwhile, how are we going to get this Valvaston info from Mr Rodney Leon? Bearing in mind Denver has told us to be careful; the last operative he sent out ended up dead at the bottom of a cliff. What was his name again?"

"Philippe Ronnier; the guy from Belgium," her husband replied. His wife suddenly changed the topic of conversation and so abruptly and bizarrely that her husband found himself rendered momentarily speechless.

"We forgot to buy some olive oil for the galley."

He stared open-mouthed at her for a few seconds before responding, "Then we'll get some when we go back to drop the girl off—and pay any extras we hadn't covered with the marina." He had spoken in the slow measured voice he used whenever he was trying to keep a lid on his anger but his wife must have missed the warning.

"But I want to cook Italian tonight..." she said, her voice trailing off at the end of the sentence as if unable to compete it. Changing the subject abruptly was one of Jeanette Ryder's foibles. At the start of their marriage, Keith had seen it as an essential part of her quirky charm. Of late he had found himself tiring of both it, and her. Her unpredictability and capriciousness now smacked of manipulation rather than charm.

"Look, we're on an assignment that could turn out to be dangerous," he reminded her, trying, and failing, to keep his growing anger and frustration under control.

"Do you think I don't know that?" She snapped back.

"But we still have to eat don't we and as yet you haven't come up with any plan to tackle Leon so what's your problem?" Her husband's mouth went square with repressed anger and then it opened wide as he yelled, "All right. I'm not lifting that bloody anchor. I'll take the inflatable and go and get your fucking olive oil." If he had hoped to intimidate or cow his wife, he was disappointed.

In response, she simply smiled back at him. "Can you get me a newspaper and some Oregano—if there is any, while you are there—oh—and you may as well sort things at the marina, if anything needs sorting? Tell them to save our space while you're at it." She delivered it all in that little girl voice she knew from experience would increase his rage even more. Minutes later she heard him angrily banging about as he prepared the small inflatable tender for use. She was only mildly surprised to hear the outboard fire up as her husband moved away from the yacht without even shouting an angry cheerio.

She lounged back in the cockpit seat and thought of the girl in the cabin below. She was so beautiful and yet what a disappointment. The Rohypnol had made her compliant and hopefully it would erased any incriminating memories of the previous night from her mind, but the drug had also taken away the part of sex that she liked so much. How can you dominate someone when they are virtually comatose, and what fun is there in subjugating someone who isn't fighting back or even aware of your presence? Still, she had been in control and, even though the girl had been as unresponsive as a piece of meat, the meat had tasted good.

She sat in the cockpit facing the shore and idly picked up the binoculars to scan the veranda high on the rocky cliff. There was still no sign of life so she went to the galley and poured herself a glass of orange from the fridge and carried it back to the cockpit with a slice of papaya on a plate. She settled back in the seat again and picked up the binoculars again and pointed them towards the veranda, just as she was about to lower them again her eyes caught a movement lower down on the beach. She frowned and lifted the binoculars again refocussing them on the tall figure on the sand as he removed his shorts and placed them behind a small tree with yellow flowers.

Well, well, well, the mystery man from the veranda going for a swim and can't afford any swimming trunks, what a shame. She kept the binoculars trained on the head of the swimming figure and then realised with a surge of adrenalin that he was swimming straight towards the yacht. She heard banging and it was coming from the cabin which contained the girl. The door was vibrating with blows hammering on it and she heard muffled shouts from the girl within. Jeanette went down to the master cabin aft and opened the concealed weapons cabinet at the side of the bed and took out one of the Glock 17s. She had done her weapons training using a Sig Sauer and, though she preferred the smooth action of the Sig, the Glock's had been cheaper and their composite bodies were more practical in a sea-air ocean environment.

She checked the pistol had a full clip and placed the pistol on the bed. Moving to the wardrobe, she selected a white jacket from the wardrobe. The jacket had side pockets large enough to accommodate the Glock and there was enough structure and stiffness in its fabric to take the weight of the gun without it being too obvious. As an afterthought, she also picked a man's wallet from beside the bed, it was her wallet and she placed it in the inside pocket of the jacket. Back at the cockpit, she hardly needed the binoculars to confirm the yacht was indeed the swimmer's destination. The swimmer would need to get through the break in the reef first and that wouldn't be easy. She could also see the young man was not an experienced swimmer. From his flailing strokes she began to doubt if he was going to have the strength to make it at all. She had no idea how strong the current through the gap in the reef was but it could be too much for this young swimmer.

Now the problem of their lack of a plan for how to get information from Rodney Leon might be on the point of being solved, she thought. The young man was from Leon's house and he was coming straight to the yacht and to her. He was almost certainly unarmed and would be too exhausted if he actually made it to the yacht, to pose much of a threat. She straightened her shoulders and felt the weight of the Glock in her right-hand pocket.

As a private investigator, she knew how to act and assume different personas, she decided the sort of woman the lone swimmer was going to meet when, if, he finally made it to the yacht. She lowered the stainless steel bathing ladder at the stern and scanned the sea in the direction her husband had taken, there was no sign of the inflatable so it had already rounded the headland. He was probably already at the marina.

Joelle was not sure if she was awake or whether she was still in the middle of a bizarre dream. It was the persistent pain in her stomach that eventually drove her to sit up on the rumpled bed. What she saw as she looked about the dark cabin only increased her confusion and growing sense of unease. It may have been the sudden action of sitting upright that triggered the cold sweat she knew precedes a bout of vomiting. She scanned the cabin with blurred vision for a sink or toilet. Clambering awkwardly over the bed she stumbled on weak unsteady legs until she found, more by chance than design, the small toilet cubicle just as her stomach heaved. She bent over and vomited what seemed like the entire contents of her stomach into the white bowl. It did not end there, she continued retching until there was nothing to regurgitate but dry heaves.

Struggling for breath and with tears coursing down her cheeks from the effort, she collapsed on to the floor beside the toilet. Her clothes were damp and chilly with sweat and clung to her body making her shiver despite the warm air in the cabin. She was not sure how long she remained there before she was woken by the urge to vomit again and only just managed to heave her body up and her head over the rim of the toilet in time. If she had thought her stomach had been emptied in the previous session, she was mistaken. Now her stomach muscles strained until she was expelling clear bile. There was a small sink close by and she managed to rinse her mouth out and then swallow a few mouthfuls of water. She began to feel slightly better but still collapsed back on to the floor trying to gather her strength.

Her mind slowly began to try to make sense of her surroundings. The floor moved like a boat at sea and she vaguely remembered something about a yacht, a friendly married couple and eating in a restaurant. It took all her strength to sit and then to stand upright. She made use of every available handhold, but still bumped against the sides of cupboards and the bed itself as she made her way towards the only door in the cabin. When she turned the handle nothing happened, she tried again and again and then started to bang on the door with her fist. Apprehension and a growing sense of fear were beginning to replace her physical distress and nausea. Fragmented memories from the previous night flashed like lightning in her brain.

The couple in the Café, the logbook, walking down the main street, eating in Bab's Place, and talking, so much talking, and the woman's face close to hers, listening. Then she remembered the woman's hand on her thigh, a beautiful yacht and, she frowned in concentration trying to see into the shadows of her memory. Something had happened, she was sure of that, but the more she tried to recall it, the more determinedly it stayed out of reach just slipping beyond the reach of her memory. Instinctively she felt that whatever had happened the previous night, it wasn't good. The couple had played on her loneliness and, in some awful way, they had cynically used her.

Andy passed the Kokonet Café heading towards the Three-In-One for a quick drink when Julie rushed out of the café and called to him, "Andy, have you seen Rodney anywhere?"

He immediately picked up the concern in her voice.

"Yes I saw him earlier this morning, I gave him a fish, why, what's happened?"

Julie took a deep breath and recounted how Joelle had not turned up for work that morning and how Rodney had come looking for her. She recounted how she had told Rodney about the friendly couple and the log book and how he seemed very concerned.

"Rodney just…he went off very fast and looked worried which is not like him at all."

"Which way did he go?" asked Andy and the urgency in his voice warned her to answer his question rather than to ask one of her own.

"He went down to the marina first because this couple came on a yacht, but ten minutes later I heard his bike and saw him going really fast back up the hill." She was breathless at the end of her story because she'd said it all on one breath. Andy touched Julie's arm reassuringly with his hand.

"Don't worry; I'll sort it out. You look after the café till Joelle gets back." He weighed whether it would be quicker to run to Rodney's house, a good mile up steep hills, or to wait for the next bus, the decision was made for him because at that very moment he heard the welcome grinding of gears and saw the bus turning ponderously out of Market Street and then head towards him. As he settled into his seat he forced himself to think rationally, in the end it would all turn out to be a storm in teacup but then, maybe…Had Joelle finally treated herself to a night out and Rodney's jealousy gotten the better of him? Even as he thought this through, he knew Rodney wasn't that kind of guy.

He remembered back to when the Belgian had gone over the cliff, when Rodney, Nahil and he had sat in Rodney's house discussing what they should do next. Rodney and Nahil had been shocked when he'd predicted the story wasn't over, that more people would follow. The other two hadn't wanted to believe it, and it was not in his nature to cause unnecessary anxiety in people just for the sake of it. Nevertheless, ever since that evening he had discreetly made it his job to watch for anything out of the ordinary on the island, anything that could herald the arrival of more trouble for them. An instinct developed over years of operating in a Special Forces unit and then as a bodyguard told him the second assault team had finally arrived on St Gilberts.

Andy alighted from the bus at the top of Rodney's drive and jogged down the steep gravel driveway. The Honda was parked on its stand and the door to the house was open. He walked around the house shouting Rodney's name checking each of the rooms in turn, the blue fish he had given Rodney earlier that morning was still in the kitchen sink. He went out to the garden continuing to shout when he looked up and saw a white yacht at anchor just beyond the reef. With a cold sense of certainty he ran back inside to get a better view of the boat from the veranda.

The sea beyond the reef was dark-blue but the water within the lagoon was a swirling mix of aquamarine and turquoise, then he saw the lone swimmer, his arms thrashing the water as he swam towards the break in the reef. Even as he watched, the swimmer stopped, trod water to lift his head to check his bearings and adjust his direction before continuing onwards towards the break and the yacht beyond. Despite the distance, Andy recognised the swimmer. Why was Rodney taking on a swim so clearly at the limits of his capability?

Andy forced himself to think rationally, he was a better swimmer than Rodney and could make the yacht without too much difficulty, though the suck and flow of water through the break in the reef would not be easy. But Rodney was almost at the break in the reef and no matter how fast he set off in pursuit there was no way he could make up the distance between them, not before Rodney either drowned or reached the yacht. What then? What if the yacht decided to up-anchor and sail off with Rodney on-board? Andy frowned in concentration as he watched Rodney's increasingly erratic strokes and began to wonder if Rodney would even reach the yacht. It looked more doubtful with each floundering stroke. Andy chewed on his lower lip, he could use the Honda, get back to his house and launch the Avon but then it would take too long to bring the Avon around the coast to Anse Raffin. He squinted against the bright blue of the lagoon at the distant figure ploughing towards the break when a name came to him, Jean Claude, Rodney's uncle.

Jean Claude lived a short way along the coast and had a wooden sailing dingy with an outboard motor as back-up to its triangular main sail and jib. Andy picked up the keys to the Honda from the table in the kitchen and ran out to the bike. It refused to start so using brute strength he pushed it some way up the slope turned it to face down the drive again and jumped astride it. He put the bike into second gear, depressed the clutch lever and let the bike roll down. He waited till the bike had picked up speed before releasing the clutch. The back wheel locked, skidded on the loose gravel, the engine coughed and spluttered into life freeing the back wheel. He accelerated down the rest of the drive, turned the bike, gave the engine some revs and roared back up the track towards the road turning right when he reached it and headed down towards town.

A quarter mile later he turned off the road and took a rough track heading steeply down towards the sea. Pitted and ridged with deep gullies where torrents of rainwater had cut deep gouges into the orange soil, the track was almost unrideable. It took all of Andy's concentration to stay on the bike as he weaved to avoid getting his front tyre jammed in one of the deep gullies. He stood on the bike's footrests and leaned back to keep his weight distributed towards the rear of the machine. In low gear, and with the fingers of his right-hand keeping a light tension on the front brake leaver he coaxed the Honda down ducking low under the branches that joined overhead and flinching as they plucked at his arms.

At last the track broadened and levelled allowing him to accelerate towards the sunlight reflecting off the sea ahead shining through the tropical foliage in bursts of white light. Now he could see Jean Claude's half brick, half wood, house set back off the beach and in the shade of two large Casuarinas trees.

The wheels of the bike bit into the sand causing him to slew to one side. He cut the engine, kicked the stand out and dismounted. As he walked towards the shack he heard the Honda fall over onto its side on the sand behind him.

Harassed office and city dwellers would find the setting of Jean Claude's little home a slice of paradise. High palms, dazzling white sand and a tap water clear ocean lapping the shoreline. To a local these natural features are unremarkable, commonplace—or simply home and a bit of a liability if a tsunami ever came in from the west instead of the north. Andy could see both the beauty and potential of the location but he had also once been inside Jean Claude's house, though only once. Jean Claude was a widower and had been for more than twenty years. The Spartan conditions in which he chose to live would have made a stretch on Raynauld Island correctional facility seem inviting by comparison. Apart from the few fish he sold at the market or to hotels and the occasional toddy at Toffies, he tended to keep himself to himself and had a reputation for not suffering fools gladly.

As Andy drew close to the house, he saw Jean Claude sat in a wooden rocking-chair on the narrow veranda and he took a deep breath. A fresh sense of urgency swept through him and as he approached the seated man he began speaking as rapidly as he could in Creole to explain why he needed to use the other's boat to help Rodney out of a fix.

"For god's sake, speak English, son," growled the man on the veranda, he was tall with grey hair and still managing to look distinguished despite the ragged state of his clothes. Andy thought that Jean Claude's features held more than a passing resemblance to the actor Morgan Freeman and Jean Claude could certainly generate a similar gravitas when he wanted to. He stood up and faced Andy. "You saying you want to use my boat for something?" He asked.

"Yes I think Rodney's in some sort of trouble."

"Nothing new there, that boy's never out of trouble," replied Jean Claude laconically. Andy had no time to trade words with this curmudgeon, he preferred action to words but he took another deep breath and started mentally to assemble his next sentence. The older man saved him the trouble of having to say it by suggesting, "But this time it really is serious, right?"

"Yes," said Andy.

"OK son, you get my boat but you get me along with it."

Andy hadn't expected that. "B, buh, but it might be dangerous…" he began to stammer.

"It bloody well better be," growled the older man who turned and disappeared into his house letting the door swing closed behind him. Seconds later he re-emerged, like a magician, and made towards the dingy. As he walked, Jean Claude was unwinding an oil-stained cloth from around an ancient rifle. Andy blinked in surprise as he recognised a short magazine Lee Enfield rifle Mark Three. The last time he'd seen one of those was in his Special Boat Service days and it had been slung over the shoulder of an Afghan astride a pony in the Khyber Pass. But then the Afghan's rifle was in a far better state of repair than Jean Claude's.

"Will that thing fire?" Asked Andy, less sceptical of the rifle's capability to fire than of the .303 ammunition contained in a grimy transparent plastic bag swinging from Jean Claude's left-hand. Andy could see that some of the bullets were connected to the five round stripper clips that were used to help load the rounds into rifle's magazine. The older man replied with a withering look causing Andy to shrug his shoulders and smile despite the circumstances. He had only ever met Rodney's uncle on a couple of occasions, not counting the many times they had passed each other on the street in town, so he didn't know him beyond the taciturn persona Jean Claude presented to the world at large.

However, he was beginning to think he might actually warm to the guy after all. Jean Claude's boat was already in the water though tied to a metal ring set in the planks of a rough jetty that Jean Claude had built himself. Andy untied the painter, followed Jean Claude into the dingy and directed.

"Go out past the reef and towards Anse Raffin. There should be a yacht lying at anchor there, aim for that."

Once Jean Claude had the engine going and they had moved off towards the open sea, he turned to Andy, "Here take hold of this," he commanded pointing to the long wooden tiller and as soon as Andy had a grip of it Jean Claude stooped over the rifle and began thumbing rounds into the magazine using one of the strips of five.

Every time my ears went underwater, the sound of the sea hitting the reef came as a hissing noise which grew louder the near I got to it. I could also feel the unnerving force of the sea pulling and then pushing me back again as the current ebbed and flowed. The hissing noise had become a roaring wall of radio static when, for the umpteenth time, I trod water and lifted my head to see if I was still on target to make the gap in the reef. A few seconds of disorientation followed as I searched in vain for the pinnacle of coral until I realised I was already in the gap itself. The strong current pushed me back and then sucked me forward again.

I felt small, insignificant, and scared. I waited for the next wave, took a deep breath and when it came, lowered my head and swam with all the power and speed I could manage—which wasn't that much—until I sensed I had passed out of the gap and in the open sea. With arms so tired I could hardly lift them out of the sea I somehow paddled my way towards the yacht rising and falling on the large swells ahead of me. The yacht had a stainless steel ladder at the stern and I gratefully got my hands on the rungs and with some difficulty heaved myself on to the deck where I lay coughing and gasping for air. I had taken in a few mouthfuls of water on my swim out to the reef and could still taste the salt in my mouth.

I had not allowed myself to imagine who I'd face once I'd reached the yacht. I had a vague notion of a sinister middle-aged couple dressed in expensive, sporty sailing gear with a tough crew of grimy vest wearing muscle-bound thugs. Instead, an attractive blonde woman blocked out the sun as she leaned over me holding out a white fluffy towel.

"Here, you'd better take this," she said handing me the towel then she turned and picked up a glass of orange juice from a tray nearby and held it out to me.

"And I'm sure you could do with a drink as well after that swim of yours, very impressive by the way. Have you just popped in to say hello or was there anything in particular you wanted?"

She let the question hang in the air so I took the opportunity to gulp some of the orange juice down before rising unsteadily to my feet. I had to grab for a nearby rail, the motion of the yacht coupled with my tired leg muscles made staying upright difficult.

"My, you are a big boy," she said a little flirtatiously and I was not sure whether she was referring to my height or being sarcastic because of something connected to my sodden, clinging, trunk-style underpants. But older women and innuendo was familiar territory to me and gave her a quick smile.

"Thanks for your hospitality," I said looking down on her. "I believe that you have a Miss Joelle Kelly onboard and I'd like to see her please." Even to my ears, it sounded a bit stilted and formal especially considering the bizarre nature of my arrival on to her yacht. However, she smiled and nodded.

"Yes. Joelle had a little too much to drink last night so we left her to sleep it off in one of our cabins below. I'll take you to her if you want?" I nodded, and she invited me to go ahead of her down the companionway. Despite the welcoming towel, glass of orange juice and her motherly easy manner, I hadn't dropped my guard. I still half expected the husband to appear from behind one of the solid looking teak doors with nasty scowl on his face and a bloody great gun in his hand. However, the saloon was not only beautiful—it was also empty of people, at least as far as I could see. There was a banging noise coming from one of the cabins and we headed towards it.

There were some business-like locks on the door that looked out of place as if they had been added to the original specification. The woman gave me a reassuring smile and set about unlocking the door without explaining why her guest had been locked in there in the first place. So I asked the question.

"For her security," was her enigmatic and rather sinister reply. The door swung open before I could come up with a suitable follow-up question and Joelle stood in the open doorway in front of me wearing a short yellow miniskirt and clinging black top combination that always got my pulse racing when I saw her in it. However, now I could see that her hair was dishevelled and she wasn't her usual immaculate self. She stood with her hands on her hips and her legs planted firmly apart to maintain her balance against the roll of the yacht.

"Rodney?" She said in a tone that suggested that I was last the person in the world that she had expected to see. "What are you doing here?"

Before I could answer, the blonde woman spoke, "Ah, so you really are THE Rodney Leon?"

Both Joelle and I must have gaped back at her because she smiled turning from Joelle to me and then back to Joelle again.

"I take it from your expressions that I'm right then," she said pleasantly then added towards Joelle, "Well, love, he swam all the way out here just to check you were alright, aren't you a lucky girl?" The sentence had started out light and pleasant enough but by the last few words of it the woman had been unable to disguise a nasty sneer in her voice. Joelle had also picked up on the change in the woman's voice and balled her fists.

"Why did you lock me in here, you…you pig?" she snapped and I could see she was about to advance on the woman who was stood to my right. Suddenly, the woman's leg came upwards with amazing speed and force, and the foot at the end of it caught Joelle a vicious kick between her open legs. Joelle immediately jack-knifed forward clutching her groin and let out a shriek of pain as she fell to the floor of the cabin where she lay curled up in a foetal position whimpering in pain. I turned and considered giving the woman a belt with one of my fists but I'd never hit a woman in my life and my brain was still processing what had just happened. I hesitated for a second and then, surely foolishly, moved towards Joelle to comfort her instead.

I walked past the woman into the cabin and bent down towards Joelle who was still curled up on the cabin floor. Turning my back on the woman was a mistake because just as I had reached Joelle and stooped towards her, I felt myself jolt forward slightly and a millisecond later it was as if a grenade had exploded in my scrotum as the woman's foot slammed into my dangling testicles, the wet cloth of my trunks offering neither support for my parts nor protection against the kick. I had to reach out and put a hand on the deck at the side of Joelle as I lurched forward to prevent myself from collapsing on top of her.

The pair of us remained side-by-side in our separate worlds of pain until I eventually managed to turn to face the door. The woman was still there watching us and I noticed a pistol in her right-hand though she was not even bothering to point at us, merely letting it hang down by her side. She smiled at me and said conversationally, "I just wanted to make sure that you two didn't get up to anything naughty while we wait for my husband to return. We don't approve of any hanky-panky onboard this yacht."

Despite the pain I didn't like that sneering tone of hers so, pushing down on one knee, I painfully started to get to my feet. I'd no sooner managed to stand and face her when she moved forward with that lightning speed of hers. I was only aware of a blur of movement as her foot snapped out and caught me between the legs again, this time from the front. I went down even faster this time and heard her chuckle as she watched me double up like a pocket knife and crumple to the floor.

"You don't look so big now, sunshine," she said and seconds later I heard the bolts sliding to on the other side of the door. I don't know how long we remained fighting the waves of pain shooting through our lower bodies. In my case the initial explosion of pain in the testicles had quickly extended to my lower stomach causing me to cough and retch. In the end I lay still with my head resting on the cool wooden floor forcing myself to take slow deep breaths.

Joelle shifted her position so she was now sitting with her knees drawn up to her chest and her arms wrapped around them, her face sunk down on the top of her knees. I groaned, closed my eyes, and writhed some more. When I opened my eyes again I found that my face was only six inches or so away from her and that I was staring straight at her crotch. The front of the yellow miniskirt now pinned against her chest by her brown legs and the rest of it rumpled beneath her bum. She was wearing shiny white panties that were so sheer and tight that they looked as if they'd been melted on to her skin and the thin material clung to the swollen outer lips and then disappeared into the deep cleft that separated them. The pristine white of the shiny fabric was marked by a dark line of stains running down the centre of the gusset, the natural result, I guessed, of a day or so of continuous wear.

Suddenly, I felt guilty at staring at her and, as if she had sensed my line of gaze and read my thoughts, Joelle spoke into the silence, "They locked me in here and I haven't been able to wash or change in what seems like days."

Anyone else might have found her concern over her appearance misplaced considering the predicament we were in but I knew Joelle and understood how important personal cleanliness was to her and so empathised with her distress.

"How are you now?" I asked.

"A little bit better I think," she replied and then added, "The bitch toe-ended me in the clit." My mouth fell open at this last statement, coming from any other girl on the island it would not have merited a raised eyebrow but from Joelle? Had she visited a few of those dodgy websites herself? I had certainly never heard her use intimate and explicit language like that before and I wondered if that brief remark heralded a new seismic shift in her usual restraint and modesty.

I didn't know what to say so instead asked, "Is there any way we can break out of this place?"

"I couldn't see anywhere but you might," she replied. I checked the door, the walls, and even the narrow glass windows set high up, but we may as well have been locked up in a police cell on St Gilberts.

I helped Joelle on to the bed telling her, "Just because we're imprisoned doesn't mean we have to be uncomfortable." Good old Rodney, I thought, always helping women on to beds. She sat upright in the middle of the mattress with her legs stretched out in front of her and she made an effort to pull the front of her skirt down so it almost covered her knickers.

"What's going on, Rodney? Are they kidnappers? Why have they done this to me, to us?"

I presumed she meant the couple who owned the yacht and though I had only met the woman once so far that was more than enough for me. I gathered my thoughts to explain the train of events that had led me to swim out to the yacht but then I saw her shoulders shaking as she started to weep.

I kneeled astride her outstretched legs and wrapped my arms around her and let her cry into my chest. We stayed that way for some minutes until her sobs eased and she sniffed and lifted a hand to wipe her eyes. Gently, I eased her body back to a lying position on to the bed but just as her back reached the mattress, her knee came up to counterbalance her weight. I gave an involuntary gasp expecting yet another strike to a sensitive place and one still tender and aching from two previous assaults within the past few minutes. Fortunately, her knee stopped its upward move at the moment just short of hard contact though I still felt her knee lift everything slightly. Thankfully, there was no force behind it and the anticipated pain never came.

However, Joelle had heard my gasp and immediately sat upright and in what I can only believe was a reflex action, perhaps an attempt on her part, to undo or relieve any pain she had caused, her hand came up between my legs to gently cup the much offended parts.

"I'm sorry, Rodney, I didn't mean to…" our eyes locked in the intimacy of the moment as our faces drew together. She had always been the only one able see through and past the blue eyes and into the confusion of my mind and now, for the first time, she didn't seem disappointed at what she saw there. I cast aside all my experience with women, my gigolo tricks, as we embraced. It was as if we were holding on to life itself. I lowered her gently back on to the bed our eyes never breaking contact then I felt her hand slide up to the growing hardness.

Our faces moved closer until our vision blurred then my lips were on hers and our bodies melding together. My hands moved slowly and gently over her body as it arched up towards me and then the need we both felt quickened our breathing and desperate hands removed any remaining clothing and threw it aside. Our love making in the close heat of that cabin was urgent and primordial and its intensity left us gasping for air and our bodies drenched in sweat.

I've heard it said that in times of war both soldiers and civilians often feel an urgent need to have sex, something to do with a biological need to perpetuate the human species in times of danger. I am sure that others would say that that would explain what had just happened between us that it was a sort of primordial reaction to our situation, but not me. I would have wanted to make love to Joelle no matter what yes, even in light of the injuries we had both just sustained. The nature of our situation probably heightened the moment, but I knew as our bodies slid together, we connected at a much deeper level than sex. It went beyond anything I had experienced before. It involved letting go and, for the first time, the thought of commitment did not terrify me—it made sense.

Together, and without a word being spoken, we let trust and love take over, nothing was held back, everything offered; our bodies, our minds, our hopes, and our futures. We lay joined in spirit just as our bodies lay joined, me to her and her to me. At last I had found someone I could love and trust without reserve. After a short lifetime of knowing her, I had at last found Joelle.

Our passion spent, at least for the moment, we pulled our underwear back on. Neither of us wanted to give our captors the satisfaction of seeing us naked nor the woman and her sneering voice an excuse to try to cheapen the moment we had just shared. Then we lay side-by-side in silence until we heard a rattling sound.

"What's that noise?" Joelle said in a whisper.

"I don't know; is it the anchor coming up?"

"Or going down?" She finished. I didn't have that much experience on boats so I wasn't sure which it was.

"Where are we anyway?" she asked.

"We're on a large yacht just off the reef at Anse Raffin," I told her.

She looked up at me. "Did you really swim all the way out from the beach just for me?"

I thought for a moment before answering, "Do you know something—I did! So it looks like this is another fine mess you've got me into." She managed a smile and a little chuckle at that. Then we felt, rather than heard the throb of the engine and sensed a change in the motion of the yacht. It was starting to cut its way through the sea instead of wallowing on it. We looked at each other with our heads only inches apart on the bolster pillow.

"Do you remember that day we finished school early and went to Lolas Beach to paddle in the sea?" Joelle asked unexpectedly. Though the question itself took me by surprise, I remembered the day well enough, even though it seemed a lifetime away.

"Jeez that's going back a bit, but yes, of course, I remember it, were we six or seven at the time?"

"We were seven," confirmed Joelle adding, "Do you remember those Sargent Major fish swimming around tickling us so much we couldn't stop laughing?"

"Of course I remember them; how could I forget? You know something, Joelle, I guess that was one of the happiest, if not THE happiest, day of my school life—correction my whole life." As I spoke our eyes locked again.

"Mine too," she said wistfully.

"Just you and me and no else to make our lives a misery."

"Just you and me and a few thousand Sergeant major fish," I corrected, she chuckled.

"Those Sergeant major fish were cheeky and fun weren't they Rodney?"

I thought for a second before replying, "No Joelle it was us—we were fun."

Pleased with her morning's work, Jeanette Ryder smiled broadly. Rodney Leon, the person central to their assignment and his girlfriend, if that's what she was, securely locked in the cabin below. It seemed that despite Keith's little temper tantrum that morning, her decision to bring the girl on to the yacht had turned out to be a fortuitous one after all. The girl's presence on the yacht had acted as a lure bringing their quarry to them, unarmed, undressed, and clearly alone.

When Keith returned, they would work out how best to get information on the Valvaston wreck site from Leon. Having the girl as well could only help, perhaps, she thought, the initial enquiry had originated from her internet café therefore she might know something that would be helpful to them. Extracting the information from either one of them in front of the other may prove to be entertaining, providing of course, that Keith didn't get all moral again. She pressed the button to raise the anchor and heard not only the noise of the wince but more thumping on the door below. Let them make as much noise as they wanted, the yacht was far from the shore and the cabin so well soundproofed that even if they were closer, little if any sound would be heard off the yacht.

She remembered how she had subdued them both without even having to show the Glock let alone use it. What a buzz, and it had gone some way to make up for the previous night's disappointment. Jeanette started the engine and turned the yacht towards the headland so as to meet Keith on his return journey return and so save a little time. Rodney Leon was not what she had expected at all. Denver had primed her to expect a killer, someone with the skills to take out a seasoned operative like Ronnier and make it look like an accident. Instead, Leon had turned out to be nothing more than a boy. She put him in his early to mid-twenties despite his size.

He was, she admitted, the most attractive male she had ever seen and his blue eyes and long lashes were truly remarkable, but she couldn't see a killer or a criminal mastermind in him at all. If anything, he was a bit naive and gauche. The way he'd walked down the beach, hid his shorts behind a tree, and then just swam for the yacht unprepared, unarmed, and nearly drowning himself in the process showed that.

He was no trained fighter either. If Ronnier had been any good at all, and she had no reason to think that Denver would employ anyone who wasn't, then the lad in the cabin wouldn't have stood a chance against him. After all, despite literally towering over her she had still managed to deck both him and his girlfriend. How glad she was that she had left her rubber soled deck shoes on when Leon had started to swim out. She had caught the girl with a peach of kick to the vag and felt the hard ridge of her shoe sole hit through to the pubic bone.

From the way the girl had shrieked as she went down, the kick must have been a lucky one and caught her right on the button. If that hadn't been fun enough, moments later she had felt the impact as her right instep met Leon's bollocks. That would teach him to turn his back on her to help his beautiful local tart. The temptation had just been too great to resist. The follow-up kick from the front was the cherry on the cake, how she'd enjoyed seeing the look of surprise and pain on his face when her foot slogged into his crown jewels for the second time. This was what S&M was all about, stuff role-plays.

She'd physically dominated them and soon she would dominate them mentally too. The anticipation of what lay ahead was already making her moist. Yes, a good morning's work and she looked forward to seeing the amazement on Keith's face when he finally returned and she told him what she'd achieved. She might even be in line for an apology from him; in fact she would demand one.

As she glanced over the top of the cockpit hood she saw the small tender around the headland with Keith sat in the stern of it. She started the engine and pressed button to start the winch drawing in the anchor and reversed towards where the anchor was lying. Once up, she wanted to close the gap between the yacht and the tender.

Jean Claude lowered the battered binoculars he normally used to spot shoals out at sea. He had once been proud of his eyesight but age, that cruel thief of a person's talents, had changed all that. Now he always sailed with the binoculars in the wooden stowage locker onboard. He passed them to Andy who watched the man stowing an inflatable tender aboard the yacht then talk with a blonde woman in the cockpit. After a few moments of arm waving discussion they dropped the anchor and the yacht swung out with the current. He lowered the binoculars noting the direction of the wind as he put them down.

"Could you lay me alongside that yacht using only the sail?" He received another one of those withering looks as Jean Claude switched off the outboard engine and quickly raised the small sail. With expertise that came from years of daily practise, the older man manoeuvred the dingy on wind and current and set a course that would lead towards the stationary yacht. A short distance away from the yacht he spilled the air from the sail and lowered it. The momentum of the dingy drifted it slowly in against the large inflated fenders dangling like huge fruit at the yacht's stern.

Andy took the painter and tied it to one of the cleats on the yacht and climbed aboard as silently as he could. He went to one side of the companionway and stood with his head cocked, listening. The couple were having a heated debate in the saloon but he could only catch snippets of it when they raised their voices or moved so the sound of their voices reached him more easily.

"But what are we going to do with the girl?" The man was asking, the woman replied but he couldn't catch what she said. Then the man spoke again, "But Leon might not tell us anything."

"He will," answered the woman and there was certainty in her voice. Andy had heard enough and silently began to descend to the saloon.

We were still lying on the bed facing each other when we felt the throb of the engine die away and heard the rattling sound of the anchor chain again. Moments later we also heard the muffled voices of a man and a woman the sound coming from the saloon area. I stood up from the bed and walked over to the cabin door to see if I could hear what they were saying.

"What's going on?" asked Joelle also rising to her feet. I raised my hand to show I was listening when suddenly we both heard the sound of fighting coming from the other side of the door. Joelle quickly came over to stand beside me at the door and we looked at each other with raised eyebrows then we both leaned in to listen at the door. The commotion only lasted a few seconds only to be followed by raised voices and then someone speaking quietly, then silence. Joelle turned to look at me again, I shrugged my shoulders, it was then that we heard the bolts sliding on the other side of the door.

Slowly the door swung open, we held our breath. Andy's grinning face confronted us. He held the door open and I followed Joelle out of our cell. Over the top of her head, I could see into the saloon and a man sat on one of bench seats clutching his chest. His face bore all the hallmarks of a run in with Andy. His lip was split and blood was still pumping from a nose which looked broken. Physically, he looked a bit older than the woman and had dark hair to her blonde but they were obviously a couple since both dressed in outfits that co-ordinated with the other. Newly married I guessed.

The woman stood a little apart from the seated man, her head turned away from him and towards the companionway. My eyes followed her gaze and I was amazed to see Uncle Claude stood halfway down the steps holding an ancient rifle which he had trained on the couple. He looked stern but I knew him well enough to recognise that he was as happy as I had ever seen him. It was clear that he was not only comfortable with Andy's talent for violence and mayhem, but that he actually approved of it.

"She has a gun…" I started to warn Andy but he lifted a black pistol to show he had already relieved her of it.

"And fast feet," added Joelle.

"N-No sw-sweat," replied Andy adding, "She's a-already t-tried that and she c-came off worst." I glanced down at the woman's legs and her right shin sported a nasty red weal surrounded by a large darkening bruise. I suddenly realised that it was not nerves that made Andy stammer but adrenalin, perhaps the two states amounted to the same thing in him.

"So what gives you the right to come to our Island and start kidnapping folks?" growled Jean Claude and he waved the barrel of the rifle towards the couple. He looked impressive and his voice resonated with authority. The man's head was still down with blood still pouring from his nose and on to the expensive upholstery which gave me a little lift. He was obviously still dazed from the beating Andy had given him so it was the woman who replied.

"This young woman was recovering from having drunk a little too much last night and we were about to drop her ashore when this young man swam out from the beach and boarded us of his own accord. Why don't you ask him what he's doing here?" I had to hand it to her, the voice was calm and firm, in fact the voice of a balanced and reasonable person.

"Bullshit," snorted Jean Claude, our self-appointed brief in the case of Islanders versus Outsiders and on the basis of the brief exchanges so far, he was doing a damned good job of it to. "We may be a small Island but we still have laws and you two have already broken enough to get you a decent spell on Raynauld."

"Where?" Retorted the woman and before Jean Claude could reply she seized the stage by continuing in that so reasonable voice of hers, but there was steel and determination in it. "I'll tell you what we are doing on St Gilberts. We are investigating the death and possible murder of a Belgium citizen named Philippe Ronnier. We have reason to believe that Rodney Leon, and maybe others in this cabin now, are implicated in Mr Ronnier's death."

I felt my stomach flip at her words and an unpleasant sense of apprehension course through me. The woman swung her gaze around the cabin looking at each of us in turn, it was neatly done. Joelle's and Jean Claude's faces must have registered complete incredulity; whereas I'm sure my facial expression exuded pure undiluted guilt. I glanced discreetly at Andy's face but his expression remained resolutely neutral.

"In fact we had intended to visit the Island Chief-of-Police today to discuss our suspicions with him," she continued. Then she reached into the breast pocket of her jacket.

"Steady," growled Jean Claude in warning; obviously he had watched too many TV detective serials. She slowly withdrew her hand which thankfully wasn't holding a mother-of-pearl handled Saturday Night Special, but a man's wallet. Holding it aloft with her right-hand she flipped it open with her fingers in a well-practised move to reveal what looked like an ID card.

Andy stepped forward and read aloud, "Jeanette Ryder, private investigator, Licensed Johannesburg, South Africa." The apprehension I'd felt seconds earlier now roared through my body like the sea through that break in the reef. In the case of the Islanders versus the Outsiders the Outsiders had just moved in front. I looked to Jean Claude, our self-appointed advocate, and saw his mouth open as he began to speak.

"You want to visit the Chief of Police, good, I'll tell my cousin to expect a visit from you, better still I'll take you to meet him myself." If I hadn't been watching the woman's reaction so closely, I would have missed the barely perceptible change in her demeanour. Suddenly, from being in command, she became less sure of herself, a little older perhaps and physically smaller in some indefinable way. Jean Claude picked up on it too.

"You're full of shit, lady. The police examined that case and know for a fact the man fell in an accident, pure and simple. So who sent you here and for what? Who's paying you to sail your fancy yacht all the way from South Africa to this little island of ours?" As he spoke Uncle Claude had lifted the barrel of the rifle to point straight at the seated man.

"What's the name of the person who sent you?" he asked again, only this time with a lot more emphasis in his voice. The seated man didn't even look up; he was well out of it. The woman looked around the saloon again, first at me then at Andy and then at Joelle, it was as if she was looking to us for support, she didn't receive any.

"WHO SENT YOU?" Roared Uncle Claude and he noisily drew back the bolt on the rifle and lifted the rifle to his shoulder as if he was about to shoot the seated man. I knew Jean Claude better than anyone else on that boat but in that moment even I wasn't sure if he was going to pull the trigger or not. I held my breath; I guessed we all held our breath, tense as we waited for the big bang. It seemed like an age and my lungs felt about to burst, but with each long second that passed I became more certain that Claude wasn't going to pull the trigger after all. The woman had clearly reached the same conclusion and gave a little nod as if to say that she knew the threat was nothing more than a bluff. She took a deep breath and began to speak.

"Look, you are not going to shoot that thing so why not put it down so we can talk?" Her voice was firm and reasonable again, obviously she thought that she now had the measure of us but Jean Claude's voice cut across the saloon before the echo from her words had died.

"Yeah in the same way you had no intention of going to the police. You're not interested in some accident that happened way back, what are you interested in? By the way, if you try anything then I will shoot you, or your husband, or the both of you. Is that clear?" She gave the barest nod of her head in reply.

"So what's there to talk about," asked Uncle Claude lowering the rifle from his shoulder but continuing to point it at the seated man. I thought that if he'd just point the rifle at the woman instead of her beaten husband, it might knock some of that infuriating self-confidence out of her.

"What do you know about the Valvaston?" It was as if the whole yacht reverberated at the mention of that name. I was almost beyond controlling any facial expression now, my mouth was dry and I felt light-headed and dizzy. Jean Claude's face and Joelle's could only have registered more bewilderment but before we could stop ourselves, Andy and I exchanged the briefest of eye contact but it was enough for the woman to notice it.

If Jean Claude was confused, there was no trace of it in his voice as once again he broke the silence following the woman's question.

"If you aren't going to answer my question of who sent you here and why, then you'll get nothing from us, lady. Just pull up your anchor and sail back to wherever you came from." As an afterthought, he added, "By the way, I know you filled up with fuel and water at the marina yesterday along with supplies. So there's no reason for you to even set foot on St Gilberts again." This seemed to put the woman off her stride I could see it in her face. Uncle Claude's knowledge of the couple's movements gave the impression that nothing took place on St Gilberts without it being public knowledge. This was not just an impression, basically it was true, and it obviously made the woman uncomfortable.

Uncle Claude knew they had refuelled and taken on water the previous day because he drank Baka at Toffies with Albert Raguin the marina owner, another man who pissed away his profits there.

"Look maybe we can work something out. We're prepared to pay for any useful information you can give us on the Valvast—"

Jean Claude cut her off in midsentence, "We're leaving this yacht now. Then we're going to watch you sail off, and if you don't sail off very soon then I'm going to start putting holes in the side of this fancy yacht of yours along the water line." His voice dropped lower and there was convincing menace in it.

"Don't even think of ever coming back if you value this boat or your own lives." The threat against the yacht clearly carried more impact for the woman than Jean Claude's earlier threat to shoot her husband because I saw her shoulders drop a little in capitulation—if that's the right word. Up to then we hadn't moved from the positions we had taken just after Andy released Joelle and me from the cabin. A bit like school kids in an end of year school play.

Now Joelle and I moved towards the companionway while Andy kept the couple covered with the pistol, not that he needed a weapon on current form. As Joelle came level with the woman she stepped towards her. The woman turned and gave Joelle a look of contempt that turned into another one of those sneers of hers. With impressive hand speed, Joelle's right fist shot out in a straight punch striking the woman full in the face.

Not for Joelle one those feminine slaps you'd see thrown in catfights in the Katcholo Club over straying boyfriends, or the neighbourly fallouts in the fish market. The woman's nose burst like a ripe plum under Joelle's fist and a shower of blood cascaded down her face, blouse and over the front of her white jacket. She slumped on to the bench seat beside her husband, who also still had his hand to his face. Together they sat like a couple of bookends—coordinated bookends.

I looked at Joelle and wondered that she had ever been bullied at school. Jean Claude gave a nod of approval and I saw Andy's eyebrows raised in surprise—or salute—I couldn't tell which. I was about to put my hands on Joelle's shoulders and steer her towards the companionway but she clearly had never needed steering by anybody in her life.

Andy was the last to board Jean Claude's dingy and cast off the painter as he stepped on. He removed the magazine out of the pistol then threw the empty pistol back onboard the yacht, emptied the clip of bullets into the sea and then threw the empty clip towards the cockpit and we heard it clatter around inside. Jean Claude got the outboard going and we headed back towards the break in the reef that I had swum through earlier. Before we reached it, Joelle spotted the yacht's anchor lifting clear of the water.

"I think you two have a lot of explaining to do," Jean Claude shouted above the noise of the underpowered engine.

Andy and I exchanged a brief look and both nodded at the same time before I replied, "OK but it's going to take some time. Let's sort ourselves out first then meet at my place around five."

We looked at Jean Claude who simply nodded in agreement before growling in disgust, "And for god's sake, Rodney, get some damned clothes on, you look a disgrace."

I looked down at my trunks and grinned but couldn't resist a dig back at him, "Don't think you need to bring that big cannon with you this evening, Uncle Claude." I nodded at the rifle propped against the side of the boat next to him. He scowled again and muttered something about ungrateful sods under his breath. Joelle turned to look at me and then at Andy.

"This story had better be good you two."

I gave a rueful smile. "After seeing the way you punch, I'd be afraid to disappoint you." She narrowed her eyes gave a mock stern look and raised a clenched fist. I had a few questions of my own and turned to Uncle Claude, "I didn't know I was related to Raymond Matine St Gilberts Head of Police."

"You're not," growled Claude curtly.

"But you said…"

"Yes I know what I said, but if some of those outsiders like to think that we are all inbred savages—if it helps—why bother to put them right? I could have said I was related to the President—she would have believed it."

"Then why didn't you?" I asked.

"If she'd said she was going to see him then I would have," he replied. "Anyway, the President was in my class at junior school."

"I didn't know that," I said genuinely surprised.

"There is a lot that you don't know about me," he mumbled back.

"Jeez, remind me never to play you at poker," I said and Claude just stared impassively back at me, *I rest my case* I thought.

Andy grinned and Joelle patted Claude on the back which brought a rare smile to his face and perhaps even set a personal record for him because it lasted for a whole half a second. Claude stopped the dingy just short of the beach at Anse Raffin so Joelle and I had to wade to the beach in thigh deep water. We watched him turn and set off for the break again. Andy stood with him in the stern he said he wanted to go Jean Claude's to pick up the Honda. He'd use it to return to my house later with Nahil. I recovered my shorts from behind the bush, shook the sand off them and put them on. Then we headed up the steep trail that led to the gate that gave access to my garden. Being the pervert I most surely am, I couldn't resist taking a few peeks up Joelle's billowing miniskirt at her peachy bum moving beneath the shiny white panties as she climbed up the trail ahead of me.

"Keep your eyes on the path," she commanded without even looking round. *Was I really so predictable*?

"Listen, my name is a byword for integrity on this island so I have no idea what you are on about," I shouted back up. She snorted at that but carried on climbing up without looking back so I sneaked another look. I was so happy I felt ready to explode in a combination of lust and love.

"Your garden is lovely," she said looking around at the colourful blooms. She walked up to the Allamanda and gently reached up to draw down one of the clusters of funnel-shaped yellow flowers.

"Who planned it?"

"My mother originally but Aunt Mert added her own touches and I've dabbled here and there," I replied.

"I approve of your dabblings," she said and I was sure there was a hint of something else in her voice, was she flirting with me?

"Well, in that case I'll just have to do some more dabbling," I replied. We both looked at each other and our smiles turned into laughter. We entered the relative cool of the house still chuckling and I put my hand around her waist and felt her lean into me. We walked towards the veranda, the sun was still fierce outside and I left her looking down at the turquoise and aquamarine colours of the lagoon below while I poured us long glasses of juice diluted with water. We must have both lost a couple of litres in sweat in our exertions on that bed on the yacht so we drank in dedicated silence both draining our glasses. I refilled them and we half drained them before putting them down on the low table. I showed her around the house, she had been in it before but that was years ago, when we got to the bedroom she asked if she could use the shower. I got her a clean towel quickly checking that I'd left the bathroom halfway respectable that morning and was about to leave the room so she could change in private when she started to speak to me so I stayed. Her muffled voice came through the material as she slid the black top over her head.

"Have you got anything that I could borrow to wear until I get home?"

"I guess I might have something in the wardrobe," I replied, not sure if I had anything that wouldn't bury her like a tent. She was still undressing and continuing to speak to me in a conversational tone.

"I'll wait outside," I offered but she shook her head.

"No it's OK Rodney it's your room," so I stayed put. I knew from our time together in the cabin that she was not wearing a bra and now her pert naked breasts jiggled as she unfastened the yellow miniskirt and let it slip to the floor. Her skin was the colour of golden amber and my eyes took in her exquisitely tiny waist following the curving lines as it flared out to wide full hips and a flat belly. Her legs were beautifully shaped and toned from walking up and down St Gilberts steep roads every day. I watched transfixed—if that's the word—until she finally bent over and peeled down the flimsy white panties before stepping out of them. She scooped up the panties with the other discarded clothes and wrinkled her face in disgust as if the pile contained the plague. She looked around the room before dropping them on the floor at the foot of the bed and stood looking down at them for a moment as if remembering something in the past. I wondered if old ghosts from the school playground were surrounding and taunting her again. Sensing the light mood we had shared moments before slipping away I reached into my wardrobe and pulled out from my collection of tee-shirts the most garish and tasteless one I could find. With a flourish I presented her with it. She blinked and came out of her reverie back to the present. She took the shirt from me and held it up staring in shock at the lurid colours. Then her eyebrows shot up and then down again into a frown, "Rodney Leon if you think I'd even be seen dead wearing this. I'd rather walk home naked than put that thing on." As if commanded to do so, I surveyed her naked body from her head to her feet taking in the dark triangle between her legs. St Gilberts women do not normally wax or shave down below, unlike many of the tourists I'd known, but Joelle was very neatly trimmed, I wouldn't have expected anything less from such a fastidious person. She let out a huffing noise and strode over to the wardrobe and selected a plain white tee-shirt.

"This will do—if that's OK with you?" She checked, I nodded and grinned. She started towards the bathroom and I watched the muscles of her buttocks as she walked. When she reached the door she turned to face me and I made a quick pretence of looking into the wardrobe again so as not to be caught gaping.

"Why don't you make yourself useful by joining me in the shower and rubbing my back?" She said and the smile on her face was anything but innocent.

I managed to rescue the fish Rodney had dropped off in what seemed like a lifetime ago, but was in fact only that same morning. With Joelle's help I made a spicy fish soup and rang Andy's home from my home phone Nahil answered almost immediately. Andy had obviously brought her up to speed on the events of the morning and she sounded put out that she had missed the excitement.

"I wish I'd seen Joelle punch that woman's lights out," she said delighted at the thought of the rough island justice Joelle had dished out. While she was on the line I asked her how she felt about Joelle and Jean Claude learning our secrets about The Belgian and the secret cavern. She had no problem with Joelle but she was not sure about Jean Claude. I guessed she was thinking about where Claude drank Baka and Toddy at Toffies, it was after all a popular hangout for some of the local police, including Paul Henri. After a moment's hesitation she said that she was OK with it.

"Jean Claude's not a blabber mouth even when he's pissed out of his skull—come to think of it I haven't even seen him pissed for a couple of years now," she said at last. I chuckled glad she was onboard and asked her to bring some bread along to eat with the soup. Meanwhile Joelle went through my shorts, tracksuit bottoms and finally my underwear in a search to find some clothing that would both fit and protect her modesty when she sat down. I thought that she might settle for a pair of boxer shorts but she chose a pair of trunk style briefs similar to the ones I had swum out to the yacht in. Impressed at how good they looked on her, I asked her to twirl around 360 degrees and we both laughed as she turned round and round like a music box figurine. The tee-shirt hid just how snug a fit they were because it came down to her knees.

The purr of the Honda's four-stroke engine coming down the driveway told me Andy and Nahil had arrived. Uncle Claude came on foot and arrived ten minutes later. We sat around the big table in the lounge and Nahil dug her elbow into Andy's ribs and then grinned across the table at me and Joelle. I knew she was grinning because Joelle was wearing my clothes and also because we were sat together as a couple. Nahil did not have a jealous bone in her body, unlike some of the other local women, in fact she had always been open in her admiration of Joelle's good looks, style and business success. I knew the two of them were going to get on. I made sure everyone had a drink in front of them. Andy, Nahil, Joelle and I opted for bottles of beer while Jean Claude commandeered the rum bottle. I placed the silver napkin ring on the table and watched as it went around the table. Andy and Nahil seemed happy to leave it to me to start off by telling the story of how we had watched the tsunami hit Al Solere from Kasper's Edge. I recounted how Andy and I had visited the beach the next day and discovered the secret chamber under the church at St Francis Mount and undertook a more detailed search of the chamber the following day with Nahil.

"Oh so you two have found that place as well," said Jean Claude and we turned to look at him in astonishment.

"Don't look so surprised, you surely didn't think that you were the only young people on the island who go exploring in places they shouldn't?"

"You've been in it as well?" I asked feeling deflated we were not the first discoverers of the secret chamber.

"No, but when I was not much older than you two," he said nodding towards Andy and then me, "I heard three local lads boasting that they had come across a secret chamber under the church at Al Solere. Word got around as it does and next thing the town priest went to the church with a couple of police officers to take a look inside the chamber. They found nothing of interest and since then the church has been locked up."

"By the way," I added after Jean Claude had finished speaking, "that padlock is still in place on the church door so we broke in. If we have to tell anyone about the napkin ring it's probably best to say that I found it on Al Solere beach instead of in the cavern."

Andy nodded in agreement and legitimised the fib, "Anyway, technically speaking you did find it on the beach; it just happened to b-be a b-bit of beach surrounded by the cavern wall. Besides, the whole church mount bit is on A-Al Solere beach isn't it?" They nodded agreement except for Claude whose poker face never changed. I went on to explain Andy's wrecker's theory as best I could.

"The whole village including the priest, showed false lights to lure ships on to the rocks so the villagers could plunder the wrecks." I asked Andy if he wanted to add anything but he just shook his head. Once again it was Uncle Claude, who had something to say.

"Yes I'd go along with that. The history of this island has passed from generation to generation by word of mouth in story form long before anybody thought to write it down. Those folks of Al Solere have always had a bad name, as if there was something not right about them, or the place, so I guess if anyone was going to be wreckers it would be them." Everyone looked to me to carry on from where I'd left off but Uncle Claude's revelation about the secret chamber had knocked me off my stride. I took a swig of beer followed by a deep breath and continued the second part of the story involving the Belgian man. Nahil and Andy chipped in when they had something to add to what I was saying and to give their own unique slants to the story. Finally the story reached the current day and the events that led me to swim out to the yacht. I explained why I believed both the Belgian man and the couple must have traced me through the internet enquiry I'd made in the Café in February when I searched the web for information on the Valvaston.

"Did you say February?" Asked Joelle so suddenly that everyone turned to look at her and then at me as they waited for my confirmation.

"Yes it was February why?"

"Well, that couple, the Ryders, the ones on the yacht, wanted to check the log entries for January and February to see if their friend had visited the café," she replied.

"What's this log business," Asked Claude who had never crossed the door of the café and to whom paperwork was something that only others did, those who had nothing better to do. Joelle quickly explained the purpose of the log books and how they were used.

"Then maybe the Belgian guy followed the same trail," said Andy picking up the thread and I couldn't help but notice how calm his voice now was; there was no trace of a stammer in it. That was unusual for Andy when speaking to a group with members he did not know well. He was obviously already comfortable with Joelle and Uncle Claude.

"Yes he visited the café as well," said Joelle. "I'll check with Julie tomorrow to see if he asked to check the log like the couple did. Oh—and by the way—yes; they could have traced your enquiry, they could have traced the computer identification number and its location at least as far as AirTalk—our internet service provider."

I noticed how she had tried to avoid computer jargon but Jean Claude was starting to scratch and shake his head.

"Now that Joelle and Uncle Claude know everything that has happened so far I am sure that you can both see why we kept it a secret among ourselves?" I said and they both nodded. "And, now that we are all up-to-date let's have something to eat before we get down to the next important thing which is what is going to happen next?" Everyone agreed with my suggestion.

We ate the soup and bread in dedicated silence. Joelle and I cleared away the dishes to the kitchen and then once again we all sat facing one another across a table clear apart from the drinks and the silver napkin ring. I looked at my glass which was nearly empty of beer and decided that I was ready for a tot of rum instead. I glanced towards the bottle in front of Jean Claude but he must have caught the direction of my glance because he quickly snatched up the bottle and tipped the last of its contents into his glass. He gave me a defiant look as he replaced the empty bottle back on the table. Well, I did owe him for rescuing me and I knew he wouldn't let me forget that.

I invited Andy to tell the group why he thought we had not heard the last on the Valvaston story. He replied in a clear calm voice with only an occasional trace of his usual stammer.

"For one, whatever was on this Valvaston it must be important enough for the three people we know of so far to have travelled around the world to come here looking for it. The B-Belgian travelled from Europe, the couple, those p-private investigators, were sailing a sixty-two foot Hallberg Rassey you'd get no change from a couple of m-million quid for one of them! The Belgium had an accident which killed him and the couple have sailed off into the sunset never to return—we hope. Not one of them got what they came for—the whereabouts of this Valvaston ship." He pointed down to the silver napkin ring on the table.

"I believe both the B-Belgian and the couple were working for someone else. The woman said as much when Jean Claude asked who sent them. That's why I think more will come out following the same trail." I looked around the table and everyone was silent in thought. Jean Claude, whose English was better than I thought was following the proceedings keenly, now he broke the brief silence.

"So what are you suggesting, that we just sit back and wait for them to make the next move?" I liked the "We" bit, Uncle Claude had obviously decided if there was to be any more action then he wanted a piece of it.

"I'm not suggesting anything just yet, I'm asking for ideas," I replied. Andy immediately came up with one.

"Do you remember me saying I had a friend who's into maritime history?" I had to think for a second then remembered our get together on the day the Belgian had gone off Kasper's Edge.

"Yes," I said at last. "The one who was in the Marines with you?"

"Yes that's the one," he replied, "well I did call him and he said he'd see what he could find out. Maybe it's time to chase him up maybe tell him my need for the info had just got urgent."

"I didn't know you were in the Marines," said Jean Claude and from his expression I guessed Andy had just risen even higher in his estimation.

"Yes I'll tell you about it sometime," replied Andy.

"I'll see what I can find out about the Valvaston on the web," offered Joelle.

"Won't that bring more trouble?" Asked Nahil and I could see where she was coming from after all it had been my internet search that kicked all this off in the beginning. Joelle nodded to show she had already considered that as a possibility.

"If Rodney's enquiry was traced to the Kokonet Café then it's already the first point of call for any further visitors. It will make no difference if I do another, more comprehensive search."

"I can help you with that," I volunteered, she smiled at me and nodded. Out of the corner of my eye I caught sight of Nahil grinning again.

"What else should we be doing and what can I do?" Said Jean Claude obviously determined to be involved. Andy was the first to respond.

"Well, for a start Jean Claude you are the only one here who visits Toffies so you're main source of information on what the police are up to in their enquiries into the Belgian's death."

"They aren't enquiring anymore, that's the answer to that one," Jean Claude said shortly. Andy continued without missing a beat.

"And we need to make sure that the couple in their yacht really have sailed off and not just dropped anchor again around the back of the island. Jean Claude you know all the fishermen on St Gilberts." Jean Claude nodded. "One of them at least, would notice a strange yacht on anchor away from the marina." Jean Claude nodded slightly in agreement and then grunted something about keeping his ears open. I suddenly had another idea.

"About that secret chamber, I'd be interested to know what those three lads, though I guess they'd be old..." I saw Claude's brow draw down and quickly rephrased, "They'd be grown men by now. I wonder what they found in the chamber. When we got there, the tsunami had already churned everything up."

Claude grunted again and then rumbled, "I do see them from time-to-time though I don't know how I'd bring up the subject without it looking suspicious?"

"Good point," I conceded and then added as an afterthought, "Speaking of security, watch out everyone when Dan Meme is around; he's as sharp as a knife and will pick up immediately on anything unusual going on. He's a Toffies man as well." I looked at Jean Claude to make sure my point went home. Joelle waited until everyone was quiet before asking Andy a question.

"Andy, this friend of yours, the one in the UK, where will he be looking to find his information on this Valvaston ship?" Andy sat up straight and put his hands on the table as if that somehow helped him to think more clearly.

"Well, without asking him I am not really sure but I guess he'll visit, or at least phone, places like Lloyds Registry of Shipping, The National Maritime Museum, The East India Company Office Library..." He had been counting them off on the fingers of one hand and frowned as he tried to think of some more likely places, after a few more seconds of frowning in concentration he finally shrugged and opened out his hands in defeat. "And other places like that I guess." I looked at Joelle, she had asked for a reason and I was interested to know what that reason was.

"What's on your mind, Joelle?" I asked.

"Well, I think it's just as important to know who's on our case as it is to know what's so special about the Valvaston. If someone else has been doing research on the Valvaston then they would have left a trace just like Rodney did. There'll be a signature in a museum visitor's log, the name of a lender of a book or the name of someone requesting documents and stuff. Whoever sent those people out to St Gilberts must have trod the path that your friend in England is going to take on his search. Why not ask him to check who else is showing an interest in the Valvaston as he goes along?"

"Great idea," agreed Andy.

"I'll call him tomorrow. I think you're spot on, the list of people interested in an obscure sailing ship that sank hundreds of years ago is not going to be very long is it?"

"Smart girl," said Jean Claude approvingly and I turned in surprise to see him looking at Joelle with open admiration and felt a sense of pride on her behalf. I looked across towards the veranda, the sky was getting as the sun fell lower on the horizon. Jean Claude had noticed it to and started to stand. He must have been thinking about his walk home in the dark and the steep track leading down to his shack. It was either that or fact the rum was finished.

"OK," I said, "why don't we all meet up again at the same time next week and share what we've found out?" Everyone agreed and Jean Claude turned to leave, I offered him a lift on my bike but he said he'd feel safer on foot. I didn't know if he was casting doubt on my ability to ride the bike or on the bike itself but I was glad, I didn't fancy bouncing down that track with Jean Claude riding pillion.

Andy and Nahil stayed back to chat and share a few more drinks. When Andy went into the kitchen to look for another beer I followed him in and asked him if he would teach me a few moves of self-defence when he got the time. He readily agreed as I knew he would and he suggested I call around his house any time the following day. I hate violence but recent events had shown me it's not always possible to avoid it. I remembered my humiliation at the feet of the blonde woman, literally. Indeed I could hardly forget it as my delicate parts were still swollen and tender from the two kicks the woman had given me, a fact confirmed during my shower with Joelle. She'd joked that she liked the effect of the swelling as it made them look even bigger but I knew her humour was a brave attempt to neutralise the bad memory of what had happened to us on the yacht. She also felt twinges of pain below and I had seen the angry bruise where the hard edge of the blonde woman's shoe had cut into the flesh between her legs. None of this, however, had prevented us from engaging in a round two follow-on from our yacht cabin get-together. The second session began in the shower and continued atop a couple of towels strewn on the bed. It was gentle and loving unlike the frenzy of round one and lasted much longer as well, it was unlike anything I had experienced before. Afterwards as we lay together on the bed I offered to tell her what I knew about the Valvaston, this was all before the meeting, but she said she'd wait for the meeting to hear all about it. We discussed what to tell the others about our experience aboard the yacht and both agreed to say little as little as possible. We'd both been tricked into entering the cabin and had ended up being locked up inside, that was all we needed to say. It was the truth with some details omitted. Joelle confided that she thought she'd been drugged the previous night onboard the yacht. She was not a big drinker of alcohol but had enough experience of it to know it shouldn't have left her in such a state so quickly. What's more she had no recollection of her night aboard the yacht apart from boarding it and sitting down in the saloon. Nothing at all, for example, on how had she had ended up in the cabin and what, if anything, had taken place when she was in there? She had no answer to those questions but sensed that she had been abused in some way by the couple when she was out cold.

When Andy and Nahil rose to leave I offered them the spare room to stay overnight but Nahil gave me a cheeky smile and said that they had to get home. Andy was too pissed to chance the Honda but luck was on their side, as I walked with them up the driveway to the road we heard a bus coming down the hill. Running the rest of the way up they managed to flag it down and clamber aboard. When I got back to the house Joelle was in the kitchen, dish cloth in hand finishing off the dishes and glasses. I stood behind her and wrapped my arms around her.

"Am I useful or what?" She joked.

"So useful I don't want to let you go." I agreed and she turned in my arms and looked up into my face.

"I mean it, Joelle, I want you here living with me and I'll do whatever it takes to make you want it to."

She smiled up at me, "I already do want it," and that was it. When I'd woken that morning, Joelle was out of my league and beyond my grasp, now in only five words she had agreed to live with me. Up to that point, the little silver napkin ring had brought me only bad luck; now, it had brought me the best luck of all—it had brought me Joelle.

Richard Denver picked up the phone and heard Jeanette Ryder's voice at the other end of the line.

"Good morning Mr Denver how are you this morning?"

"Is this a progress report?" He asked ignoring her greeting.

"Well, yes it is. We have gone as far as we can on this one Mr Denver so this is a report on what we have done so far and so it is our final report."

"It's also your first." Denver reminded her tersely unable to conceal the disappointment from his voice.

"You asked us to undertake a confidential mission to find who entered your web site seeking information on the Valvaston to question them and find out what they already knew about it. We succeeded as regards the first part of the mission but not the second. St Gilberts is a small place Mr Denver and it's impossible for visitors to avoid notice the instant they set foot on the island. Most of the islanders are related to one another in some way so it's difficult, bordering on impossible, to elicit information without raising widespread suspicion."

"I thought I was employing you for that very talent," said Denver not bothering to disguise the bitterness in his voice.

"Point taken, but you were also employing us for our expertise and judgement. We have not left the Island empty-handed and I can offer a suggestion as to how you might take things forward from here." She waited for her words to sink in and heard Denver's breathing pattern change when he spoke the tone of his voice sounded more upbeat.

"I'm listening." She smiled to herself before continuing.

"You told me that Ronnier traced the Valvaston enquiry to the internet café on St Gilberts—the Kokonet Café. We can now tell you the man who made that enquiry is Rodney Leon, a young man in his early to mid-twenties. Although Leon looks a bit of a beach bum he lives in one of the most beautiful and expensive homes on the island. His girlfriend is a young woman named Joelle Kelly who also happens to be the owner, and manager, of the Kokonet Café."

"Did they kill Ronnier?" interrupted Denver.

"I can't say for certain, the local police have closed the case listing it as an unfortunate accident. Personally I don't think Leon's a murderer, he's certainly not the sort who could stage a killing to look like an accident."

"You've actually met this Leon then," Asked Denver, his voice betraying rising excitement.

"Yes I have that's how I'm so sure he's not a killer. He swam out to our yacht."

"He what?"

"Yes he swam out to us. We befriended Joelle Kelly, the manager of the internet café, and invited her on to our yacht for a friendly drink in the hope of carefully eliciting some information about the island and what she knew about Rodney Leon. Then we had no idea of her relationship with Leon. The next thing we knew Leon was swimming out to the yacht to check what his girlfriend was doing with us."

"How extraordinary. What's he like?" asked Denver.

"Oh he's young like I said, and tall, about six and a half foot, striking in looks and a local lad, he is Creole going by his skin colour but with mixed blood. He's got unusual aqua-blue eyes so somewhere in both his parents ancestry there's some blue-eyed Caucasian genes. His hair is a little straighter than the average local to. Though he's physically big he is not violent or combat trained. In fact he comes across as fairly inoffensive even simple…no, not simple, that's the wrong word; he's…er…unsophisticated—that's it, he is an unsophisticated local boy who speaks English well."

"So you reckon there's no way he could have taken Ronnier out?"

"No not him but he does have some interesting friends. One is white and, from his accent, I'd say British. He is shorter, five seven or eight and I heard Leon call him Andy presumably short for Andrew. Now, I suspect he is capable of killing someone even a professional like Ronnier and I'd take a guess that he could make it look like an accident to."

"I take it you've met him as well?" queried Denver.

"Yes he followed a little after Leon had boarded us. Presumably he thought Leon might need some back up because came out to the yacht in a wooden dingy with an older man armed with a rifle."

"He did what?" Denver sounded incredulous.

"The one they call Andy physically attacked my husband and me while the older man, a local, threatened to shoot us if we didn't reveal who'd sent us and why."

"I hope your injuries were nothing too serious," ventured Denver his voice failing to register any concern.

"Broken noses, both of us, along with many other assorted bruises. The older man kept his rifle trained on us so we were unable to defend ourselves."

"Bloody cowards," sympathised Denver, adding, "Was there any mention of the Valvaston?"

"Well, you will appreciate that we were not in the strongest of bargaining position, however, as a diversion and to move things along I took a chance and casually mentioned the name Valvaston. I got a noticeable reaction from both Leon and the Englishman, I'm certain the name meant something to them. As for the older man and the girl—Joelle Kelly, both looked genuinely baffled when I mentioned the name. Unless they are the better actors than I give them credit for, I'd say the name meant nothing to them."

"But you say it did mean something to Leon and this Englishman, the one called Andy?"

"Yes, from their reaction I'm certain of it. I told them we'd pay money for information on the Valvaston, they weren't interested and just clamed up. Don't forget they had the upper hand."

"Please tell me you never mentioned my name," said Denver and there was an underlying threat in his voice.

"Of course not," Jeanette Ryder protested. He had insulted her and the indignation in her voice carried genuine conviction.

"The old man pointed his rifle at Keith and threatened to shoot him if we didn't tell who had sent us. We refused and for a second it looked as if it could all go nasty but thank god he was bluffing. We've built our reputation on client confidentiality, once that's gone we're as good as finished. Confidentiality and a reputation for getting results are the only reason clients use us again and again and refer us to others." Denver grunted in acknowledgement—and to cut short the woman's public relations spiel.

"You said you had a suggestion for a way forward."

"Yes, the sense of community on St Gilberts effectively rules out any infiltration by outsiders. What you need is someone working on the inside for you, a member of the community, someone who has social status and the power to go with it." Jeanette Ryder paused for a second before continuing.

"Do you know much about the company Carlten SA Limited?"

"No."

"Well, we have been doing some research into your network of companies, and Carlten SA Limited is one of your South African based company's. It is also the main buyer of construction materials from a company called Ramatec?"

"No, I didn't know that either. Why…?" said Denver starting to feel a shade uncomfortable.

"Well, Ramatec is also the main supplier of building materials to many of the smaller Islands in the mid and southern Indian Ocean, including St Gilberts. Virtually all the building materials contracts with St Gilbert run through one man on the island, St Gilberts Minister for Construction and Public Works. It's a big title for a man with not that much to do, we've checked. This official thinks his position of control over the Island's construction budget also gives him the authority to demand backhanders from Ramatec to ensure he continues to push orders their way. His name is George Ferrari and I'm sure you could persuade him to apply a little pressure on Leon to tell you what he knows." Jeanette Ryder could almost hear the cogs turning in Denver's brain in the silence that came down the line.

"OK, I'm impressed, but how the hell did you find out all this?" Asked Denver.

"It's what you employed us for," she reminded him, in a mild rebuke for his earlier comment.

"I can't reveal my sources but you can rely on the information I have just given you. As I said, confidentiality is important to us and that applies to our informants as well."

"I see," he replied. "Then let me thank you for your work so far. Please adjust your invoice to increase the amount to reflect the personal inconvenience and injury that both you and your husband have suffered on this assignment."

"It's already on its way," she said. The conversation over, Denver replaced the phone as he sat back in his chair to think.

He had reached another of those decision points. Was it time to give up or to push on? Denver knew there was only one answer to that question. At heart he was still more treasure hunter than businessman. When he had searched for, and discovered the Levia containing the largest haul of gold and silver coins ever found, it had not been about profit. The wealth it gave him was a spin-off and, to him, incidental. Searching for shipwrecks fit his personality, his love of gambling and his tendency to dream. He had a passion for quests and an innate bloody-mindedness that drove him to take on what others regarded as difficult or impossible. The prospect of finding the wreck of the Valvaston was currently the only thing in life he was genuinely excited and optimistic about. Denver was a historian and an adventurer, entering a sunken wreck was not only exciting on a physical level it was also like floating into a time capsule. It felt as he had somehow floated back through the centuries and was experiencing life in another period.

Denver's business partner, Gerald Carr, would have had no problem in deciding if the quest for the Valvaston was worth pursuing, he would have abandoned it at the onset. But Denver was not Carr; in Denver's mind there was still hope of finding the wreck.

Both Ronnier and the Ryders had established there was a link between the lost ship and St Gilberts. Denver had unearthed the ship's manifest in the National Maritime Museum. From it he had discovered the Valvaston carried only one passenger and its cargo consisted of cotton, linen, spices and tea, all of which would have perished centuries ago. The only item of intrinsic value aboard the ship that could have withstood the passage of time and immersion in the sea for so long was the blue diamond. If Rupert Stillwood-Hamilton had kept the stone stored in a container perhaps a casket, preferably made of bronze or some other inert metal there was a slim chance of finding it within a wreck. A lot would depend on whether the ship had remained intact when it went down, and whether it grounded at a reasonable depth for salvage work to take place on it. For there to be even a remote possibility of recovering the diamond he would need to be the luckiest person in the world. Denver could not believe that a young beach bum, if that's what Leon was, would be able to carry out even a rudimentary salvage operation on a sunken wreck. In fact he doubted the knowledge and the necessary equipment existed anywhere in the Gilberts Island group. Besides, even if they had found the diamond what could they do with it? For one, the sale of a blue diamond of that size would soon arouse interest around the world no matter how secretly the sale took place. Yet according to Jeanette Ryder young master Leon appeared to be wealthy even though, according to Jeanette Ryder he didn't look to have been raised with money. He had a big house, but then, with the money he would have made from Stillwood-Hamilton's stone he could have bought the whole island, or better still, bought a palatial property in a developed and civilised country. It just didn't add up.

He sighed and called his secretary in, "Can you get me John Maynard on the phone please."

Five minutes later his phone rang and when he picked it up, his secretary simply said, "John Maynard on the line for you" and put him through. Denver smiled he and John went back a long way and knew each other when Denver was still a struggling owner of a ragtag marine salvage company. In those days he had not only been Denver's friend but he had also acted as his legal adviser on marine matters. They had drifted apart since Denver had literally struck gold with the Levia but Denver had paid Maynard generously for his help in securing his treasure trove and there was no animosity or resentment between them.

"Hi John long time no see, how are things?"

"Fine Richard, and you?"

"Can't complain, but I often wish I was back in the old marine salvage business again they were good days. Oh, how's Mary and the kids by the way? Those two lads of yours must be big by now."

"Yes they are and Mary's just fine, thanks for asking. So Richard, you're missing the excitement of the old days? Don't forget we were both a bit younger in those days Richard I'm not sure I could stand all that running about and diving in cold water now," said Maynard wondering when the pleasantries would end and Denver was going to reveal the real reason behind his call.

"Not that much younger," corrected Denver. "Look, I'd like you to find out the legal situation on territorial waters surrounding St Gilberts in the Indian Ocean. I'll pay whatever your current rates are of course."

"No need for that Richard."

"No I insist John—you know I always valued your professional advice as well as your friendship." Maynard's eyebrows rose at that but his voice remained even as he took the details from Denver before replacing the phone.

Two hours later John Maynard rang Denver back with the information he'd asked for.

"With respect to the territorial waters surrounding St Gilbert and all the islands that fall within its legal jurisdiction," Maynard began formally, "the government of St Gilberts claim the following." Maynard coughed to clear his throat before continuing.

"The Government of St Gilberts by the power invested in it by the people of St Gilberts claim exclusive rights over all wrecks lost within its territorial waters. By the way, they consider their territorial water to extend to 19.3 kilometres or twelve miles. In effect they have adopted the same exclusive rights approach as China and the Philippines." Denver took notes as he listened before replying,

"Thanks John, we'll have to get together sometime and catch up."

"Love to Richard, just call me and we'll arrange something." John Maynard would have been surprised to learn that his old colleague had been serious about that drink.

The next call Denver placed was to George Ferrari in St Gilberts after several abortive tries his secretary finally managed to connect him through and Denver found himself speaking to Ferrari on a surprisingly clear line.

"Hello Mr Ferrari my name is Richard Denver I am not sure if you have heard of me or not." There was a moment of silence then he heard a man breathing heavily at the other end of the line before he received a response.

Mr Ferrari spoke in accented English, "Er no I don't believe I have."

"Well, I own companies in Europe, North America, South America and South Africa, and Asia." Denver listed the names of several international organisations and then paused for a second to let the information to sink in. Ferrari sat straighter in his chair. Denver sensed both the physical and mental shift of the listener. He had the man's full and undivided attention so he continued.

"As well as my business interests I am also a historian with a real passion for marine archaeology and maritime history. Currently I am researching the background to a seventeenth century ship that may have sunk off St Gilberts somewhere and I am trying to find out where. The ship, outward bound from India was making for England with a cargo of tea, cotton and spices. The ship never reached its destination and I am trying to trace what happened to it." Ferrari was confused, not only by the other's strange accent and rapid speech, but also why Denver had rung him at all.

"Very interesting Mr…?"

"Denver."

"Oh yes sorry, Mr Denver, but I don't see what any of this has to do with me."

"Mr Ferrari, I own a company in South Africa called Carlten Sa Ltd, it is the main buyer of construction materials from a company called Ramatec who in turn supply most of the building materials to St Gilberts. I believe you know that already, Mr Ferrari. It may seem a tenuous link to you but it is a link between us nevertheless and I always like to do business with people I know something about." Ferrari's initial confusion at Denver's call now slid to bewilderment and a growing sense of unease. It came down the line in the tone of his voice.

"Business? Link? What do you know about me? I'm afraid that I am still not sure why you have called me, Mr Denver, or indeed, how I can help you." Ferrari had just provided the cue that Denver had been waiting for.

"Mr Ferrari, I understand what makes the wheels of business run smoothly, I apply the same principles to my personal interest in maritime history. I am calling you from the UK because I need someone on St Gilberts to obtain some information for me and I am prepared to pay whoever supplies it to me, very handsomely. You are the first person on St Gilberts I have approached and that is simply because I came across your name through the connection I mentioned earlier. If you are not interested, or cannot obtain the information, then I will pay someone else who can and will." When Ferrari spoke Denver could hear the note of interest in his voice.

"Perhaps you should tell me what information you want and how much you are prepared to pay for it."

Denver nodded to himself and replied, "I want to trace the whereabouts of a wrecked ship, the one I mentioned earlier. I believe someone on St Gilberts already knows where it is but so far this person has kept the knowledge to himself. If you could find some way of persuading him to part with that information then I am prepared to pay you five thousand US dollars or the equivalent in any currency you choose." Denver heard Ferrari cough at the other end of the phone line.

"Five thousand dollars for information about a worthless wreck seems a bit too generous to me."

"Perhaps it is but I also have conditions, to be agreed before I disclose both the name of the vessel and the person I believe has the information on its whereabouts. The conditions are that my name and the nature of my enquiry will not be mentioned at any time. Second; the name of the wreck must not be repeated to anyone other than to the local person whose name I will supply if you agree." There was silence down the line but Denver waited giving the other man chance to think.

At last Ferrari replied, "OK, assuming I accept your offer how do I know after I provide you with the information you won't forget to pay me?"

"Mr Ferrari, getting the information will, I think, not be too difficult; what I am really paying for is your confidentiality. If I don't pay you then I won't be sure of your confidentiality will I?"

Ferrari avoided the implied question and replied with one of his own, "Why the secrecy? Is this wreck associated with anything illegal or dangerous?"

"Absolutely not; it sank over three hundred years ago with a perishable cargo. The fact of the matter is that I am a high-profile personality followed everywhere and every time I step out of my house by the press and others—particularly those in the marine salvage business and, quite frankly, it drives me nuts. I can't even pursue a personal interest—or hobby—if you like without being followed every inch of the way by some goon trying to stick a camera in my face."

There was another pause down the line before Ferrari asked his next question and Denver heard wariness in the other's voice. "Just out of interest, because of course, if I accepted your conditions I would not break any of them, but how could you sure of my continued silence after you have paid me?" Denver's voice was conversational but there was no mistaking the warning it carried.

"Mr Ferrari, you are also a high-profile and respected public figure, at least on St Gilberts. An Island I've heard where news travels fast and everyone knows everyone's business. I know how important your reputation for honesty must be to you and how you would do anything to make sure that it is not damaged in anyway. That being the case I have no hesitation in trusting you to meet the conditions I've set should you accept my offer." Ferrari waited, holding his breath in silent dread, he knew from the other's tone there was more to come and that he wasn't going to like it when it came.

"Besides, Mr Ferrari, we both have mutual friends at Ramatec who have assured me of your ability to keep a secret. Do you understand my meaning?"

Ferrari understood all too clearly, Denver knew about the backhanders he'd been taking from Ramatec for years and would use the knowledge against him if he stepped out of line. Ferrari's voice was flat and empty of any emotion when he replied, "OK I accept. Give me the name of the ship and the local with the info."

"The ship is the Valvaston and the name of the local man is Rodney Leon."

"Right foot back, lift the heel slightly and keep your hands higher, is your wrist straight? Now again, but I want it a lot faster this time and aim a little lower." Andy watched as I practised the same blocks and punches over and over again until my arms felt as if they were going to drop off. We were at his house standing in his back garden close to the boat shed and near the beach. He was putting me through another afternoon of combat training. Nahil stood on the patio area close to the house watching, mostly giggling, though at times doubling up with laughter. Sometimes she disconcertedly went quiet and when I looked back she'd be mimicking my moves with a big grin on her face as she joined in the lesson.

"Won't it take years of dedicated practice before this is of any use?" I asked looking for an excuse to pack in but Andy assured me if I learnt just one or two moves until they became instinctive, I'd be a force to reckon with.

"First we need to build muscle memory so the reaction is automatic."

"How long will that take; we've already been at this for hours?"

"Fifteen minutes," contradicted Nahil. I shook a fist at her and she shook one back.

"Just a little more muscle on that frame of yours and you'd be awesome," said Andy, adding, "But bloody hell, Rodney! That hand speed of yours is pathetic—perhaps it's your height. Those arms and legs of yours are so long it must take longer for the message from the brain to reach your hands and feet. If you and Joelle ever have a row, she'd make mincemeat of you with that killer right-cross punch of hers. It'd be on your snout before your guard was even halfway up." He stood back and looked at me appraisingly.

"With your size, that stubble and those piercing m-mince pies..."

"What?"

"M-Mince pies, cockney rhyming slang for eyes; look, never mind. At least you look a tough handful, Rodney, and sometimes that's enough. If we bump into any trouble, you scare 'em and I'll hit 'em." This and other attempts at encouragement even had me joining him on some of his early morning jogs along the beach.

It was almost a week after the yacht couple had locked Joelle and me in one of their cabins followed by the meeting at my house on the same day. A lot had changed in my life since then. The biggest change was Joelle moving in with me.

She brought so many clothes I found my stuff pushed out of the wardrobe and the cupboard draws so I had to find space in the wardrobes and cupboards in the spare rooms. A new batch of female tourists landed on the island but now that I was with Joelle I felt no temptation at all to slip back into my old ways. Mornings were for combat training and jogging, in the afternoon I helped Joelle at the Kokonet Café. On two afternoons I joined Andy fishing. These activities all helped to distract me from the fact I still lacked a sense of where I was going in life. At times I felt as if I were living in the slipstream of Joelle and Andy's lives. Once Julie understood that I was not after her job at the Café we got on really well. She had only known me by reputation before, that reputation not being a good one. However once she'd got over her disappointment that I wasn't the demon everyone had painted me to be, and she realised we both shared a similar sense of humour, everything went smoothly. I often covered for her when she had to leave the counter for any reason. Joelle's internet searches were turning up bits of information on Indian Ocean shipwrecks in general but nothing specific on the Valvaston. I had no idea what uncle Claude had been doing since the day of the rescue but Andy told he expected a call from his mate in England in the next couple of days. Our second meeting was due to take place the following evening.

I had left the Kokonet and was heading towards the museum, because it had occurred to me earlier there may be some useful leads in the old documents stored there, especially the ancient Creole ones relating to Al Solere. As I walked I remembered the school lesson the teacher told us about Marcel Leste's account of the night he escaped the tsunami. Suddenly the large portly figure of George Ferrari stepped in front of me blocking my way. Startled, I stumbled slightly as I tried not to walk into him. My mind, now back in the present, I was about to apologise in a reflex response but then I stayed silent and simply smiled at the man. I knew of Ferrari rather than knew him. He was some big wheel in the St Gilberts Island government, big deal I thought; St Gilberts government was hardly Washington. Ferrari was a big fat fish in a tiny rock pool. Does he think he's so important that all lesser mortals should step aside when he walks through town? I gave a theatrical sigh of resignation and made to walk around him but he stretched out his arm to block me.

"Ah, Rodney, have you got a moment," he asked in a surprisingly pleasant voice. A little dazed by the unexpected interruption I let him lead me to one of the street benches under the shade of a spreading Geiger tree.

"Do you know who I am, Rodney?" he asked peering up at me through thick lenses spectacles.

"Yes, you're Mr Ferrari; you work for the government."

"That's right, Rodney, I'm the Minister for Construction and Public Works." Was I supposed to say wow or something? Instead I looked back at him with an expression that made it clear I had yet to be impressed.

"I'd like to ask you a question, Rodney, and I want you to answer it absolutely honestly, is that clear?"

"Fire away," I said confidently enough though I was starting to feel the first tentacles of apprehension sliding their way through my gut and yet I was still intrigued to hear what he was about to say to me.

"Rodney," he said in a low serious voice looking directly into my eyes through those glass pebble specs of his, "tell me what you know about the Valvaston."

The name hit me like a jolt of electricity that scrambled my thoughts for a second. With recognition and shock surely written clear across my face, I gathered my wits and replied with a limp, "What?" It was said as I composed my features with an effort. "The Val-ston what?" Out of my many guises I had fallen back on an old favourite; youthful innocent and ignorance with just a dash of stupidity thrown in. But Ferrari wasn't buying it.

"I think you know that name very well, Rodney, and I'm going to ask you again; tell me what you know about the Valvaston."

However, since I had chosen ignorance as my defence I felt obliged to continue with it. What I really wanted to do was get away from this unwelcome inquisitor as fast as I could to somewhere quiet to try and workout what was going on. I remained seated and replied as convincingly as I was able.

"Seriously, I don't know what you are talking about. What is this Valvaston thing anyway?" He continued to look up at me in that disturbing way of his and in moment of defiance I locked my eyes on to his and let my focus bore through the thick lenses and into his eyes. The irises of his eyes were so dark they merged into the black of the pupils giving them an inhuman quality that was unnerving. However when it comes to eyes I can do unnerving as well as anyone, and better than most. After a few seconds of staring each other out I had the satisfaction of seeing him break off and make a show of checking his wristwatch.

"Well, I'm sorry you have decided to take that approach, Rodney, I had hoped that you were going to be more cooperative, but we'll see, we'll see." He got up and walked off leaving me confused, shaken and with a sense of foreboding that something awful was going to happen. Instead of carrying on to the museum, I doubled back to the Kokonet Café and gave a sigh of relief to see Joelle there. I led her to the office and shut the door behind us I recounted my meeting with Ferrari to her.

"Do you think Jean Claude has let anything slip at Toffies?" She asked.

"I don't know," I replied. "I guess that's something we should bring up at our meeting tomorrow evening."

"Yes," she agreed. "But it is worrying all the same. We don't know what Ferrari is going to do and we don't know who else, if anyone, he's working with." Joelle was right, and once again I felt again the tentacles of fear coiling in my stomach.

George Ferrari walked thoughtfully away from his brief meeting with Rodney Leon. Although he hadn't got the information Denver wanted the meeting had gone much as expected and he had learnt something. The look of recognition and shock on the boy's face on hearing the word Valvaston had been almost comical. The name clearly meant something to him. He had seen Leon about town but had never met him up close or spoken to him before. Close up the lad was a giant and though he couldn't control his facial expressions he was certainly no pushover. Richard Denver had confided that the person with the information, meaning Leon, had kept the information to himself. What had he meant by that?

Ferrari could only assume that Denver had already sent others to ask Leon the same question and they'd come away empty-handed. Ferrari wondered what pressure, if any, they'd used on the lad. Ferrari cursed himself for not demanding more than the five thousand US dollars Denver had offered. Nevertheless, he consoled himself with the knowledge that if he asked for payment in Euros, he could probably quadruple its value by exchanging it for Gilberts Island rupees on the black market. The job of getting the information wasn't going to be as straightforward as Denver suggested.

Ferrari had an aunty who ran a vegetable stall on the market and earlier that morning he had asked her a few casual questions about Leon. He'd discovered Leon normally lived alone but had recently paired up with a local girl, the one who ran the Kokonet Café and that she was now living with him in his house.

"About time that young man settled down and stopped running with all them white girls," his aunt had said shaking her head. "Made poor Mert tear her hair out with shame." There were few secrets on St Gilberts, thought Ferrari, and pondered what his aunt had said. By 'white girls' she was obviously referring to tourists. Had Master Leon been indulging in the island hobby of illegal money exchange? He walked into St Gilberts small police station and the activity inside surprised him. He discovered from the burly duty officer, Paul Henri, a dispute between two families the previous night had resulted in key members of the warring neighbours filling the station's four cells. Ferrari had learnt that later, when he had first walked into the station Henri had lifted his sweating face from a report he was writing and then immediately straightened when he saw who was approaching the desk.

"Hello Mr Ferrari, how can I help you?"

"Have you a room where we can talk in private?" Ferrari asked.

After my meeting with Ferrari, I felt restless. The shock alone had caused adrenalin to flood my body leaving me too restless to settle down in front of a computer screen in the Café. It was a relief when Julie said goodbye for the day and it was time to help Joelle log off the computers and lock the place up.

She sat behind me on the pillion of the Honda and complained, not for the first time, "Rodney, this tear in the seat is scratchy in a delicate area." I promised her to have it fixed one day but she just leaned her head against my back so I could feel the vibration of her voice, as well as hear it.

"Hmmm-yeah sure you will," she said as I pulled away from the kerb and started up the steep road towards the house. As soon as we entered the house, Joelle started to undress ready for a shower. I hadn't managed to persuade her to scale down her obsession with personal cleanliness, but I was working on it—St Gilberts limited water supply depended on my efforts. Besides, in my eyes, Joelle was never anything less than perfect no matter what state she thought she was in. She smiled at the rapt expression on my face as I watched her undress and before either of us knew what was happening, our naked bodies were locked together first against the wall and then we were rolling on the floor. I don't know how long our lovemaking lasted but it effectively dealt with the problem of what to do with my excess adrenalin. I had also overridden Joelle's need to have a shower before she did anything else, so perhaps I beginning to make some progress there too!

Later that same evening, after we had eaten, I rang Andy and Nahil and told them about my meeting with George Ferrari. Actually, I only spoke to Andy who relayed the story speaking away from the phone—sentence by sentence to Nahil who was stood close by. When he told her the name, "George Ferrari," I heard Nahil say, "That fat shit."

Good old Nahil, I thought, always upfront—nothing two-faced about her. When I'd finished, Andy asked me what I wanted to do about it.

"I don't know for now but let's discuss it tomorrow when you come around." Andy's voice suddenly lightened. "Hey, I've got a little something back from my mate in the UK I'll tell you tomorrow."

"Tell me now."

"No you'll have to wait until tomorrow," he said amused at my impatience.

"Andy you're a bastard," I said and then winced as Joelle gave my arm a punch. "Well, maybe he doesn't know who his father is," I said to her over my shoulder and I heard Andy's chuckle down the line just before he replaced the receiver and the line went dead.

"Andy's friend in England has found out something about the Valvaston," I told her.

"Well, go on, what is it?" she said digging my arm again with her fist.

"I don't know, he said we'd have to wait until tomorrow evening."

"The bastard," she said, and flounced over to the veranda. We turned in for an early night, well early by my old standards. My last tourist work, or gigoloing as Joelle called it, had been Helen and I'd put her on her plane home only a few weeks previous now it seemed like years ago and part of a different life.

It was sometime after twelve when I heard the phone ring. Joelle moaned and turned over in the bed pulling half the sheets with her, not that it was cold enough to need any. I got up and walked through to the lounge to pick up the call on my landline phone. I don't have a line through to the bedroom, never really needed one before. The voice of Dan Meme greeted me when I picked up the receiver, what surprised me most was not the fact he was calling me after midnight but that he was speaking in a confidential voice, almost a whisper and when Dan spoke like that you listened more intently than when he bellowed. I could tell that he was speaking on a mobile and from the sounds of traffic in the background guessed that he was outdoors and speaking as he walked.

"Rodney?"

"Yes is that you Dan?"

"Yes listen, I've just left Toffies and Henri was there pissed as usual, he's been bad-mouthing you all night."

"Nothing new there then," I cut in.

"Yes but he says he's going to pull you in tomorrow," Dan hissed down the line.

"Pull me in? What do you mean?"

"Arrest you, Rodney—he said he's going to arrest you sometime tomorrow morning." A sudden wave of panic swept over me leaving taking shallow breaths in my upper chest before I managed to control it.

"He can't just arrest me, Dan, I haven't done anything; what was he saying?"

Dan ignored my question and asked, "Have you changed any money recently?"

"No not for weeks now."

"What about that lanky French geek you were with?" He asked and, from his description, I guessed he was referring to Helen.

I lowered my voice and looked over my shoulder to check Joelle wasn't standing there. "Do you mean Helen—the one with the glasses?"

"Yes, her."

"No she didn't let me change a rupee; in fact I ended up paying for most things anyway."

Dan tut-tutted disappointment of me at this confession. "I'm disappointed in you, Rodney, I really am but then if you haven't done anything wrong then I don't see that you've got any problem. Yeah you've nothing to worry about, just sit tight through a few hours in the station then you'll be out again and buying me a drink in the Three-In-One thanking me for this life saving tip off."

"But Dan, did he say anything about why he was going to arrest me?" I asked again.

"No, he just said that he'd been given the go-ahead to do it from someone high up." I felt a chill slide up my back despite the warm night and I saw in my mind's eye those black inhuman eyes magnified through the thick glass lenses.

"And what if I have done something to worry about, what should I do then?" I asked.

"Run like hell and get on a boat to somewhere else," came his laconic reply.

I walked slowly back to the bedroom, Joelle was propped up on a pillow waiting for me.

"Problem?" she asked when she saw my face.

"That was Dan Meme; he's just left Toffies, he said that Henri was there and telling everyone that he was going to arrest me tomorrow morning." I looked at my watch, "Today."

She sat up straight with concern written all over her face.

"For what?" she said her voice rising in pitch, "Is it because of those people on the yacht or something?"

"I don't know, but Dan said that Henri was boasting about getting the go ahead from someone high up and I can only think of George Ferrari."

"What are we going to do, Rodney?" she asked and I liked the 'we' bit. I rang Andy no doubt interrupting his bedroom gymnastics because he sounded breathless when he picked up the phone.

"Sorry to ring at this time, Andy, but I thought you should know that I just got call from Dan Meme he says that Paul Henri is coming to arrest me tomorrow morning."

"Fucking hell, what for?" Andy's voice was loud down the line.

"He didn't say but apparently, Henri's got the go ahead from above."

"George Ferrari?" Andy guessed.

"Yes; the fat shit," I agreed, borrowing Nahil's succinct description of Ferrari's personality and appearance.

"I'll come around now if you want, just tell me what you want me to do." I wouldn't have expected anything less from Andy, but I had no idea what I wanted or what I was going to do, or could do.

"Dan said if I haven't done anything then I've got nothing to worry, about but if I have, then I should run like hell."

"Yeah but run where? It's not as if it's a big island. There may be places to hide out up in the forest or even in that secret chamber under the church but what sort of life is that going to be after a few days?" I thought for a moment on what he had just said, in fact my first instinct had been to take off and hide somewhere, but that would not solve the problem it would just create another one of its own. I felt surprisingly calm, it was clear what needed to be done.

"No it's alright, Andy, there's no need for you to come around tonight but if you could check on Joelle tomorrow, I'd be grateful."

"No sweat," he agreed.

"They'll just take me to the station in town, if they come at all, Dan said Henri was pissed so maybe Henri was just talking big. But if I am arrested," I continued, "then get the gang together tomorrow as planned and see if you can come up with anything."

"No problem. Will do," he agreed, he made me promise to ring him again if I thought of anything else then we said our goodbyes and hung up.

The sunlight coming in through the curtains woke me after a light and troubled sleep. The events of the night before seemed surreal in the light of day but I had to assume that they were real enough. I left Joelle asleep on the bed and went for a shower but just as I was waiting for the water to run warm Joelle walked into the shower beside me. She worked the soap around her hands until she had built up a froth of lather in her hands before looking up at me.

"Let's check and see if that swelling has gone down shall we?"

It was while we were sat on the veranda a short while later having tea and toast that we heard a heavy knock on the door. As I walked across the lounge to open it I turned to Joelle and passed her my Omega watch, "Take care of this and the house till I get back will you?"

"I love you," she said, which stopped me in midstride.

I turned to face her. "I loved you first" and we both smiled. She got to her feet and came to the door with me. Paul Henri stood on the step with a couple more police behind him further back on the driveway. I hadn't heard a car engine so they must have parked the police car up on the road and walked down.

In his formal police voice and in Creole, Henri went through the caution, "Rodney Leon, I am arresting you on suspicion of illegal currency transactions in violation of St Gilberts financial and monetary law. You don't have to say anything now but anything you do say will be taken down and may be used against you in court at a later date, do you understand?" Henri was sweating profusely and I guessed most of it was neat alcohol. His dark skin could not hide the burst blood-vessels in his nose but it did emphasise the redness of his eyes. With his head tilted back as usual in an effort to look down his nose at me.

I sneered down at him, "Yeah yeah, you know this is a load of crap as well as I do so let's just get it sorted out as quickly as possible, shall we?"

Joelle spoke from my side, "You have no right to arrest Rodney; he hasn't done anything wrong." Henri seemed surprised to see Joelle in the house but he didn't respond to her challenge and simply drew me forward. One of the two policemen came forward and placed handcuffs on my wrists and led me up the drive. Joelle walked alongside wringing her hands with tears rolling down her cheeks. The two lackeys played their part to the full, one of them even stretched up so he could place his hand on the top of my head to push it down as I got into the car.

"Listen mate, I've been getting into cars all my life without your help, thanks." I said but he just gave me another shove and then, blow me, my head bumped painfully against the doorway as I got in. He got in the car beside me. I looked back at Joelle and gave her my best version of a confident 'I'll be back soon' smile, then we were on our way down the road to the town. When we drew near the Police station I hoped that they would drive around to the cark park at the back to save me the embarrassment of entering the station from the main street. To my surprise we continued straight past the station and carried on to the bottom of the road before turning right towards the marina. I half expected the couple with the yacht to be standing on the quay waiting to accuse me of attacking them on their yacht, but there was only a police launch and a blue shirted policeman at the wheel. They hustled me onboard despite my protests.

"Hang on, what's this for?" I asked, feeling that something wasn't right. When I saw Henri's triumphant smile, I knew with absolute certainty that nothing was right.

"This is your transport, Rodney. I hope you enjoy your nice little cruise to Raynauld Island!"

Andy and Nahil reached Rodney's house just as the police car was pulling away. Rodney was looking back towards Joelle who stood at the roadside and missed seeing their arrival. Joelle had her hands to her face as if in shock. Crossing over the road to join her Nahil put her arm around Joelle and led her back down the drive and into the house. They sat around the big table and Andy let the two girls talk among themselves in Creole for a few minutes before coughing and looking at his wristwatch.

"We need to work out what needs to be done and the order in which we need to do it," he said and the two young women nodded in silence.

"If this is a f-frame-up, which I think it is, then the m-more s-support Rodney has the b-better." Andy was obviously more comfortable with action than talking.

"This is what I suggest;" he said after the other two had nodded.

"We all get on Rodney's bike and head for town, on the way I'll drop Nahil off at the top of the path leading to Jean Claude's. Nahil you go down to Claude's and tell him what's happened then the two of you catch a bus into town and meet Joelle and me at the police station. What do think?" Joelle and Nahil both nodded and Joelle fetched the ignition key for the Honda.

Andy drove it up the drive and stopped with the engine running to let the two young women squeeze on to the pillion behind him forcing him up against the hard petrol tank. Once they'd dropped Nahil off he settled back on to the seat and let the bike roll down the hill in gear. He parked a little way from the police station and walked with Joelle towards the Police station. A familiar voice called behind him, "Andy, can you tell me what's going on?"

It was Rodney's Aunt Mert; St Gilberts Island telegraph, effective as ever, had already got news to her that Rodney was in some sort of trouble. She bustled towards them dressed in her Sunday best. Joelle answered without softening the news, "They arrested Rodney this morning. Henri said it was something to do with currency violations but it's not true and they've got no evidence."

"Humph, we'll see about that," she said and strode past and ahead of them and straight into the police station.

"I want to see my boy Rodney Leon," she demanded. St Gilberts is a matriarchal society that has had many female presidents, in fact, the two presidents preceding the current one, Gerard Duval, were both women, and no one carries more authority on the island than a mature woman dressed in full Sunday best. The duty sergeant nodded a greeting and rifled through the pages of the station log.

"No Rodney Leon here, I'm afraid," he said looking up to meet Mert's eye.

"But they took him this morning," protested Joelle.

Aunt Mert snapped at the policeman, "Where are the cells?" He did not reply but his eyes slid sideways to look at the door to his right and Aunt Mert started towards it.

"I'm sorry but you can't go through there…" said the policeman but Aunt Mert could and she did, with Joelle and Andy in close pursuit. The four cells were all in a line with open bars at the front so the small group of unauthorised visitors, led by Aunt Mert, could walk past them and check who was in each one. A minute later they were back at the duty sergeant's desk.

"Where is he? Where is Rodney?" Aunt Mert demanded and the policeman made a show of flicking pages again as if he was checking.

"It was that Paul Henri who came for him," said Joelle.

"So where's Henri now?"

The policeman coughed before replying, "Constable Henri is off duty at present. Perhaps he was not been able to return to the station to update the log."

"Y-you can't just pick p-people up from their homes and disappear them away without any evidence, no records and without any trial!" Exclaimed Andy in an almost stammer-free sentence.

"And you are an expert on the law of this country are you sir? May I ask you your name please—sir?" The policeman made the "sir," bit sound like a threat but before Andy could respond, the door to the road swung open and Jean Claude strode in closely followed by Nahil. Andy was only half relieved to see Claude had left his Lee Enfield at home.

"What's the hell's going on?" Boomed Jean Claude, and Andy had the satisfaction of seeing the policeman's torso visibly shrivel within his uniform.

"Rodney's not here and this one," Aunt Mert nodded contemptuously towards the outnumbered official, "doesn't even know what day it is."

"It was Henri who took Rodney this morning," Joelle interjected speaking directly to Jean Claude who nodded and leaned across the counter so his face was inches away from the policeman's.

"Where's that pisshead Henri?" hissed Claude, and Mert tutted at Claude's use of bad language.

"I am not at liberty to give you that information sir but if you want to leave a message I will make sure that he—"

"Stuff your effing message; I know where that fat bastard is," thundered Claude and Aunt Mert raised her hands as if to cover her ears. The group walked out of the station and stood in a circle on the pavement forcing other pedestrians to walk on to the road to get around them. Claude's voice was calm when he spoke to the others, "Look, why don't you three ladies go and sit in that café of Joelle's while Andy and I pay a visit to Toffies? We're sure to find Henri there and we can ask him where he's taken Rodney. We'll be back as soon as we learn anything."

"OK but make sure you don't stop for a drink as well," warned Mert, in response Jean Claude narrowed his eyes but he kept his mouth shut.

Claude strode ahead of Andy and when they reached the end of town Claude turned off down a narrow dirt track where the vegetation closed in on either side. Claude's sandals kicked up little puffs of red dust as he walked down the snaking path which eventually broadened out into a rough clearing in the undergrowth. Andy saw a high bamboo palisade with low scrambling lantana and clusters of small yellow flowers running along the base of it.

Claude stopped and turning back to Andy spoke to him in English in a low voice, "You'd better leave this to me son. If you treat Henri like that guy on the yacht then you'll either be deported or jailed." Andy grinned back and nodded to show he understood and agreed.

There was an opening and when they walked through it an untidy collection of wooden shacks with rusting corrugated iron roofs filled the space within the palisade. A rickety open sided affair looking like a poor man's attempt at a gazebo stood at the side of one of the shacks. Under its roof scuffed plastic patio chairs provided seating for the half-dozen or so customers. Andy spotted Henri almost immediately. He was sitting on one of the patio chair with his back to a corner post of the open sided gazebo. He still wore the dark trousers of his police uniform but had replaced the blue shirt of the uniform with a soiled white tee-shirt bearing the legend Tusker Premium, Kenya's number one beer. His huge fist was wrapped around a glass containing a cloudy yellow liquid. All the patrons turned to look at Claude and Andy. Jean Claude was something of a regular at Toffies, though not as hardcore as Henri, even so, most of those present nodded and muttered a greeting of sorts in his direction but the fierce look in Claude's eye discouraged anything more. Claude addressed Henri directly.

"Where've you've taken Rodney?" He spoke in Creole, his voice authoritative.

"I'm off duty so I'm not discussing police matters with you now, Claude." Andy noted that Henri's voice was still steady, suggesting he hadn't been drinking for that long.

"He's not in the police cells so where is he?" Claude moved closer to Henri.

"He's where he belongs—and where he should have been years ago—Raynauld Island." His voice was triumphant but there was a gloating undertone to it and Henri's sprawling posture only emphasised it. He lifted his glass as if in salute and a smile began to spread across his coarsened features.

Claude's voice held a warning as he said, "You can't send Rodney to Raynauld; he hasn't been convicted of anything, what about a trial and some evidence?"

"Oh believe me I have all the authority I need to send Rodney to Raynauld and besides, the police cells were full."

"Your authority being Ferrari?" asked Claude. Henri blinked in surprise at hearing the name but refused to respond to Claude's question. Claude took another step towards Henri who placed his glass down on a nearby table and straightened on his chair. Claude and Henri locked eyes for a moment longer before Claude turned and, taking hold of Andy's shoulder, turned the shorter man and steered him back out of the compound.

"I can't believe they taken him to Raynauld without a trial. Something's not right with all of this," said Claude as they walked briskly back along the track towards the main road. Back at the Kokonet Café the group all squeezed into

Joelle's office to plan their next move. Fifteen minutes later they headed purposefully towards Government House.

The intercom buzzed on Gerard Duval's desk and he leaned across to switch it to the 'listen' mode.

"There is a delegation to see you, Sir."

"Delegation? I'm not booked to see anyone this afternoon, am I?" He asked in surprise.

"No they have not booked an appointment but they say that it is a matter of constitutional importance." The president of the St Gilberts Isles raised his eyes up to the ceiling; "of constitutional importance" was a well-worn local phrase covering everything from domestic disputes, pigs straying into a neighbour's garden, to a full-blown military coup, not that there'd ever been one of those, yet.

"Well, I guess you'd better show them in then," he said resignedly. Aunt Mert swept in heading the delegation into the President's office. When Duval saw there were five in the delegation he stood up and walked over to open a door into another room with a long polished table set out in boardroom style.

"Claude, Lucy," He said, and nodded a greeting smile as each of the elders passed.

"Gerard," Claude mumbled in reply nodding at the same time.

"And you are Miss Kelly er, it's Joelle isn't it? You're the young businesswoman who runs the internet Café on Main Street?"

"That's me Mr President," replied Joelle.

"And you are?" He spoke directly to Nahil who replied crisply, "Nahil Ramyann."

"Ah yes, you must be one of Josie's nieces," he added. Finally he turned to Andy, extending his hand. "I don't believe we've met, Mr..."

"Andrew Colgan," said Andy and extended his arm to shake the President's proffered hand. The President waited until they were all seated around the table and their heads turned towards him.

"So, ladies and gentlemen, how may I be of help to you?"

It was my first visit to Raynauld Island though I had heard plenty about the place. It was the place authority figures always threatened young teenagers with if they didn't mend their ways. I had been one of those teenagers once yet here I was at the age of twenty-five, innocent of any major crime, and facing the possibility of some hard time. Raynauld had its share of real villains, a fact not generally known or made public by the press or the authorities St Gilberts who were, after all, trying to attract more tourists. I only knew all this because Dan Meme had told me. When I stepped ashore something struck me as odd but I couldn't quite put my finger on what. Then I realised what it was; apart from the sea air and the odour of turned earth and dust, presumably from broken rocks, the place didn't really have any signature odour at all. Dan often told me Raynauld stank, yet I had the opposite impression, It was odd because I lived my life surrounded by lush vegetation and an orchestra of hot greenhouse scents from the millions of flowers all around St Gilberts. Normally this background aroma barely registered in my conscious thoughts but now I missed its presence. Tourists usually brought the heavy scent of blooms to my attention in fact they always remarked on it but otherwise I took it for granted, but not anymore.

Raynauld had a few shrubby trees and short grassy patches here and there but otherwise it looked a sterile place. Wait till you get inside I warned myself. A couple of the prison warders led me to a long low concrete building and once inside they removed my handcuffs and processed me through as a new inmate. This involved stripping off my clothing and replacing them with a dark-blue shorts and shirt combination. They bagged my belongings and stored them on one of a rack of metal shelves. I was thankful I'd left my watch at home with Joelle earlier that morning it was just a pity I couldn't have left myself there as well. From the moment Henri had knocked on my door earlier that morning to now I had controlled the fear that threatened to overwhelm me. I was able to control it because I believed it would amount to a couple of hours in the police station at most. I had seen my arrest as a ruse to unsettle me, there was no evidence linking me with any crime so they'd soon release me. I'd mentally prepared myself for some unpleasantness at the police station, it was Henri's territory after all, even so, I expected nothing more serious than Henri shouting in my face and maybe a couple of slaps at worst. My ill-founded confidence took a nosedive when the police car went straight to the marina instead of the station. I had looked to the driver who'd said, "The station cells are full so you're going to Raynauld," adding to my growing sense of disorientation. At the time I managed to see a positive side to this turn of events, I would not have to face Henri's wrath because as the launch pulled away from the quayside I knew I was leaving Henri behind. A couple of hours on Raynauld might even give me the chance to meet with a few of my old classmates from school the ones who had chosen life's left-hand path.

Wearing the too tight-fitting prison uniform which now replaced my own clothes I followed my escorts to another single storey building this time built of grey limestone. For some reason it stood apart from the other barrack style buildings which I guessed made up the main prison quarters. Once inside they ushered me through an office of sorts where a couple of uniformed wardens eyed me sullenly. They shoved me into a small holding cell containing a thin mattress on top of a concrete plinth and a squat toilet from which, I knew, cockroaches would pour out of once it got dark. I sat on the bed and then lay down drawing my knees up to fit. To my surprise I actually dozed off though I had no idea for how long. The sliding bolts on my cell door roused me from my sleep and I opened my eyes to see the same two warders standing over me. Once again they led me through the office only this time I exited through a series of short corridors into a small windowless interview room bare except for a couple of chairs and a wide heavy looking table placed in the middle which dominated the room. My eyes settled on the centre of the square table two wrist manacles extended from it. The restraints looked medieval and I could think of no legitimate reason to justify their presence though their purpose was not difficult to guess at. Once again I felt fear coiling in my stomach. The warders who had accompanied me from the boat from now pushed me forward and down into one of the chairs facing the table.

"Put your hands on the table," one of them commanded.

"You've got to joking, what's going on?" I protested.

"Put your hands on the table now or I'll take your teeth out with this," said one of them raising the butt of his rifle. The other policeman moved around to my side and, leaning across the table, fastened a manacle around each of my wrists.

"What the hell's going on?" I asked again, my voice rising in pitch as I swivelled my head to try and catch the eye of one of the warders as my manacled hands pulled against the chains. I received only silence and blank dead stares in reply. One of the warders left the room leaving the other one stood on guard at the door. I looked down at the manacles around my wrists and saw bright metal where they were smooth and shiny with use. I had to extend my arms out straight to reach them and my arms are quite a bit longer than the average. I guessed that most men would need to be drawn across the table to reach them. Thinking along those lines was just too terrifying and I tried to blank my mind without success. Maybe, I thought, they manacle each new inmate at the start of their sentence to instil some fear into them to make them more compliant and easier to discipline. If so, it was certainly working on me. The minutes dragged but after what must have been an hour I heard movement in the corridor outside and then the door half opened. Someone on the other side of the door spoke to the warder inside the room ordering him to wait outside and under no circumstance interrupt the interview that was to take place inside. For long moments I sat alone listening to my own breathing and heartbeat then the door swung fully open and George Ferrari walked into the small dungeon like room in his right-hand he held a two-pound lump hammer.

Gerard Duval steepled his fingers under his chin.

"What you have just described certainly does appear to represent a miscarriage of justice. Even allowing for the fact the police cells in town were fully occupied I see no grounds for immediate imprisonment anyway. If what you say is correct…" Duval continued despite Mert's indignant cough, "and Henri was acting on suspicion with no supporting evidence, then I can see no reason for Rodney's arrest in the first place, let alone imprisonment on Raynauld Island! I mean if we were to use this approach every time we suspected illegal foreign currency exchange was going on at least three-quarters of the entire population would be behind bars and the population of Raynauld greater than that of the main island." Duval looked around the table and the group nodded in agreement.

His expression became serious. "You said George Ferrari, one of my ministers, is somehow responsible for Rodney's arrest. You claim he threatened

Rodney in the main street of town yesterday? Now why would he do a thing like that?" Silence followed this last question until Andy spoke with surprising calm.

"Rodney and I visited the beach of Al Solere the day after the tsunami and Rodney found a small napkin ring on the beach with the name Valvaston on it. He did a search on the internet to see if he could find out anything more about but it without success. However, since that internet search three outsiders have arrived on St Gilberts looking for him to find out what he knows about the Valvaston. Obviously they think he knows a lot more than he does."

"Outsiders?" Duval queried.

"Well, only a week or so ago a couple arrived at the marina to refuel and take on water. They visited the Kokonet Café a couple of times and invited Joelle to join them for a meal and then a drink aboard their yacht then locked her in a cabin. In the morning they left the marina with Joelle still locked in the cabin, and anchored off the reef at Anse Raffin facing Rodney's house. Rodney swam out to try to find her they shut him in the cabin with Joelle. They wanted to know what Rodney knew about the Valvaston."

"And you think that they traced him through his inquiries on the internet," asked Duval turning to Joelle.

"Yes it's certainly possible if their trace gave them the IP number of the computer Rodney used and the date and time he made his search. All they would need to do would be to identify the computer with that IP number and check the log to see who was using it on that day at the given time. I keep the log at the Café and it lists everyone who uses the computers. The couple Andy just talked about came into the Café and asked to see the log for the time that Rodney made his inquiries. They said they were looking to see if a friend had visited the Café," said Joelle.

"I want to know more about this kidnapping, these are serious allegations that need looking into and action taken, but let's deal with Rodney's current predicament first." Duval looked around the room and then nodded, more to himself than to the group around the table. He reached across the table and buzzed the intercom, "Pauline, will you get Raymond Matine on the phone and put him straight through to me. Oh, and find out the whereabouts of George Ferrari." Two long minutes of silence followed broken by the harsh ring of the phone. Joelle, who was nearest to it, jumped in her seat. Duvall picked up the receiver.

"Duval, oh hello Raymond," he paused as he gathered his thoughts and then opened his mouth to speak, Andy expected him to recount the group's story to the Chief of Police, but he obviously thought better of it.

"Look Raymond where are you now? Yes now, can you come here to my office. No-no, come right away." He listened for a few more seconds before continuing, "Yes, no problem, see you in a few minutes in my office. OK. Fifteen minutes is fine." He put the phone down but as soon as it touched the cradle, it rang again, "Yes Pauline, what was that? What do they mean they don't know where he is?" Those around the table saw Duval's brow furrow before he replied to his assistant at the other end of the line.

"OK, now can you get the Prison Governor of Raynauld Island on the line and put him through straight away." Duval looked around at the faces watching his progress on the phone in fascinated silence.

"The Chief of Police is on his way over as soon as his meeting with the tourist board has finished. As for George, he has not yet—" the ringing phone interrupted him and he stopped speaking and lifted the receiver to his ear.

"Good afternoon, Mr Hoareau," said the President his tone formal.

"Have you received a new inmate today called Rodney Leon?" He waited for a reply and from the length of the delay those around the table guessed the prison Governor was frantically checking with his staff before responding to the President's question.

"OK. When did he arrive?" The President scribbled on a pad. "Right, now I want you tell to tell me if George Ferrari is on Raynauld, has he visited the prison any time today?" Again there was a lengthy silence before the President exclaimed, "He is! What's he doing? Is he checking stone aggregate?" Prisoners on Raynauld laboured in the heat of the Sun to pulverise rocks to provide aggregate for public roads and other construction projects. A visit by the Minister for Construction and Public Works was not beyond the realms of possibility—though it was stretching coincidence a little too far in Duval's opinion. Duval's eyes suddenly flicked down as he concentrated on what the Governor was saying and then his voice had steel in it as he continued with his questions, "Which prisoner is Mr Ferrari interviewing? Well, find out—yes right now." More time passed as Duval waited for the prison Governor's reply. When it came, he nodded grimly and spoke back into the phone.

"Listen carefully, I want you to tell Mr Ferrari to stop whatever he is doing and come to the phone immediately. This is very urgent and I will wait on this line until he arrives, next, before you go, how many boats have you got available at your disposal ready for immediate use?"

"Good; then put Rodney Leon on one and send him back to my office with an escort immediately. After I have spoken to Mr Ferrari, he will also need a boat and an escort back to the St Gilberts. Is that all clear? Good, I'll expect to see Mr Leon arriving shortly." Duval put the phone down and looked at the faces around the table.

"I'm not convinced you've told me the whole story on this Valvaston affair but that can wait until Rodney arrives back on St Gilberts, at the moment my main concern is to prevent a possible miscarriage of justice. I suggest you get yourselves a cup of tea somewhere and then return here in about…" he looked questioningly at Claude. "How long will take the prison launch from Raynauld to reach the marina?"

"Three-quarters of an hour to one hour," replied Claude without a moment's hesitation.

"OK, I guess I'll see you back here in about an hour's time."

Just as the group left Government House to make their way back to the Kokonet Café a lean man in his late forties entered the building, the receptionist looked up and smiled in recognition, "Ah Mr Matine, please go straight up the president is waiting for you in his office."

"Hello Rodney, so we meet again," said Ferrari in that pleasant voice of his. He had a good voice for politician and he was speaking in English, perhaps to make it harder for the guard outside to understand what was being said should the warder be brave enough to eavesdrop.

"It's time to pick up where we left off in our little conversation of yesterday." He said, settling into the seat to my left side and slowly and carefully placing the lump hammer on the table in front of him making sure that I had a good sight of it. I was not sure I could trust my voice to speak so I kept quiet. Ferrari let an ominous silence settle in the small space and I gradually became aware of my own shallow breathing and consciously forced myself to breathe in lower, slower, and deeper breaths, Ferrari must have noticed it to.

"Raynauld Island," he began. "Prison life is tough. Breaking rocks is tough. You've landed yourself in a thoroughly unpleasant place where the work environment is extremely dangerous Rodney. Despite the heroic efforts of the Governor and staff to ensure the inmates' safety, unfortunate and regrettable accidents do happen from time-to-time. Inevitable perhaps, what else could you expect when you kettle the dregs of society together and supply them with sledgehammers, pickaxes, shovels, chisels and hammers, and set them the frustrating job of smashing rocks in the heat of the sun?" He paused and I felt those strange black eyes boring into the side of my face inviting me into another staring contest. I continued to stare ahead trying to ignore both the unspoken challenge and the presence of the hammer on the table between us.

"Young men just like you, Rodney, fit and active one day, then sadly reduced to a cripple the next. What are you now, twenty something? Imagine that you live to eighty years old, that's another sixty years or so of carrying a disability gained through an unfortunate accident on this terrible island. Perhaps an eye plucked out of its socket by a flying shard of rock, a limb shattered beyond the rudimentary abilities of our small island hospital to repair. Yes, imagine yourself Rodney, scarred and hobbling and bobbing around the town and the looks of pity from the young girls who remembered you as you were before, girls who once found you attractive."

"Not all girls are put off by disability," I said defiantly, a picture of Dan Meme charming a group of female tourists flashing briefly in my mind.

"Maybe you're right, Rodney, but I don't think so, and I don't think you believe it either. You'd be just another lonely loser and even more of an outcast than you already are on the island."

"I don't agree. I've got friends who'd stay friends," I replied and immediately regretted the defiance in my voice. He'd baited me, struck a raw nerve, and I'd risen to his goading. He smiled patronisingly.

"Easy for you to say, Rodney, just look at you, young, tall handsome, those eyes, I bet life has been a breeze for you. I bet you've never had to chase a girl because they always chased you." I detected an undercurrent of envy and resentment in his voice. It was the first time he had allowed any emotion to leak out and I wondered if his interest in me was not just about getting information on the Valvaston but also personal. Maybe he'd had lousy luck with the ladies and blamed it on the world in general and on me in particular?

"Look, I don't know what you want, Mr Ferrari, why don't you just ask me and I'll tell you what you want to know. Let's cut out all this drama stuff."

"Drama stuff," he repeated, rolling the words around in his mouth as if tasting them. Suddenly, he yelled into my ear, "I'll give you fucking drama, son. I'll smash your bones so you're ruined for the rest of your miserable fucking life!" I flinched in surprise at the force and hate in this sudden flash of rage. The words echoed off the walls and I struggled to keep my composure.

Ferrari was breathing hard and I surprised him, and myself, by managing to strike a note of defiance.

"You'd never get away it. St Gilberts has laws and I've got friends and relations who'd make sure you pay heavy for anything you do." I was staring him in the eye as I said this and my voice had conviction because I desperately wanted to believe what I was saying. He lifted his eyebrows high and let his mouth drop open as if in surprise but it was not real surprise he was expressing, he was simply mocking my outburst and laughing at me.

"Ho ho ho Rodney ho ho," he said leaning back on his chair and then he gave an evil little chuckle and his eyes crinkled with humour.

"A nice little human right rights speech Rodney, you should have been a politician you really should." Then the smile slide off his face like loose stools off a wet shovel blade.

"What will people believe, Rodney? That I attacked a giant half-caste and illegal money changing gigolo? Mr Ferrari, a short middle-aged and highly respected Minister for Construction and Public Works who, coincidently, is related to half of the Island's residents. No Rodney, this is the only story the public will hear."

Ferrari adopted the delivery of a television newsreader as he continued, "Mr Rodney Leon, currently serving a sentence on Raynauld Island for miscellaneous offences including illegal money changing, was the victim of an unfortunate accident during his allotted work placement. Another inmate has admitted to a momentary lapse of concentration which caused the unfortunate accident to Rodney Leon's limb. Or any other organ I choose," he added as an aside. Ferrari smiled but his eyes remained cold, black and inhuman.

"This prison is full of inmates who would jump at the chance to own up to something like that especially if such an admission brought them special privileges or even a parole date brought forward. They'd be queuing up Rodney; in fact they'd literally fall over themselves to swing a hammer at you. Oh, and as for this vast band of supporters you boast about—where are they now, Rodney, where are they now?" He gave me a second to think about that one before continuing, "Well, then let's think about all that support you could call on shall we? No parents, brought up by your Aunt Mert, a couple of uncle's on the island and maybe a couple more in the U-S of A who, if I'm not mistaken, have virtually disowned you anyway. Hardly amounts to an extended family in the local sense. Oh, and as for your many friends," he snorted in derision and started to count on his fingers.

"Let's see; there's a white man from England supposedly in the security business, though probably an ex-thug from all accounts. I could have him thrown off the island any time I want—oh, and let's not forget your assortment of old girlfriends are they supporters too? How can you be sure they don't have an axe to grind with you? All in all, Rodney, things are not looking that good for you are they? You may turn heads now young master Rodney but by the time you leave this island you'll be turning stomachs." The sad truth was, apart from Andy, I couldn't dispute most of what he had just said, however for some reason I was starting to feel more confident. My terror as they placed the manacles around my wrists had been overwhelming, now, the more he talked the more certain I became that he was not going to use the hammer on me. Why would he take the risk? Besides, I was prepared to tell him whatever he wanted to know anyway?

"What do you want?" I asked.

"Tell me where the wreck of the Valvaston is?" He replied. "Oh, and remember, you are going to be here for some time so we can check everything you tell me as we go along over the days, weeks, months and years ahead."

Our eyes met again. I took a deep breath and summarised as best I could.

"Look, I found a silver napkin ring on the beach at Al Solere a couple of days after that tsunami. I noticed the ring had the name Valvaston engraved on it so I did a search on the internet for anything to do with Valvaston and shortly after that outsiders started coming to the island to ask me about it. The truth is, I really don't know anything about the Valvaston—what it is, or where it is; I guess it must be an old sailing ship or something." I thought that would do but he continued to look steadily into my eyes as if looking for some suggestion of deception on my part, I at least knew there was none. Slowly, his right hand reached for the hammer and his fingers closed around the handle.

"Not good enough, Rodney, tell me where the Valvaston is." He picked up the hammer and I saw in his expression something that made me flinch and something in his eyes that made me afraid, not only for my body, but my soul as well. I no longer had any doubt I was in the presence of evil.

"Look Mr Ferrari, that's the truth. I have no idea where the Valvaston is, it probably got wrecked on the rocks at Al Solere or something." I was speaking fast now hoping to convince him, to distract him, anything just to stop him from doing what he looked as if he was about to do.

He spoke quietly in reply as if he was regretful, his voice almost purring, "Sorry Rodney, it's still not enough." Suddenly he raised his arm and brought the hammer down onto to my left forearm. There was a crack as the weight of the hammer and the force behind it drove the head into my flesh to make contact with the bone. As I watched him raise the hammer, my mind formed the words, "What the fuck…?" But it was only a scream of pain, fuelled by fear that came out of my mouth. I strained against the manacles, my body chilled by the sweat already covering my body. Ferrari sat silent watching me waiting for my rapid hyperventilating breaths to slow.

"Once I have made the first break, the next stage is to reduce the splintered ends to bonemeal so there is no possibility of them ever mending. You'll never be able to hold a knife and fork, wash your hair or wipe your arse using that arm again." He said all this in his soft voice, the words dripped like poisoned molasses into the electric storm of pain and terror raging in my head. Suddenly I became vaguely aware there was someone else in the room, a warder. Had he heard my scream? I prayed he had come to my rescue, that he would release me and drag Ferrari away in handcuffs.

But instead, he remained at the door and said, "Mr Ferrari—" but Ferrari cut him off in midsentence as he thundered, "GET OUT! I am not to be disturbed." The warder flinched but stood his ground.

"It's the President, Sir, he wants to speak to you right away, he's waiting for you now on the phone in the Governor's office."

"Who told him I was here?" Asked Ferrari accusingly as he stood up but then he waved his hand dismissively. "No matter." He turned towards me and bent low so that his mouth came close to my ear. "Think carefully about how you are going to answer me when I come back and ask you that question again and I will be back, you can count on that, I'll be back very soon." He looked at my manacled wrists and smiled at his little joke.

I waited in that dark cell of a room my jaw clenching as each new wave of pain surged through my body. I was afraid to move my left arm even a fraction for the fear of triggering even more intense pain. If what I had already told Ferrari had failed to appease him then I would have to make something up, but what? I was pondering this problem when the door slowly opened. I held my breath and then breathed out in relief when I saw a regular prison warder enter the room, it was Edward and I knew him from the Three-In-One. His face registered surprise and then shock when he saw my manacled wrists and the state I was in.

"Bloody hell, Rodney, I didn't know you were on Raynauld until a few moments ago when the Governor sent me to find you. He wants you on a launch back to the marina, but what the hell's been going on in here?" He looked at the lump hammer on the table and at the purple bruise on my left arm and added, "Looks like you've been having a smashing time."

Through gritted teeth, I snarled back at my liberator, "Cut the humour Ed, just get me out of these fucking things."

The group returned to Government House before an hour had passed the receptionist directed them straight up to the President's office. Duval welcomed them in though his expression offered little reassurance, "The governor of Raynauld just rang to say Rodney is on his way back; however, he is going straight to the hospital on arrival."

Aunt Mert gasped at this and Joelle's face darkened with anger. She leaned forward over the table and spoke directly at the President, "Tell us what have they done to him?"

It was not so much a question as a command and the President held up both hands. "I'm as keen to know as you are—but let's wait until Rodney can tell us for himself. The hospital is giving him a thorough going over right now."

Jean Claude's voice rumbled into the short silence that followed this last comment from the President, "If that George Farar—or whatever his name is—has done anything to Rodney, he'll have me to answer to."

"But he'll have the law to answer to first and let's not forget that," said the President and his voice held a note of warning which he aimed towards Jean Claude and Andy. The phone rang and he picked it up. "Duval," then he listened for a short while before speaking himself, "Keep him in a private room and, apart from Doctors and medical staff, do not allow any visitors in until I have seen him myself, I'll be there in about ten minutes." He replaced the phone and called Pauline, his personal assistant, into the room.

"I going to the hospital now," he told her, "but I'm expecting a call from Raymond Matine telling me when the prison Governor and George Ferrari arrive at the marina, would you put the call through to my mobile when it comes?"

"Yes Mr President." He waited until she had left the room before explaining to the seated group, "Rodney's arrived back and he's at the hospital; the doctor is examining him right now. I'll see him first and, though I have forbidden general visitors, you can visit on the condition you don't repeat outside anything that Rodney tells you. At least not until I have sorted out what I am going to do with George Ferrari and the Prison Governor. Your talking before the trial—if it comes to that—will only help their case. Have I made myself clear?" Five heads nodded as one.

"Right, follow me."

Despite the President's wish for secrecy and the group's stolid adherence to their promise not to leak the story out, word inevitably reached the street of Rodney's arrest and torture by the Henri-Ferrari duo. On St Gilberts such news is impossible to keep under wraps and Rodney's case quickly became public his status switched temporarily from disreputable rogue to that of heroic victim. Duval acted quickly and forced Henri to retire from the police force and George Ferrari to revisit Raynauld Island prison yet again though this time as an inmate under the new prison governorship of William Camille.

The phone rang in St Gilberts office for Construction and Public Works and a secretary picked up the receiver.

"Hello, Office for Construction and Public Works."

Richard Denver listened to this introduction before speaking himself, "Hello, I'd like to speak to Mr Ferrari could you put him on the line please?"

"I'm sorry sir; Mr Ferrari is no longer with this office." Denver's surprise rendered him speechless as his brain scrambled to work out an alternative question to the one he had planned to ask.

"Well, could you tell me where I could contact him, it is rather urgent?"

"May I ask who is speaking please?" The question carried a hint of suspicion, and a warning to Denver who slowly returned the phone to the cradle. He would get his Security Chief to find out what had happened to Ferrari. Denver sat back in his high-backed office chair and pondered on what he had just been told, the latest in a growing list of abortive attempts to trace the whereabouts of the Valvaston. Contacting Ferrari himself and using his own name when he did so, had been a calculated risk now it looked as if that decision might come back to haunt him. He would have to limit the damage, if any, his contact with Ferrari might bring. Yet despite this latest failure there was something about each failure that piqued his interest all the more. It seemed there was a determined and well-orchestrated resistance to his enquires about the Valvaston on this island and he wanted to know why.

So far the historical leads he had gathered were thin at best and needed enormous leaps of faith on his part to believe and follow them. But it was in Denver's DNA to follow such leads. The treasure hunter side of his personality already believed that Rupert Stillwood-Hamilton had boarded a ship called the Valvaston. That he carried with him a large blue diamond, the other and larger half of the Hope Diamond, and that now, someone on St Gilberts knew something that would take him a step, or several steps, closer to finding that diamond. The lore of finding a treasure of such historical value, the money meant nothing to Denver, was as irresistible to him as a full syringe to a heroin addict. His capital and Carr's business astuteness had made him wealthy to a point where a lack of money was never going to be an issue ever again but it was not business but the romance of maritime history that ran through his veins. Denver had already passed a 'tipping point' he had to continue his quest to whatever conclusion it took him too. He checked through a list of phone numbers and, almost reluctantly, picked up the phone and began to press keys.

"Hello, is that Jeannette Ryder?" Denver listened with growing impatience through the usual pleasantries before continuing, "Good, where are you now? Where? Sorry I didn't catch that." Denver frowned in concentration and then spoke into the mouthpiece again.

"OK so where is your nearest landfall?" He waited then screwed up his eyes as he tried to hear over the background noise at the other end of the line, "Did you say the Comoros Islands? Which one? Grande-Terre? Oh—the Mayotte Group." Having established the whereabouts of the private investigators, Denver chewed his lip in thought for five seconds before deciding.

"Are you available for immediate hire? Good; I have something unusual in mind, let me run it past you first then and tell me if you and Keith are still interested."

Typical, I thought, just when I finally get my hands on the woman I've been chasing forever, some fat shit busts my arm. The doctor told me that I had sustained a green-stick fracture; in other words, the broken bone had not completely separated. They checked the bone around the break and then placed my arm in a splint to keep it rigid. However, when the Doctor told me I'd been very lucky, his credibility dropped faster than an over-ripe Breadfruit.

The President called the whole gang; me, Joelle, Andy, Nahil, Uncle Claude and Aunt Mert back to his office. He kept preliminaries to a minimum and questioned us on the sequence of events beginning the morning of my arrest through to my rescue and arrival at the St Gilberts hospital. It was my first real contact with the President, of course I had seen him about, it's a small Island so it would have been impossible not to, but Duval impressed me. He was the same age as Uncle Claude and physically similar to. Both were a little taller than the average with grizzled hair going grey at the temples and intelligent lived in faces which gave them an air of gravitas. The President's face however, had fewer lines and was less weathered than Claude's and his eyes and mouth gave the impression of a kindly good-humoured man. When the meeting ended he waited until Aunt Mert and Claude had filed out of the room before quickly turning to Andy and me his face serious.

"I want to see you two again along with those two young women of yours, not now," he raised one hand, "my secretary will set up an appointment and send you word." Taken by surprise, we simply nodded in reply and then followed the others out of the room. From the look the President had given us, I knew we still had a lot of explaining to do.

Once we were all out of the building and on the street, Aunt Mert announced that she was going to the church to meet her Alfred but before she left, she squared her shoulders and confronted Andy and me wearing a stern expression. I knew what was coming; it was one of her, "Well, I hope this has taught you both a lesson…" speeches. I had faced so many in my formative years that I automatically adopted the same posture I had as a teenager. To his credit Andy took it in silence and waited until she had turned to walk away before elbowing me and grinning. I could see Claude was about to head off down the street himself, probably towards Toffies given the direction he was pointed. I leaned over and tapped him on the arm.

"Have you got a moment, Uncle?"

"I suppose so; why?" He asked suspiciously. I turned to the other three.

"Look, the President said that he wants to see us four again sometime soon."

"Not me?" Asked Claude and I could see that he was a bit put out.

"I guess not, Uncle Claude, but you know him better than any of us and we need your advice on what we should, and shouldn't, tell him." Claude stepped back on the pavement to let a couple of pedestrians walk through between us.

"Look," I said, "Let's get a table in the beer garden of the Three-In-one where we can talk without being disturbed." I suggested the bar in place of the Café as an extra incentive for Claude to join us and because I needed a drink myself the others didn't take much persuading either.

We got a table away from the other drinkers that gave us the privacy we needed and when we had a drink in hand I spoke directly to Claude.

"I think the President wants to see us four," I waved my hand around the table to take in Andy, Nahil, and Joelle, "because he thinks we won't say anything while you and Aunt Mert are there as well."

Claude just grunted, "Maybe."

"The question is, Uncle, if we tell him everything, including all that about that Belgian guy going over the cliff, what's he going to do, especially to Andy here? I mean, is he going to deport him or something?" Claude took some time to think, leaning back in his seat and then looked around the table at each of us in turn.

"This is just my own opinion so you'll have to make your own minds up on what you tell or don't tell him, but I respect Gerard Duval, he's been the best President St Gilberts ever had. I trust him too. He once helped me out over a fishing dispute. It was years ago when Luciana was still alive, but I remember he was honest and straightforward then, I believe he still is. If I were you, I'd tell him everything—just like you told it to me."

We got the call to report to the President's office two four days later. When we entered his office he showed us to some easy chairs arranged around a low coffee table in his office instead of the formal boardroom in the adjoining room. Once we were seated he studied us one by one very slowly and carefully, then he began to speak.

"Beyond these shores St Gilberts does not appear on the political radar of any other country, excepting our closest neighbours, who are themselves equally insignificant in the great scheme of things. I guess that Andy is more aware of this fact than anyone else in this room. Why am I telling you this? Well, just to show you that I am under no illusions about my own status, I know that, as President of St Gilberts I am simply a big fish in a very small pool indeed. Nevertheless being its President is a responsibility and a role that I take seriously. It may be an old-fashioned view of the world, and one that not many would agree with, but I see my role as similar to that of a father-figure, the head of the family of St Gilberts. Whether we like it or not, on an Island this size, we are a family, everything we do has an impact on somebody, and often, everybody else. So if someone from outside the Island is threatening one of my people then I want to know about it. You are all my people, my family if you like, and yes, I'm including you Andy." I saw Nahil smile at that. I had been watching the President's face closely during this little introductory piece. It was the sort of speech that could so easily have been pompous and patronising but not with Duval, he was genuine all right, or my ability to gauge another person's authenticity had suddenly slipped, but he wasn't finished, "I think that you lot have somehow gotten yourselves caught up in something and that you have no real idea what that something is." He looked at each of us in turn.

"Now is the time to tell me everything you know, good or bad, so together we can sort things out." We had already agreed among ourselves to make a clean breast of everything and the others left it to me to tell the story. I started at the picnic on Kasper's Edge and how we waited for the tsunami to arrive. Then I recounted how Andy and I had rode out the Al Solere the next day and entered the church. When I got to the part about finding the secret chamber he chuckled to himself and asked, "Are those strange grey plates still stacked on that stone shelf?" He chuckled some more when he saw our gaping mouths.

"Yes I'm sure that every new generation on this Island throws up a couple of adventurers who stumble on to that secret chamber and think they've found a hoard of lost pirate treasure or the lost Ark. I was one of those young adventurers myself once and I guess in a way it's reassuring to know there are still some young people around today who are able to leave behind their televisions, mobiles, and music players for a... But I've interrupted you, Rodney, please continue?"

I picked up where I had left off and told him about the silver napkin ring which I had brought with me. I passed it to him to and he turned it in his hand before returning it to me. I told him about my internet search and my suspicion that it had left a trail for somebody from outside the island to trace me. The President looked towards Joelle, she nodded back and quickly confirmed that such a trace was possible. He became serious when I recounted our experience with the Belgian man Ronnier and sucked air through his teeth when I got to the part where he broke into my house, knocked out Nahil and tied both of us up. His face displayed open shock when I described how he had attacked Andy but then how Andy had managed to pull off a last-minute rescue and save us.

"This is serious." He exclaimed, "You should have gone to the police." He raised a hand to silence me before I could respond.

"I know about your feud with Henri but it only partially explains your reluctance to go to the authorities, you could have asked to see Raymond Matine. Anyway go on what happened next?"

When I'd finished telling the whole story right up to the moment Ferrari brought the lump hammer down on to my arm, the President leaned back stretched his arms up and laced his fingers behind his head.

"Tell me," he said, "does the name Richard Denver mean anything to you?" The President had addressed the question to all of us but we turned in surprise to look at Andy who had gasped and suddenly leaned forward in his seat, his eyes shining.

"Y-Yes I've h-heard that name before." He was speaking to the whole group rather than to just the President. "With everything going on this last week I forgot to tell anyone about the call I made to Josh, my friend in the UK." We stared at him in incomprehension until he explained, "The friend I mentioned the one who I asked to dig up information on the Valvaston for us." Andy quickly brought the President up to speed on his friend in the UK though I noticed he conveniently left out any mention of being in the Special Forces.

"I can give you the details of h-how he got the information and his sources ano-nother time," said Andy, his enthusiasm enabling him to blast through the blocks he had on certain words.

"B-but basically the Valvaston was an interloper. An interloper was a ship or even an individual acting in defiance of the law that gave the East India Company the monopoly over all trade between Britain and India and, indeed, all the islands in the Indian Ocean. Interlopers were usually fast midsized Frigates carrying cargo from India to the UK. The Valvaston was such a ship and it carried a cargo of spices and cotton."

"Not a cargo to survive a shipwreck and the intervening centuries," commented Duval.

"Exactly," agreed Andy. "But following a suggestion from Joelle I also asked Josh to keep an eye out to see if anyone else had, or was, following the same trail, and he came up with only one name, Richard Denver!" We looked from Andy to the President, who nodded before adding his piece to the jigsaw of information.

"I got that name from Raymond Matine who carried out George Ferrari's interrogation. Ferrari said it was the name of the man who offered him five thousand US dollars or its equivalent in any currency of his choosing to find out the whereabouts of the Valvaston from you."

"But I don't know where it is," I exclaimed in frustration.

"We know that Rodney but clearly your internet enquiry has led others to believe that you do."

"Has this Richard Denver incriminated himself in a way we can we can bring him to justice," asked Andy practical as ever.

"Not really," replied the President, "Ferrari received no payment into any of his bank accounts. However, I have done a little research into Richard Denver and the results are very interesting. He is the head of a large organisation that comprises a conglomerate of companies in different industries and spread right across most of the globe. His personal wealth is such he could afford to buy the whole St Gilberts group with his pocket money. However, and this is the interesting bit, as far as this Valvaston is concerned, he made his first fortune in marine salvage with the discovery of a sunken treasure ship called the Levia."

"So the Valvaston could be another treasure ship!" Said Nahil, her eyes shining with excitement at the prospect.

"Well, it must have contained something of great value for Mr Denver to go to so much trouble to find it."

"Why can't we find it first then," persisted Nahil and the President smiled at her excitement.

"Well, there's nothing to stop us trying by using whatever limited resources we have, but the point is, even if Denver finds it first, if he finds it in our territorial waters, then officially the wreck belongs to us anyway."

"S-Surely whether the wreck is f-found or not this whole story, with the s-secret chamber at St Francis M-Mount, could be made into a real tourist attraction to pull people to St Gilberts from all over the world!" Andy, back on his tourist attraction idea I thought. The President sighed.

"I'm sure you are right Andrew but tourism is a double-edged sword on an island of this size, we cannot even cope with the two tourist hotels we already have. As it is they stretch what the island can supply in terms of freshwater, sewerage and refuge disposal—not to mention fuel. Diesel generated electrical power is getting more expensive every month and, added to the rising cost of imported food staples such as rice and dairy produce, we are already struggling. Extra income from tourism may cover some of the costs of imports but providing the utility services is another matter. St Gilberts main selling point for visitors is its natural beauty and on that score we'd have no problem in attracting any number of tourists; not since that famous travel writer—"Duval screwed his eyes almost closed as he tried to remember the name. "O-oh what's his name—Paul—Paul—something." He looked around at each of us but we shook our heads and shrugged our shoulders, we didn't know either.

"Anyway, ever since he listed St Gilberts as the most beautiful tropical island on the planet, the phone in our office of tourism has been ringing non-stop." I missed a little of what Duval said next because I was trying to mentally recall, had the President just said "the phone in our office of tourism"? So the office charged with the job of fielding enquiries from abroad regarding tourism relating to the whole Gilberts Island Group, only had one phone? I returned to the present Duval and was still speaking.

"For us to be able to cater for more tourists some of that natural beauty would inevitably be sacrificed. Tourists bring income to the island but they also bring ecological and financial costs. I know the standard of our hotels falls well below what the tourists have come to expect these days, especially if they have visited other places such as Mauritius and the Seychelles. But it's not just the hotel buildings. As a people we don't do customer service very well, it's not in our nature."

"What do you mean by that?" asked Nahil defensively.

"Well, enough tourists have taken the time to provide feedback to us and on our performance as a tourist destination for us to have no illusions about our customer service. Many have reported that the service they received across the island, not just in the hotels; was slow, indifferent and even rude to the point of surly." None of us in the room could argue with that. We are not rude or bad people; it's just that as a nation we are suspicious of outsiders and tend to keep strangers at arm's length until we know and trust them. Once trust is established, all barriers come down and the visitor becomes part of the family and we are the friendliest people in the whole world, but how often does that ever happen to a tourist on a one-or two week vacation? *Even to a local insider like me*, I thought, but said nothing.

We sat in silence for a few moments reflecting on St Gilberts growing tourist industry and the insights the President had shared with us. I was glad Duval, with his obvious regard for the Island's ecology and its people, was in charge of steering us through such complex issues. Suddenly, the President took a deep breath and slapped his hands down on to the low table in front of him.

"So, let's get back to the problem of what to do about Richard Denver. Now it just so happens that I have the telephone number of his office here on my desk, let's give him a ring to see what he has to say for himself shall we?" He stood and walked over to his desk, and, using the intercom called for his secretary to come through. He handed her a sheet of paper with the telephone number on it and waited till she had left the room. Two minutes later the phone on the desk rang and the President lifted one finger to his lips signalling that we should remain silent then he lifted the receiver. With the phone to his ear he looked first at us and then down at the desktop waiting for the connection to be made.

"Hello this is Gerard Duval. Yes I am the President of The St Gilberts Island Group." His secretary had clearly already announced his status when she had put the call through.

"It is a group of Islands in the Indian Ocean north of Madagascar," Duval explained patiently.

"I would like to speak to Mr Denver please, er no, I have not made an appointment." The president's brow came down in irritation he wasn't used to being stalled on the phone, especially by a secretary.

"Well, when can I speak to him? This is a matter of some importance. No I don't want to give you an outline first. I want to speak directly with Mr Denver. Where is he now; do you have a number that I can contact him on? OK, well, when is he due back then?" Duval's voice had increased in volume slightly and I could see that he was losing his temper with the person at the other end of the line.

"So what do you suggest?" He said after listening in silence to what was clearly a lengthy explanation from the other speaker.

"Well, I guess that will have to do then, yes my name is Gerard Duval, D-U-V-A-L," he spelled it out, "and I am the President of St Gilberts. I want Mr Denver to call me urgently on a matter of importance my number is..." He put the phone down annoyance written across his face.

"Well, I guess you caught the gist of that. Our Mr Denver is not in the office at present and they won't say where he has gone or when he is due back. They gave me some excuse about security and their need to avoid the possibility of Mr Denver's kidnap or something like that. She said Mr Denver worries the paparazzi might learn of his whereabouts and cause a nuisance taking pictures." Duval shook his head dismissively to show that he found the excuses over dramatic and then an open-handed gesture as if to say "Well, I did try," he returned to his seat at the low coffee-table.

"Well, there doesn't seem to be anything more we can do for the present. I will try to get Denver again and will let you know if I do. For your part you must promise to tell me immediately if anyone else contacts you about the Valvaston, and straight away this time, is that understood?" He looked at us all in turn and waited for each of us to agree in turn.

"Oh—and as for your friend in England, Andrew, please send my thanks to him for his efforts and let me know if he comes up with anything else. We need to clear this mystery up." Andy agreed, thanked the President and joined us as we filed out of the office.

Richard Denver's secretary frowned with worry and annoyance. The telephone conversation with Gerard Duval had caught her off guard and at one point in it she found herself close to babbling which was not like her at all. All that flannel about the paparazzi, security and kidnapping for God's sake, what had she been thinking? All of it had been a hastily improvised smokescreen. In truth she had no idea where her boss Richard Denver had disappeared to and, more importantly, when he was due to return. He had never gone off like this before and no one else in the organisation, not even Mr Carr, would say where Denver had gone. Richard Denver had rung her at her home on the Saturday evening and simply said that he was going to take a couple of weeks off work and that had been it. The timing of the call meant she was not in work mode or she might have asked for more details of his itinerary but it was all too late now. Perhaps her mention of Mr Denver's possible kidnap had stemmed from her own imagination, an attempt to explain his sudden and unexplained disappearance. She had also tried to contact George Kirkham, Denver's head of security. He was the logical person to contact in the current circumstances and she also knew Kirkham enjoyed a close friendship with Denver going back many years to when they worked together in marine salvage. The security man was also not available and nobody knew where he was either, or indeed, when he was due back.

She contacted Gerald Carr to express her concerns and he reassured her that he had received a call from Denver—a message left on his answering machine. It was the same message that she herself had received off Denver; that he was taking a couple of weeks leave. It was out of character for Denver to disappear without leaving an itinerary and Carr, more concerned than he let on, fretted in private. If Denver was having a break down he shuddered at the effect it could have on the stock value of their myriad companies when word of it reached the share market.

"Do not breathe a word of this to anyone," he'd warned her and "transfer all his calls through to me until I say otherwise. Leave it to me to organise a discreet search to see if I can trace his whereabouts and check he's OK." She thanked Carr and felt a weight lifted off her shoulders.

Richard Denver made his own travel arrangements, a novel experience for him. When you have fame and money then travel, and the logistics of travel, pose few of the barriers and hurdles that confront most people. Since he had decided to opt for as low a profile as possible, booking the flights to Mayotte did give him a brief insight into one of the jobs he had been delegating to others for years. Although Mayotte was still sometimes described as belonging to the Comoros Archipelago, in 1974 its people voted to forgo independence and remain part of the overseas collectivity of France thus separating itself from the other islands in the group. It was a decision that saw them prosper compared with the other islands of the Comoros Archipelago. Travelling with his head of Security and long-time friend George Kirkham, Denver found himself perversely enjoying the discomforts and minor privations of their four-leg journey to Mayotte. From London their first stop was in Paris followed by Kenya then Reunion before they reached their destination of Mayotte in the Southern Indian Ocean. Mayotte, a small group of islands halfway between northern Madagascar and northern Mozambique had been the Ryders nearest landfall when they had received his call.

George Kirkham left Denver's marine salvage firm shortly after the discovery of the Levia and had joined an American security firm based in London. He took to the work and quickly rose through the ranks. Seeing his potential his employers gave him a posting to the United States to work in within the parent company and continue his training to a higher level than was available in the UK. He returned to the UK a year later to take up a senior post in the London branch and it was while he was in this job that Richard Denver head-hunted him to front his own security department. Denver's friendship with George had been allowed to lapse in recent years mainly through neglect on Denver's part rather than through any disagreement. Even so Denver had occasionally been offhand and even downright rude to Kirkham but Kirkham had remained loyal. He remembered the Denver of old when they both worked aboard Denver's salvage vessel. George had just left the army at the time after a stint in Northern Ireland. Army life had suited George but he clashed with his commanding officer and one particular disagreement led to an exchange of punches. The incident looked set to stymie his future career prospects in the forces so he had left. By chance he met Richard Denver who was looking for crew at the time. Despite no previous sailing experience Denver took George on as crew and the two men found they got on well together. Perhaps it was Kirkham's military background that enabled him to accept the sudden changes in Denver's behaviour. Kirkham was able to remain calm while absorbing the other's abrupt commands and brusque put-downs Denver occasionally threw at him when he was under stress. On the journey from the UK, as they shuffled through airport security checks and sat side by side in aircraft seats, George saw glimpses of the old Denver gradually emerging during the long journey. Now, forced to spend hours in each other's company they managed to re-forge some of the links that had lost over the intervening years.

On the final plane journey from Reunion they looked at a map of the islands off the East coast of Africa. Together they agreed that it would probably take several days sailing to reach St Gilberts from Mayotte. The Ryders had said they would meet them at the airport. Their plane landed on the small adjoining island of Pamandze sometimes called Petite-Terre because the runway was situated there, a narrow landing strip built on land partially reclaimed from the sea. The runway was so narrow that, as the plane dropped low on its final approach, it had disappeared from view beneath the aircraft giving the passengers the unsettling sensation that they were about to land on the ocean itself. Jeanette Ryder stood waiting for them in the small airport as they cleared customs. She had commandeered a taxi to take them across the causeway from Pamandze to the tiny coral atoll of Dzaoudzi on which the main administration centre was based along with a French Foreign Legion detachment HQ.

"See that Island over that's Gran Terre the largest of the Mayotte Islands ferry barges can take you over to it but we won't need to go there—unless of course you want to?" Jeanette Ryder looked at the two men who both shook their heads.

"We're anchored in the sheltered hollow between Pamandze and Dzaoudzi."

Jeanette Ryder had not been sure what to expect when she had agreed to let Richard Denver and a colleague, to join them on their yacht on a clandestine journey back to St Gilberts. The decision to agree to Denver's proposal had been a source of friction between her and Keith. From the moment she'd replaced the phone, turned, and told him that she had just agreed to on their behalf his mood had changed. Even now she was not sure what annoyed Keith the most, the proposal itself, or the fact she'd accepted it without consulting him first. Since that moment there had been a subtle, but tangible, breakdown in the telepathic closeness they'd enjoyed since the early days of their marriage. Jeanette Ryder knew that her acceptance of Denver's proposal was not the only thing causing the growing rift between her and her husband, the sexual chemistry between them, once so intense, had also waned. Her husband had been comfortable with the safe sadomasochistic role-playing in Johannesburg but was clearly uncomfortable with the real thing.

Stuff him she thought with annoyance but then; remembering he was not only her husband but an intrinsic part of her lifestyle, the business, and her sailing partner on the yacht, chewed her lip in worry. Maybe it was worth throttling back her growing attraction to women and her addiction to violent sex, for the sake of their marriage and the life it gave her. On the other hand, how could she deny her contempt for his weakness, his lack of adventure and the fact he was turning into the antithesis of the man she thought she had married? When they had first met in that hotel she knew herself to be bisexual with a healthy interest in sex with both men and women. Over the last few months the sex with her husband had become stale, predictable and frankly disappointing, and so she had found herself drawn more and more towards women. Perhaps that stupid computer tart, Joelle had started the rot.

Keith had behaved differently after their departure from St Gilberts and, while he behaved differently, she actually looked different. Joelle's parting punch had broken her nose and, despite the swift application of an ice pack, the pain and the bleeding had just gone on and on. For days her nose had remained swollen and discoloured. It was now also permanently blocked, which forced her to breathe through her mouth causing her mouth to be constantly dry and her breath rancid. Keith commented on her snoring which kept him awake at night and, though he never said anything, she suspected from the way he leaned away from her when she spoke that her mouth needed a slug of mouthwash. When the main swelling finally went down the real damage to her nose became even more apparent. The break had changed the shape of the nose itself. Now it spoilt her otherwise symmetrical and attractive features. The broken nose was now the focal point of her face and it was not a focal point to be proud of.

When they reached a reputable hospital the consultant had confirmed the nose was broken and suggested surgery to repair not only the cosmetic damage to her nose but also to clear damaged cartilage and bone obstructing her breathing. She had readily agreed to surgery but because her injury was little more than two weeks old the consultant advised against any operation until the inflammation had subsided. She would have to wait another six months before he could operate. So now she struggled on with her breathing and still flinched each time she confronted her reflection in a mirror. She had a score to settle with that little island bint and Denver's offer of a return to St Gilberts looked like it might provide her with the opportunity to do exactly that.

The Ryders used the internet to gather information on all their clients. The first time Denver had hired them they had checked his background now they ran another, more extensive search printing off any pages of interest. Richard Denver, they found, was a man whose life consisted of three broad stages, at least if you believed the press.

The first stage was the young Richard Denver. A rugged marine salvage engineer, pictured in press photos dressed casually, a burly man's man with a broad open face split with a confident smile. The accompanying text contained words such as "young, reckless, risk taking, adventurous, determined and tough."

The second stage began with the discovery of the Spanish treasure ship the Levia. The press coverage on Denver by now increased a thousandfold, showed a successful young man enjoying the attention that being young and rich and famous brings. There he was at the wheel of an expensive sports car, or walking a red-carpet with a beautiful actress in tow to attend a film premier. The pictures were different and so were the words that came with them; "Playboy, party, rich, wealthy, lucky, and arrogant."

Stage three began when Denver entered the business world after going into partnership with his old friend Gerald Carr. The press photos of this stage showed a middle-aged man formally dressed in dark business suits carrying papers, signing papers, getting in or out of dark limousines and always seemingly oblivious to the camera that was capturing his image. Now, fleshier in both body and face he no longer smiled at the camera, his jowly face remaining grim and humourless. The accompanying text for the pictures contained words such as; "powerful, relentless, driven, forceful, and magnate."

Jeanette Ryder had prepared herself to meet the stern businessman at the height of his powers and one whose high-powered lifestyle would leave him unprepared for Mayotte's earthy reality. Now she watched with surprise and growing interest at the two large men walking out of the airport carrying holdalls. They were talking to each other relaxed and grinning as if they had just exchanged a joke. Relieved their baggage was small and carried in soft-sided grips, hard cases would have taken up space and been more difficult to stow—smiling she walked towards them. Both had dressed casually in jeans and loose polo shirts and she instantly recognised Denver as the shorter of the two men though at six foot he was hardly short. The taxi sagged under the combined weight of passengers and luggage, but still made it across the causeway to Dzaoudzi. It continued through some narrow dusty and crowded streets lined with women wearing brightly coloured kangas while others, swathed in yards of red and white cotton, were selling produce spread out on cloths on the roadside. Woven baskets containing charcoal stood to one side. The women had stacked small pyramids of fruit and vegetables, vanilla pods, mounds of peppers and chilli on the cloths along with some huge Jackfruits. Other baskets contained rice and other dark roots. Denver thought Dzaoudzi a pretty place with its palm trees, bougainvillea bushes, and mango trees which were alive with squabbling fruitbats.

It all reminded Denver back to a time in his early twenties. He was at university studying to be a marine engineer. His work experience placement consisted of a few months at the Masinga Dam project in Kenya one hundred and sixty kilometres north-east of Nairobi, it wasn't exactly marine work but it was connected to water. Masinga is a dry arid area desperate for water and power and the dam had been constructed to alleviate the problem. At the end on his placement he took the opportunity to visit Malindi and Mombasa on the Kenyan coast and Dzaoudzi now brought back memories of that visit to the African coast. He had been young then, the work practical and interesting, and Africa exciting and stimulating. As a result the placement had been one of the happiest times of his life. Now he savoured the myriad scents and odours rushing in through the open taxi windows and let them transport him back through the years to a happier time.

The French influence on the island was clear in the street signs, the style of the shops and cafes, and in the tourists themselves. Where the locals covered themselves in yards of material or flowing robes, the tourists opted to wear as little as possible. Red dust blew in through the open windows swirling about them irritating their eyes and settling over their clothes. Denver smelt diesel and petrol fumes, copra, rotting refuse and sewage, but there was also an underlying current of fresh sea air, fish and an intriguing top note of spices, coffee and ylang-ylang, the perfume essence he'd read was an export of the island. When the taxi finally dropped them off at the quayside Jeanette Ryder paid the driver off in Euros while the two men knocked the dust off their shirts and trousers.

"Sorry about that," she apologised but they simply shrugged and smiled back at her. Along the quayside locals were spit-roasting kebabs and deep-frying green bananas.

"They're roasting fruitbats," said Jeanette Ryder "They taste quite nice actually and since the island is swarming with the blighters, it's the freshest meat you can get here." The two men hefted their bags and followed her to a floating jetty and towards the lone white man stood next to an inflatable. Jeanette spoke over her shoulder as they walked, "We've heard Anjouan, one of the independent islands in the Comoros Archipelago, has more character, is a damn sight cheaper and the people are friendlier too."

"That's when they're not shooting at you or killing each other," interrupted the man on the quayside, his hand extended in welcome. "Hi. I'm Keith."

"Will this hold all four of us and the luggage as well?" asked George Kirkham after he had shook the others hand. He eyed the inflatable dubiously.

"No problem at all," replied the man as he helped them board from the jetty. The small outboard took them the short distance to a sleek white yacht. The couple were proud of their beloved Hallberg-Rassey.

"Welcome aboard Wave Ryder. We're all fuelled up; the water tanks are full to burst, so we're ready to go whenever you are." He waved down towards the companionway leading down to the saloon inviting them to descend. "Probably not up to your usual standards but nevertheless—"

"It looks absolutely fine to me," interrupted Denver letting out a sigh of appreciation as he looked around well-appointed saloon.

"Then perhaps I can interest you gentlemen in an ice-cold beer," asked Keith Ryder.

"Now you're talking!" exclaimed George flopping down on to one of the bench seats. The two men looked around at the workmanship in the mahogany and teak trim about the saloon and nodded appreciatively. The quality of the accommodation far exceeded Denver's expectations and he felt a further releasing of the internal stress and tension that had become a constant part of his physiology over the last few years. The Ryders had considered giving Denver their large cabin and then decided against, giving him the larger of the remaining cabins instead. They gave his companion one of smaller ones. All the cabins, apart from the one they used for their occasional sexual forays, offered a high level of comfort and were close to amenities.

The Ryders were pleasantly surprised to find their guests not only pleased with the accommodation but almost childlike in their appreciation of Jeanette's cooking. It augured well for the days ahead when they would be in close proximity with their two guests. Denver and his companion were in fact the first two guests, prostitutes aside, that they had ever let sail with them since owning the yacht.

"See those buttons there?" Keith pointed at the steering pedestal directly in front of Denver who was gripping the wheel.

"With those buttons you can raise and lower the anchor, or set and sheet the sails!" Denver nodded appreciatively.

"From what you've shown me so far Keith, it looks as if a yacht like this could be sailed single-handed."

"It could," agreed Keith adding ruefully, "A bit lonely though, and if anything went wrong with the equipment or you had an accident in the galley or something…" Keith let the thought hang in the air but when he looked to see Denver's reaction to the hypothetical scenarios he could see from the other's face that Denver considered the risks reasonable and acceptable. Denver and Kirkham soon worked out that Jeanette was the dominant partner in the Ryders marriage. There was something in the way she addressed her husband as the two of them moved and worked effortlessly about the yacht.

Keith however, was better company and was certainly the better of the two at explaining the workings of the yacht. Denver was an eager student and his previous sailing experience, coupled with his engineering background, meant that he quickly grasped the purpose of each control and the mechanics working them. He studied the yacht, its rig and sails and the Perkins engine. Keith for his part enjoyed the other man's obvious interest and enthusiasm to learn more.

Showing Denver the features of the Hallberg-Rassey 62 was for Keith, what it must be like for a proud parent to be asked to describe the qualities of their favourite child. He explained the Mastervolt Whisper Ultra electricity generator and showed him how all the navigation, communication and sonar equipment worked, much of which Denver seemed already familiar with and, if anything, his knowledge exceeded Keith's own. Both Denver and his companion relished any opportunity to undertake sailing duties and, it seemed, the more physical the better. Keith thought that they were like men of action finally released from tedious desk duty. Strong winds ensured an exhilarating voyage from Mayotte towards St Gilberts and the four of them stood turns at the helm throughout the day and night. Keith Ryder was secretly impressed that neither of the two men had fallen ill with seasickness. The up and down, and side to side motion of the yacht was relentless hour after hour, so much so, movement below deck became a nightmare. Table edges and cupboards rose to strike at the limbs of all those making their way to the heads, their cabin, or to the galley. Stomachs lifted as the bows came slamming down, falling through space to hit the trough of the grey swells. It was worse than being drunk it was as if it was not them but the world itself that was drunk, thrashing and reeling beneath them and around the hull.

During one of the quieter spells Kirkham and Denver were studying a map on the chart table as Keith Ryder pointed out the course they were currently following.

"At present the South-West Trade winds are pushing us," said Keith Ryder making a sweeping gesture with his hand across the map to show the direction of the wind.

"If we continue at our current speed then we should make St Gilberts at roughly midday tomorrow. However, since you want to arrive after dark we will cut back on the sail tomorrow morning and take our time, going on the engine if needs be." Kirkham asked a question.

"If the wind is blowing in that direction and we want to go here," he pointed at St Gilberts on the map, "Then why are we heading in this direction?" He laid the edge of his hand on the map at a tangent to the island, "Couldn't we just go straight towards the island with the wind blowing at our back?"

"Well, we'll actually travel faster with the wind on our beam than when it's behind us. Not only that but it's damned uncomfortable sailing with a following wind, the sails fill and then spill causing the yacht to roll horribly from side to side. Chances are we'd all be seasick after a few hours of it. They call it the 'Death Roll' apparently."

"Sounds unpleasant," said Kirkham.

"Oh believe me it is," Keith assured him. "I know we've been thrown around a bit since we left Mayotte but with the Death Roll the motion is different and almost certain to have you heaving. Anyway, I'm about to get myself a juice, what about you gentlemen?"

"A beer for me," replied Kirkham and Denver opted for the same.

"Did you sleep well?" asked Jeanette Ryder as Richard Denver entered the saloon. He was running a hand through his tousled hair and blinking through sleep encrusted eyes at the bright early morning light pouring in through the side windows.

"Like a baby," came his prompt reply. Unlike Keith, Jeanette Ryder had found it difficult to connect with either of the two guests and Denver in particular. She wasn't sure whose fault that was, hers or Denver's. So far her attempts at conversation had not progressed beyond hearty greetings and even some of those had been awkward and stilted. Perhaps it was because he was so unlike the man she had been expecting—the ruthless, cynical businessman. Instead she had welcomed aboard a reasonably mellow and easy-going middle-aged man, more marine engineer than corporate suit. To her surprise, in a rush of insight, she realised she would probably have found the ruthless businessman easier to relate to than the chilled engineer. Nevertheless, she decided she would have another try. She took the seat across the table from him.

"I've got some water on to boil. Is it coffee again or do you want tea for a change?"

"No, coffee's fine, thanks," he replied still rubbing the sleep out of his eyes but behind the rumpled exterior his mind was working. How best to broach the question he had already decided to direct at the wife rather than the husband? He decided to employ an elliptical approach—the opposite of his usual style—but what the hell?

"Jeanette, you and Keith have a lovely yacht here. Don't you ever worry about pirates when you're far out on the ocean?" Denver saw from her expression that his question had taken her by surprise.

"Well, yes we are aware of the danger and this yacht is fitted with state-of-the-art tracking technology in case it is ever stolen and we are still alive to search for it. And of course, we always have the radar warning system switched on..."

"So what if you get a warning and their boat is faster than yours; have you any means of defending yourselves?" interrupted Denver.

"Well, we have firearms onboard and both Keith and I know how to use them. Why do you ask?" There was caution in her voice as she wondered where the conversation was going.

"I really am interested in how you keep a yacht like this safe on the open seas; after all, it must be an extremely attractive target to any yacht thief. I was also thinking about tonight and when I go ashore to visit Leon in his home. After what they did to you and Keith last time, and with Ronnier's inexplicable death, maybe it would be wise to carry some protection."

"You are not intending to shoot anyone, I hope," Jeanette said coolly.

"No, of course not, all I want is an uninterrupted discussion with Rodney Leon. More importantly, I don't want them to shoot us!"

"Well, if that's all you want," she said in a flat noncommittal voice and Denver couldn't decide if her voice had had a note of doubt or disappointment in it.

"Yes absolutely. I thought if George and Keith carried a pistol then at least we could ensure we are in control of the proceedings rather than them. We would also be in a better position to discourage violence or stop an escalation of it should any start."

"Keith?" Jeanette Ryder exclaimed, her voice an octave higher. "No Mr Denver. I will be accompanying you ashore, Keith will be staying on the boat."

"But I just thought that Keith would be—" Denver began to protest.

"Look, Mr Denver," cut in Jeanette Ryder, her tone formal. "If, as you say, you simply want an uninterrupted discussion without any trouble, then which is going to look more threatening; three men bursting in on them, armed or not, or two men and a woman?" Denver thought for a moment, she did have a point.

"OK, you're on the team." Jeanette Ryder gave him a tight little smile which Denver did not return, instead the muscles underneath his fleshy jawline hardened, and for a brief second his eyes bored into hers.

Denver the ruthless businessman had just made his first appearance.

With sails stowed, blinds drawn on all the windows and portholes and all deck and rigging lights extinguished, Wave Ryder dropped anchor a safe distance from the reef off Anse Raffin. From the deck Denver used a pair of binoculars to look up at the villa high on the cliff. He saw light streaming through the trailing vegetation from the open space of the veranda. The house was traditional and yet ultramodern in the way it blended in beautifully with its surroundings. The balcony veranda was empty of people and he lowered the binoculars and descended to the saloon. George was leaving his cabin holding two pairs of military style night vision goggles.

"Where did you get those from?" asked Denver.

"From my travel bag," replied Kirkham breezily. Denver frowned.

"Jeez George how the hell would you have explained those to customs if they'd found them and asked?" There was a note of annoyance in Denver's voice but George recognising the symptoms of pre-battle nerves in Denver, simply smiled back at him.

"Essential kit for observing the nesting Green Turtle as she comes ashore at night. Look I've even brought a book on their laying habits if you want to see it? We'll need these when we try to find that break in the reef in the dark. From what I've seen so far it won't be easy at night without these." He held up the goggles.

"I've brought two pairs Jeanette should have one pair as she's the one steering the inflatable and I thought I'd wear the other pair. I've worn them before and have a better idea of what to look out for in terms of any alarms or defences we may have to breach." Denver nodded his agreement but remained silent. When he was younger, back in his marine salvage days, a jaunt like this would have been meat and drink to him but now he doubted his ability to meet danger and physical challenges. He hoped that he up to whatever he was going to meet in the next few hours. George was speaking to Jeanette and showing her how to wear the goggles, Denver shook his head to bring himself into the present and with an effort he tuned into their conversation.

"I've taken a look at that cliff, I know it's dark but I can't see any path up to the house," said George.

"There is one," replied Jeanette as she remembered how Leon had made his way down to the beach on the day he'd swum out to the yacht.

"It's to the left of the beach, I'll show you when we reach the shore."

It was one of those blazing hot days where you are reluctant to leave the shade. We spent most of the day in the cool of the Kokonet Café. I was picking up more and more knowledge about the business, and computers in general, every day. I reckoned the more I learnt the more useful I'd be to Joelle. My pride wouldn't let me take any money off Joelle. She knew I was strapped for cash now that I no longer had any money changing scams going or any income from 'gigolo' activity. And so quietly, and without fuss, she started to pick up most of the day-to-day expenses. She usually bought most of the food and drink. She'd been to the market earlier in the day and brought back a big Red Snapper, my favourite fish and, so as not to let it stink up the café, we left Julie to lock up and went home early to get it scaled and ready for the oven. Joelle made a Creole sauce of tomatoes, mushrooms, peppers and chillies all fried in oil with some tomato puree thrown in. With the fish baking in the oven Joelle suggested we go down for a paddle. I still had a cast on my arm but readily agreed thinking I could put a plastic bag over it but then, when I looked around for one in vain, I just followed her outside anyway. The cast was driving me mad in the heat and I had resorted to using one of Aunt Mert's knitting needles to scratch underneath it so covering it in a plastic bag could only have made it even more uncomfortable. We slipped out of the house and down to the beach and stood cooling ourselves in the sea. We were up to our waists in the sea, well, at least Joelle was, it was only halfway up my legs, when we started throwing seaweed at each other. I heard voices behind and turned to see Andy and Nahil coming down the trail to join us.

"Checked the house and saw you were out, then heard your shouting and thought we'd come and join you." Neither of them had their swimming stuff but they tipped their pockets out on to a corner of the cloth Joelle had spread on the sand they walked straight into the sea with their shorts and tee-shirts on. I know some tourists like to get all their kit off on the beach, I've even encouraged a few to do it myself, women that is, but on St Gilberts public nudity is generally frowned on. Besides, I find stripping off in front of people I know more embarrassing than in front of people I've never seen before and therefore unlikely to see again. As the sun fell lower we made our way back to the house and waiting in the garden was a box of beers that Andy had left there before joining us on the beach.

"Well, that's us sorted for tonight," I said, and we made our way indoors. After we had eaten we just sat and talked for an hour or so before Nahil went through my CD collection and put on some Sega music. The two girls got up and began dancing. Reluctantly, for I'd just gotten comfortable, I rose to join them as did Andy. I showed Andy, for what seemed like the umpteenth time since I'd known him, how to dance the Sega like a local instead of embarrassing Nahil, and the rest of us, in the Katcholo Club with his robotic arm and leg movements.

"No, no, not that way. Look, just imagine your feet in deep soft sand—especially your big toes, yes, that's more like it, now wave your arms like this." I flinched as I tried to lift my left arm in its cast. It was at that moment that the expression on Andy's face suddenly changed causing me to look around to see what was capturing his attention. Even as I turned a sense of foreboding was already turning the fish dinner rancid in my guts then I caught sight of the three people who had just entered the lounge through the unlocked door. Yes I should have locked it but I doubt if even a seven-lever mortise lock would have kept out the trio that had just sauntered in.

I immediately recognised the woman from the big yacht, the one who'd put the boot into Joelle and me and then locked us in a cabin. She looked different though, and then I realised that it was her nose, Joelle's fisty-work. Had the woman returned to exact some sort of revenge? Nahil reached over and switched the CD player off and I turned my attention to the two men, surprised that the woman's husband was not one of them. Both were large men like middle-aged doormen. The taller, broader and tougher looking of the two men studied me as if measuring me for a coffin. I guessed he was assessing how much of a risk I posed, I was taller than him and perhaps my shoulders made him think me more formidable than I actually am. He'd obviously dismissed Andy, surely the most lethal person in the room, as insignificant. In the brief silence that followed I noticed both the yacht woman and the tall tough guy looking to the shorter man as if waiting for some directions as to what they should do next. As if on cue the man in question began to speak.

"Everyone stay calm, we're not looking for any trouble. I just want to have a chat with Rodney Leon here." And he looked directly at me. My stomach hit my ribcage at that and I could only gape back at him in shock. On another level my mind was working frenetically and had seized on his switch from the plural to the singular from the "we" to "I" in his sentences.

"And who the hell are you to b-break into someone else's h-house and demand a chat?" It was Andy and he looked as if he was about to move forward and physically assault the man. I broke the tense silence that followed his challenge by answering Andy's question.

"Mr Denver I presume." Every head in the room turned towards me and then back towards the shorter of the two men stood fore square in the centre of the lounge. He gave a brief smile confirming my assumption and looked relieved, as if I had made something easier for him, perhaps it had solved the problem of how to begin his little "chat".

"Yes that's right, my name is Richard Denver and I came because I want you to tell me everything you know about the Valvaston."

"Yeah right," snorted Andy derisively. "If you are not looking for trouble then what's with the guns," he demanded. I hadn't noticed any guns and none of them seemed to be carrying anything other than some funny goggles and a torch, but I trusted Andy's assessment—after all it used to be his job as a VIP bodyguard. Denver's face remained calm as he replied, "They're simply a precaution, for our own protection, just in case you become as rough as you have been with my previous emissaries."

"Emissaries," repeated Joelle not understanding the word.

"Yes," replied Denver his voice still calm. "Philippe Ronnier died in suspicious circumstances and this woman and her husband were assaulted by you, you and another man who doesn't appear to be here at present. He had a rifle then I believe."

"Ronnier? From Belgium, right?" asked Andy.

"The very man," replied Denver smoothly without taking his eyes from mine. Nahil's voice, full of anger and indignation, suddenly cut into this exchange, "That pig-shit madman knocked me out, tied me up and then tried to kill us all, and you're the one who fricking sent him?" This last bit was delivered at full volume which, coming from Nahil, would have flattened a less substantial man. I saw a frown of incomprehension cross Denver's face and then a look of real surprise in his eyes. Before he could recover Joelle confronted him hands-on hips.

"This woman," she pointed accusingly at the woman whose nose she had remodelled, "and her husband drugged me and locked me and Rodney in a cabin on that yacht of theirs. They're nasty people and I'm glad I smashed her face in."

"Pigshits," muttered Nahil in support and glowered across at the yacht woman before balling her tiny hands into fists. She looked ready to take the three of them on single-handed with or without their guns.

I guessed it was my turn so I simply lifted my left arm to show him the cast and said, "George Ferrari, was he another of your emissaries?" Denver's mouth fell open in genuine surprise that, or he was an actor of Oscar winning potential. He shook his head from side to side as if all that we had just told him really was breaking news. I studied his face carefully and his shock looked genuine enough and he really had no reason to act otherwise? He was still the one with the initiative—and the guns.

"Surely you're not going to believe all that crap?" Spat the woman suddenly moving forward, she had drawn a pistol from her pocket and was aiming at Joelle. The expression on her face was chilling. There was something at the back of her eyes that screamed 'unhinged'. She strode towards Joelle and raised the pistol and I could see from the way she held it that she was not going to use it shoot Joelle but to pistol-whip her with it. It would have been like hitting her with a hammer so I lunged forward to intercept the blow but Denver reached her first.

"What the hell do you think you are doing?" he hissed, grabbing her upraised armed.

"Get the fuck off me." She snarled, but the other, taller man, also took hold of her and expertly prised the pistol from her hand and pocketed it. Joelle had her fists raised and her right foot back behind her, I saw she was ready to continue her apprenticeship in cosmetic surgery on the woman's face. Andy, I guessed, was calculating the odds of annihilating all three of them in a burst of controlled aggression, Nahil meanwhile stood ready to back him up. Perhaps it was only me who'd picked up the vibes coming from the two men and realised that they were genuinely not looking for trouble. I turned my attention away from the struggling woman with the killer feet, bent nose, and crazy eyes; she was clearly as stable as an oven-roasted grenade. The attitude of the two men on the other hand did not strike me as particularly threatening. Maybe Denver really had come for a chat. If Andy was an expert at spotting potential danger, and then dealing with it, then my strength is empathy, and the confidence I have in my ability to assess the person in front of me. Perhaps it has been that self-same confidence that has enabled me to meet tourists free of the wariness and suspicion levelled at them by the rest of my fellow citizens who liked to keep people at arm's length for quite a long time until they were convinced they could trust them. Somehow, I just knew that these two guys were not dangerous to us anymore, they just wanted information and I was happy to give it to them. I raised my voice above Denver's as he tried to pacify the woman.

"I'll tell you everything I know about the Valvaston, but only if you tell me why it's so important for you to find it. Do you agree?"

"So you know where it is," asked Denver instantly distracted away from the woman by my offer. Did I imagine it or was there a note of pathetic hope in his voice at odds with his otherwise quiet air of authority?

"You haven't answered my question," I replied staring him in the eye and, despite the odds, feeling more in control with every passing second.

"Don't listen to him; he—" started the woman but Denver cut her short with a slap across the face.

"For God sake; will you shut up, woman?" She snuffled and glowered balefully at him but stayed quiet.

“I said I came here for a chat and that’s what I meant. Yes Mr Leon, you tell me everything you know then I’ll tell you everything that I know.” He laid heavy stress on the word “everything”.

I nodded and suggested we sat down around the table. For some reason I couldn’t put my finger on, I just trusted that he was going to stick to his side of the agreement.

“You start,” he said, and so, in much the same way that I had relayed my story to the President a week earlier, I told Denver about the tsunami and how Andy and I visited Al Solere the following day. I told him how I’d found the silver napkin ring on the beach. I didn’t mention the secret chamber, and not because I wanted to keep it a secret, but simply because it made for an easier story to tell by omitting it.

When I came to the bit about finding the silver napkin ring, Joelle walked over to the low cupboard and fetched the silver ring off the top of it where I had left it as an ornament. Denver’s eyes studied the ring so intently that I stopped speaking because I could see his attention was elsewhere. He traced lovingly over the lettering on the ring with his thumb and, it seemed, wistfully.

“It seems in remarkable condition for something that has been in the sea for a few hundred years. Was there any sign of a wreck site?” He asked at last.

“No but I’m sure the ship did wreck off Al Solere probably the people of the village lured it on to the rocks so they could plunder whatever was on it. At least that’s what we think. Tell them, Andy.” Andy related his wrecker theory and described the dangerous nature of underlying rock shelves on that particular stretch of coastline. I watched the faces of the two men. From the way they nodded occasionally as Andy explained his wrecker theory and described the treacherous coast at Al Solere it was obvious he was starting to convince them of the truth of my story. I picked up the tale when Andy had finished his part.

“Look, Mr Denver, the village of Al Solere was wiped out by a tsunami hundreds of years ago, I mean totally, it was as if a giant brush scoured the beach, the village, and all of the people there had never existed. Since then, two more have swept over the beach. We saw the last one and the waves went halfway up the cliff, so anything that was there then is unlikely to be there now.”

“And the same applies to the rocks on which the ship could have been wrecked,” chipped in Andy. “They’re just below the surface and a wooden ship would have been smashed to pieces on them and the pieces scattered and washed across the ocean floor. Look, if it wasn't so late and dark we could take you to the place and you'd see it for yourself."

"Or," I added, "to the museum so you could read the historical record of how the village of Al Solere disappeared overnight." All eyes turned towards Denver who was chewing on his lower lip in thought. When he finally raised his eyes, it was to me he looked.

"So what you're telling me is that you simply found this ring on the beach and did an internet search on the name Valvaston. You really don't know anything at all about the Valvaston at all or where it is?" I nodded.

"That's why I did an internet search."

"OK," he said suddenly, and his voice had a ring of authority in it, "so how do you explain all of this?" He lifted both arms and rotated his torso to indicate he was referring to the house, "And that?" He pointed his open hand at my Omega watch, it could not have been anything other than a cheap or midranges watch to him, but obviously he considered it out of place on my wrist.

"You see, Rodney, no offence meant, but I'm finding it difficult to match a young man like you with all of this." He waved an open hand at the room. "What sort of employment can St Gilberts offer to provide the income for this? Look, even I'm impressed—the house—the location it's perfect, it must be worth a small fortune." His eyes went hard and he leaned over the table towards me his voice low, "So tell me how you got it all, Rodney, because I really want to know." There was no mistaking the undercurrent of menace in his voice. I knew to get him off my case everything depended on the answer I was about to give and whether he believed it.

"My parents left me this house," I said and pointed towards the large monochrome portrait on the wall behind them. Denver and the woman turned on their seats to look up at the monochrome family photo and at the young couple, one black, one white and their child whose skin colour fell somewhere in between and whose light-coloured eyes stared back into the camera lens.

The tall man however did not spin around to look at the portrait; instead, his eyes never left my face. I took the fact that he still considered me a threat as a sort of compliment; at least he was showing me some respect.

"They're your parents," asked Denver over his shoulder, his eyes still on the portrait.

"Yes," I answered simply.

"And the kid, that's you right?"

"Right again," I replied.

"So what happened to them?" he asked bluntly.

"Plane crash," I replied equally bluntly.

Denver turned back to face me and said, "Sorry," then after a brief pause he asked "When did it happen?"

"About a month after that picture was taken," I replied. Denver's face remained impassive but his eyes gave me the impression that he was looking inward.

"O—K," he said drawing it out so it led into his question, "so what did your parents do to enable them to afford a place like this?"

"My father was a famous basketball player in the States." The taller man's head finally turned to look at the portrait.

"What's your dad's name, Rodney?" He asked over his shoulder and his tone was surprisingly light and friendly.

"Jusha," I replied.

"Juice-sa?" He repeated the name trying to match my pronunciation and failing, then suddenly he exclaimed, "JUICE LEON! Your dad was Juice Leon!" he turned back to look closely at my face. He seemed more relaxed now, even a little excited.

"You've heard of him?" Denver asked the other man.

"Why yes, when I was in the States I followed the basketball whenever I could. In fact the firm I worked for provided VIP security for a few of the players." Turning to me, he said, "Your dad was quite a celebrity, Rodney, and that crash involving… what was it… an inter-Island light aircraft or something like that—even made the front page of the daily's across the States." He looked at me and suddenly the excitement drained out of his face.

"Yeah sorry, it must have been tough losing both parents like that." I looked back at him and then straight at Denver. I'd made up my mind I wasn't going to answer any more of their questions. Denver owed me an explanation and now I wanted to hear it.

Denver knew it was his turn and he stared down at the table, still considering all he'd just heard. When his head rose, his eyes were bleak and he looked tired, tired with the drained, emptied out tiredness that comes when your last great hope floats to the surface belly uppermost and you know that's the end of it.

His eyes settled on my left arm resting on the table in front of me and the scuffed white cast encasing it.

"You have to believe me when I tell you that I never meant for any of those things to happen to you, to any of you," he said.

Andy snorted in derision, "Men like you always say you never m-meant for anyone to get hurt, but the t-truth is you don't give a f-flying fuck just so long as you get what you want or what you p-pay for. I know, I've worked for guys like you d-doing m-much the same job as I guess you're d-doing right now," he nodded towards the taller of the two men. "But you turn a b-blind eye to the effect your m-money has on those around you. W-when you w-want something you don't give a shit who gets trampled on so you can g-get it."

Andy paused for breath so I spoke into the brief lull, "What did you hope to get, Mr Denver? What brought you all the way to St Gilberts? What could be worth all that has happened to us and to that Belgian man?" Denver had remained silent throughout Andy's outburst and my challenge, now he nodded in acknowledgement. He knew he owed us an explanation of why he'd started the train of events leading up to now. Denver wiped his face with a handkerchief and took a deep breath. Six pairs of eyes turned in his direction as he began to speak.

"I guess you're right about me not knowing the lengths that some people I employ go to, and you're also right that I pay for results rather than the means by which they are achieved. I can only apologise and try to make it up to you somehow." I thought for a moment that Andy might have more to say on that score but he kept quiet I guess he also wanted to hear what Denver had to say.

"Difficult to say where it all began, when I was a kid probably, the books I read, the films I watched, but I grew up with a love of history and a fascination with lost and buried treasure and an appetite for adventure." Denver allowed a wistful smile to pass briefly across his face. "When I was about your age," he nodded towards me, "I came across some documents in an auction that connected them with some research I'd been doing a year previous in the British Lending Library. It gave me a trail to follow that eventually led to the discovery of a sunken Spanish ship called the Levia it was full of gold and silver coins, the largest haul ever recorded." Denver paused as if savouring the memory and no one around the table spoke into the silence because we knew the interesting bits were still to come.

"Yes, I made lots of money and even became famous in the process but nothing could, or ever has, matched the excitement of following that trail, nothing has even come close. The excitement slowly builds and builds and as a new piece of evidence is uncovered I really can't describe it." His eyes were shining with excitement as if in his mind he was reliving the moment and then the light faded and he refocussed on the faces around the table. "I guess it is difficult to imagine if you've never been there." He said almost apologetically. I noticed the other man looking at Denver as if he was seeing him for the first time.

Denver shook his head, coughed to clear his throat and then sat up straight in his chair. He had re-joined us in the present.

"Alright, you want to know about the Valvaston. The Valvaston was a Frigate, a wooden sailing ship carrying tea, spices and fabrics from India and, I believe, a passenger who had with him the most valuable diamond on earth. Do you want to know more?" He was smiling now and I could see that he was enjoying the opportunity to share something of his passion for history and treasure hunting with a willing audience. His excitement transmitted through to me though I was already gripped now, I just had to know the whole story so I nodded willing him to continue. When I looked around at the others, I saw their eyes were shining and their heads nodding for him to tell them more. Even the yacht woman had calmed down and I saw her move her head in an almost imperceptible nod.

"A few years ago at an auction I bought the private journal of a man named Thomas Pitt. Thomas Pitt was the grandfather of William Pitt the Elder who became Prime Minister of Britain. William Pitt's son known as William Pitt the Younger later also became the Prime Minister of Britain at the ridiculously young the age of twenty-four..."

As the minutes slid into hours Denver told us a fantastic tale steeped in history and larger than life characters that lived and died hundreds of years before. He told us of private journals, letters, and dishonesty. Just as riveting were the stories of how he had personally uncovered and then followed clues, connected the clues and then slowly continued accumulating evidence. A trail that had finally led him to my house. I was now part of the story, his story, as well, a late addition to the history of a lost blue diamond.

I pictured a well-dressed dandy boarding a ship from a port in India to begin a voyage back to England and his country mansion. The man carries a blue diamond of great value he believes will solve all his financial problems for the rest of his life. The ship never arrives at its destination instead it's wrecked on the rocks of St Gilberts notorious Al Solere, not so far from my house. I looked across the table at Andy. Denver's story had fired him up to but then, when I looked at Nahil her expression was sceptical and Joelle's eyes were still hostile.

The ability to empathise with others is a double-edged sword. On the one hand it enables a person to see, and to some extent, experience the world through the eyes of others which means you also end up living in a world of nuance, caring and compromise without the decisive certainty and simplicity enjoyed by those who lack empathy and see the world through only one lens. In a flash of insight I realised that I was less afraid and suspicious of outsiders than most of my fellow islanders because I felt I could trust my powers of empathy to work out if someone was a threat while they couldn't and so they have to fall back on stereotypes instead.

I believe I have expanded my world view without ever having leaving St Gilberts because of my ability to empathise with the many foreign tourists I met or I went with. I saw and experienced St Gilberts through their eyes by noting what they found novel and attractive, strange or uncomfortable about my island home. I feel I can sometimes tune into to another's mood and maintain just the right amount of tension and unpredictability to keep a romance fresh and exciting enough to keep their attention and attraction for me alive. An insight into why someone has done the things they've done tends to push you towards a tolerance and an understanding of them. You are less inclined to judge them badly which can put you at odds with others whose capacity to see another's viewpoint is limited.

After hearing Denver's story and the way he told it, I could not help feeling some understanding and tolerance towards him despite the fact that he'd been the instigator of our troubles. The others, the Belgian, the couple on the yacht, Ferrari; they were different. Denver was a man pursuing an obsession like a besotted teenager, a drug addict, the others were simply ruthless money chasing bastards. I felt sure that, given Denver's power and wealth, many would behave in a similar way if they found something they wanted as badly. He had asked others to obtain information for him without inquiring too hard as to how that information was going to be obtained. I considered the couple on the yacht. He had asked them to use their initiative as private investigators to find out what I knew about the Valvaston. He hadn't told them to kidnap Joelle and then me well, at least I believed him when he said he hadn't.

Yes, he had offered a bribe to Ferrari to get the same information but again Denver seemed genuinely surprised that Ferrari had used violence on me. He expected Ferrari to use his authority to lean on me but the hammer was Ferrari's idea. However I could see Joelle and Nahil were not so forgiving and would see my reading of Denver's part in our misfortunes as naive and weak.

Rising to my feet, I asked who wanted tea and who wanted coffee. I saw Joelle give a look that asked, *what the hell do you think you are doing offering these thugs hospitality?* Nahil also gave me gave me a look that said pretty much the same thing, but I didn't care I needed a few seconds on my own away from the scrutiny of Denver and Co. I was thinking about the secret chamber beneath St Francis Mount Church and how easy it was to overlook a bluestone, not just in our search, but in all the searches that had been made there so far.

After the coffee was finished and questions from both sides all answered Denver drew things to a close by taking out his wallet and offering to give us a roll of notes. For, as he put it, to compensate us for the unpleasantness we had suffered as a consequence of his quest for a lost diamond.

Joelle, who had become increasingly agitated, suddenly sprang to her feet at this and told Denver to "Go and shove your blood money; we don't want it."

Nahil nodded and murmured in approval. My spirits, however, sank at Joelle's rejection, apparently on behalf of all of us, of his offer. As far as I was concerned, a wad of cash would have been most welcome, but I knew if I wanted to keep Joelle, this was not the moment to contradict her. I glanced across the table towards Andy and he briefly met my eyes and ever so slightly he shrugged his shoulders in a gesture of sympathy. Maybe Denver picked up on this little exchange because when he put his wallet away, he added as if in an afterthought, "Well, if ever in the future any one of you guys need any help in anything at all, then make sure you get in touch. I'll do whatever I can, and that's a promise." With that he fished in another pocket and pulled out a small business card holder and passed me an embossed card bearing his name and contact details. We followed them to the edge of the garden and watched as the two men and the woman carefully negotiated the path down and on to the beach.

After Denver and the woman were aboard, the tall guy pushed the inflatable out from the sand and then boarded himself. A few minutes later, we lost sight of them in the dark as they headed towards the reef we stayed listening to the sound of the outboard until that too was swallowed up by the night and the boom of surf crashing down on the distant reef.

"Why don't you ring the police?" demanded Joelle. She was standing in the kitchen doorway facing me with her hands planted firmly on her hips and her eyes blazing. Andy and Nahil stood awkwardly behind in the lounge looking at each other not wanting to witness our first row as a couple. I shrugged and held up my hands.

"Call the police? Are you crazy, look at the time! Any cop still awake at this time will be pissed out of their skulls." I saw her lips compress so I went for a compromise, "Look, I'll ring the President's office tomorrow first light, OK?"

"But it's Sunday tomorrow," she retorted.

"So what; I'll still ring anyway," I snapped back, and to my utter astonishment, she nodded her acceptance. I guessed she'd remembered I had good cause to be suspicious of the police.

Andy and Nahil slept in the room they always used when they stopped over. Unfortunately there was not much of the night left and it seemed we no sooner lain our heads on the pillow than morning sunlight was pouring into the bedroom. Joelle turned over and got out of bed, she tried not to disturb me but I was already half awake. A few moments later I heard the sound of cups clacking and cutlery scraping on plates and it was that which finally roused me out of bed. I already knew Joelle was up but now I saw both Nahil and Andy sat on the veranda eating buttered toast and drinking tea.

"They've gone." Andy nodded towards the horizon and I understood that he was telling me that Denver and the others had sailed off in the yacht. I joined them on the veranda carrying a glass of orange and a plate of buttered toast and we chatted about the previous night while looking at the clear aquamarine waters below. The sun was rising and close to the reef the sea was a deep lapis lazuli blue.

"They headed North on the engine," said Andy between bites of toast. "They'll be long gone by now."

"Nope," I countered, "I bet they've gone up to Al Solere for a look around."

Andy held out his hand as if to shake mine. “Fifty rupees says they’ve gone.”

I shook it and said, “Fifty rupees says that they are still pissing about at Al Solere.” Joelle reminded me about my promise to ring the President’s Office and I reminded her that it was Sunday morning. She put a frown line on that pretty forehead of hers so I shrugged and picked up the phone hoping that no one would answer my call also hoping at the same time that Joelle wasn’t going to turn into a nag, no I decided, I won’t let her even if she tries. I dialled the number and smiled back at her with the phone against my head confident I’d go straight through an answer machine. To my surprise, someone answered the call immediately. The voice of Pauline, Duval’s secretary, came down the line and she threw me off balance.

“Hello, is that you, Rodney?”

“Yes,” I replied realising she must have one of those caller display phones. “The President is not in his office now but he will be calling in later at around five pm to pick up some paperwork, is it urgent?”

“No it’s OK I’ll give him a call him then,” I replied thanking her and replaced the phone.

Twenty minutes later, the four of us, carrying some drinks and eats in shopping bags, were walking up the road towards Kasper’s Edge. I won the bet and relieved Andy of fifty rupees. Out at sea, a safe distance off the rocky shelf, the big yacht was stationary. Closer in, Denver, his tall friend and bodyguard, and the yacht woman’s husband were in an inflatable dingy moving slowly over the jagged submerged shelf of rocks close to the shore. Every so often, Denver would slip on a diver’s face mask, lean over the side of the dingy, duck his head underwater and look around. Then the inflatable would move on to another section.

We made ourselves comfortable on the same spot we’d used the day of the tsunami and Nahil recounted to Joelle, yet again, how the Belgian man had brought her and me to Kasper’s Edge only to end up going over the edge himself. Now, since we were at the location she could point out where everyone had stood and the part they played, or—in my case—not played. It was not a story I wanted to hear but Joelle seemed riveted so I opened two beers for Andy and I and we stood a little away from them and watched the men in the inflatable searching for a lost wreck. Bored after a while, we sat down again on the grass.

“Tell me how the tsunami came in,” Joelle asked, and before either Andy or I could open our mouths, Nahil was in full flow again. Nahil told her how we’d scrambled back up the narrow cliff face path just in time and then gone up even higher up the little hill to our left. When Nahil had finished I gave a brief resume of the follow-up trip Andy and I made the day after. Andy chipped in occasionally and I noticed no stammer as he spoke, he clearly felt relaxed speaking to Joelle, I was glad because she was one of the gang now. Joelle's interest in the story surprised me, I knew she'd already heard the story several times already but maybe Denver's revelations of the previous night had renewed her interest and given her an appetite for more detail. Had it also, I wondered, given her an appetite for treasure hunting as well?

We stayed there chatting and drinking for several hours taking advantage of the shade of nearby trees to save us from the worst of the sun. It was shortly after our supply of drinks had run out and we were thinking about making our way back to the house when Andy looked out to sea and exclaimed the inflatable was heading back towards the yacht.

"I think they've had enough," He suggested.

"Doesn't look as if they found anything either," I added, and we watched the small dingy grow smaller as it headed out to sea towards the waiting yacht. Shortly after the three men were onboard and the dingy stowed we saw the yacht turn to face into the wind and then sails go up. The beautiful white yacht leaned over as the main sail filled and we watched in silence as it sailed off towards the horizon.

"I guess they really are going," said Joelle in a tone that suggested she found it difficult to believe they were leaving. I was sceptical myself but Denver's resignation to the fact he would never find his blue diamond seemed genuine enough to me the previous night. So as I watched the white sail in the distance I believed it was the last time I would ever see Denver again.

I rang the President's office again at five pm and again the secretary answered my call almost immediately, didn't she ever take any time off? "Hello is that you Rodney?"

"Yes it's me, is he back yet?" I asked.

"No but I expect him any time, are you sure you don't want to leave a message?"

"No it's OK I'll call back later," I said hoping that I hadn't given the impression that I didn't trust her in some way. Twenty-five minutes later, and before I made that repeat call, the phone rang and when I picked up the receiver the authoritative voice of Gerard Duval came through the earpiece.

"I believe you've been trying to contact me."

"Yes," I replied. "It's about Richard Denver..."

Duval, with a note of impatience in his voice, cut into my brief pause, "Yes Rodney, I have tried to contact him many times but nobody in his organisation seems to know where he is, or at least that's what they're telling me."

"I know where he is—or at least where he was last night and this morning." An audible intake of breath came down the line with the satisfying knowledge I now had his full and undivided attention.

"OK Rodney, tell all."

After I'd completed my account of the previous night and what I'd witnessed from Kasper's Edge that morning, Duval sounded thoughtful.

"I am shocked that he came armed but unfortunately, they will be clear of our territorial waters by now and, apart from diplomatic disapproval there is little more that we can do, especially against a man like Denver. However, I do think it's time we revisited that secret chamber, especially now that we know what we're looking for, only this time we'll do a proper job of it. Robert Chan is an old friend of mine, I guess you already know he's curator of the museum, but in his youth he took part in many archaeological digs abroad. I'll ask him to lead a proper archaeological exploration of the chamber. Do you and Andy want to be in on it?" I looked down at the cast on my arm and then at the faces of the other three gathered around me at the phone to listen in.

"Definitely, we wouldn't miss it for the world," and I saw frowns of concentration as they tried to guess what I had just agreed to.

If I am ever invited to take part in another archaeological dig, I will refuse without a second's hesitation. Boring doesn't come close to describing the finicky and painstaking torture Robert Chan orchestrated within the dank confined space of that miserable little chamber. My broken arm exempted me from digging duties which fell to Andy and a younger member of the museum staff. Chan still had me holding lamps at various heights and angles for endless photos to be taken. In addition I helped Mr Chan log and package the various artefacts as they emerged during the dig.

Andy and the staff member carefully scraped up the sand floor and washed it through a sieve. I guessed Chan about the same age as the president, but he looked and acted much older. He was a stickler for procedure and detail and a slave-driver which, since Andy and I received no pay for our labour, pissed me off. That and the fact Chan treated us like a couple of junior school misbehavers.

Andy, perhaps because he was ex-military, could take it in good humour and, at first, so could I.

Chan was meticulous and obviously knew what he was doing so if anyone on St Gilberts could find the blue diamond in that cavern it was going to be him. That belief kept me motivated, even excited, as I approached the church each morning with yet another long tiring day stretching ahead. I must confess it made me grind my teeth when Chan's reedy voice rang out across the church.

"Rodney, stop dilly dallying and log those plates as I told you to—at least half an hour ago. Come on, get it done, boy." We'd set up some trestle tables in the church itself on which to lay out the bits and pieces recovered from the chamber. With each day that passed and another section of the chamber was systematically excavated, examined and found empty of anything of value. My optimism began to wane. I say nothing of any value, because the artefacts we collected looked like a pile of rubbish to me.

Chan, on the other hand, would stand hands-on hips, long strands of grey hair framing his features, grinning and ridiculously happy with his haul of rotting cloths, clothing and grey pewter plates and cups. I didn't tell him that Andy and I already had a few of the self-same plates at our homes and we'd picked the best of the bunch. That revelation could have triggered a heart attack in him or, maybe have driven him to press the President to reintroduce the death penalty for us. Yeah, I guess I am moaning about Chan and the dig, only because we never found the blue diamond or indeed, anything I would class as treasure.

Something I did gain during my time under Chan was some of his objectivity about the site itself. Before the dig, Al Solere had always given me the creeps, the church, and secret chamber especially so. Now, after a week of working there day after day, all those previous misgivings about ghosts and spirits that had swirled about in my head were pretty much gone. At the end of the dig I no longer gave them a passing thought and much less feared them.

So the search for the diamond ended and Chan returned to his museum to catalogue and prepare his new collection of 'junk' for display to the public. I went back to life as before, sometimes working in the Kokonet Café and sometimes helping Andy out, well as best as I could with the plaster cast still on. Wearing a cast in the tropics is not pleasant and when the day finally came for its removal I invited Andy and Nahil to the house for a little party. I also invited Uncle Claude but he said that he'd leave us youngsters to it and stick with his own age group at Toffies. After food and drinks we eventually turned the music up and the girls started to dance. I couldn't stop myself glancing at the door to see if Denver and his mob were about to gate-crash again and once or twice I saw Joelle doing the same.

The next morning, Andy and Nahil borrowed the Honda to return home and as we watched them disappear on to the road at the top of the drive, I asked Joelle how I could best thank her for all she had done for me when I'd had the cast on. I half expected her to suggest we go into town to have dinner together somewhere posh, at a tourist hotel perhaps. She surprised me by suggesting we spend the day at Al Solere. My wallet sighed with relief, but to be honest, I was not keen on her idea at all. My fear of spirits had dwindled but I had already spent too much time there of late and the Belgian guy's death ensured the place still held uncomfortable memories for me.

However, ever the gentleman, I agreed readily enough and we packed a few eats and a few drinks into two rucksacks and set off on foot up the road towards the turnoff to Kasper's Edge. I wondered if Joelle felt she'd missed something of importance in the Valvaston adventure that Andy, Nahil and I had shared before she joined the gang. When we arrived at Kasper's Edge she was not content with simply looking down on Al Solere from the top but insisted we took the zigzag path down to the to the beach itself. Joelle was clearly less concerned about the presence of Al Solere's ghosts than Nahil and I had been on our first visit. Working there on a daily basis for a week had desensitised me but Joelle, who had never visited the beach before, already seemed oblivious to the possibility of bad spirits. The solitary white church atop the hill at the edge of the beach fascinated her.

"I want to see inside," she begged so we climbed the steps to the top and walked along the side of the church to the door. The padlock was still firmly in place and, as there was no Andy on hand with a lock pick it open it, we had to content ourselves with walking around the church walls. There was a nice stretch of short grass at the side of the church with shade from a large feathery casuarinas tree and we spread a cloth over its long thin fallen needle leaves and lay down on top side-by-side.

Joelle's long hair fell lightly over my chest as she leaned over to kiss me and a slight cooling breeze coming in from the sea lifted the strands so they brushed and caressed across my skin. She lifted her head slightly so we were eye to eye and I saw the look in her eyes that left me in no doubt what we'd be doing very soon.

"But can we be seen by anyone up there?" she said, and I knew she was referring to Kasper's Edge.

"Probably," I murmured into her ear giving it a little nibble at the same time.

"And if they have a camera phone with them then we could even end up on YouTube," she teased, adding, "And customers in the Café will be able to watch us."

"Then we'd better be good," I said between our gentle touching of lips.

"Not much pressure then," she mumbled.

"Hopefully only in the right places," I said, lifting her shirt over her head.

I am almost certain no one spied on us from Kasper's Edge, after all it's not a place many visit, but if someone had, we would surely have satisfied, and maybe even impressed, the most discerning of voyeurs. I lay back with Joelle's arms and legs still entwined with mine and together we enjoyed the sensual pleasure of the occasional sea breeze tracing a cool path across our sweat covered bodies. I freed one of my hands to reached into my rucksack and bring out a bottle of beer. It was no longer chilled but it still felt cool and after my exertions I had a raging thirst and no doubt Joelle had the same. I rooted about some more in the rucksack until I found the distinctive shape of bottle opener. I gave Joelle the first drink and thought she was going to finish the whole bottle in one go but she passed it back to me with a bit left at the bottom.

"Well, you have some more, haven't you?" She'd seen my pained expression.

"Three more."

"Well, there you are then." We drank the other bottles down quickly one after the other and felt all better for it if not a little light-headed. Joelle with an uncharacteristic lack of modesty suggested that we go for a dip in the sea to cool off and clearly had no intention of covering up to do so.

"I hope that camera is still rolling," I said, "because even I'd like to see a re-run of this part myself." I admired the beautiful curves of her body as she stretched and was about to suggest an alternative exercise to swimming when she headed for the beach.

There is something about swimming without any clothes on that is, what's the word I'm looking for—liberating! And, when you have the girl you've always wanted to be with swimming naked with you, and brushing against you, then you could throw in a whole heap of other positive words as well. We stood together in the surf and began to provide further footage for any cliff-top film buff but the surf had raised the coarse coral sand and, while friction is the physical and joyous point of contact between lovers, abrasion is not. Holding hands we made our back up the steps to the church and to the cloth we'd spread out in churchyard. Joelle glanced back up towards the cliff and modestly donned her underwear.

"Why does your underwear have to fit you in such a sexy way?" I said, staring at the knickers that hugged and outlined every contour. Putting my shorts back on to hide my growing appreciation, I rescued the plastic bag with the samosas from the rucksack and we sat in companionable silence for a few minutes munching our way through them. I enjoyed the sexual tension I could feel building again guessing what we'd be having for deserts. Alas, Joelle broke the spell by a sudden change of subject.

"The stonemason here must have been a busy man," she was shaking the last crumbs off her fingers.

"He certainly was," I agreed, and told her about the stone shelves in the secret chamber and the stone steps leading down into the chamber itself. I stopped mid-sentence and looked at her. "Why? What made you say that?"

"Say what?" she asked looking confused.

"That the stonemason must have been a busy man."

"Oh that? I was just looking at all those grave stones there." I followed her gaze towards the small collection of gravestones mostly shaded from the sun by the shadow of the church and by the tall trees at the perimeter of the plot.

"Yes, there's a fair bit of work in all of them," I agreed.

Joelle looked thoughtful, "I don't know how long the village was around before the wave washed it away but I guess it went back a fair way, after all, they had enough time to build this church. So you'd think there'd be a lot more graves than that."

I had to agree, "Being short of land perhaps they doubled up in the graves or something."

Joelle looked at my face to see if I was being serious and then gave me a push when she saw one of my eyebrows rise.

"Did Chan's archaeological interest extend as far as the church and the graveyard?" she asked.

"No, just the chamber, we were really only looking for the diamond."

Joelle shrugged her shoulders. "But he didn't find the diamond, and yet, you say Chan is going to set up a new Al Solere exhibition at the museum."

"That's right," I agreed wondering where she was going with this.

"Surely the best record of the people who once lived here is in Marcel Leste's account, which is already in the museum, and the names and dates on those tombstones over there. I'm just surprised Chan, being an archaeologist, didn't take more interest in the graveyard."

Come to think of it, she was right. Why didn't he check up here? I thought.

"Maybe you should be running the museum, not Chan," I said. She looked at my face to see if I were making fun of her but this time I didn't get a shove, so I guess she decided I wasn't.

Together we walked among the tombstones looking at the names and dates and reading those stones that had a eulogy, in Creole, carved into the stone. Some of the old Creole was difficult to follow but together we could make sense of most of it. I stopped at one of the stones slightly apart from the others and which looked ever so slightly different. Then I saw there was a date of death carved on to the stone but no birth date.

"Joelle, come and have a look at this one."

"Why, what is it?" She asked but came over without waiting for an answer.

"This one," I said pointing to the stone. "Look there's no birth date; why's that do you think?"

"How should I know? Read the inscription." Joelle squatted in front of the stone and stared hard at the faint inscription, her lips moved as she quietly read the words carved into the stone:

August 1669

The nobleman who died on our shore.

In an angry sea, all men are equal.

She looked back at me with a questioning expression on her face. "So?"

"Don't you see it, Joelle?" I said trying to contain the excitement in my voice. "The date is 1669, the year that Denver told us the Valvaston set sail from India!"

"Was it 1669?" she asked not convinced.

"Yes, I think he said it was May, surely a boat from India could have reached St Gilberts by August of the same year? Remember how Denver said that this Rupert guy was some sort of high-up in England? How he liked to dress as if he was something special. Imagine what our lot here would have thought finding a guy washed ashore if he had on one of those fancy shirts with frills and things on his collar and cuffs?"

“Well, his arrival would hardly be a surprise if, as Andy says, they wrecked his boat in the first place!”

“Well, Andy doesn’t know that for sure,” I said defensively. “Anyway, even if they did wreck it,” I continued, “once they realised there was someone a bit special on-board it would make sense to give the guy a nice grave just in case his country’s navy come looking for him. They could point to the grave and say, ‘We did our best to save him but he was dead on arrival and there he is.’”

“Hmm…” was Joelle’s only reply, that and a sceptical rising of her eyebrows. “OK Rodney, so let’s suppose you’re right and this grave belongs to Rupert Still… whatever his name was, then, so what? If he’d come ashore with the diamond the villagers would have taken it off him but there’s no record of Al Solere being anything other than dirt poor. More likely, if they found it at all, they’d think it was a bit of blue glass or a pebble and sling it away on the beach or keep it as an ornament. Either way, one of the big waves would have washed it away.”

My spirits sank. I couldn’t fault her logic and yes, as she said, even if Rupert Stillwood-Hamilton was in the grave in front of us, so what? Joelle must have seen the disappointment in my face, her expression softened and she reached out and touched my arm. Suddenly, I knew how Denver must have felt that night in my house knowing his search for the diamond was over, and his quest had ended in failure. Now I realised just how much hope I had invested in all of this Valvaston stuff without even really realising it. Was it finally the time I let go of it all and move on? No, I just needed a little more time to think about what the discovery of this grave might mean—if it meant anything at all.

It was a Monday morning and I had left Joelle in the Kokonet Café to take a walk down the main street. As I passed the Three-In-One, I glanced in and saw Andy quenching his thirst with a bottle of beer. I joined him at the bar and we were soon laughing and joking as more beer flowed.

“Let’s go out in the beer garden,” he suggested and we ambled out into the sunshine and sat under the shade of one of the white sail-like canopies Bengy had put up for that purpose. As usual we talked about nothing in particular but eventually I got around to telling him about Joelle and my visit to Al Solere and about the grave I thought might belong to the man Denver had told us about, the high-up called Rupert Something-Hamilton.

“I’m sure Joelle thinks I’m mad. I think she’s getting fed up with the whole Valvaston thing.” Andy listened as intently as the consumption of several beers allowed and then told me something that showed the Valvaston story was still very much on his mind too.

"I was in the Kokonet last week and did a few searches on the Hope Diamond, you know, the diamond Denver reckons makes up the other half of the one lost on the Valvaston." I nodded keen to know more, disappointed with myself for not thinking to do the same search.

"So?" I prompted impatiently. Usually when Andy is talking to old friends like me his slight stammer disappears but now in his interest and excitement it surfaced again. He reached into his pocket and pulled out some folded sheets he'd printed off from his internet search in the café there were some of his handwritten notes in the margins.

"I s-saw pictures of it; the Hope Diamond; it's aw-awesome. Not the b-biggest diamond around b-but it is the largest b-blue diamond. What makes it so famous is its history—all the stories and myths c-connected to it—some of them c-clearly made up but s-some are fact." Referring to his notes again, he gave me a rundown of the history of the Hope Diamond starting with John Baptiste Tavernier, Rupert Stillwood-Hamilton's alleged partner in crime. He told me how a collection of diamonds, which included a blue diamond; were sold to Louis XIV who had them cut and facetted. He described the later theft of some of the royal jewels, including the blue diamond, in 1792 and the appearance, twenty-one years and one day later of a large blue diamond in London.

"It's been p-proven to be n-none other than the B-Blue diamond Tavernier sold to the King of France, only re-cut to a round shape. Philip Hope a Dutch born heir to a banking fortune bought the diamond and generations later sold it to help clear f-family debts. After exchanging hands a f-few more times it was bought by Ned Mclean owner of the Washington P-Post as a p-present for his wife Evelyn Mclean. After she died her entire collection of jewellery was sold to H-Harry Winston for one p-point one million dollars and he later donates it to the Smithsonian Institute in Washington DC where it remains its most viewed exhibit."

It was probably the longest non-stop speech I'd ever heard from Andy and we both sat back and took a swig of our beer. We tried to weave in parts of Denver's story to fit in with Andy's information.

"In 2001," he continued, "some experts v-valued the H-Hope Diamond at two hundred and fifteen million p-pounds—that's as-assuming anyone w-would want to own a diamond with s-such a background and one so widely believed to carry a curse. If the H-Hope Diamond really does h-have a twin then the value of b-both diamonds must s-surely increase with the added history, in effect they would b-both b-be even more priceless than they already are." We both frowned trying to work out how something already priceless could further increase in value.

"Well, you know what I mean," said Andy at last, and we raised our bottles and clinked them together in a toast before up-ending their contents down our throats.

"It looks as if you have been doing some serious studying," I said and he nodded.

"I've got time to spare."

We both have, I thought, but didn't say it, I didn't need to. We fell silent for a moment, each lost in our own thoughts. I wondered if Andy was getting finally getting bored with St Gilberts, not beyond the realms of possibility for an action man like him. I sometimes wondered why he'd stayed as long as he had. There was nothing to stop him marrying Nahil and the two of them taking off to the UK.

Sometimes when I'd introduced women I dated from the tourist hotels to Andy and Nahil, some of them had later given me a knowing look and said Nahil was only going with Andy to get a British passport but I knew comments like that always revealed more about the world view of those who spoke them than they did of Nahil. Nahil was Gilbertise through and through, it was the only place she'd ever call home and the only place she'd ever want to live. I considered them my closest friends and knew I'd be gutted if they left.

"This Valvaston thing," I said at last, "I don't want it to be over."

"I know what you mean," agreed Andy. "I don't want it to be over either."

After our little session in the Three-In-One, I did not see much of Andy for a day or two and I spent my time, either helping out in the Kokonet Café, or doing odd jobs around the house. A neighbour, whose niece was getting married, came around to see if I would let him cut some of the Parrot's Plantain in my garden. They were having the reception in his house and he wanted to decorate it with the Plantain's long broad leaves. I helped him select and cut some and gave him a load of flowers to take as well as well. But these were minor distractions; I still lacked a sense of direction and purpose.

Before Joelle and I became a couple, I spent much my time with female tourists. It provided me with a source of income, admittedly unreliable, but an income of sorts nevertheless, more crucially it also gave me something of interest to occupy my day. I often killed time dreaming up little scams even though I mostly never carried them through. I don't care what others think, I know being a tour guide and companion, gigolo if you insist, requires a high-level of people skills. You need to be able to engage with different personalities, different age groups and of course, people from different cultures. You also need to create opportunities to interest and entertain them and to make them want to give you some money since nobody I have ever met wants to think they are paying for companionship let alone sex.

Now I sagged under a lack of something to occupy my brain and a lack of purpose, the sultry heat added to my general apathy and I found myself looking forward to the coming rains. In an attempt to shake off the blanket of boredom settling over me I made my way into town with the intention of saying hello to see some familiar faces and my old contacts in the shops and small businesses along the seafront. I wanted to see if they had any work for me to do and, even if they hadn't, the exercise of looking would at least kill a bit of time.

I had just left the General Store when I heard someone shout my name from across the street. It was Christopher in the Post Office and, after waiting for a bus to pass; I crossed and entered into the relative dark of the public side of the little office.

"Got a parcel for you, Rodney, it came in yesterday." Christopher turned his narrow lemonade bottle shoulders to me as he reached into one of the wooden pigeon-holes behind him and brought out a largish package wrapped in brown paper.

"It came recorded delivery so you'll need to sign here. That's it, all yours now." He handed me package almost reluctantly and I got the feeling that he expected, or hoped, I'd open it there and then in front of him. Christopher had one of the most unusual haircuts on St Gilberts, a big fan of Elvis Presley he'd tried to copy the star's trademark hairstyle along with the quiff. Having afro hair didn't help. He'd buzzed his hair short with clippers over the whole head except for the fringe which he grew long and plastered in women's hair gel to make it stick up. Unfortunately, he still didn't look anything like his hero and I suspected that it hadn't improved his pulling power with the opposite sex either.

I thanked him and took the package tucking it under my arm before walking out nonchalantly, as if receiving a package from abroad was an everyday affair for me. However I was far from nonchalant in fact I was galvanised with a nervous energy. As I'd picked up the package I had seen, on a small white label stuck in the top right corner on the thick padded envelope, the name of the sender—it was Richard Denver.

I walked a short way up the street before crossing over to the seaward side and down some steps that led on to a short sandy beach. It had a small wooden jetty that was mainly used by fishermen who wanted to take their catch straight to the market. The jetty was their closest landfall to the town. Usually, however, housewives pack the jetty when the boats come in so as to pick the best fish for themselves. They'd crowd around the fishermen, still tying off their boats, as if they were pop stars who had just landed. Now I had the beach to myself all the boats being out at sea. I walked over the wooden boards of the jetty, worn grey by sea and age, and smooth by countless feet, until I reached the end where I kicked off my sandals and sat down letting my feet dangle in the sea. I placed the package beside me on the jetty and carefully opened it. Inside were four separate sealed plastic wallets; two of these appeared, at first glance, to contain books or diaries. As for the other two; one contained papers, the other, letters. I tilted the package to let the sunlight fall inside and a white envelope caught my eye since it was the only thing not protected in a plastic wallet. I reached in and took the envelope out and saw with a start my name 'Rodney Leon' written by hand on the front of it. I sat staring at the envelope for some time before carefully peeling open the flap and reaching in and taking out the folded letter. Again I waited my heart was pounding before I unfolded the paper and spread it out on my lap. I had to tilt the paper before I could read anything on it because of the sunlight reflecting off the white surface and hurting my eyes. The letter was also hand written.

Dear Rodney,

Several weeks have passed since we met and I have had time to reflect on how my search for lost treasure has caused you and your friends much unnecessary discomfort. I do hope your arm has now fully recovered.

I also realise the explanation and apology I made to you on the evening we met fell short of what you deserved, hence this letter. I hope you will not be insulted when I say I saw something of my younger self in you. Like me you seem to be looking for more out of life than you already have—some excitement or a goal perhaps?

Enclosed with this letter you will find four packets. The packets contain all the documents I have connected to my search for the Valvaston and the blue diamond I told you about on the night we met. I still firmly believe that Rupert Stillwood-Hamilton boarded a ship bound for England in May 1669 and that he carried with him the other half of the blue diamond we now know as the Hope Diamond. The name of the ship he boarded was the Valvaston and that it never reached its destination. What happened to it remains a mystery but I suspect you and your friend Andrew are correct in assuming it was wrecked off the beach as you suggested.

The enclosed documents are now yours to dispose of as you see fit. They are unlikely to lead you to any lost or sunken treasure, as they failed to lead me, but do not underestimate their intrinsic value. In particular, the journal of Thomas Pitt and the letters of Rupert Stillwood-Hamilton to his sister, both are of considerable value in their own right, if combined they may be worth even more still, especially if you highlight the historical links between them and the Hope Diamond.

Finally, my offer of help was genuine and remains available to you, and each of your three admirable friends.

Good luck for the future.

Yours,

Richard Denver

I read the letter through several times and then placed it carefully back in the white envelope and then in turn back in the larger envelope with the plastic wrapped packets. I controlled an impulse to take out the plastic wallets to see what they contained; sitting at the end of the jetty with the ocean lapping around my feet was not the place to do it. The slightest gust of wind and the papers would be in the drink. I stood up, stamped the water off my feet and on to the sun and sea bleached wooden boards, then slipped them into my sandals and carried the package to the Kokonet Café. Joelle was in her office and she looked up and smiled when she saw me through the window. I walked in and sat down across the desk from her, I'd removed Denver's letter from the package and passed it to her without comment. Suddenly tense her brow furrowed as she read through it, then she relaxed, sank back in her chair and read through it again, this time more slowly.

"Well, maybe he wasn't so bad after all," she conceded at last. "But what did he mean saying you reminded him of his younger self and that you were looking for more out of life than you already have?" I could see she took it as a personal slight. I moved to dispel that notion from her head.

"I'm sure he was referring to my interest in searching for the Valvaston on the internet." But I could see my spin on Denver's comment didn't wash from the way she looked back at my face intently checking my expression.

"Are you unhappy with the way things are now?"

"No of course not. I—"

"Please don't tell me you wish you were back chasing those foreign blonde women again?" She spat the words "foreign" and "blonde" at me and her eyes were blazing as if she'd worked up a head of steam. Many of the local lads have a thing about foreign women and blondes in particular. I guess they look so different in their colouring from local girls. Yellow hair pale skin and light-coloured eyes make them appear exotic that, and a reputation for being sex mad and wild in bed, a reputation totally overstated in my experience. Nevertheless it had become a rite of passage for local boys to sleep with a blond woman if they wanted to brag in the Three-In-One.

My mother was the blondest of blonds and I have aqua-blue eyes so the combination is hardly exotic to me. Besides, I've enough experience of foreign women in and out of the bedroom to qualify me to at least have an opinion on their libidos and sexual experience. Nevertheless many local women, including it seemed, absolute stunners like Joelle still felt threatened by some foreign women, and blondes in particular. When I replied the indignation in my voice must have been clear and obviously genuine.

"Of course not! After our time together, I'm sorry you can even think that."

I quickly lowered my voice when I noticed one of the customers turn from their computer screen to look at us through the office window.

"What Denver is getting at, is not to do with us, which, by the way, is the best thing that has happened to me, no it's to do with me and what I am doing—or not doing—with my time. You have the Café—"

Joelle cut in, "No Rodney, we both have the Café," but both of us knew that wasn't really true. Yes, I helped out now and then, but Joelle and her assistant were so on top of everything they could surely manage much better without me in the way.

"Yes Joelle but I want something that…" I was struggling for words, unusual for me, but I was unsure of what I wanted to say, "I just want to be good at something that means something." I trailed off, not sure myself what was I was trying to say? The only thing I'd been good at so far was gigoloing but even there I was never going to be in Dan Meme's league nor did I want to be. What else could I turn my hand to? Joelle's expression changed, she was looking at me with understanding and compassion now, though to be honest, I preferred the blazing eye look, it made me feel less pathetic. She reached out across the desk and laid her hand on my forearm where the cast had been.

"Whatever you do or don't do, Rodney, I will always love you just as you are." I blinked, as a couple we'd never gone in for declarations of love, we'd never needed to—or at least I never thought we had—but I placed a hand over hers and smiled back at her in silent appreciation.

"I think Andy and Nahil should be there when I open these packets, after all they've been in this right from the start," I said and Joelle nodded in agreement.

"I'll call Nahil's mobile and ask her to come around with Andy tonight. We should get some food and drinks in," she prompted, I reached in my pocket to check my wallet but she quickly produced a few notes and pushed them into my hand. As I left the office and headed towards the market I smiled ruefully with the irony of it, I was still taking money off women after all.

Relaxed and with our stomachs full of Unicorn fish curry, Bitter Gourd with rice. Joelle had mixed a rum punch to go with the food and now we each took a full glass to the veranda to sit, or sprawl, on the padded chairs. Below us the swirling blues, turquoises and aquamarines of the ocean by day had given way to orange and glittering silver as the sun fell lower on the horizon. I considered letting Andy read out some of the contents of the packets but then decided my spoken English was better than his and besides, he had a dislike of public speaking.

Anyway, I'm a bit of a show-off at heart and was looking forward to seeing their faces when I told them what I'd received in the post that day. I also fancy myself as a mimic and the arrival of the package had perked me up and I felt like having fun. I'd already looked through the packages earlier and found that Denver had helpfully placed paper markers on all the relevant pages with handwritten notes summarising important facts at various stages. I remembered how Denver had spoken with an accent I'd vaguely recognised, through my contact with British tourists, as being from the north of England.

I mimicked his flattened vowels and exaggerated them as I read out his letter to me. Nahil slapped her thighs and hooted at my take on Denver's voice and my attempt to copy his stern facial expression, even Joelle smiled. Next I picked up the book, *Travels in India* by Jean-Baptiste Tavernier. I opened it at the paper marker between pages 100 and 101, inside there was a fold-out page showing pen sketches of the collection of precious stones, including the Blue diamond, that Tavernier presented to the King of France. It was the diamond known then as the Tavernier Blue later to become the French Blue and finally the Hope Diamond. I adopted a French accent and spoke in the wheezing tones of a frail old man stooping and shuffling around the table as I showed them the open page and sketch of the Tavernier Blue.

Andy took the book from me and studied the diagrams with interest so I returned to my place and picked up the dark leather-bound journal of Thomas Pitt. My next voice came from an old black-and-white film I had seen on television years before. The film had been set in the Second World War and the character, whose voice I was about to imitate, was that of the Commander of the Royal Air Force. I placed a straight finger across my upper lip to stand for a moustache and tried to reproduce the plumy English tones of the actor. I used Denver's brief note on the paper page marker as my script and then picked out a couple of the key sections from the journal itself.

My audience, though smiling, were now clearly more interested in the contents of the journal than me but I kept up the voice just to keep things light-hearted. According to Denver's notes, the journal linked both Rupert Stillwood-Hamilton and Jean-Baptiste Tavernier to a large blue diamond. Denver then noted that the stone Tavernier presented to the king of France was half the size and weight of the original blue diamond Rupert Stillwood-Hamilton had bought in the hut in India.

Next, I turned my attention to the packet of letters from Rupert Stillwood-Hamilton to his sister. I quickly referred to Denver's notes again and picked out the envelope Denver had marked with one of his pieces of paper. I let my voice drop an octave and read the letter in a seduction special voice.

"My Daarh-ling Elizabeth..." I began and Nahil clasped her hands to her mouth and let out a hoot that was far more amusing than anything I was supplying. Speaking as if I were Rupert Stillwood-Hamilton, I explained, using

Denver's notes and my own imagination, how Elizabeth was my beloved sister was waiting for me in back in England with debt-collectors hammering on the door.

"I am counting the seconds until we are in each other's arms again and I am nuzzling your little titties again. Oh, and rest assured that all our worries about finance will melt away on my return and we will be able to live in the manner which our birth right deserves. My pocket is bulging with desire and something hard." I paused for a second, "A hard bluestone that will leave you breathless when you see and feel it." OK—so I embellished a little as I went along but surely I wasn't that far from the truth. After all, historians do much the same thing; they connect known facts with informed guesswork? *At least Nahil is enjoying my use of artistic licence,* I thought. Later however, she read the letter herself and expressed disappointment at not finding the part I'd just read, she thought I'd been reading from the letter word for word. Andy was chuckling at my different accents and at Nahil's reaction to them. Joelle on the other hand wore a warm smile and was looking directly into my eyes. She was happier than amused but I could live with that.

Finally, I took out the photocopied sheets of A4 taken of pages from the journal of Gerald Aungier. Headed; British East India Archives the journal entry made in June 1669. I glanced down at the paper marker and read Denver's handwriting summarising the key points from the journal entries. So, what voice to use for Gerald Aungier? Was he even British, his surname didn't sound British, but who was I to tell if a name was British or not? Perhaps he was a Scottish man and I had spent a week with woman from Scotland. At the end of a week with her I had learnt a few more different swear words and could do a reasonable impersonation of her accent; I launched into it now.

"This wee bonny lad called Rupert was last seen boarding the Valvaston on the twenty-fifth of May 1669, aye, and he was pissed out of his wee skull as well." Andy shook his head in despair obviously finding my attempt at a Scottish accent unbearable. Joelle and Nahil were also frowning but that was because they were still trying to make sense of what I had just said. I put them out of their misery by sliding the sheets of paper across the low table towards them.

A few minutes of silence followed broken only by the occasional murmur as the other three, read, and then exchanged packets of papers with one another. When everyone had finished reading and were sat back relaxing Andy spoke, "I've brought a little reading matter and a couple of p-pretty pictures myself courtesy of the Kokonet Café's printer." He reached into his back pocket and brought out some sheets of folded white paper which he opened out flat and laid on the low table so we could all see the coloured pictures that filled the top page. A few minutes earlier Joelle and Nahil were amused by my antics and mildly interested in the documents Denver had sent to me. Now the two of them acted as if they'd been connected to the mains supply as they leaned over the photos cooing in delight. *What is it with women and diamonds?* I thought, shrugging my shoulders, but I still leaned over to take a closer look myself.

There was a photograph of large blue cushion-shaped diamond looking more like a sapphire to me. It was in a setting surrounded by small clear stones that I took to be more diamonds. Below there was another picture of the same blue diamond but alone and without the setting and looking much smaller. The third photograph which was towards the bottom of the page showed a red diamond in what looked like the same setting as the first photograph. As we crowded around the table in interest Nahil took the paper up to take a closer look at it and Joelle leaned in at her side to look over her shoulder. Since I was on the other side of the table I turned my attention to the text on the sheet of paper that now lay on top of the table. I read a couple of lines:

For many of the millions of visitors to the Smithsonian Institute's Museum of National History each year, at the top of their list of things to see is the Hope Diamond, making it certainly the most viewed gemstone in the world...

I realised Andy was speaking and broke off reading to listen to what he was saying about the photographs on the page Nahil held in her hand.

"The top photo shows the Hope Diamond as it is today in a platinum setting designed by Cartier surrounded by sixteen white diamonds. The next photo down shows the actual size of the Hope Diamond but without the setting. It was about the size of a nutmeg and not a big one at that."

"But it's only small," complained Nahil.

"Believe me, forty-five and a half carats is hardly small," Andy said smiling. "In fact, it makes it the largest blue diamond in the world."

Nahil frowned not convinced and Joelle pointed at the page and asked, "Then what's this red diamond here then?"

“That’s a photo of the Hope Diamond taken in the dark after it has been subjected to ultraviolet light,” said Andy. I walked around the table to look over their shoulders at the picture of the diamond glowing with a strange red light.

“That’s weird,” said Nahil and I couldn’t disagree with her assessment.

“Do all diamonds glow red like that after being under ultraviolet?” I asked.

“No, apparently not, it’s only blue diamonds and even then none react to the same extent as the Hope Diamond.”

“So you’ve become an expert,” I said half impressed and half mocking.

“N-No it’s all in there,” he pointed at the papers on the table, “read for yourself.” I took up the papers and started leafing through them. It was all there, even a time-line showing the history of the diamond and when each owner took possession and when they passed it on. The timeline started with Jean-Baptiste Tavernier and carried on to the present day and the Smithsonian Museum. Another page listed all the mishaps that supposedly befell them. It was all there except where the diamond was found and who discovered it. There was some speculation around Tavernier and how he came by the original stone but that’s all it was—speculation. I pushed the papers across the table towards Joelle and she looked at my face, smiled and picked them up.

“Imagine if we’d found the other half of that diamond in the cave under the church, just think how rich we’d all be,” exclaimed Nahil suddenly. We were sprawling in our seats the papers left behind on the table. The slight breeze had changed direction and brought the sound of the surf crashing on the distant reef.

“I doubt they’d allow us to keep it,” said Andy. “I’m sure the President would consider it the property of the people of St Gilberts.”

“Rubbish,” exclaimed Nahil. “I am a Gilbertise; if we find it—then finders keepers.”

“OK so what if we could keep it; what the hell would we do with it?” I asked looking around to the other three. Nahil smiled wistfully she tilted her head to one side then back on to the cushion behind. She put a finger to her mouth in thought as if she didn’t know where to begin.

“First I’d make sure all my family had everything they needed and then my Aunt Josie and all my uncles and aunts, and then all my cousins as well. All my family would have enough money for weddings. For Andy and me, a new car, new clothes from Mauritius, a new mobile for me, and a new boat for Andy, one with a cabin so he can keep out of the sun.” Her reply was exactly as I had expected, it was all about family and friends. Nahil, like most Gilbertise, did not see herself as a single entity but as part of an extended family group. Her happiness was dependent on happiness of others and of the whole group; if others were unhappy then the chances were she'd be unhappy too. Nahil looked at Joelle.

"Yes of course I'd make sure that Rose and Tocile and all my brothers and sisters were OK," Joelle said slowly and with less enthusiasm. I knew she felt differently about her foster parents and relatives than Nahil because Joelle, unlike Nahil, had never been encouraged to feel a part of any extended family group. Joelle's face brightened once she got past the family bit.

"Then I'd upgrade all the computers in the Café and get in the very latest software, the ones I have now are all old news. I'd like to travel abroad to see something of the world, with Rodney of course." She quickly glanced across at me and I saw how she keen she was that we shared the same hopes for the future. I nodded and smiled back at her. She was about to ask me what I would do if I suddenly became rich but I beat her to the punch by looking across at Andy and directing the question at him. Andy was a cool guy who'd seen more of the world than any of us so I was intrigued to find out how he'd deal with a massive windfall. He lay back in the chair almost horizontal, with his hands behind his head and smiled broadly at us all.

"Yes, I guess a newer and bigger boat would be nice, but sometimes thinking and dreaming about a bigger boat is better than actually having one, if that makes sense?" The frown of concentration on Nahil's face showed that it didn't make much sense to her at all. Maybe she was going back over the sentence to see if she had misheard him, but I knew what he meant all right. I remembered the time when I had dreamed of owning a motorbike and of all the things I would do when I finally did. However, once I got a motorcycle it was not long before I took it for granted, except when it broke down, which was frequent. It seemed as if I had gained a bike but lost the pleasure I used to get from thinking about, and looking forward to, actually owning one. The same was true of my first mobile phone and other such gadgets many of them earned from the foreign women I had escorted and pleasured.

"I get you," I said. "It's like the taste of a new stick of chewing gum once you've put it in your mouth the nice taste soon wears off."

"That's it." He agreed. "I've worked around rich, and very rich, people for long enough to know that wealth isn't all it's cracked up to be. It can make you a prisoner so you need to employ guys like me to make sure you and your kids aren't kidnapped or harmed. In the end, a life based purely on leisure without purpose much beyond pleasure, must feel pretty pointless." Andy sounded relaxed, his stammer all but gone, but there was something in his words and tone that made me wonder, what he'd said had struck a chord in me. Not because I lived solely for pleasure, but that my life lacked purpose. Others around me were busy with jobs and families and things to do. I ambled pointlessly around the house, garden and the island. I could no longer even claim to be serving St Gilberts virgin tourist industry.

Nahil and Joelle looked serious as they considered what Andy had said.

"Hmm I guess you're right," said Joelle. "I hadn't thought about it like that."

Andy nodded. "Besides, how impossible would it be to keep the discovery of a diamond of that size, colour and history a secret? For a start, how the hell would you find someone rich enough to buy it?"

"Mr Denver," shouted Nahil and we looked across at her to see her grinning triumphantly and her fist in the air.

"Yes, he'd certainly be interested," agreed Andy. "And if anyone could raise the money then I guess it's him. The problem is; according to the law of The St Gilberts Island Group, any wreck, and presumably treasure, belongs to the government and the people of St Gilberts."

"But we are people from St Gilberts," protested Nahil. Andy smiled and nodded agreeing before wagging his finger.

"Yes and hopefully, we'd benefit from whatever you had found once the government has decided what to do with it."

"Those pigshits," muttered Nahil before adding, "If I found the diamond I'd keep it a secret, sell it to Denver and then…" she stalled as her mind tried to follow it through.

"We'd have millions of rupees; how could we keep it a secret and explain all the gifts to family, relatives and friends? And our bank accounts would show enough money to buy the whole island a couple of times over." Andy put his arm around her shoulder.

"There's always Swiss bank accounts, but, yeah, you're right, if we found it and kept it, we'd eventually have to leave the island because you can't keep something like that a secret. It would be on all the news channels, CNN and all the others; it'd make front page news all over the world." Nahil had started a light-hearted discussion on what we'd do if we found the diamond and became rich and yet the subject had left us flat and subdued.

"Well, if I found the diamond," I said into the brief silence that followed Andy's last statement, "I'd buy everyone on the Island a pair of baggy pants and a big hat and make it the national costume!" Everyone laughed, but it was more to release the slight tension and lift the gloom, rather than in any appreciation of my wit.

Despite Joelle's and my protests, Andy and Nahil, refused the spare room and made their way back home in the small hours of the morning. It seemed that we had no sooner gone to bed ourselves before the alarm went off and Joelle started moving to get out of bed. I lay an arm across her to hold her down and managed to persuade her to sleep a little longer promising to take her to the Café on the motorbike instead of her having to catch the bus. So we slept on another hour or so until Joelle shrieked and almost spring from the bed.

"I'm late. Have you seen the time?" She was running about snatching up items of clothing and heading for the bathroom then she turned and snapped accusingly, "It's all right for you, Rodney Leon, but I have a business to run." She stormed towards the shower unaware of just how much her words had stung me.

Yeah, I thought, *kick a man when he's down and in bed*, but Joelle's annoyance at being late for work irked me, she was after all the boss, it was her Café, so why the big fuss? I got out of bed and threw some clothes on and made my way to the kitchen to put the kettle on and walked to the veranda. Joelle's annoyance, had set the tone for the day, the sky was grey with low cloud and a light drizzling rain. The usual vivid blues, turquoises and aquamarines of the sea now replaced by flat sweeps of navy-blue and greys giving way to dark charcoal blues for the deeper water beyond the reef.

"I'll eat breakfast at the Café," she said when she finally emerged from the bedroom in a haze of perfume. I put down the cup of tea I had been about to offer her and nodded in silent acknowledgement. I scooped up the keys to the Honda and, as we left the house, Joelle cursed when she realised it was raining so she stayed under the cover of the back porch while I turned the bike around and tried to kick-start it. I tried again and again until it was obvious to both of us that I was never going to get it to start that morning. Joelle fished in her handbag and brought out a small collapsible umbrella which she opened out and started walking up the drive towards the road.

"I'll catch the bus," she said over her shoulder as she walked up the drive with the gravel crunching under her shoes. I sat on the bike watching her march up without looking back as the rain ran off my hair and into my eyes forcing me to squeeze my eyelids shut. When I opened them, Joelle had disappeared from view on to the road.

I went back into the house and dried off with a towel. The house seemed empty and dark without the usual sunlight streaming in. I tossed the bike keys on the cupboard top and went to the kitchen to pour myself some tea from the pot, it was still hot and I took it to the veranda and sat facing out to sea. Thirty minutes later I stood and took a jacket off the peg before leaving the house. I walked up the drive towards the road. Joelle had gone so at least the bus had turned up. I was about to cross over to the same stop to catch the next bus into town when, for some reason I stayed put and flagged down a bus going in the opposite direction instead.

The road was slick with rain and the driver only managed to get up to second gear as we climbed, passing the turnoff to Kasper's Edge. Once we passed the highest point he shifted down to first gear for the steep descent and the gearbox growled and roared all the way down. I felt the heat from the hump near the driver's seat covering the differential as they held the bus from careering down and off the road. I had no idea why I'd caught the bus or when or where I intended to get off it. When we reached the flat coast road I looked through the rain spattered window at the choppy grey waves glimpsed through the boles of coconut palms as we sped along picking up speed. Takamaka trees, mangrove and the Giant Milkweed with its green leaves and mauve star-shaped flowers lined the shore on this part of the island.

For no particular reason, I got off the bus at Anse Forbans, a tiny collection of huts scattered around a large stone-built general store. The outer walls of the store were painted white and had been used as a canvass by talented artist Ronny, the owner's sixteen year old son. He'd painted groups of dumpy islanders wearing colourful clothes and sporting outlandish hairstyles on every exposed stretch of the white walls. He had also painted backgrounds for each group, the town centre, Lolas beach, people around a table inside a house, another was a beach where breadfruits were roasting on an open fire, a couple kissing on memory hill, and so on.

I recognised some of the characters immediately, a boggle-eyed black tee-shirted Dan Meme dripping in gold chains and bangles, Christopher from the Post Office, his distinctive Elvis hairstyle and sloping shoulders exaggerated even more in the painting. There was new mural still only half finished which showed an immensely fat bespectacled man breaking rocks with a pickaxe, Ferrari? Yes, it had to be; I chuckled but still found myself involuntarily touching my newly healed arm.

My eyes swept over the murals, there was no doubting his talent for caricature and love of bright colour but I sighed with relief at not spotting myself among the characters—hold on—one mural showed a hotel swimming pool with a busty white girl, skin a garish pink and hair, a birds nest of yellow paint stretched out on a sun lounger wearing a bikini. I almost missed the two feet sticking out on either side at the foot of a tall palm tree. My eye travelled to the top of the painted palm, sure enough, a dark grinning face with goggling blue eyes, presumably the owner of the two feet far below spied down through leaves and coconuts, on to the sunbathing woman below.

You little bastard Ronny. I thought, and almost entered the store in search of the artist but then I shrugged and considered buying a beer to drink outside on one of the concrete bench seats under the covered porch. Instead, I walked back towards the beach and found a rough wooden shelter, open at the sides, but with palm roof in reasonable condition. Underneath was a bench made from wooden plank worn smooth with use atop three uprights set into the sand. A place where the elders could sit, shaded from the sun, and watch the world go by. Anse Forbans does not have a sandy beach the shelter was over what little sand there is, the rest consists of large dark slabs of rock that meet the sea.

It is one of the few points around the island unprotected by a reef. The ocean reaches the shore in great unchecked swells that rise as they approach land and then thunder on to the rocks in a frightening explosion of water spray and sound. Avoided by swimmers and fishermen alike, tourists occasionally visit Anse Forbans little outpost but only stop long enough to buy an ice cream from the store and shoot half a dozen photos of the paintings on its walls.

I had slept badly the previous night and suddenly I realised how dog-tired I was, my legs ached and I sat on the wooden form and I felt the spray from the sea and rain on my sandaled feet and legs and, when the wind blew stronger, I felt the spray on my face to. The sky was unnaturally dark for this time of the morning and the cloud seemed so low I could have reached up and touched it. I sat and watched the rollers coming in still not sure why I had chosen to leave the bus at Anse Forbans or what I was going to do here, I had simply drifted here without any destination in mind and that just about summed up my life. It was a depressing realisation, and I tried to push it to the back of mind and replace it with something more positive.

The image of a glassy blue stone lost in the vastness of the Indian Ocean and covered with hundreds of years of sand and silt, appeared in my mind's eye. I closed my eyelids and let my mind drift to wherever it chose. I was on the deck of a wooden sailing ship staring into blackness all around. I strained my ears for the sound of breakers. I could hear waves and the hiss of surf on a distant beach but no breakers though there was something else, for the first time after all those weeks at sea there was the faint smell of damp vegetation and land. It came briefly and then was lost again as wind and spray blew into my face.

The deck tilted and heaved beneath my feet threatening to break my grip on the rail and pitch me over the side into the blackness of the sea. Landfall in a heavy sea in unknown waters and on the blackest of nights was every sailor's nightmare. Desperation and fear edged the voices shouted across deck as deckhands scurried about grappling with loose lines and deck cargo. Then one voice carried over the roar of the wind and sea, "Single light on the starboard bow! A ship's light!"

I opened my eyes and found my chest heaving and my fingers gripping the plank so hard my knuckles ached. I let go and flexed my fingers and nearly pitched forward off the bench. The intensity of the daydream, if that's what it was, both surprised and shocked me, it had seemed so real. Perhaps I'd been absorbing more historical information over the last few months than I realised. All that time spent with, and listening to Robert Chan, during those days in the dank cavern under St Francis Mount church and then, as we transferred the sodden trophies from the cavern to the museum, listening to him discussing the finer details of sailing ships of the seventeenth century with Andy, knowledgeable in his own right on nautical matters.

Yes, all of that plus the evening we'd spent listening to Richard Denver tell us the history of the bluestone, followed by a read through the documents he'd sent me. It wasn't surprising that some of it must have lodged in my brain. Now the weather, the closeness of the waves crashing on the rocks nearby, must have helped prime my mind and senses with the cocktail of information needed to produce a daydream of startling clarity. The rain turned from a fine mist into a regular downpour until it was battering down on the thatch covering the thin boards of the roof over my head and it started to blow in through the seaward side soaking my shorts and legs. I pulled the jacket close around me and once again closed my eyes and almost immediately it seemed, the dream continued.

I WAS Rupert Stillwood-Hamilton and I was shaking with fear. I was looking down at my loose white shirt, more like a woman's blouse with its frills and voluminous sleeves, at the leather belt around my waist and the sheaved knife it held. Around my neck was a lanyard on which hung a leather pouch containing the bluestone which I never removed day or night. I wore the lanyard like a bandolier, underneath my shirt so the pouch hung under my armpit out of sight, and where I could constantly feel its presence.

Now I squeezed my arm tight against it and felt the hardness of the stone against my chest and inner arm. I looked around at the crew, blurred, dark shapes moving back and forth across the deck. Sometimes I caught a glimpse of a face I knew. Paul Henri, wearing oilskins slick with rain and spray towering above two smaller men as he pulled on a rope. I saw Albert Raguin clinging to a rail and rigid as if the force of the wind and the motion of the ship had paralysed him. The man at the wheel was white, Denver? No, it was his tall friend, the one called George. Who was the captain?

I couldn't see but his voice rang out again, "Any other lights out there, lad?"

"None, Captain." I looked out at the single light moving as if on a ship at sea. Our ship was in great danger I sensed it, and those all about me felt it too I could see it in their faces. An hour earlier the captain had ordered the lead to be cast to assess what depth of water lay beneath us and he had just called for it to be cast again when our keel touched the rocks.

The first contact was so light that only the man at the helm had sensed its true significance. I looked up to see if we had lost a spar and saw the topmast shudder but otherwise there was no immediate sign we had run on to rocks. A second later I was thrown across the deck and towards the helmsman. The deck was now moving differently beneath my feet, turning and lifting so I found it impossible to keep my footing even with both hands gripping a rail in support. I looked for the other ship and, as I turned my head, a lightning flash revealed a white church atop a high hill that met the sea less than quarter of a mile away. On the hill front of the church swung a single lantern. We had been lured on to the rocks.

The captain bellowed for the first mate. I saw the dark shapes of deckhands swarming up the companionways and onto the upper decks many straight from their bunks and in various stages of undress. Their sailing experience had read the import of the light bump more accurately than I, even though they'd been asleep at the time. As they rushed on to the upper deck the second impact flung them across the planks and into a sprawling heap of tangled humanity. I kept my two-handed grip on the rail but felt my feet slide across the planks as the deck canted over. From below came the crack and splinter of a timber hull being torn open on jagged rock teeth. More ominous still, was the hiss and rush of sea water gushing in through the opening. There were four boats but only two were any position to be lowered into the water. The helmsman, still at the wheel, fought to turn the ship hoping the next wave might lift her free but the wheel spun free in his hands sending him reeling in the direction he had been turning, his head struck the edge of a rail and he collapsed to the deck with dark blood pouring from a long cut right across his forehead. Fear; chest panting, muscle trembling fear, of the sort I'd never experienced before. The crew were no better, their hands tore at snagged and snarled ropes in a vain effort to untangle and free the boats for lowering. Close to one they were trying to free, a dark figure slowly turned to face me. He was wearing a hood which threw his face into shadow until he was staring directly at me. I gasped in horror I was staring into the face of a rotted corpse, the face of Christopher Henri my old classmate and son of Paul Henri, Christopher the drug mule. Suddenly to my right another figure with a white face shadowed beneath a sou'wester hissed a single word at me, "Wreckers," and I saw it was Andy.

Wreckers, so if I survived the sea I would be murdered on the shore, the realisation drained the hope out of me. Why try to board one of the two Jolly boats? What was the point? At that moment, with all hope gone, I found I could think more clearly than at any other time since the ship had first hit the rocks. I checked the lanyard across my neck and, out of habit, squeezed down on the hidden stone beneath my shirt feeling the pressure in my armpit. The diamond was to have built my future but, for that future, I needed to survive the present. I had to both survive and keep the diamond. Time was running out; fear and panic took possession of me again. I needed to react, to decide a course of action, to move, to do something, anything; but all I could do was to stand rooted, my thoughts again scrambled and the noise of the wind, the sea, and the cries of the crew, all around filling my head like the scream of a boiling kettle. I must survive but amid the mayhem and clamour there would be no rescue, no redemption, only death by drowning or death at the hands of the wreckers on a godforsaken foreign shore. Everything else amounted to half chances and fractions of half chances. I had lost control of my fate, my destiny, there was nothing I could do, nothing to save both myself and the stone—unless…

My eyes snapped open and for a brief moment ghostly transparent shapes continued to move across my vision as I gazed towards the rollers crashing on to the rocks of Anse Forbans. I blinked until my vision cleared and gulped shallow breaths of the damp sea air with my heart pounding so hard I could hear it above the sound of wind, rain, and sea. Again, I found my hands gripping the bench so tightly the fingers were stiff and claw-like and my knees locked in a similar muscular tension. My shorts jacket and tee-shirt clung to my skin, damp, hanging cold and clammy with spray or sweat—I didn't know which. I shivered as wind blew across my wet body chilling me further till I stood up and stretched out stiff limbs. I recalled that conversation with Andy in the beer garden of the Three-In-One, and how neither of us had wanted our Valvaston dream to end. I smiled, because now I knew it hadn't.

"Whoa! Let me get this straight," exclaimed Andy. He was shouting to me from his lounge while I was in the kitchen wringing my sodden tee-shirt out in the sink with one of his fluffy white towels draped around my shoulders.

"You want me to help you dig up a dead body?" Nahil was out at the covered market in town helping her mother and Aunt Josie with their vegetable stall. Covered or not, I doubted the market would do much business in this rain but at least we had his place to ourselves and it was just as well given what I was asking Andy to help me with.

I had gone to Andy's house from Anse Forbans which entailed a bus journey and then the last drenching quarter of a mile on foot, for that is how far Andy's house is from the nearest stop. Andy walked into the kitchen and leaned against a tiled worktop. He was trying hard to sound sceptical and doing a damned good job of it, but I knew him too well for him to be able to hide his underlying interest and excitement from me.

"I'll put the kettle on and then we'll go over it again," he suggested, but I guessed he would need very little convincing to help me with my grave robbing plans. It constituted a risk for both of us but especially for him, a grave robber's hands are hardly 'the clean pair of hands' he needed to have to stay on St Gilberts. I was relying on that element of risk to tempt Andy on board with my little scheme, besides, weren't we both well in with President Duval after our last pat-on-the-back meeting with him?

"Think about it Andy," I said turning to face him. "You're on your way home from India with a diamond that'll not only clear your debts and set you up in luxury for life. But, not only that, it's going to make you famous and put you in the history books. Then what happens? Wreckers lure your ship on to rocks next thing you know it's sinking. What do you do?"

"Shit myself," replied Andy.

"Yes-yes," I agreed impatiently not allowing his flippant remark to side-track me, "Yes, yes, but after you've shit yourself? Think about it, Stillwood-Hamilton came from England right, so he knows about wreckers and has a good idea what's in store for him—even if he does manage to reach the shore alive."

Andy nodded and drew a finger across his throat.

"Maybe," he conceded grudgingly.

"That's right," I said. "If he reaches the shore alive, they'll kill and strip him of everything—including his polyester Y-fronts and gold fillings—and then dump him—"

"Did they have gold fillings in those days?" interrupted Andy, but I ignored the question and his grin, and motored on.

"If he reaches the shore dead or alive the wreckers will strip off him anything of value and dump him." I repeated, "He's desperate to achieve two things; one; stay alive and two; keep the diamond. So what are his options?" Before Andy could reply to this question, I answered it for him, "Try to get on a boat with the rest of the crew and fight his way ashore. Or, get on a boat with the crew and head out to sea taking his chance in the storm in an open boat. Or, swim ashore and run like hell or, swim ashore and pretend to be dead on arrival?"

Andy frowned. "If he tried to swim ashore, he probably would be dead on arrival."

"Would he?" I queried. "Don't forget those rocks at Al Solere are below the surface so it's not as if he's getting battered over a reef. He'd just be swimming in on the surf."

Andy looked doubtful, "In those seas—at night, I wouldn't fancy it."

"But what other chance has he got?" I asked.

Andy thought for a moment, "Well, to be honest, I think I'd take my chance in the boat with the others. I mean, if you're in for the chop as soon as you set foot on the beach then why go through the effort of having to swim there? At least with the boat you'd still have some strength to fight with?" He had a point.

"OK, so he goes with the boat and lands on the beach but whether he fights or whether he pretends to be dead he still wants to keep that diamond because without it he's nothing—a nobody."

"He's still alive though," countered Andy.

"Yes but he may as well be dead," I said. "That's how important it must have been to him." Andy shrugged his shoulders, neither agreeing nor disagreeing.

"Suppose it was you, what would you do with the diamond?" I asked.

Andy thought for only a moment before answering, "Depends on the size of it, but I'd either swallow it or stick it up my arse."

"Exactly," I exclaimed triumphantly. "That's just what I thought; it gives him the best result in any outcome. If the locals turn out to be friendly after all, he still has the diamond. If he pretends to be dead and they don't stick a pike through him just to make sure, then he's still alive and he still has the diamond!"

"And if he is dead?" queried Andy.

"Then he dies with the diamond," I said with emphasis like a barrister making his final case for the defence.

Andy nodded and summarised, "So what you're saying is; our friend Rupert swallows the diamond and either washes ashore dead or the wreckers kill him when reaches the shore. The locals see from what's left of his clothes he's a man of substance and fear his country may send the navy to come looking for him. As a bit of insurance just in case someone actually does trace him to Al Solere the villagers give the nobleman a proper grave and bury him in it just in case." Andy had summed it up quite well so I nodded in agreement.

"There is no record of Al Solere being anything other than a dirt poor village so I'm guessing they never found the diamond; if that's the case, then if it was inside Stillwood-Hamilton when they buried him—then that's where it still is today."

Andy sucked in air through his teeth and then slowly nodded. "It's a long shot but you could be right."

"I'm sure of it, Andy, it all fits. Isn't it what we'd do in his situation?" I had a sudden thought, "Do you think if he'd swallowed the diamond, it would have dissolved in his stomach acid?"

Andy replied without hesitation, "No chance, diamonds are the hardest things in nature. You'd probably have to take stomach acid and heat it in a furnace before it could mark a diamond. If old Rupert was dead, or killed on arrival, his guts would be pretty damn cold pretty damned quick. Besides, he would have stuck up his arse anyway, I've heard visitors have smuggled phones into prison in their rectums and, you just try swallowing even an almond nut without chewing it first, this blue stone is even bigger than the Hope diamond and…" he looked sideways at me and added, "That must have been some dream you had at Anse Forbans."

I nodded ruefully. "Yes it was and I wasn't even properly asleep at the time."

We had a cup of tea and then organised when, and how, we were going to excavate the grave. We decided to do it the following day when hopefully the rain would have stopped but the soil was still soft, damp, and easy to dig. Andy's inflatable was still not fit to take out to Al Solere so I agreed to wait until it was dark to avoid the possibility of any of my neighbours seeing me, and then carry two spades, a rake, and two trowels up the road to the turn-off to Kasper's edge and hide them in the trees there. Andy agreed to bring his sieve, as I didn't have one, wrapped in a plastic bag.

Together in the morning we would stroll up the road to the turn-off to Kasper's Edge and pick up the spades and trowels as we passed. Any one seeing us would have no idea of our mission. As we drank our tea we floated an alternative idea, that we tell Gerald Duval my idea and let Chan organise the dig. We talked about it but dismissed it; Gerald Duval would never agree to violate a grave in a Christian churchyard on the half chance there was something valuable inside it. If we told him he would make sure we didn't violate it either.

We'd be in a limbo of not knowing and I wasn't having that. If we wanted to know for sure if the diamond lay in that grave we'd have to do the deed ourselves and without anyone else knowing, except of course for Joelle and Nahil.

When Joelle arrived home from the Café, I was already cooking the dinner, pork curry and pigeon peas—one of her favourites. It was obvious as soon as she walked through the door that her mood had softened since the morning. She gave me one of those 'let's make up' smiles and followed it by wrapping her arms around my neck and giving me a kiss on the lips.

"I've been thinking, Rodney, why don't I take tomorrow off so we can go somewhere for the day? If it's nice, we could have another picnic, just you and me." Was it the hesitation or the expression on my face that gave me away? Well, sooner or later she would have guessed I was up to something especially when I got around to taking those spades up the road later in the evening after it was dark.

"You're going to do what? Please tell me you're joking. You're not serious right? Rodney, please tell me you're joking." I shrugged as if that was answer enough. She gave me a long despairing look took a deep breath and let it out in a shriek of frustration before storming off to the bathroom. I heard the bolt snapped noisily in place. No bed gymnastics tonight I thought, and walked over to the veranda, before I reached it, I saw it was dark outside. I gathered all the garden tools I thought we'd need the next day and, picking up the torch I'd got ready for the occasion set off up the road.

When I returned over an hour later, Joelle was already in bed and seemingly asleep. I showered and slipped in alongside her. She turned, moaned and then threw her arm across me. Unfortunately, that only confirmed she actually was asleep. There was no way she could have forgiven me that easily or that quickly.

Breakfast the following morning was a subdued affair and I thought that she was going to go off in a mood again for the second day running. However just before she left the house she must have thought better of things because she turned and walked back up to the table where I was still sipping tea.

"What time is Andy coming?" She asked.

"Any time now," I replied.

"You know that you are both taking a hell of a risk, especially Andy."

"He knows, but he thinks it's there as well." She pulled a face as if surprised at Andy's gullibility.

"Well, be careful, the pair of you. I know Duval was friendly enough with us all last time but he's not going to go along with grave robbing, this is a Christian island, remember that—and just think what Aunt Mert would think?" It was a cheap shot and she knew it. She was telling me that if we were caught our crime would shame everyone in our social circle, our family, friends, and most of all our partners, her and Nahil. I nodded grimly; I didn't need a lecture on how things were on St Gilberts.

Joelle had worked her way up to become a respected member of the business community, my plan threatened to turn her into a laughing stock and outcast—something she had hoped never to be again. Could I really be so selfish? When the door closed behind her I sat in a crisis of indecision and almost decided against going through with it but Andy's arrival lifted my spirits and returned my confidence. He joined me for a cup of tea before we set out.

"By the way, don't wear that tee-shirt," he said as we rose from the table, "Every fisherman off the coast will see you. Haven't you got something that'll blend in with the scenery a bit better?"

We chatted on the way up the drive and I learnt he had faced a similar barrage from Nahil who was also not keen on what we were about to do.

"Well, she's afraid you'll be kicked off the island. If you leave you know she'll leave with you but it'd break her heart, she loves St Gilberts—it's the only place she knows."

Andy nodded, serious for a moment before he slapped me on the back and grinned, "Buck up, mate, if we play things carefully, none of that's going to happen." His voice was calm, no stammer, I wanted to believe him.

We took a quick look about us before we ducked off the road and down the overgrown trail leading to Kasper's Edge. The spades and trowels were exactly where I'd left them the evening before and we collected them on our way down. When we reached the edge I experienced a few butterflies in my stomach. If someone had told me a few months earlier that I could seriously consider digging up a grave at Al Solere of all places, I would have laughed in their face.

"Dig up a grave in St Gilberts most haunted place, no chance." Is that what the lure of treasure does to people? Is that what it had done to me? And, in that thought, I felt I understood Denver a little more. Of course the week spent on Chan's archaeological dig had also desensitised me and reduced Al Solere's psychological fear factor. The narrow zigzag trail down to the beach was greasy from the previous day's rain, providing a genuine physical danger to make up for the taming of the ghosts. Carrying the tools didn't help but we set off down nevertheless.

Halfway along the path, we dropped the tools down ahead of us picking them up again when we reached the flat ground. Our eyes scanned the cliff edge and the sea behind us for watchers as we made our way up the steps to the top of the mount. When we reached the grave we checked again but saw no one in any direction, our eyes met and I knew he was checking me to see if I was still ready to go through with it, I nodded. Andy had brought a large plastic sheet in the bag he had used to also carry the sieve and he spread it out alongside the grave and weighted down the corners with some large stones.

Andy suggested that we place all the soil we excavated on to the sheet so it would be easier to keep it together as we sieved for the stone. It would also leave less of a mark on the ground when we replaced the soil back at the end. I looked down at the grave and felt the enormity of what we were about to do.

We stood both with a spade in hand. Andy had done the digging in the cavern so I bowed to his greater experience in excavations and waited for him to start.

"How deep down do you think it'll be?" I asked, not able to bring myself to say 'body'.

He thought for a few seconds before answering, "I'd be surprised if there was that much soil here so I guess not very deep." He looked around at the area in general.

"Will the body or bones still be there?" I asked, and before he could answer I added, "Or will the body have disintegrated without a trace? If so how will we know when to stop digging?" I was playing for time and needing reassurance.

He shrugged and grinned. "When we reach Australia," he replied but then became serious again. "It's difficult to say and I'm no expert. It's got a lot to do with the climate and the nature of the soil. Heat, moisture and soil acidity speeds up decomposition but there's only one way to find out." With that he slowly and carefully pressed the blade of his spade a short way into the soft damp soil. After that we worked slowly and in silence.

"Remember what Chan told us," said Andy as we laid aside the spades and stooped with our trowels.

"Always work the trowel back towards you." The soil was still soft from the previous day's rain but dried almost as soon as it reached the sieve and was given a shake or two. Andy had originally bought the sieve to grade aggregate when laying a new concrete floor in his boathouse. The mesh was wide enough to let the soil through but close enough to pick up anything the size of a fingertip upwards. We had been working steadily for about two and half-hours when Andy's trowel struck something hard. We concentrated our efforts around the area and slowly uncovered a brown dome-shaped object larger than a coconut shell. We uncovered more earth until Andy reached down and pulled the object out by hand. I gasped and fell back as he turned the skull towards me.

"Fucking hell, we've found him!" Andy leaned back in amazement, as if the possibility of finding anything at all had never even entered his head. His obvious lack of superstitious fear for the gruesome relic in his hand gave me some courage as well and I leaned in cautiously to have a closer look.

"Alas, poor Rupert, I knew him well," intoned Andy and I mentally said a prayer of apology on his behalf to the ghosts of Al Solere and particularly the owner of the skull who must surely have been frowning on our mornings work.

Having located the head we could work out where the rest of the body-bones lay and set to scraping thin layers of soil with our trowels and then running it through the sieve. It soon became obvious that we were not going to uncover an intact skeleton. Most of the bones had either disappeared into the soil or been reduced into tiny fragments. The exception to this was the pelvis and the two thigh bones which, though obviously degraded, were just about recognisable for what they were. I was scraping close to the area of the pelvis when my trowel struck what I took to be another stone.

I stopped to look more closely and saw the glint of something glassy. I held my breath dropped the trowel and reached to pick it up. We had been working in concentrated silence for past fifteen minutes or so and Andy hadn't noticed that

I had stopped. My fingers trembled as they pushed the damp soil off to reveal the blue stone underneath.

"Oh my god, Andy, it's here, I've found it!" I held it up and saw light reflected in blue glints within the stone itself. At that moment I wasn't sure what I felt; was it triumph, elation, or was it fear or dread? My stomach turned in apprehension of something with no name and no face. The low sun caught the stone and as we gazed in awestruck wonder at the sparks of blue light within. I had no doubt that here was the stone Richard Denver had crossed the world to St Gilberts to find.

I looked across at Andy and saw his hand extended across the grave. I assumed he wanted to hold the stone himself but when I made to pass it to him, he gave a little shake of his head and his extended hand waved it away. Then I realised he wanted to shake my hand. I transferred the stone to my left hand and clasped his extended hand. Andy spoke in that funny British officer voice he sometimes used when telling British jokes in the Three-In-One. He never stammered when he was mimicking another's voice.

"Rodney, bloody well done, old chap, well done, a first-class effort." Then he slipped back into his own voice but his voice was quiet and serious, "I'll tell you something, Rodney, when you suggested we come here and dig up a grave, I agreed because you're my best mate and because I need to do something bonkers every now and then. Oh, and yes, your theory did make some sense but, to be honest, I never really expected you to find the bloody thing! You proved me wrong; in fact you've proved everyone who's ever doubted you wrong. You've done what Denver with all his millions and billions and Chan with all his book learning failed to do and I'm proud of you mate, and you should be bloody proud of yourself too."

It was a long speech coming from Andy, and he'd delivered it without faltering as well. I must confess as his words sank in they moved me. Perhaps it was the moment, or maybe it was because no one had ever said anything like that to me before—that they were proud to know me and that I should be proud of myself. In fact I couldn't remember when I'd last felt proud of myself or, even if I ever had. This realisation reached deep inside me and touched a neglected part of my soul. I had done something special, something others had tried and failed to do.

For an awful moment, I feared tears might roll from my eyes but with a major effort and a deep breath, I kept a lid on them and forced a grin back at him. "Turn it in, mate; you'll want to have my fricking baby next!" He grinned and held out his hand out, this time for the stone.

"I see Rupert had the stone shaped in India before he set sail," said Andy holding the stone up to the light. "I'm no expert but it looks like a bit of a shitty job as well, a rushed job." I'd been expecting to find something similar to a piece of broken blue glass rather than a facetted jewel. Even to my untrained eye I could see the facets gave the rough stone a little shape but there was no symmetry to it. It was the size of a very large nutmeg. Andy held the diamond so it caught the sun.

"When I was studying the Hope Diamond in the Café, I read a link on the old Indian diamond cutters. They used to rank size over brilliance so when they cut, their aim was to keep the diamond's size rather than to heighten the internal refraction."

"What?" I asked gaping at him. He grinned.

"Bloody hell; I know a word that Rodney Leon doesn't. Look, to make a diamond sparkly, you have to cut it so light entering the stone bounces off the facets like they're internal mirrors. To create the best shape and the right number of facets for that to happen usually means you have to lose more of the diamond in the cutting. The Indian cutters, on the other hand, liked sparkly diamonds but thought it was better to keep as much of the diamond as possible and sacrifice a bit of the sparkle." I nodded understanding and he passed the blue diamond back to me so I could see what he meant.

"Still I'd need a shoe horn and a dozen pints of beer to get that thing past my throat," he commented as he passed it back.

"What the hell are we going to do with it?" I asked.

Andy's voice was serious again, "I'm more worried about what it's going to do to us."

We covered our tracks well and put everything back just as we'd found it, bar the diamond. We tipped the soil back into the grave and pressed it down, Andy sprinkled dry dust over the top to cover any sign of recent excavation. On our way back to the road, we left the tools in the same place as I had left them the previous evening, I'd pick them up when it was dark. Andy put the sieve and plastic sheet in a shopping bag.

"Let's get the gang together tonight at my place and decide what we're going to do with it," I suggested.

Andy looked at me and frowned. "It's your diamond, mate—do with it what you want."

"No way, Andy, all four of us have suffered and taken risks because of this thing—it belongs to all of us. Besides, whatever any of us do with it, it's going to affect us all one way or another." My voice must have held conviction because he never argued, just nodded in acceptance as we approached the road. When we reached the drive down to my house we parted and Andy promised to return back with Nahil as soon as he could.

The four of us were sat around the table in my lounge. Earlier I'd rung the Kokonet Café and asked Joelle to come home as soon as she could. On hearing my request, she immediately feared the worst but I reassured her everything was cool without letting on what it was all about—despite her protests. While I waited for the others to arrive, I checked the cupboards and fridge for food and drink and found them all mostly bare.

Here I am, I thought, *with one of the most valuable diamonds in the world, with not even enough spare cash for a few bottles of beer and a packet of fish.* I peeled potatoes, softened them in boiling water and put them on a tray. I poured a little oil over them and sprinkled curry powder over the top then placed the tray in the oven. It would give us something to eat at least. For drinks; tea, coffee, or Tamarind juice would have to do; besides, we were going to need clear heads anyway.

I sat out on the veranda and placed the diamond on the low table in front of me. A few moments ago, I had been impatient for the others to arrive. Now, as I thought things through, I was glad that I had some time alone to think. What would I do with millions in cash? What would wealth bring me that I didn't already have; a new bike, or even a car, or why not both? What about a motorboat? I frowned as a new set of questions came to me: but to take where, to do what?

I imagined myself driving up and parking a new sports car outside the Three-In-One. Dan and Bengy would be happy for me but, try as might; I could not conjure up any other smiling faces. Miserable sods, stuff them all. How many would be jealous and resentful of me and think "He's never really been one of us, different, like an outsider, not a true Gilbertise, an idle waster, a gigolo."

In their eyes, the money would only make me more of what I already was, and a show-off to boot. I could move I could go abroad but then there was only one house I wanted to live in and that was this house, the house I was already in.

Deep down, there was only one place I wanted to live as well—St Gilberts. Yes, I was unhappy with parts of my life but could I change those parts with more money? And what parts were they; not the house, not Joelle, not my friends, Andy and Nahil?

Suddenly, I realised that being the richest man on St Gilberts wouldn't make me any happier or make me feel any better about myself. Even giving the money away in good works and charity would be seen as trying to buy peoples favour or even that I was patronising others with handouts. Andy had been shrewd, finding the diamond would alter the balance of everything, especially that which was most important to me and I had a horrible foreboding it would not be for the better. For a fraction of a second I wished I'd never found it, but it was only for a second.

I snatched it up and clenched my fist around it, "I did it! I found it, and no one can ever take that fact away from me."

Nahil was passing the café when Joelle stepped out on her way home in response to my call. Nahil had received a call off Andy telling her to meet him at my house so the two of them caught the same bus and arrived at the house ahead of Andy who I guessed was still making his way up from his house. The two girls walked in still talking and only stopped their chatter when they saw me standing near the table.

"What's happened, Rodney?" they asked. Joelle's expression was serious and concerned.

"Relax, everything is just fine there's no problem, no problem, except what to do with this?" They both frowned with incomprehension. "I found it! I've found the diamond," I said, and waved towards the table suggesting they should sit first. I produced the stone from my pocket and placed it on the table in front of them. Nahil drew back with her hands to her mouth and then just as quickly leaned in for a closer look.

Joelle tilted her head slightly and stared at the stone with a fixed, trance-like expression on her face. Nahil surprised me slightly by asking if she could hold it, the Nahil I knew would just have snatched it up. I nodded and shrugged to show that she had no need to ask. She picked it up and held it to the light. Joelle's eyes followed it all the while, her face impassive. I waited until they turned back to the table having examined it from every angle.

"Tell us how it was when you found it," asked Nahil. So I told them of my strange daydream at Anse Forbans and how I came to believe Rupert Stillwood-

Hamilton either swallowed the diamond or pushed it up the other end before making for the shore. Then I gave them a blow-by-blow account of that morning's dig with Andy and how my trowel had turned over the mud caked stone.

"He couldn't swallow a thing that big," exclaimed Nahil pointing at the stone.

"OK, so he stuck it up his arse then," I replied and she snorted with laughter which relaxed us all a bit more.

She was still chuckling when Andy arrived carrying the same plastic bag he'd used that morning to carry the sieve and plastic sheet. I had the bizarre notion that he had either forgotten to put the bag down or was not aware that he was still carrying it even though he had changed his clothes. He must have noticed me staring at it because he held up the bag and grinned, "Brought this along for a little experiment."

He reached in the bag and brought out the bug catcher I'd seen outside his house at barbecues and on those evenings we'd sat late into the night drinking. Andy's place is more prone to mosquitoes than mine and the Ultraviolet bug catcher was one of many methods he'd experimented with to wage war on them. The gadget did kill plenty of the little bloodsuckers but there were always plenty more to take their place so we still got bitten, another reason most of our get-togethers took place at my house instead of his. He set the contraption on the table and though it could work on batteries but he hadn't got any with enough juice to power it. Batteries were just another one of the many expensive imports to St Gilberts. Instead, he connected it to an extension lead that just about reached one of my plug sockets.

"OK," he said and I flipped the plug socket and the bug zappers blue lights came on.

"Probably best not to look at the light," Andy warned. "Ultraviolet is not good for the eyes." He stood holding the diamond close to the lit tubes with his own face turned away. It was not dark outside so I drew the blinds and stood ready by the light switch. The minutes dragged by as Andy held the diamond near the ultraviolet bug catcher then he signalled for me to switch the lights off. He reached over and flipped the switch on the gadget switching it off so we were thrown into darkness—though not quite. A little red sun floated over the table held by between Andy's finger and thumb.

"See the intense orange-red phosphorescence? That reaction to ultraviolet light is exclusive to dark-blue diamonds," he said triumphantly. If the diamond had inspired awe before, Andy's demonstration had just raised that awe several notches. He placed the diamond on the table and we gathered around the table to stare down at the stone glowing red, as if it contained a furnace within.

"So what are we going to do with it?" I asked when the lights were back on and we'd retuned to our places at the table. I expected a continuation of the discussion we'd had a few nights earlier but now the others seemed subdued. Andy's little demonstration had brought home to us just how special this diamond was. It wasn't just the potential monetary value of the stone but the history that went with it and its connection with the ill-fated Hope Diamond. I set myself to play devil's advocate and challenge any frivolous suggestions such as buying new boats, cars, clothes and the like.

I was deadly serious. I wanted, rather I needed, a solution to the responsibility the discovery of this diamond had placed on me. A windfall of a few thousand or even a few hundred thousand rupees in cash would have made the evening more of an occasion to enjoy. A local lottery win where everyone simply envied your outrageous luck and then looked forward to the next draw hoping then it would be their turn next to celebrate. With this diamond nothing was going to be straightforward or simple, we knew that.

It was however Andy who played the role of devil's advocate most effectively. His background as a VIP bodyguard had given him more experience of being around serious money than the rest of us and he understood the problems and drawbacks that great wealth brings. He also had a clearer understanding of the difficulty of transporting such a valuable gemstone, of finding buyers, of banking the payments and of how life in general could become more restrictive in proportion to how much wealth we had.

We were not long into our discussion before it became clear we were concentrating not on what we'd do with the money we'd get from selling the stone, but on what to do with the stone full stop. We had surely broken some law in digging up the grave and besides, the diamond was legally the property of the Government of St Gilberts rather than ours anyway. To sell it we would need to risk smuggling it out of the country. We put forward various solutions to this problem but Andy, as always, spotted the flaws in each suggestion.

"We could of course ignore the history of the diamond and offer it as a new find," Joelle suggested.

Andy nodded but said, "Possible, but I think the way the diamond's cut would be difficult to explain. Selling this diamond would be like introducing a second version of the *Mona Lisa* by Leonardo De Vinci to the art world."

"Suppose we just give the diamond to the President to give to Chan for his museum?" said Nahil, I looked at her and her face was serious. Maybe all the talk of the problems the diamond could bring was beginning to make her think it was more trouble than it was worth. It had certainly given us a lot to think about.

Andy thought for a moment, "It's a possibility but who's going to pay to see it?"

"Tourists," answered Nahil crisply.

Andy nodded agreement before adding, "I seem to remember Duval wasn't too keen on increasing the number of tourists visiting St Gilberts because we haven't got the facilities or the resources to cope with them when they come. Besides, St Gilberts couldn't afford what it would cost to protect something as valuable as this." He pointed to the diamond on the table.

"I could break into the museum and steal it myself without raising a sweat. Imagine what someone with Denver's resources could do. Armed villains from all over the world, not to mention those Somali pirates just up the coast, would descend on the island in droves. They'd just march in a take it. Who would stop them—the police?" We sat in silence absorbing this and I waited, knowing the moment had finally arrived.

The idea which had started to develop in my mind earlier, while sitting alone waiting for the others to arrive well, now was the time to reveal it. For my plan to work it was essential for them to want it to work as well because I needed the support of each one of them. I needed the special talents each of them had. I needed Joelle for her business intelligence and skill at negotiating. I needed Andy for his street smarts and experience in anticipating and working out the angles that I'd never see coming until they hit me in the face. And finally, and perhaps most importantly, I needed Nahil; out of all of us, she was the only one who had always, unquestionably, been on the inside, a true Gilbertise.

Nahil was part of the fabric of St Gilberts interconnected society. Her relatives dotted the length and breadth of St Gilberts and most of the outlying islands to. Living with Andy was the only thing she'd ever done, the only action that might have dented her status but it was a very small dent, if it were a dent at all, her standing as a true Gilbertise was unquestioned. Nahil had an insight into the mind-set of the average Islander the rest of us couldn't boast. Through her network of contacts she would be the one who ensured the correct story passed into folk-lore. First, I needed to change the focus of the current discussion.

"At the moment we are concentrating on what to do with the diamond but, as Andy said, this diamond is so big there's no way it's not going to change our lives. Even if we did nothing with it, or even if I picked it up now and threw it in the sea, the knowledge we once had it, and the thought of all the things we could, or should have done with it, would eat away at us for the rest of our lives."

Nahil leaned in and I guessed she was getting ready to snatch the diamond away from me if I tried to follow through with my last comment about throwing it in the sea. I leaned back in the chair and put my hands behind my head.

"If it's going to change our lives then why don't we decide now what exactly we want changing or, just as important, what we don't want to change in our lives?" Andy's eyebrows raised a little and he gave me a quizzical look but then nodded me to continue as if in approval.

"I'll kick off if you want," I said, and I could see that I had their full attention. "OK. Things I don't want to change first." I turned and placed my hand on Joelle's arm. She sat at my side and she gave a shy smile. If I hadn't said her first then I'm sure I would have had to duck one of her deadly punches.

"Then of course there's you guys," I waved towards Andy and Nahil, "I hope you two are going to stick around on the Island because we'd be lost without you." They smiled and nodded, though I wasn't sure if in agreement they'd stay or just in acknowledgement of the question.

"Next there's this house, I like it here and I don't want to live anywhere else so I want to stay on St Gilberts, but as a free and respected man." The others nodded and I could see they were thinking things through from their own perspectives. I guessed we shared similar hopes for the future and continuing to live on St Gilberts, perhaps the opportunity to take a trip abroad in the future, keeping the friendship that meant so much to all of us. One by one the others expressed the same and when everyone had said their piece we realised how in line each of our needs were. We saw how little change we really wanted in our lives. I thought the discussion had grounded us and put our find into perspective but Joelle sighed in frustration looking first at me, then Nahil and Andy and then back at me again.

"My head's spinning, one minute we're saying all the good things we'll do when we're rich, the next it's nothing but problems. Well, is this thing going to be good or bad?"

She pointed down towards the diamond on the table and said, "I don't think we can win any way we play it." Her eyes met mine and held, was she blaming me for all of this? If so, then of course she was right too. I put my hands on top of the table, it was at last the right time.

"Yes; we will win. I have an idea..."

Four days later, we entered the President's office. Joelle and Andy each carried a sheaf of papers. Nahil and I carried our hearts in our mouths. Five long hours later, we left and made our way home to our separate houses drained by the intensity and effort of the meeting. Two days passed then without warning the President summoned Andy and me to his office. I returned to my house to find Joelle already there. Apparently, word had gone around: "Andy and Rodney are walking towards the Government Building." So she'd left the Café early.

"Is everything OK?" she asked, her face showing concern.

"Yes, everything's fine," I reassured her.

"Nothing's going to affect our plan, is it?" she asked.

"No," I replied, "the meeting was not even connected to that. In fact he surprised us, but in a good way—I think."

She turned and leaned in closer. "Tell me more." So I led her to the veranda where we stood, leaning on the rail looking out across the sea to where the setting sun, glowing red-orange like our diamond had, was dropping into the sea.

"He asked Andy and me if we wanted to become consultants working for and directly answerable to him. Oh, he'll pay us to, said he'd find the money no problem."

"Consulting?" She looked up at me puzzled, unconvinced. "Consulting in what?"

"Investigating things."

"Things?"

"Yes, like unsolved crimes, missing people, or anything that needs investigating." I'm sure I sounded like an over enthusiastic schoolboy, trying too hard to convince. I wanted her to be happy for me but instead she frowned some more.

"Crime, what crime?" she asked.

"Yes that's exactly what I had thought too, but Duval told us St Gilberts and its outlying islands have more mysterious things going on than most people realised, more than I realised anyway."

"Such as what?" she asked her voice dripping scepticism.

I couldn't disguise my frustration. "Shit, I don't know, he didn't say, no doubt he'll tell us if we accept the job."

"Isn't that the sort of thing we have police for?" She persisted. I took a deep breath as if dredging up the last of my patience.

"Yes it is, and they do solve most—well—some things. It's the ones they haven't—and can't—that we'll be working on. Besides, you know as well as me that our police are not the sharpest knives in the drawer, there're still a few Henri types among them. Look he needs people he can trust, independent people who are not in the system that's all." I was trying hard to convince her but it was having the opposite effect, yet I persisted because it was important to me to have her on side, but she was frowning, unconvinced.

"Yes, but why you and Andy?" she asked.

"Why not?" I replied indignantly. "Duval thinks we have the right mix of qualities he's looking for; we impressed him with the way we dealt with all the stuff Denver threw at us over the Valvaston."

Her expression softened as she asked, "Will it be dangerous?"

"No, I don't think so," I lied, Duvall had said the opposite, guessing correctly that would be part of the job that appealed to us.

Joelle was silent for a while and we both watched as the sun finally slipped beneath the sea leaving the evening sky a darkening blue-grey.

"So will you take the job," she asked at last.

"Yes," I replied.

"Is it what you want, Rodney?" I didn't need to think about the answer to that, Andy and I had spent some time sat on the bench outside Government Building doing just that. We had exchanged thoughts on Duval's description of the current mysteries awaiting resolution, and realised our lives were suddenly going to get very exciting, and we'd grinned at each other and at our luck.

"Yes, it is," I said simply; and at last she smiled and nodded.

"Then I'm happy too, Rodney, is Andy going for it as well?" I nodded. Her eyes turned towards the table and the travel documents on top near the silver napkin ring.

"When will he expect you to start all this consulting then?" she asked, and I knew what she was thinking.

"Don't worry, I'll make sure we'll have plenty of time to sort out our plans for what we are going to do with the diamond first; I promise."

The fifteen knot east wind that had pushed the sixty-two foot yacht up from the Atlantic had abruptly died away forcing the lone sailor, a middle-aged man, to switch on the engine. It was perhaps as well, according to the charts, the keel of the sixty-two footer would scrape the riverbed if he wasn't careful. Fortunately the charts were good so, if he was sensible, the risk was small but still enough to make him feel alive.

When Richard Denver finally said goodbye to the Ryder couple in Madagascar, he'd been as glad to see the back of them as they were of him. His only regret was leaving the boat. So much so he had bought his own but that was after his meeting with Gerald Carr, his business partner. During a surprisingly amicable discussion, the two men had thrashed out an agreement that left the day-to-day running of their business empire to Carr. Denver was to remain a partner, but a sleeping partner. This arrangement suited both men; it gave Carr what he had always wanted from the start, and gave Denver time to pursue other interests.

Shortly afterwards, Denver announced that he was planning to spend some time travelling, a sabbatical, and both men agreed to review the new arrangement on his return. Denver would, of course, continue to have full use the travel section of their parent organisation to help him with any logistical support he needed on his travels. The two men parted, each feeling they'd got the better half of the gentleman's agreement.

When Denver announced that he intended to buy a yacht, many of his business associates assumed that with his wealth, he was intending to buy a large ocean-going vessel complete with crew, a typical billionaire's super yacht but Denver wanted adventure and he wanted to sail. The Hallberg-Rassey 62 was a nice size, big but not too big, and manageable for single-hander sailing if you were fit and knew what you were doing. He had finally taken possession of the yacht during the summer from the Island of Orust, in Sweden, one hour's drive from Gothenberg. The yacht; fitted with extra communication equipment and personalised fittings, left him with little change out of three million euros, a mere bagatelle.

After the standard initial engine checks and adjustments, full service and a few minor tweaks in the handling and to the engine and, with the help of two hired crew he set off. They sailed across the Atlantic stopping in Horta in the Azores. From there Denver and his crew sailed to St Georges in Bermuda where one of the crew members left to join another yacht he'd previously agreed to crew to New York. After a two-week break in Bermuda, Denver continued with his remaining crew member on to the United States. They tied up at Little Creek, Virginia.

Denver's logistical backup had pre-warned Immigration of his arrival and they agreed to drive out to the marina from Norfolk International Airport and sort out the formalities on-board Denver's yacht. When they left, Denver had a cruising licence obviating the need for further port-by-port check-ins as he continued his journey in US waters. One of the officials asked Denver for his autograph and Denver smiled as the man told him how he thought Denver's discovery of the Levia was like a true-life Dirk Pitt, Clive Cussler story. The back-up team also contacted the Woodrow-Wilson Memorial Bridge to schedule his passage through the bridge.

The Hallberg-Rassey 62 needed the bridge lifted to allow its mast through. The air-draft of the sixty-two was nearly eighty-seven foot to the masthead but the antenna, lights, and Windex made it closer to ninety, far too high to fit under the bridge even under highest central arch. His time slot was one am.

Denver's remaining crew of one had left him at Little Creek this time to join a yacht sailing back towards Bermuda thus leaving Denver in sole charge of his yacht for the first time. As he left marina sailing single-handed he found himself revelling in the experience. The trans-Atlantic crossing had been hard work, especially at the beginning, but as his fitness improved, along with his confidence and dexterity about the boat, he found himself enjoying the physicality of sailing. It was as if all the lights in his brain had suddenly been switched on. Slimmer, his hair longer with the grey showing through, his face tanned and weathered by the sun and wind, he looked a younger man than the one who'd stepped aboard the Ryders yacht in Mayotte. His journey up the Potomac River was a joy. The sun glittered off the surface of the water and his yacht drew admiring looks from other yachters as they passed on the river. He watched the courting couples as they walked hand-in-hand along the bank.

It was dark when he passed under the raised bridge and he made his way cautiously towards the Alexandria City Marina. Afraid of running aground, he'd considered anchoring in the Washington Channel and having a launch pick him up and take him to Cantina Marina from where he could take a car into town. In the end he decided to chance the Alexandria alternative since it gave him the freedom of being able to walk ashore. It was close to one-thirty am when he tied up at Founder's Park North T-head a stretch recently dredged to twenty-one feet, enough to accommodate the keel of his yacht.

His people had done their work well because two dock hands waited to guide him in and help secure the aft spring line, stern line and then the bow line as he positioned the fenders and finally cut the engine. They brushed aside his offer to help them with the two heavy 50 amp power cords needed to connect the yacht to shore power but accepted his offer of coffee aboard the yacht once everything was secure. They sighed in admiration at the interior but did not overstay their welcome and twenty-five minutes later, he had the yacht to himself again. He showered and shaved before collapsing gratefully onto his bed in the master cabin.

The voice of George Kirkham calling his name from the quayside woke him early the next morning and Denver presented a tousled figure as he emerged, on to the deck blinking in the bright morning light.

"Welcome aboard, George. Where's your stuff?" The other man lifted his arm to show Denver a large black grip and Denver nodded cheerfully.

"Let me show you to your cabin and give you a quick tour of the yacht then I'll wash the sleep out of my eyes, throw on some clothes, then we'll go ashore and get some breakfast."

"Sounds good," said Kirkham.

"Or have you eaten already?" asked Denver looking at the other's face. Kirkham shook his head.

"Too early when I got up."

"Good; then follow me, mind your head on that lintel, it's caught me a few times."

"Where will we be sailing to?" asked Kirkham.

"Time's no problem for you, right?"

"Nope I'm as free as a bird. Carr said I could take as long as I want."

"Good old Gerry," retorted Denver. "How the hell is he still managing to make money when everyone else in the world is losing their shirts and being credit-crunched into oblivion?" Kirkham laughed.

"The guy's got the Midas touch and no mistake."

"God bless him, he sure has," agreed Denver.

"So where are we headed, the Atlantic!"

In reply, Denver shrugged his shoulders, "I've got a few ideas but let's discuss them later this evening when we've got some food inside our bellies." He turned to face his friend suddenly serious. "But first; are we set?"

"Are you ready for this?" asked Kirkham his brow furrowed in concern.

"As I'll ever be," replied Denver.

It was seven am but they found a small café open and chatted amiably catching up on all the organisational news they then reminisced about their trip to St Gilberts. It was still not quite eight am when they left the small café and caught a taxi into the city centre and to the intersection of 10th Street and Constitution Avenue.

"Have you seen it already?" Enquired Denver and his friend shook his head.

"No; thought I'd wait, besides, from what I saw yesterday, the queues to get in are horrendous."

"What about us?" asked Denver.

"Should be no problem," replied Kirkham. "They told me to give them a call when we reached the door." As he spoke, Kirkham reached into his pocket for his phone. As they approached the impressive columned entrance of the white domed building, an attractive woman in her mid-thirties stepped out to meet them and ushered them through the door closing it firmly behind them before locking it. She stopped inside and turned to greet her two visitors.

"Mr Denver." She extended her hand towards the shorter of the two men. "My name is Mary Moreland; we are so glad you could find the time to visit us and thus give us an opportunity to thank you properly for your invaluable contribution to our new exhibition." Denver managed to hide his surprise at this greeting with a ready smile and a firm handshake. The woman turned to the other man, "And you must be George Kirkham; we spoke over the phone yesterday." She offered her hand to him.

"Well then." She said clapping her hands together as if about to make a public announcement, "Let's go straight to the second floor. Rowland Berris, Chair of the Board of the Smithsonian and Doug Furno, acting Manager over the Department of Mineral Science, are waiting for you. By the way, Doug is also a Specialist Gemmologist." The elevator was to the right and as they stepped inside Mary Moreland nodded a quick greeting to the security guard stood behind a desk to one side of it. As the lift doors opened on the second floor two men stood waiting and the older of the two stepped forward with his hand extended.

"Good morning, Mr Denver, allow me to welcome you formally to the Smithsonian National Museum of Natural History." Denver shook his hand and also that of the other man introducing George Kirkham as a friend and colleague. Neither of the two Smithsonian men showed any surprise at the informality of dress of their two visitors. Rowland Berris, Chair of the Board had a personal theory that the wealth and success of a modern businessperson showed in how they chose to dress. The wardrobes of those on the way up tended to reflect quality, taste, and money, whereas those who had already made it no longer felt the need to impress so dressed however-the-hell they wanted. Richard Denver and his tall companion dressed like a couple of tourists but still managed to exude confidence and wealth.

"Your generous gift of documents to the people of St Gilberts detailing the provenance of the St Gilberts Leon Blue really made our new exhibition the runaway success it is. As well as filling in some historical gaps surrounding the history of both diamonds, it gives the exhibition a 'story' and that's so important. I think your documentation is as interesting, if not more so, than the diamonds themselves."

They were still stood as a group near the elevator and Rowland Berris got the impression Denver hadn't heard a word he'd said. In fact, Denver actually looked confused or at least bemused as if his attention was elsewhere. Not used to people zoning out when he was speaking to them, Berris turned to see the object of Denver's attention. Apparently, he had been staring at the promotional posters for the new exhibition.

"Are you OK, Mr Denver?" He asked in an attempt to bring him back. Denver shook his head and apologised but Berris also shook his head as if to make out it was him that was at fault. "No, no, I'm sorry, Mr Denver, you must be tired did you fly in this morning?"

"Er, no, I arrived by yacht," replied Denver and Berris's eyebrows rose a centimetre.

"Really! Where from?" Denver considered for a moment; what had been the origin of his odyssey, was it Britain, Orust in Sweden, or had his journey really begun much further back in time than that?

"Little Creek," he replied at last, his mind still on the colourful photograph posters overhead. One of the men who had met them on the second floor as they exited the elevator, the one introduced as Doug Furno, spoke at last, "Mr Denver, have you seen the St Gilberts Leon Blue yet?"

"No…in fact…no…I haven't." Denver replied and as he answered he noticed a large poster-sized photograph of a tropical beach, a high cliff and a white church atop a mound of volcanic rock that met the beach and the foam topped waves breaking across the white coral sand. The picture made him catch his breath and for a second he felt as if he was back on the Ryders' inflatable about to lean over the side and plunge his head under water searching for signs of the wreck of the Valvaston.

Richard Denver, celebrated treasure hunter and business tycoon, felt nervous, his stomach churned beneath his diaphragm raising it so that his breathing was shallower. Doug Furno lightly rested an arm on Denver's arm and led him towards the Harry Winston Gallery. Denver had visited the gallery two years previously when its sole occupier had been the Hope Diamond. Now the area around the gallery, and the gallery itself had undergone considerable change and renovation to prepare it to house its latest addition. Denver suddenly realised that Doug Furno was speaking to him.

"We selected the key pages, including your helpful notes, from the documents you gave to the people of St Gilberts and copied them to poster size for wall mounting. We also included potted biographies on the author of each of the documents. They add to the richness of the exhibition and make fascinating reading, especially the journal of Thomas Pitt, and Rupert Stillwood-Hamilton's letters to his sister. Both were colourful, larger than life characters. The documents are important historic artefacts in their own right."

Denver felt an uncomfortable jolt at seeing his own handwriting alongside the text on the enlarged and beautifully finished wall mountings. It was all there on the large cream-coloured boards, the trail that he had followed for so long. There were selected pages from Jean-Baptiste Tavernier's Travels in India. The Journal of Thomas Pitt and Rupert Stillwood-Hamilton's letters to his sister, and pages from Gerald Aungier's Journal. The storyboards led the reader on a journey through history joining supposition and fact to connect the renegade Rupert Stillwood-Hamilton with a large blue diamond, the other half of the Hope Diamond.

Denver read again, the story that had occupied so much of his time had fuelled so many of his hopes for so many years. At last the storyboard ended and they were stood at, and looking into, a glass case in which sat the Hope Diamond in its platinum setting designed by Pierre Cartier surrounded by sixteen white pear-shaped and cushion cut diamonds with its chain containing forty-five diamonds. Close by in the same glass case was a much larger diamond of the same dark-blue as the Hope but not so expertly cut, or mounted, though no less striking for that, in fact the lack of a setting meant that more of the diamond itself was visible. Its simple presentation gave it an aura that drew his eye away from the extravagantly set Hope Diamond to rest on the lone diamond. Next to it lay a silver napkin ring with the name Valvaston in relief running around it.

"Fabulous, isn't it?" said Furno with genuine enthusiasm. Denver and Kirkham nodded, silently transfixed by the two diamonds.

"How can you be sure the two stones were originally one?" asked Kirkham.

Doug Furno's grin broadened, he was obviously glad of the opportunity to explain the Institute's previous research.

"First, let me tell you how we linked the Hope Diamond with the French Blue and so with the blue diamond Jean-Baptiste Tavernier presented to the King of France on his return from India. Perhaps you are already aware of some of the studies we conducted on the Hope Diamond over the years?" He continued without waiting for a response.

"Back in 2005, a study of the Hope Diamond showed precisely how it was cut from the larger diamond, the French Blue. In other words the Hope Diamond was linked directly to the 115 carat diamond Tavernier sold to King Louis XIV of France in 1668."

"The French Blue?" queried Kirkham.

"Yes, remember the diamond Tavernier sold to the King of France, known as the Tavernier Blue, the one later recut and renamed the French Blue?"

"Hmm and how the devil did they prove that?" Asked Kirkham still confused.

Doug Furno, clearly comfortable in lecture mode, looked delighted at the other's question. He paused for a second to check he still had his audience's attention, satisfied that he had, the smooth flow of information continued.

"Well, a team of researchers, Steven Attaway—engineer and gem cutter, and Scott Sucher and Nancy Attaway, both gem-cutting experts and led by our own Jeffery Post spent a year working on it. They used all the available data on the French Blue including sketches of the French Blue from pre-Revolutionary France. The information they gathered was accurate and detailed, and from it they prepared a computer model of the French Blue. When they entered the precise measurements of the Hope Diamond into the computer as well, they could, using advanced computer virtual reality technology, place the Hope inside the French Blue. It fitted perfectly in only one way, but at that orientation you could clearly see that it did fit, and why they cut it the way they did. They cut the corners off the French Blue, changed, but only slightly, the angle of the bottom facets, and so produced the Hope Diamond."

"OK," said George in the brief pause that followed. "That links Jean-Baptiste Tavernier to the Hope diamond but what evidence is there, apart from the documents Richard provided, linking the diamond from St Gilberts to the Hope Diamond?"

"A good question," replied Furno with obvious enthusiasm.

"A few years ago, I would have said that we couldn't link the two stones, but now, fortunately, we can. A study released in January of this year again by Jeffery Post, though this time helped by the guys at the US Naval Research Laboratory, shows how to fingerprint individual blue diamonds. This is how it works. Submit a blue diamond to ultraviolet light for more than a minute then take the light away, in a darkened room the diamond will show phosphorescence that has components of blue and red light. This reaction to ultraviolet is due to the impurities that exist in Blue diamonds, specifically, high levels of Boron and a low-level of Nitrogen. The interactions between these two elements cause the phosphorescence.

"With the Hope Diamond the phosphorescence is predominantly red, red-orange in fact. Yet when they submitted sixty-six other blue diamonds, including the Blue Heart Diamond, another large, it's almost a thirty-one carat diamond, (also in one of our collections by the way,) to the same ultraviolet test, the colour of their phosphorescence was mainly blue. So you see the specific characteristics of a blue diamond's phosphorescence, in other words the relative intensities of the blue and red components, and how quickly it fades, are specific to each diamond." Furno noted with satisfaction that his audience, including Rowland Berris, were hanging on his every word. After a brief but dramatic pause, he continued more slowly.

"When we ran the ultraviolet test on both the Hope Diamond and the St Gilberts Leon Blue, their phosphorescence spectra and fade time were identical. At some time in the past these two diamonds were part of the same stone."

A long silence followed Furno's last statement. Denver felt light-headed, had his heart had stopped beating? Then he realised he was holding his breath. He needed silence and solitude to process the swirling emotions that threatened to overwhelm him. He had a lump in his throat and, to his surprise, felt the tears just a second away. He knew he had reached the end of…of something; a quest, a dream, an obsession perhaps. If only there was a quiet room somewhere he could sit, absorb the information, but now was not that time. Rowland Berris broke the silence.

"The Hope Diamond has always been the most popular of our exhibits, the history behind it, and the diamond itself. It has always fascinated people. But now! The discovery the Hope now has a larger twin with a history equally exciting and more current, well! The fact we can prove the two stones were originally part of a larger whole by the ultraviolet test and the documents you provided makes for…" He searched for a suitable superlative, "A breath-taking exhibition. It's easy to understand why the volume of visitors to the National Museum of National History has shattered all previous records—bearing in mind we already averaged around eight million visitors a year before!" Berris was grinning and Furno's smile spread right across his face. Denver in contrast looked serious and thoughtful.

"You said earlier the President of St Gilberts gave the stone and the documents to the Smithsonian."

"That's right," agreed Berris.

"So what, if anything, do the people of St Gilberts get out of their extraordinarily generous gift?" The smiles on the faces of the two Smithsonian men faded slightly as they caught something in Denver's tone, a drop in the temperature. They straightened slightly as they considered the question and Berris was the first to reply.

"Well, they've gotten quite a lot actually. A diamond of this importance and value is not easy or cheap to guard once its whereabouts becomes known. Unless it creates income through its sale, or as a tourist attraction, then protecting it would quickly drain the finances of a small island like St Gilberts. When President Duval contacted the Smithsonian Institute he already had a proposal telling us what he expected from the Smithsonian in return for the diamond and the supporting documentation. Initially sceptical, we sent our experts, including Doug here out to St Gilberts to verify the authenticity of the diamond. Once we realised it was genuine we saw the Duval's proposal as win-win deal for the both of us. Don't forget, the diamond and the documents still belong to the people of St Gilberts."

“Normally, we don’t enter into merchandising agreements with outside bodies,” Berris paused before raising both his arms and his eyebrows. “But to be perfectly honest, once we realised what St Gilberts were offering us, we, the Smithsonian, were absolutely desperate to agree a deal. To get a treasure of such intrinsic and historical value we would have agreed to almost anything just to get it. From my first discussion with the President, he made it clear St Gilberts did not want to attract a high volume of tourism to its own shores, it simply didn’t have the resources to cope with them.

“He was keen to build the island’s infrastructure, water reservoirs, sewerage, waste disposal, and of course hospitals, schools, roads and the like. He is understandably wary of letting in multinational organisations and hotel conglomerates. There are only two hotels on St Gilberts and that’s how they want to keep it, at least for the moment. We signed a contract covering all merchandise that used the St Gilberts Leon Blue Diamond and its associated story. It’s in our shops now. The usual stuff; coffee-table books, picture postcards, tee-shirts, DVDs, full-size imitations of the diamond itself, small plastic figurines of Rupert Still-Wood Hamilton and his sister, wrist bangle versions of the Valvaston napkin ring, etcetera, etcetera…” Berris threw his arms wide to encompass the contents of the room.

“The profits we are getting so far are even better than the sale of plastic dinosaurs when Jurassic Park first came out. Remember, the Hope Diamond was already the most popular museum exhibition in the world. I have no doubt whatsoever the St Gilberts Leon Blue will be even more popular than the Hope. Yes, the people of St Gilberts are going to do very well out of this exhibition year in year out and far into the future as well…. What’s more; they’ll have no security problems and none of the headaches that come with owning a treasure like this.” Denver and Kirkham nodded approval.

“One more question, if you don’t mind?” said Denver. “I didn’t get chance to read all the storyboards as we walked round, but I assume Rodney Leon discovered the diamond; do you know the actual date he discovered it?” Berris frowned in thought and turned to Furno, who was also frowning in concentration and stroking his chin.

“You know something, Mr Denver, that’s an excellent question,” said Furno, a sheepish expression replacing his earlier smile.

“Our first concern was to check the authenticity of the diamond and the supporting documentation. Then we had the problem of arranging safe transport from St Gilberts and to the Institute and then we got caught up in the design and construction of the new exhibition, oh, and of course the negotiations with the two Gilbertise negotiators."

"One of whom was Rodney Leon," added Berris. Furno looked at Berris, his expression still rueful.

"You know something; I do believe we've overlooked that particular detail." Berris looked at his colleague.

"Surely we can make a quick phone call to the island to get an answer to Mr Denver's question? What's the time difference there?" Furno looked down at his watch but Denver raised his hands showing his open palms.

"No, no, there's no need for that; it was just casual interest."

"But no; you're right; we should at least know the day and date when Rodney Leon first discovered it, now I wish I'd thought to ask him when he was here."

"He was here?" echoed Denver in surprise.

"Why yes, as I just said he was one of the negotiators, he and his beautiful partner Joelle. They were the two representatives sent by the President." Denver shook his head his mind reeling. Berris's earlier comment that Leon was one of the negotiators hadn't registered at the time.

"Yes, a most attractive couple, very striking," Berris said picking up on Furno's description of Leon's girlfriend and feeling relaxed enough to add a little humour.

"Apparently, our female employees were more interested in catching a glimpse of Rodney Leon than of the St Gilberts Leon Blue, and Joelle, his girlfriend, had every man in the building falling in love with her. I joked at the time that if were to sell postcards just showing those two, St Gilberts would be as wealthy as an Arab oil state in no time."

Furno smiled politely before adding, "They were tough negotiators though. Rodney clearly had a vision of the result he wanted to come away with, but Joelle was the one with the business brain. She knew how to trade options, how to negotiate hard, she was the one who pushed and kept going when the going got tough. She's a very impressive lady," concluded Furno with frank admiration.

"Got you too, did she?" Chuckled Berris and Furno actually blushed. As a group, they moved away from the glass cabinet containing the two blue gemstones, the climax of the exhibition.

"So what do you think?" Berris asked, indicating with a sweep of his hand, that he was referring to the exhibition as a whole. Denver and Kirkham turned taking in the room their eyes catching only snatches of the story as they turned; how diamonds form deep below the earth's crust and brought to the surface, a labourer in a Galconda gravel pit, a seventeen century Indian jeweller, Jean-Baptiste Tavernier, Rupert Stillwood-Hamilton. The separate journeys of two diamonds parted so long ago in India finally reunited under a bulletproof glass case in the Smithsonian Institute; the climax of a geological love story.

The final storyboard described the formal handover of the St Gilberts Leon Blue and the documents Denver had sent to Rodney Leon. There was a photograph showing both Rowland Berris and Doug Furno along with several other people, presumably representatives of the Smithsonian Institute. They all stood on one side of a small stand on which rested the papers, journal, letters and other documents Denver had posted to Rodney Leon; on the other side of the table, stood an extraordinarily beautiful young couple.

Their dark skin looked so perfect it may have led some to assume their features had been airbrushed, but Denver knew better. He had a vivid recollection of entering Leon's house to the sound of Sega music and seeing four young people laughing and dancing. In the photo Leon had obviously tried to tidy himself up, the stubble was gone he'd squeezed his wide shoulders and tall frame into a white shirt and cheap suit but he still looked a million dollars.

Denver recognised the beautiful girl at his side with the long melting brown eyes and flawless honey-coloured skin. He studied the photograph. She was just as he remembered; the same composure, poise and quintessential femininity. She oozed class. In the photograph, Leon's hand reached towards the outstretched hand of Berris passing him the box containing the Blue diamond. Everyone in the photo was staring at the camera lens and smiling. Denver himself smiled; if that young couple weren't careful, Hollywood or some advertising agency would be chasing after them. He shook his head regretfully at the thought.

Berris coughed to regain the guest's attention.

"Well, gentlemen, I'm afraid that I will have to ask you to excuse me as I have a meeting across town and I had better leave now if I'm going to make it through the traffic. It's been a pleasure to meet you both and I hope you can see that we intend to take very good care of the valuable documents and artefacts you so generously passed to the people of St Gilberts. I'm sure Doug can stay a while longer and can arrange some refreshments for you." He looked down at his watch.

"Ten am! If I'm not mistaken, they'll be letting the public in about now so I suggest you make your way to…?" and he looked enquiringly at Furno.

"I thought the Atrium Café on the ground floor," Furno said and Berris nodded in approval and turned to shake both Denver's and Kirkham's hands.

"Well, enjoy the rest of your visit. I hope you find time to visit us again." Even as the sound of his footsteps faded down the corridor outside they were replaced by the noise of the advancing hordes of visitors he had earlier been so enthusiastic about. Furno and Kirkham made their way out of the Harry Winston Gallery but Denver did not follow them. He called to say that he would follow them down shortly, but first he wanted to take another look at the exhibition.

"Make mine a Latte," he shouted at the departing backs of the two men.

He was alone in the Gallery for only a few moments before the public began to stream in. He stared intently at the St Gilberts Leon Blue as if trying to see deep into the dark heart of it. In some respects he still saw it as his diamond—The Denver Blue perhaps—but no, he remembered the young man, Rodney Leon sat across the table from him, the young man who had made everyone tea. At that time, he had appeared little more than a teenager, now he had the other half of the Hope Diamond named after him.

"Good on you, kid!" he thought, but when a young woman with a child stood next to him suddenly turned to look at him, he realised he must have said it out loud. The woman turned her back to him and moved slightly away. He walked from storyboard to storyboard seeing enlarged copies of his own handwriting everywhere and even a potted biography describing him, among other things, as an adventurer and avid treasure hunter, he allowed himself a wry smile.

All told, the biography was really quite flattering, more than he deserved, and he smiled some more. He watched as scores of people milled around the Gallery following the separate histories of each diamond before finally gaping in wonder at the two blue diamonds in the glass box their faces expressing wonderment. The photo of the Smithsonian staff and the island couple was also attracting a lot of attention.

"Look at his eyes!" He heard one girl exclaim to her friends as he made his way out moving against the flow of those entering the gallery. Finally, he squeezed out through the door and headed towards the stairs that led down.

When Denver and Kirkham left the Museum, they crossed Constitution Ave made their way up 10th Street in amiable silence passing the Internal Revenue

Service offices and the Old Post Office Pavilion before Kirkham spoke, "Fancy a few beers?"

"Now you're talking," replied Denver.

Kirkham grinned, it was exactly the response he wanted—hoped for. "And what about some grub?"

"But you've just bloody well eaten in the museum!" Exclaimed Denver in mock outrage and Kirkham mollified him in the most reasonable tone of voice he could manage.

"Not now—I mean later—after a few beers."

Denver thought for a few moments licking his lips as if in anticipation. "You know something, George, I think a good Thai Red Curry would hit the spot."

"Sounds good to me," Kirkham agreed.

They were approaching Pennsylvania Avenue side-stepping to avoid kamikaze pedestrians. The sun was out and the noise of the city all around them. Kirkham looked sideways at the expression on his friend's face before asking.

"Do you think the kid already had the diamond when we visited him that night on St Gilberts?"

Denver did not answer straightaway and Kirkham was beginning to think his question had been lost in the background noise when Denver suddenly turned his head to face him.

"I'd like to think so." Kirkham stopped walking and positioned himself in front of his friend his large hands gripping Denver's biceps forcing Denver to stop and face him and the endless pedestrians to swerve around them.

He held Denver at arm's length examining the expression on his friend's face. "You're shitting me?" Then Kirkham corrected himself as he read the other man's face. "But no, you're not!" Denver and Kirkham burst out laughing in the middle of the busy street solid as two rocks in the river of humanity that swirled around them.

"For some reason, I don't think we've heard the last of Master Leon," said Denver thoughtfully.

"Let's get that beer," said Kirkham slapping his friend on the back.

"Hell, it's going to be like old times."

"Like the best of old times," added Denver.

Joelle and I stood watching Nahil and Andy walk up the drive towards the road. I would have offered them the Honda to use but it was still off the road awaiting a new rear wheel chain sprocket from South Africa. The existing one, worn and as smooth as a ten rupee piece meant the cog could no longer grip the chain links besides; Andy had shifted a fair few bottles of beer.

"See you at eight tomorrow morning," Andy reminded me.

"At the marina," I shouted back, adding, "We'll put that new police boat through its paces." Nahil's grin was as wide as Andy's. Her man had a new job on St Gilberts and she was as excited about it as he was. Her constant fear that Andy would get bored and leave St Gilberts had, for the moment, receded, and now she took joy in his excitement. In contrast, Joelle's face was shadowed with concern but she smiled back at Nahil and then at me. The light was fading fast but we stood and waved until they reached the end of the drive, where they both turned and waved back and then disappeared from view onto the road. We returned inside and went to the veranda to clear up the glasses and bottles strewn on the low table.

"Let's watch it sink," said Joelle and I nodded. We stood at the rail to watch the sunset, as we had for so many nights before. We both loved the moment just after the sun disappeared below the horizon when, for a short while longer, its light continued to reflect off the high clouds and the dark blue sky in a wash of delicate pinks and reds. We had now seen a small bit of the world beyond our shores and we had returned to St Gilberts excited at what we had seen and with a sense of pride in what we had achieved but it was a relief to be back as well.

"Did we make the right decision? I mean, about the diamond?" She asked, seeking reassurance. "We could have had it all."

I looked at her face and shrugged my shoulders. "I know."

"But it was so much money, Rodney."

Please write a good review on Amazon.

Yours.

Rodney Leon.

“I know, but so much trouble too. If we’d kept it for ourselves, how could we have stayed on St Gilberts, stayed here?” I waved my hand at the house. “Besides, what more could we have bought with it?”

Her mouth moved as if she was about to answer but then her eyes looked down as she seemed to change her mind and she remained silent.

“Anyway, it’s done now and I can live with it, I can live with it very well but I can live with you even better.” She smiled in reply and moved her hand along the veranda rail till it covered mine, connecting us. It was a quiet low-key gesture, the sort that always says more than whoops and yells. I turned my hand in hers so I could pull her around to face me and in that moment felt the world, and St Gilberts, changing and adapting to suit us. We had passed through a doorway and found ourselves in a better place on the other side.

At long last, and for the first time, we were where we belonged; we were home.

THE END